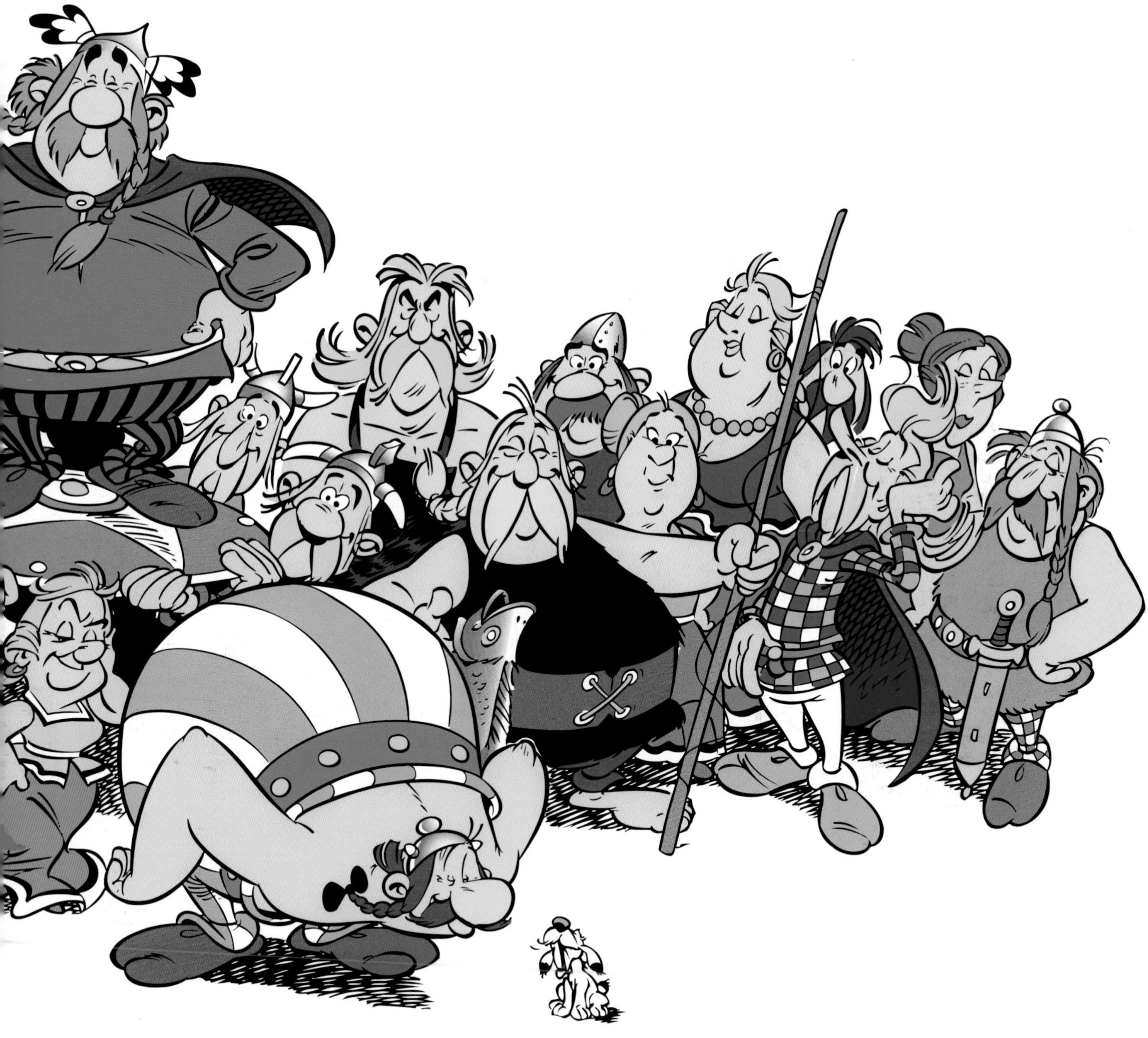

Asterix Omnibus 7

ASTERIX AND THE SOOTHSAYER, ASTERIX IN CORSICA, ASTERIX AND CAESAR'S GIFT

Written by RENÉ GOSCINNY

Illustrated by ALBERT UDERZO

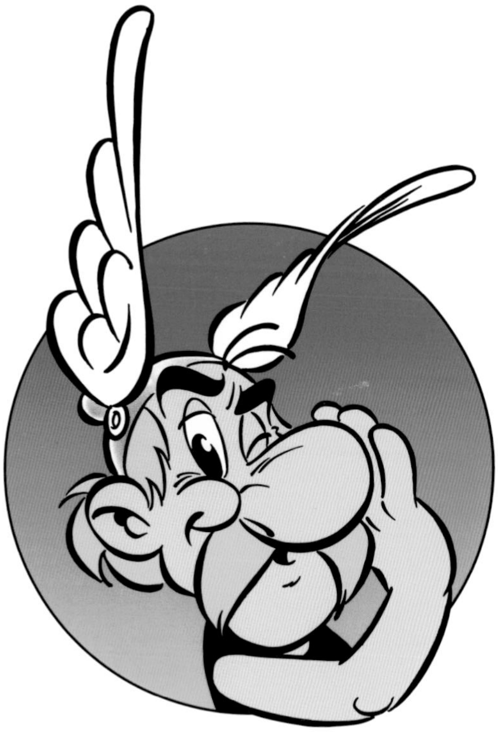

Orion
Children's Books

ORION CHILDREN'S BOOKS

This omnibus © 2013 Hachette Livre/Goscinny-Uderzo

ASTERIX®-OBELIX®-DOGMATIX®
Exclusive licensee: Hachette Children's Group
Translators: Anthea Bell and Derek Hockridge
Typography: Bryony Newhouse

Asterix and the Soothsayer
Original title: *Le Devin*
© 1972 GOSCINNY/UDERZO
Revised edition and English translation © 2004 Hachette Livre

Asterix in Corsica
Original title: *Astérix en Corse*
© 1973 GOSCINNY/UDERZO
Revised edition and English translation © 2004 Hachette Livre

Asterix and Caesar's Gift
Original title: *Le Cadeau de César*
© 1974 GOSCINNY/UDERZO
Revised edition and English translation © 2004 Hachette Livre

The right of René Goscinny and Albert Uderzo to be identified as the authors of this work
has been asserted by them in accordance with the Copyright, Designs and Patents Act 1988.

First Published in Great Britain in 2013 by Orion Children's Books Ltd
Paperback edition first published in Great Britain in 2014 by
Orion Children's Books Ltd
This edition published in 2016 by Hodder and Stoughton

7 9 10 8 6

A CIP catalogue record for this book is available from the British Library

ISBN 978 1 4440 0835 7 (cased)
ISBN 978 1 4440 0836 4 (paperback)

Printed in China
The paper and board used in this book are from well-managed forests and other responsible sources.

Orion Children's Books
An imprint of Hachette Children's Group, part of Hodder and Stoughton
Carmelite House, 50 Victoria Embankment
London EC4Y 0DZ
An Hachette UK Company

www.hachette.co.uk
www.asterix.com
www.hachettechildrens.co.uk
Asterix and Obelix

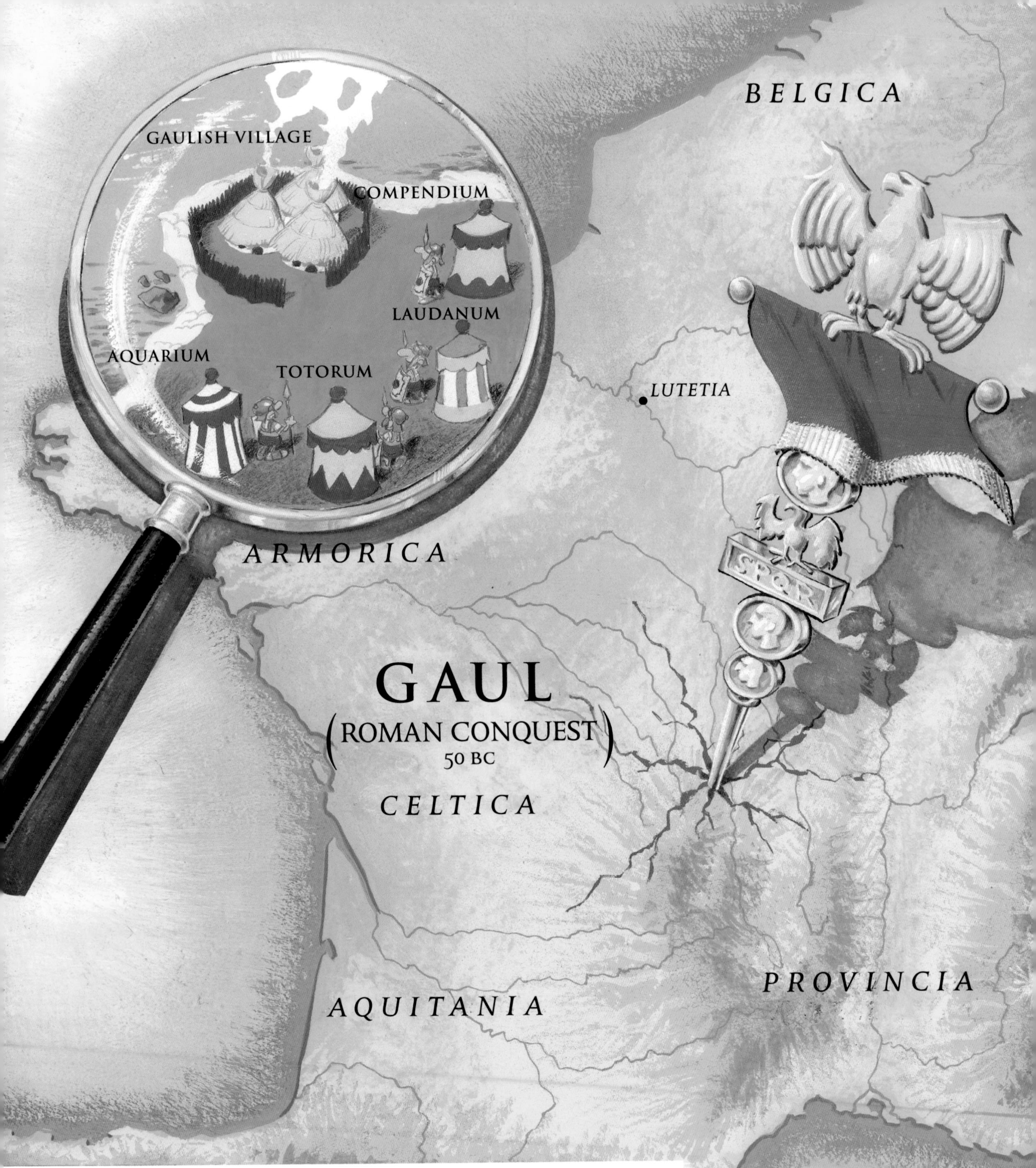
BELGICA
GAULISH VILLAGE
COMPENDIUM
LAUDANUM
AQUARIUM
TOTORUM
LUTETIA
ARMORICA
SPQR
GAUL
(ROMAN CONQUEST 50 BC)
CELTICA
PROVINCIA
AQUITANIA

THE YEAR IS 50 BC. GAUL IS ENTIRELY OCCUPIED BY THE ROMANS. WELL, NOT ENTIRELY ... ONE SMALL VILLAGE OF INDOMITABLE GAULS STILL HOLDS OUT AGAINST THE INVADERS. AND LIFE IS NOT EASY FOR THE ROMAN LEGIONARIES WHO GARRISON THE FORTIFIED CAMPS OF TOTORUM, AQUARIUM, LAUDANUM AND COMPENDIUM ...

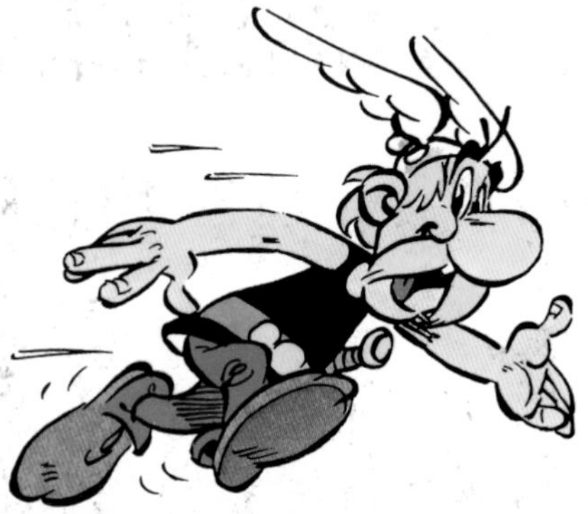

ASTERIX, THE HERO OF THESE ADVENTURES. A SHREWD, CUNNING LITTLE WARRIOR, ALL PERILOUS MISSIONS ARE IMMEDIATELY ENTRUSTED TO HIM. ASTERIX GETS HIS SUPERHUMAN STRENGTH FROM THE MAGIC POTION BREWED BY THE DRUID GETAFIX . . .

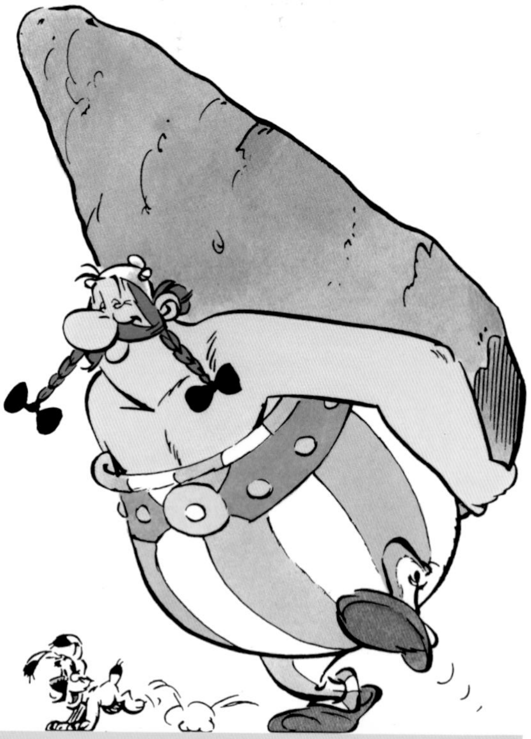

OBELIX, ASTERIX'S INSEPARABLE FRIEND. A MENHIR DELIVERY MAN BY TRADE, ADDICTED TO WILD BOAR. OBELIX IS ALWAYS READY TO DROP EVERYTHING AND GO OFF ON A NEW ADVENTURE WITH ASTERIX – SO LONG AS THERE'S WILD BOAR TO EAT, AND PLENTY OF FIGHTING. HIS CONSTANT COMPANION IS DOGMATIX, THE ONLY KNOWN CANINE ECOLOGIST, WHO HOWLS WITH DESPAIR WHEN A TREE IS CUT DOWN.

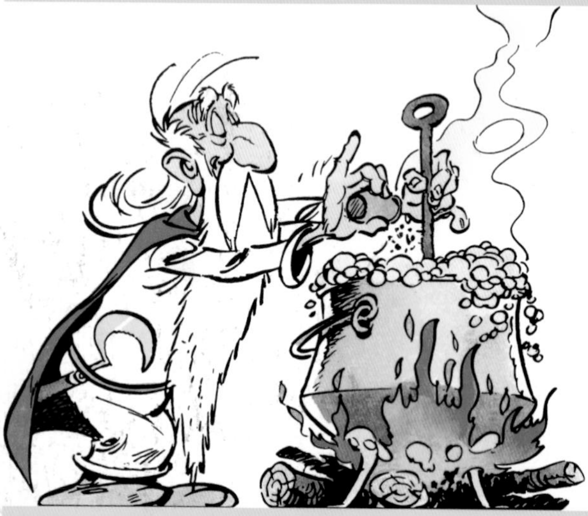

GETAFIX, THE VENERABLE VILLAGE DRUID, GATHERS MISTLETOE AND BREWS MAGIC POTIONS. HIS SPECIALITY IS THE POTION WHICH GIVES THE DRINKER SUPERHUMAN STRENGTH. BUT GETAFIX ALSO HAS OTHER RECIPES UP HIS SLEEVE . . .

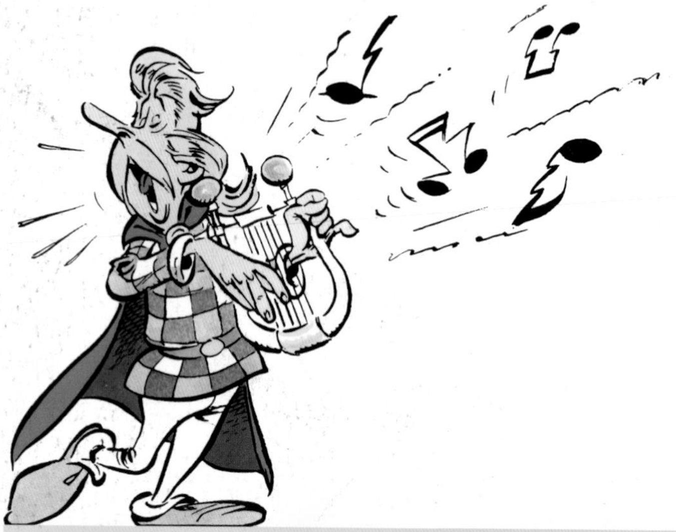

CACOFONIX, THE BARD. OPINION IS DIVIDED AS TO HIS MUSICAL GIFTS. CACOFONIX THINKS HE'S A GENIUS. EVERYONE ELSE THINKS HE'S UNSPEAKABLE. BUT SO LONG AS HE DOESN'T SPEAK, LET ALONE SING, EVERYBODY LIKES HIM . . .

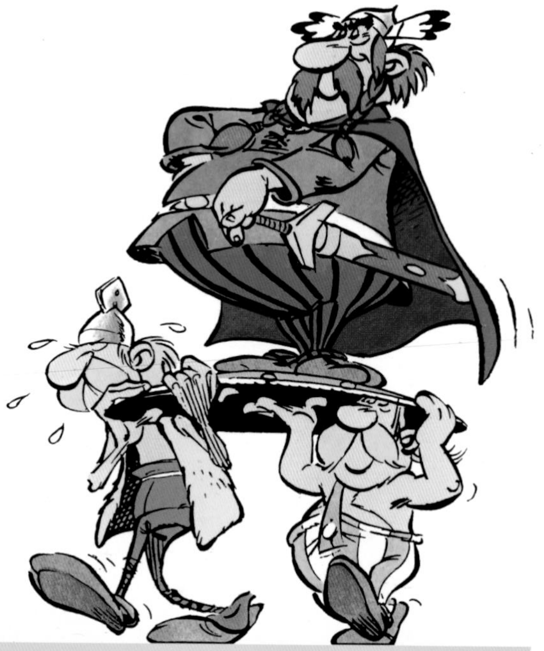

FINALLY, VITALSTATISTIX, THE CHIEF OF THE TRIBE. MAJESTIC, BRAVE AND HOT-TEMPERED, THE OLD WARRIOR IS RESPECTED BY HIS MEN AND FEARED BY HIS ENEMIES. VITALSTATISTIX HIMSELF HAS ONLY ONE FEAR, HE IS AFRAID THE SKY MAY FALL ON HIS HEAD TOMORROW. BUT AS HE ALWAYS SAYS, TOMORROW NEVER COMES.

R. GOSCINNY ASTERIX A. UDERZO

ASTERIX and the SOOTHSAYER

Written by René GOSCINNY

Illustrated by Albert UDERZO

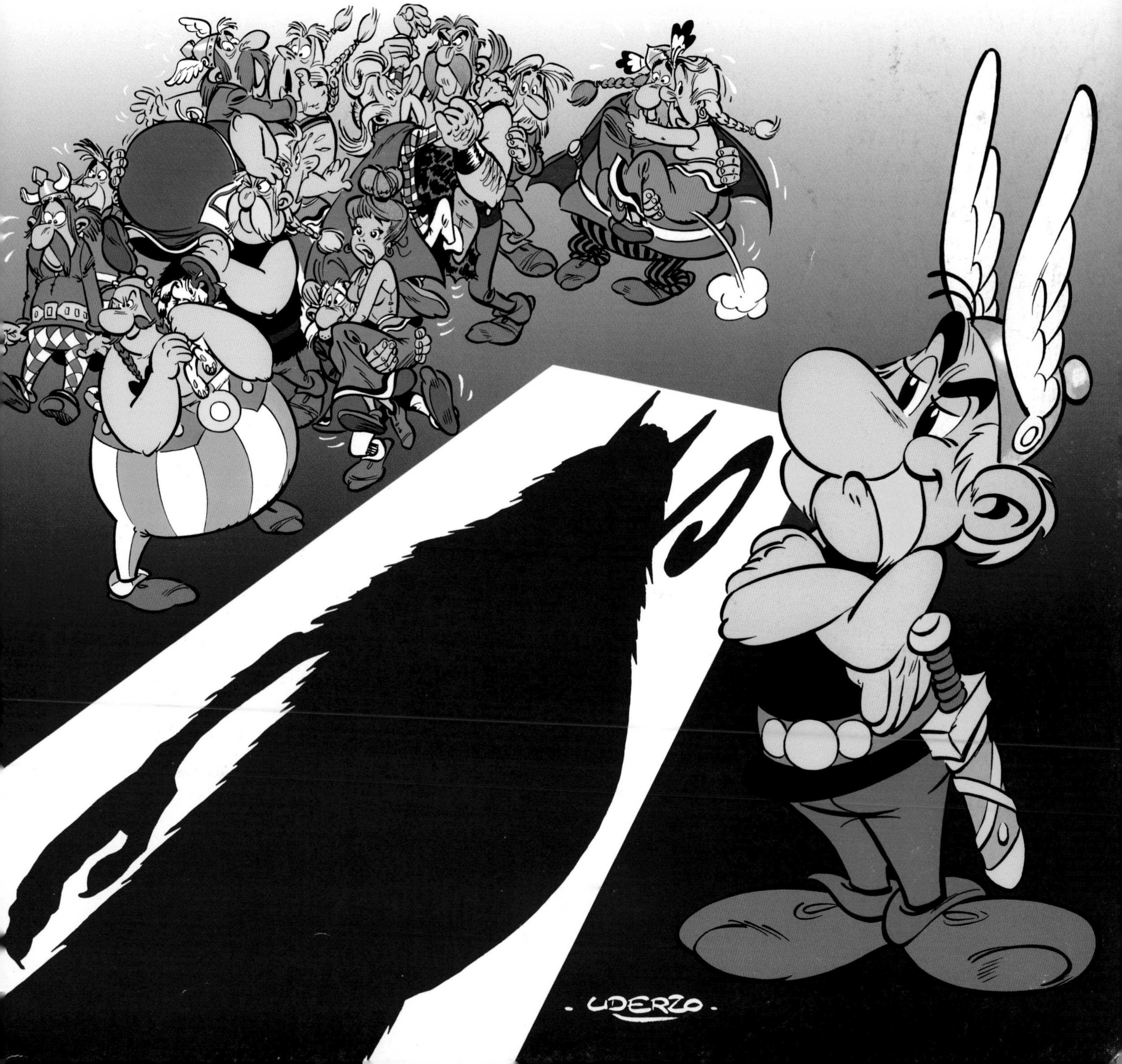
UDERZO

GOSCINNY AND UDERZO

PRESENT

An Asterix Adventure

ASTERIX AND THE SOOTHSAYER

Written by RENÉ GOSCINNY *and Illustrated by* ALBERT UDERZO

Translated by Anthea Bell *and* Derek Hockridge

Orion
Children's Books

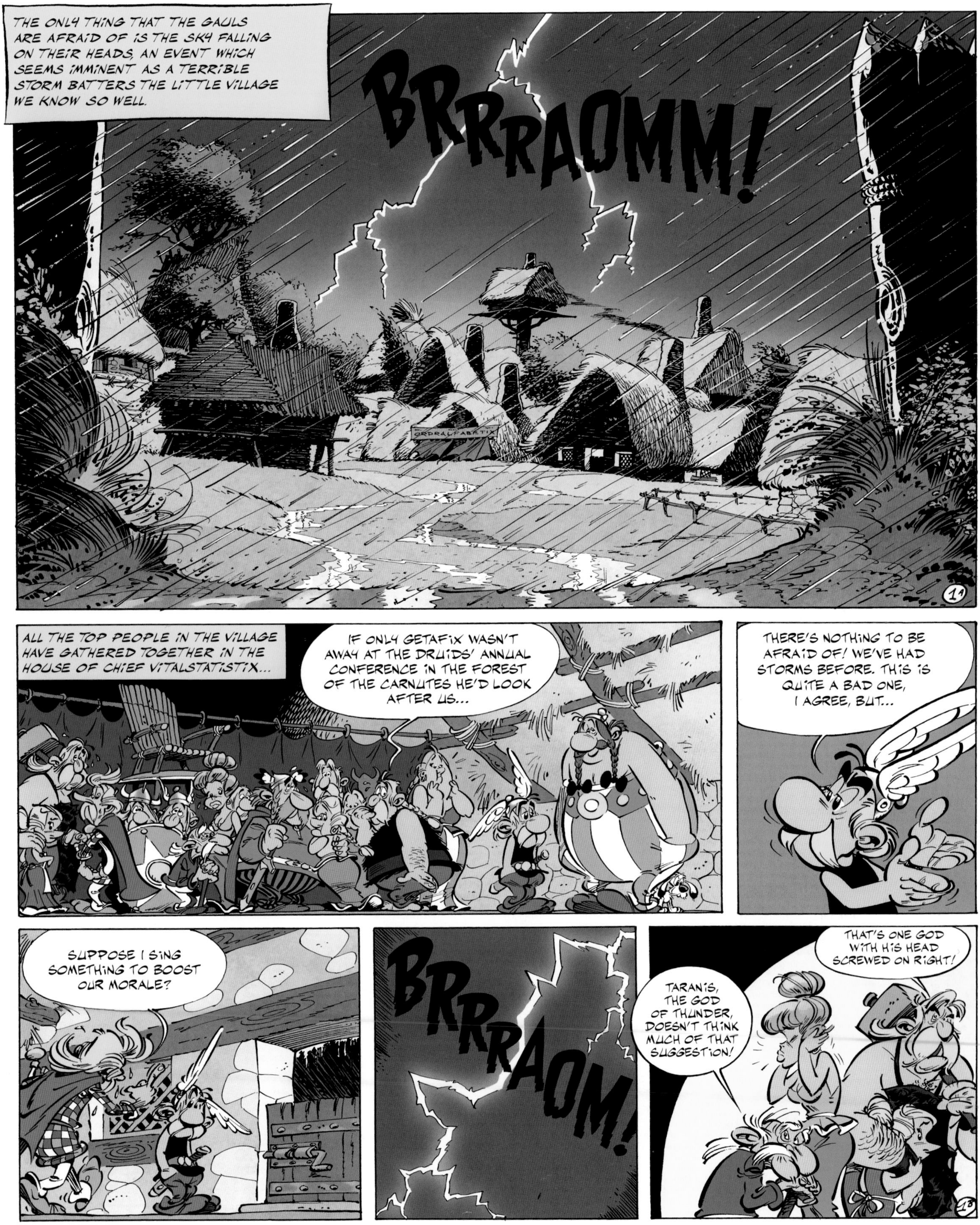
THE ONLY THING THAT THE GAULS ARE AFRAID OF IS THE SKY FALLING ON THEIR HEADS, AN EVENT WHICH SEEMS IMMINENT AS A TERRIBLE STORM BATTERS THE LITTLE VILLAGE WE KNOW SO WELL.
BRRRAOMM!
ALL THE TOP PEOPLE IN THE VILLAGE HAVE GATHERED TOGETHER IN THE HOUSE OF CHIEF VITALSTATISTIX...
IF ONLY GETAFIX WASN'T AWAY AT THE DRUIDS' ANNUAL CONFERENCE IN THE FOREST OF THE CARNUTES HE'D LOOK AFTER US...
THERE'S NOTHING TO BE AFRAID OF! WE'VE HAD STORMS BEFORE. THIS IS QUITE A BAD ONE, I AGREE, BUT...
SUPPOSE I SING SOMETHING TO BOOST OUR MORALE?
BRRRAOM!
TARANIS, THE GOD OF THUNDER, DOESN'T THINK MUCH OF THAT SUGGESTION!
THAT'S ONE GOD WITH HIS HEAD SCREWED ON RIGHT!

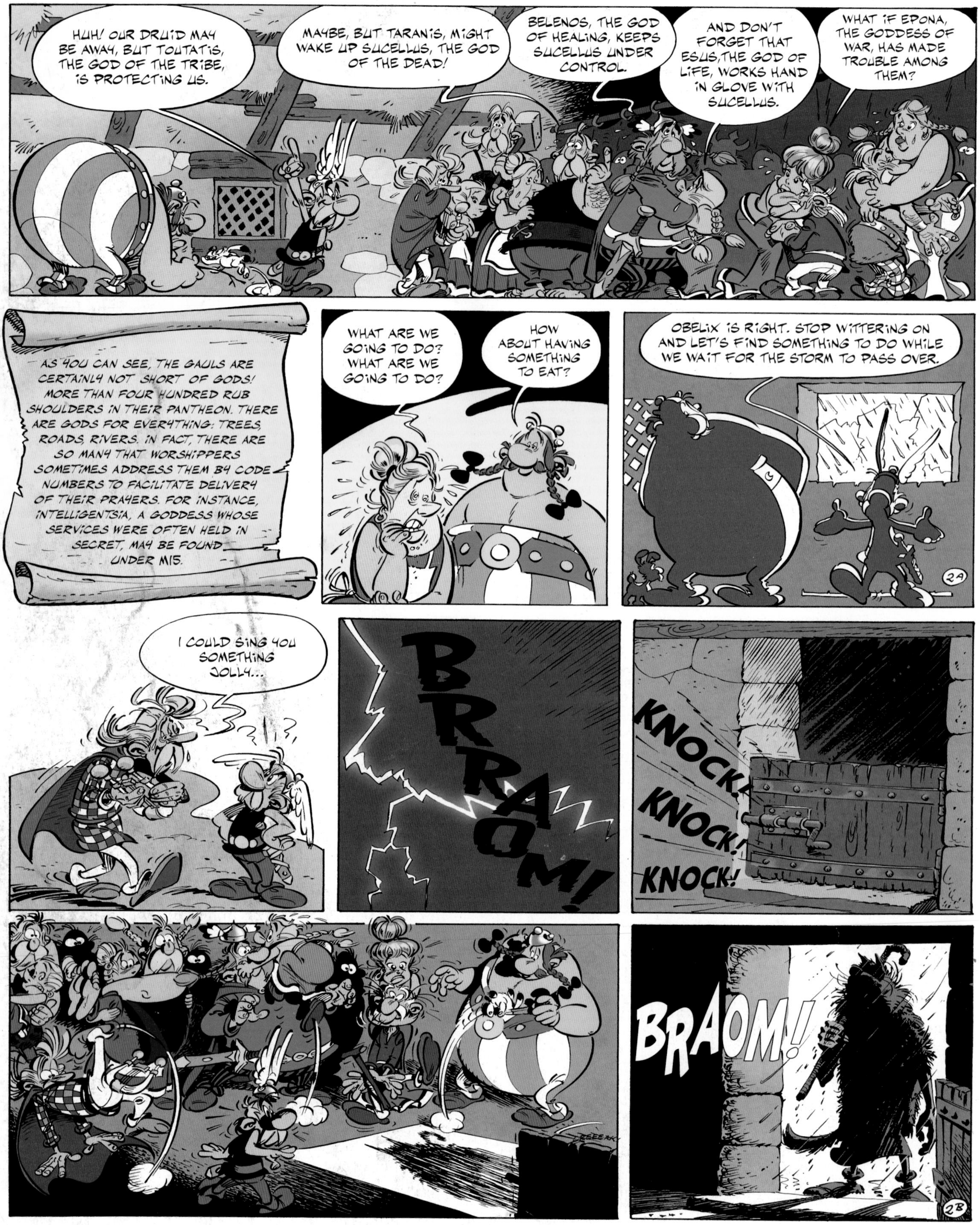
HUH! OUR DRUID MAY BE AWAY, BUT TOUTATIS, THE GOD OF THE TRIBE, IS PROTECTING US.
MAYBE, BUT TARANIS, MIGHT WAKE UP SUCELLUS, THE GOD OF THE DEAD!
BELENOS, THE GOD OF HEALING, KEEPS SUCELLUS UNDER CONTROL.
AND DON'T FORGET THAT ESUS, THE GOD OF LIFE, WORKS HAND IN GLOVE WITH SUCELLUS.
WHAT IF EPONA, THE GODDESS OF WAR, HAS MADE TROUBLE AMONG THEM?
AS YOU CAN SEE, THE GAULS ARE CERTAINLY NOT SHORT OF GODS! MORE THAN FOUR HUNDRED RUB SHOULDERS IN THEIR PANTHEON. THERE ARE GODS FOR EVERYTHING: TREES, ROADS, RIVERS. IN FACT, THERE ARE SO MANY THAT WORSHIPPERS SOMETIMES ADDRESS THEM BY CODE NUMBERS TO FACILITATE DELIVERY OF THEIR PRAYERS. FOR INSTANCE, INTELLIGENTSIA, A GODDESS WHOSE SERVICES WERE OFTEN HELD IN SECRET, MAY BE FOUND UNDER MI5.
WHAT ARE WE GOING TO DO? WHAT ARE WE GOING TO DO?
HOW ABOUT HAVING SOMETHING TO EAT?
OBELIX IS RIGHT. STOP WITTERING ON AND LET'S FIND SOMETHING TO DO WHILE WE WAIT FOR THE STORM TO PASS OVER.
I COULD SING YOU SOMETHING JOLLY...
BRRAAOM!
KNOCK! KNOCK! KNOCK!
BRAOM!!

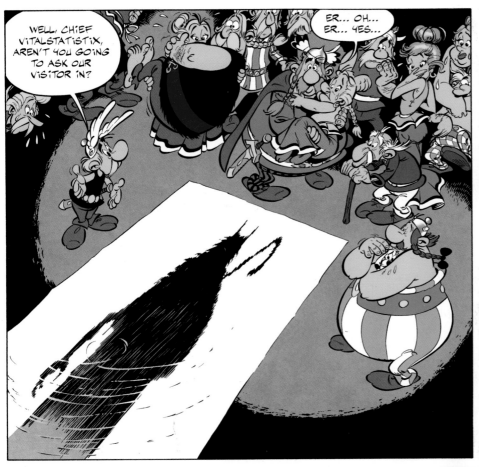

WELL, CHIEF VITALSTATISTIX, AREN'T YOU GOING TO ASK OUR VISITOR IN?

ER... OH... ER... YES...

JUST HOLD THAT A MINUTE.

EH?

WHO... WHO ARE YOU?

A TRAVELLER CAUGHT IN THE STORM. GRANT ME THE SHELTER OF YOUR ROOF UNTIL THE WRATH OF THE GODS HAS BEEN APPEASED!

IT LOOKS AS THOUGH THE GODS HAVE HAD A BRAINSTORM UNDER THE INFLUENCE OF THE GODDESS MANIA...

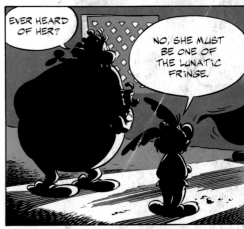

EVER HEARD OF HER?

NO, SHE MUST BE ONE OF THE LUNATIC FRINGE.

COME IN, TRAVELLER. MAKE YOURSELF AT HOME. WHAT CAN WE GET FOR YOU?

HE MUST BE VERY HUNGRY.

I'VE GOT SOME BOAR LEFT, AND A LITTLE GOAT'S MILK.

BRING IT ALL IN. I'LL KEEP HIM COMPANY WHILE HE DRINKS HIS GOAT'S MILK.

15

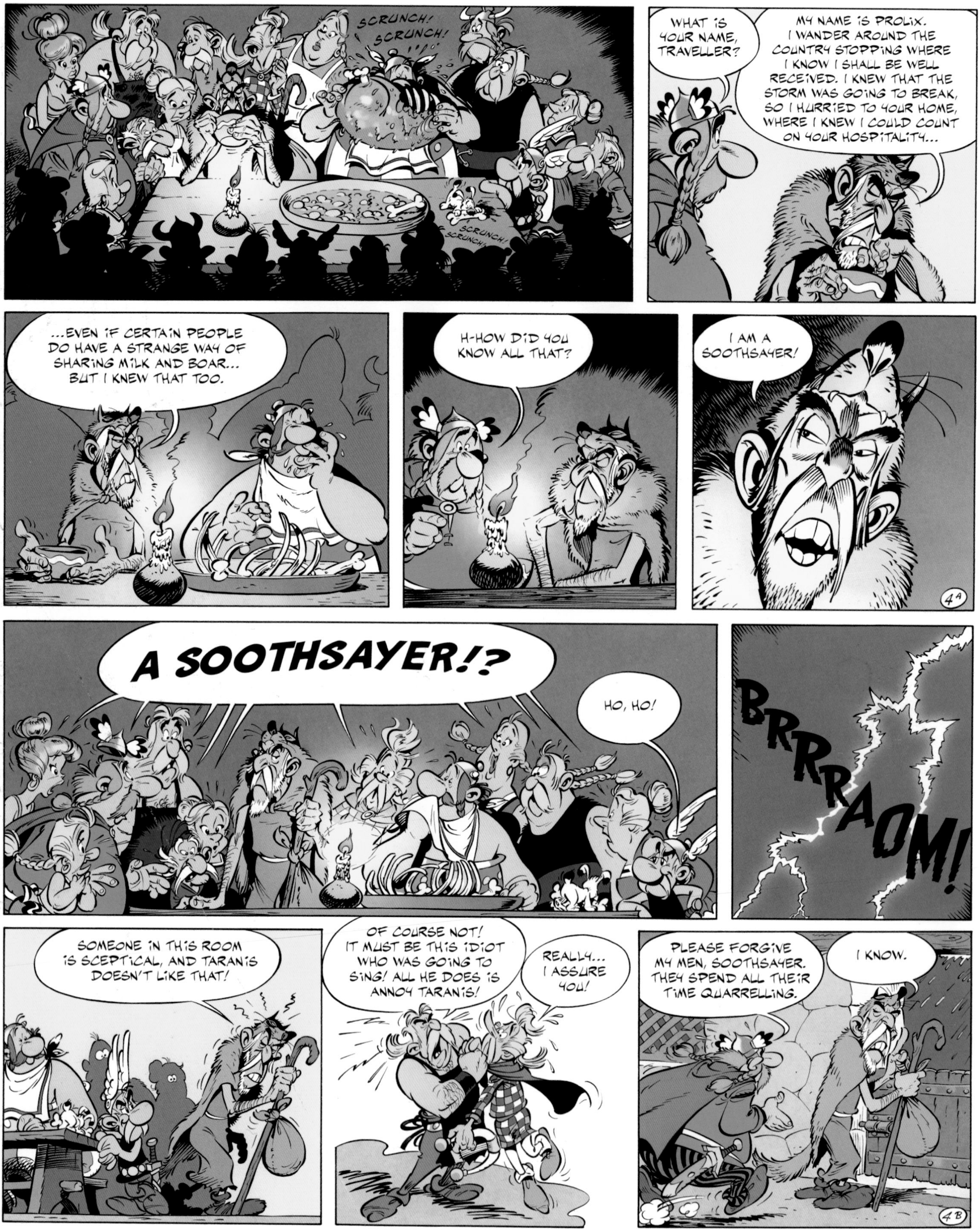
SCRUNCH! SCRUNCH!
SCRUNCH! SCRUNCH!
WHAT IS YOUR NAME, TRAVELLER?
MY NAME IS PROLIX. I WANDER AROUND THE COUNTRY STOPPING WHERE I KNOW I SHALL BE WELL RECEIVED. I KNEW THAT THE STORM WAS GOING TO BREAK, SO I HURRIED TO YOUR HOME, WHERE I KNEW I COULD COUNT ON YOUR HOSPITALITY...
...EVEN IF CERTAIN PEOPLE DO HAVE A STRANGE WAY OF SHARING MILK AND BOAR... BUT I KNEW THAT TOO.
H-HOW DID YOU KNOW ALL THAT?
I AM A SOOTHSAYER!
A SOOTHSAYER!?
HO, HO!
BRRRAOM!
SOMEONE IN THIS ROOM IS SCEPTICAL, AND TARANIS DOESN'T LIKE THAT!
OF COURSE NOT! IT MUST BE THIS IDIOT WHO WAS GOING TO SING! ALL HE DOES IS ANNOY TARANIS!
REALLY... I ASSURE YOU!
PLEASE FORGIVE MY MEN, SOOTHSAYER. THEY SPEND ALL THEIR TIME QUARRELLING.
I KNOW.

ASTERIX'S SCEPTICISM HAS NO EFFECT. SUBJECTED TO THE INFLUENCE OF SO MANY GODS, WHO BOTH PROTECT AND THREATEN THEM, THE NATIONS OF ANTIQUITY WOULD LIKE TO HAVE ADVANCE NOTICE OF THEIR WHIMS. HERE WE MUST INSERT A PARENTHESIS...

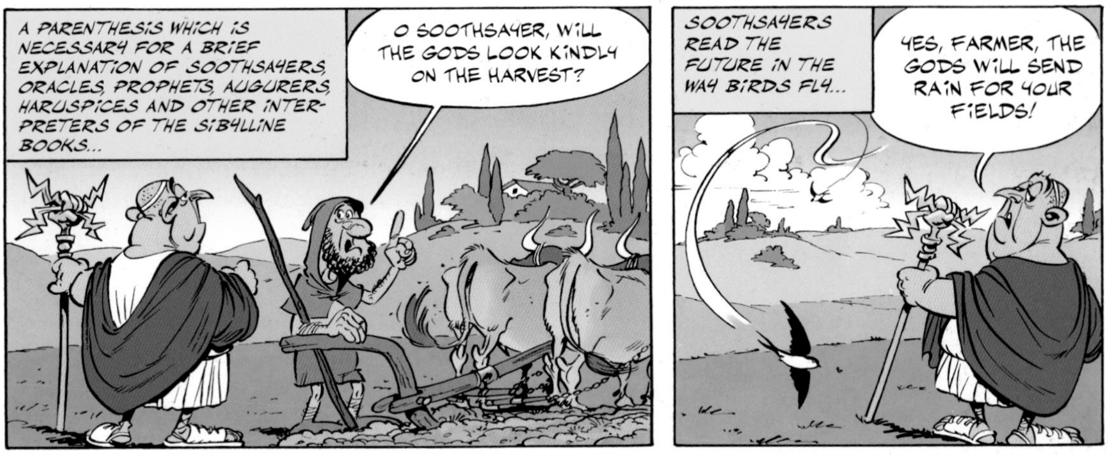

A PARENTHESIS WHICH IS NECESSARY FOR A BRIEF EXPLANATION OF SOOTHSAYERS, ORACLES, PROPHETS, AUGURERS, HARUSPICES AND OTHER INTERPRETERS OF THE SIBYLLINE BOOKS...
O SOOTHSAYER, WILL THE GODS LOOK KINDLY ON THE HARVEST?
SOOTHSAYERS READ THE FUTURE IN THE WAY BIRDS FLY...
YES, FARMER, THE GODS WILL SEND RAIN FOR YOUR FIELDS!

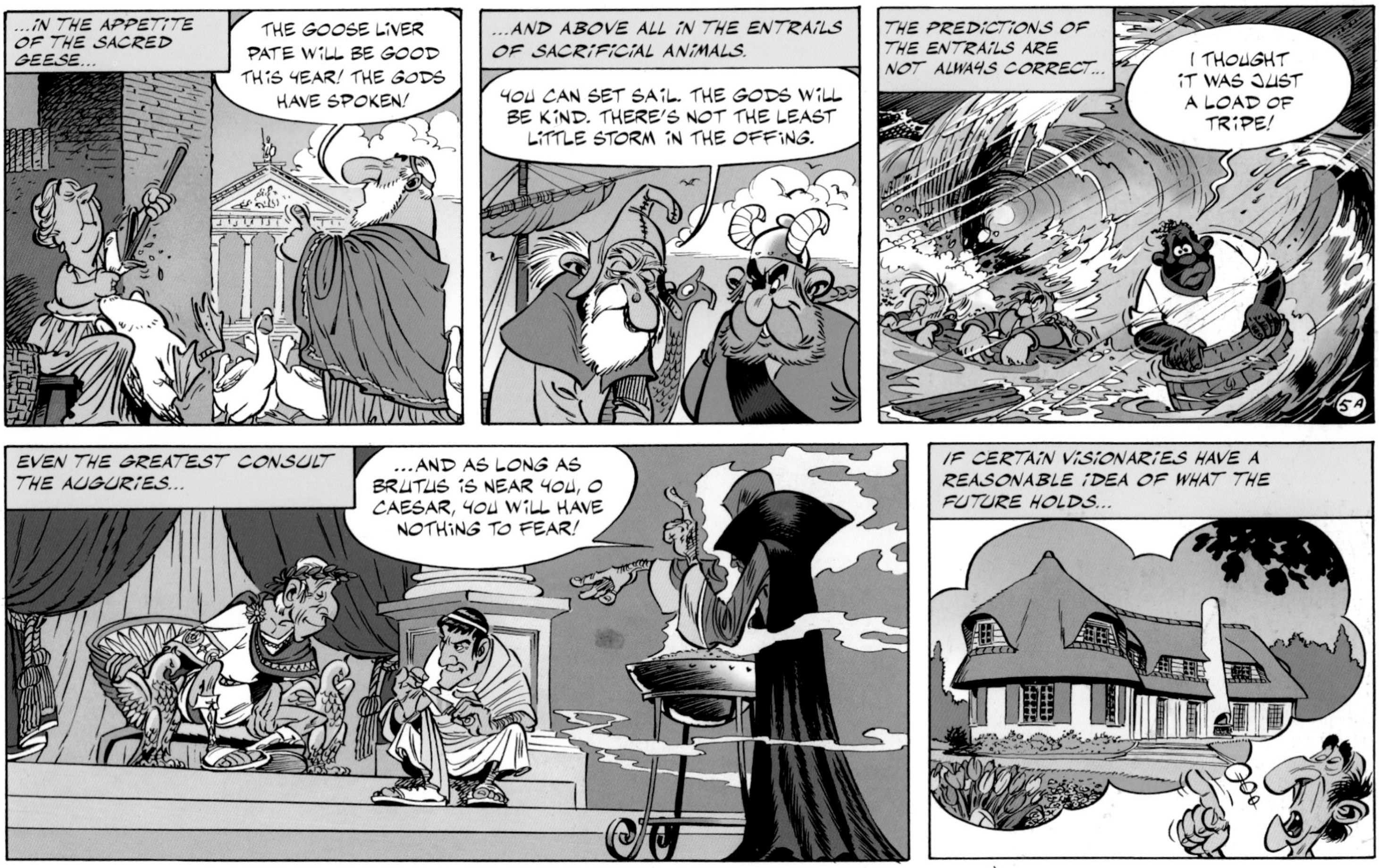

...IN THE APPETITE OF THE SACRED GEESE...
THE GOOSE LIVER PATE WILL BE GOOD THIS YEAR! THE GODS HAVE SPOKEN!
...AND ABOVE ALL IN THE ENTRAILS OF SACRIFICIAL ANIMALS.
YOU CAN SET SAIL. THE GODS WILL BE KIND. THERE'S NOT THE LEAST LITTLE STORM IN THE OFFING.
THE PREDICTIONS OF THE ENTRAILS ARE NOT ALWAYS CORRECT...
I THOUGHT IT WAS JUST A LOAD OF TRIPE!
5A
EVEN THE GREATEST CONSULT THE AUGURIES...
...AND AS LONG AS BRUTUS IS NEAR YOU, O CAESAR, YOU WILL HAVE NOTHING TO FEAR!
IF CERTAIN VISIONARIES HAVE A REASONABLE IDEA OF WHAT THE FUTURE HOLDS...

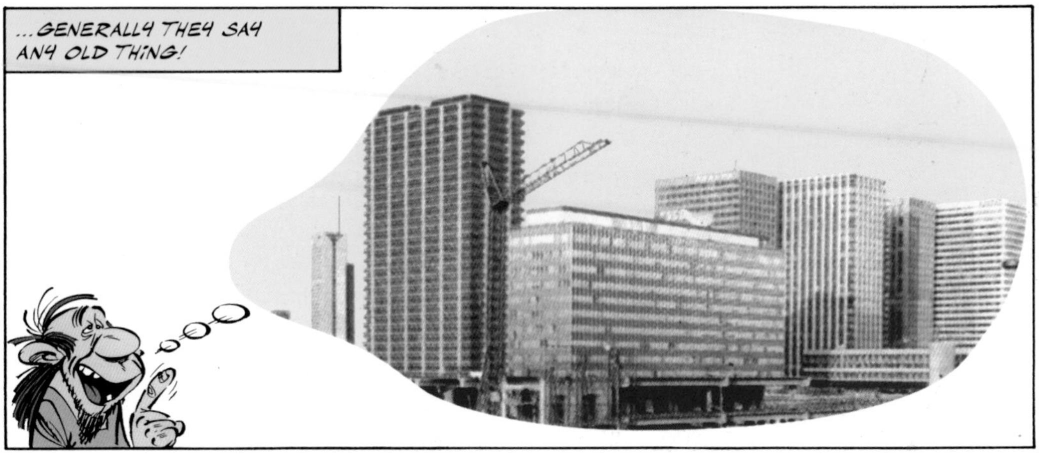

...GENERALLY THEY SAY ANY OLD THING!

IN SHORT, THEY ARE CHARLATANS WHO THRIVE ON CREDULITY, FEAR AND HUMAN SUPERSTITION. HERE WE CLOSE THE PARENTHESIS.

5B

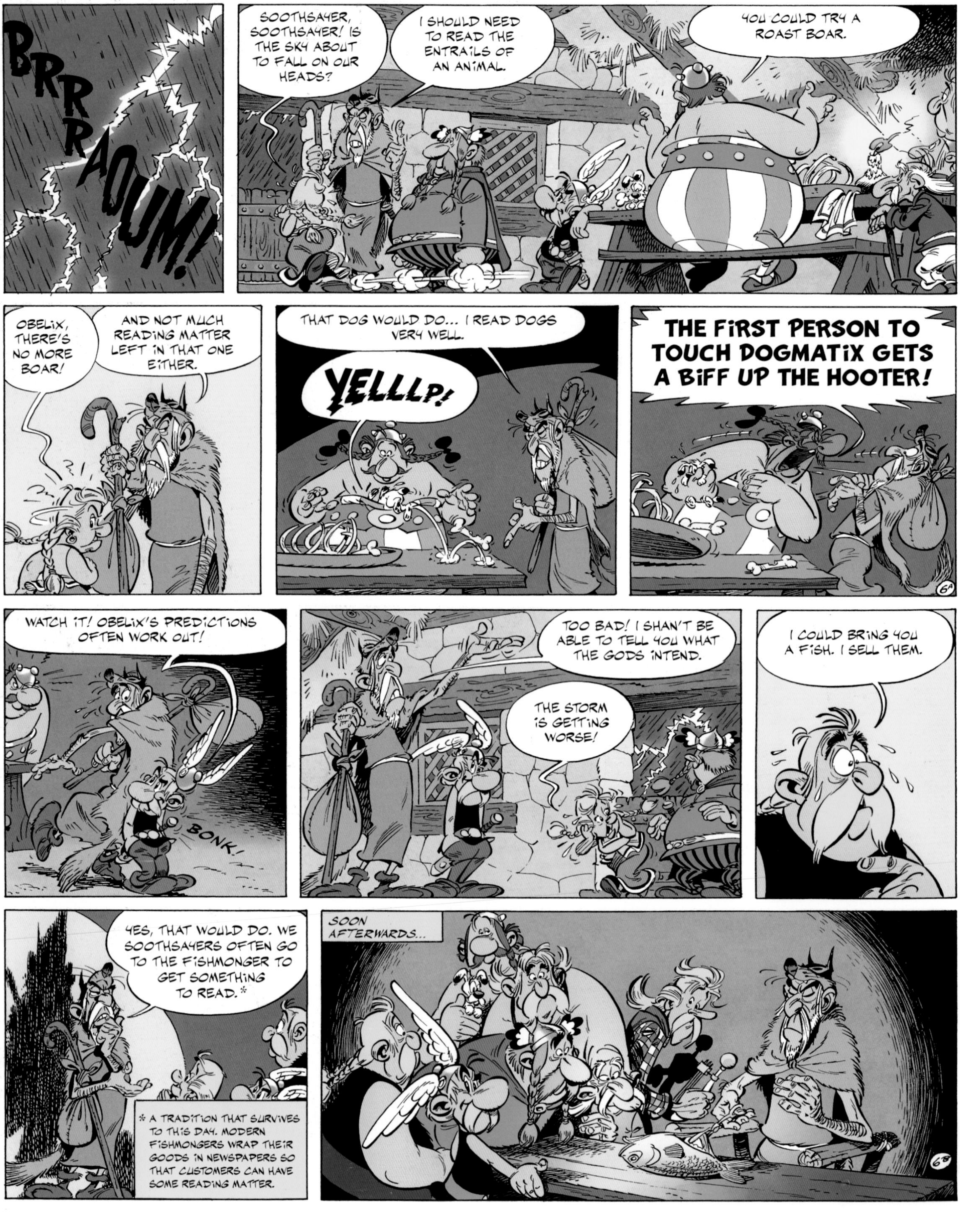
BRRRAOUM!
SOOTHSAYER, SOOTHSAYER! IS THE SKY ABOUT TO FALL ON OUR HEADS?
I SHOULD NEED TO READ THE ENTRAILS OF AN ANIMAL.
YOU COULD TRY A ROAST BOAR.
OBELIX, THERE'S NO MORE BOAR!
AND NOT MUCH READING MATTER LEFT IN THAT ONE EITHER.
THAT DOG WOULD DO... I READ DOGS VERY WELL.
YELLLP!
THE FIRST PERSON TO TOUCH DOGMATIX GETS A BIFF UP THE HOOTER!
WATCH IT! OBELIX'S PREDICTIONS OFTEN WORK OUT!
BONK!
TOO BAD! I SHAN'T BE ABLE TO TELL YOU WHAT THE GODS INTEND.
THE STORM IS GETTING WORSE!
I COULD BRING YOU A FISH. I SELL THEM.
YES, THAT WOULD DO. WE SOOTHSAYERS OFTEN GO TO THE FISHMONGER TO GET SOMETHING TO READ.*
* A TRADITION THAT SURVIVES TO THIS DAY. MODERN FISHMONGERS WRAP THEIR GOODS IN NEWSPAPERS SO THAT CUSTOMERS CAN HAVE SOME READING MATTER.
SOON AFTERWARDS...

BY BORVO, GOD OF SPRINGS, AND BY DAMONA THE HEIFER, AND NO MATTER WHAT THE SCEPTICS THINK, I SEE THAT THE SKY WILL NOT FALL ON YOUR HEADS, AND THAT WHEN THE STORM IS OVER THE WEATHER WILL IMPROVE...

OH! WHAT A RELIEF..

I ALSO SEE THAT THERE'S GOING TO BE A FIGHT.

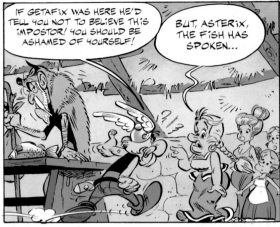

IF GETAFIX WAS HERE HE'D TELL YOU NOT TO BELIEVE THIS IMPOSTOR! YOU SHOULD BE ASHAMED OF YOURSELF!

BUT, ASTERIX, THE FISH HAS SPOKEN...

THE ONLY THING YOU CAN PREDICT FROM EXAMINING THAT FISH IS THAT ANYONE WHO EATS IT WILL BE ILL!

AND WHY DO YOU THINK THAT, MAY I ASK?

BECAUSE YOUR FISH IS NOT VERY FRESH!

PERHAPS IT WAS A BIT STALE... BUT I'M CERTAIN THAT IF I READ THIS DOG WE SHOULD GET CONFIRMATION OF...

NO ONE HAS EVER READ US, AND NO ONE IS EVER GOING TO!!!

SO YOU THINK MY FISH ISN'T VERY FRESH, DO YOU?

WELL, NOT TO PUT TOO FINE A POINT ON IT... NOW IT'S BEEN READ YOU SHOULD CLOSE IT UP AND PUT IT BACK ON THE SLAB...

SPLATCH!

PAF!

PAF!

PAF!

TCHONC!

TCHONC!

TCHOC!

TCHAC!

BANG! BANG! BANG!

WOOF! WOOF!

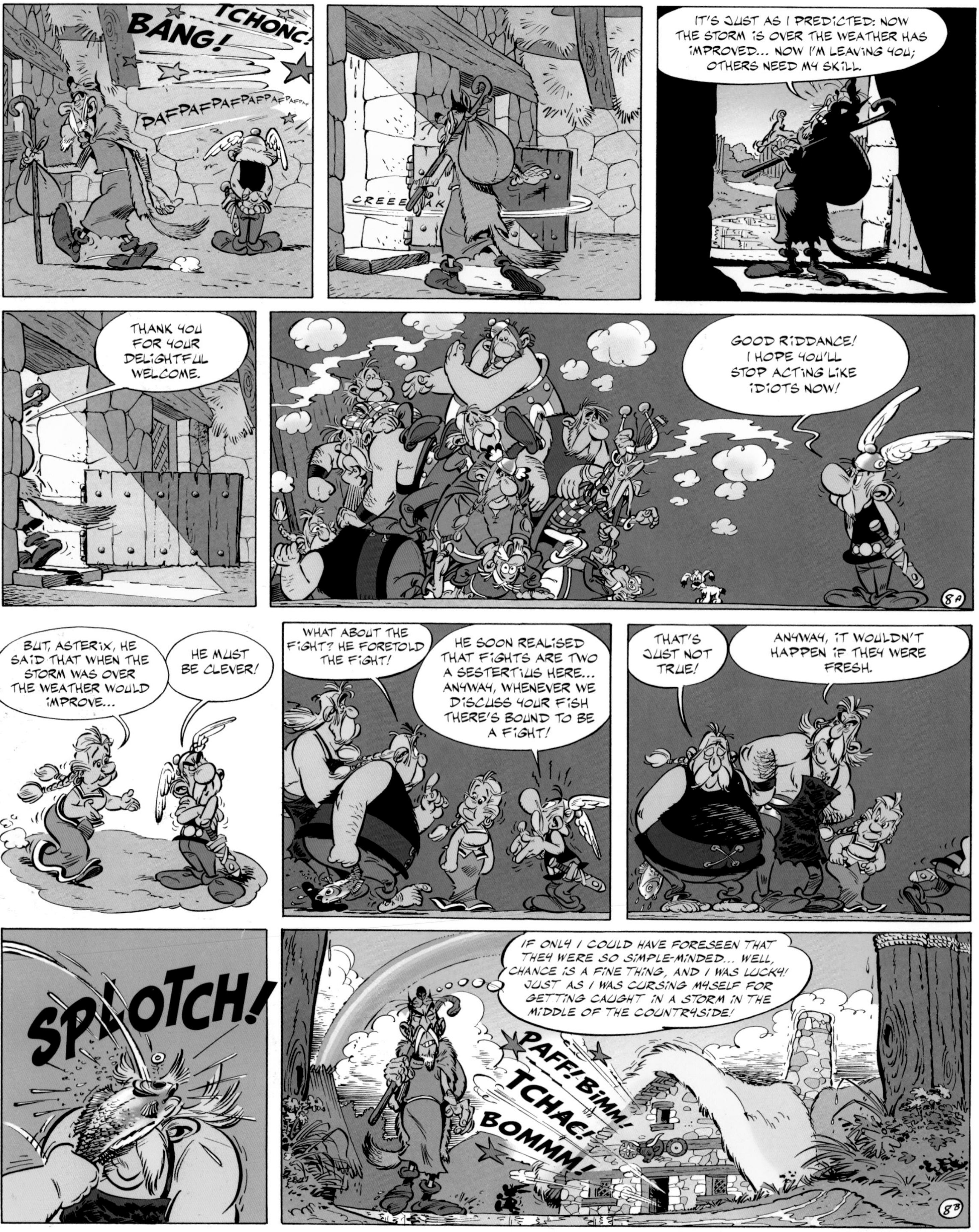
TCHONC!
BANG!
PAFPAFPAFPAFPAFPAFPAF
IT'S JUST AS I PREDICTED: NOW THE STORM IS OVER THE WEATHER HAS IMPROVED... NOW I'M LEAVING YOU; OTHERS NEED MY SKILL.
THANK YOU FOR YOUR DELIGHTFUL WELCOME.
GOOD RIDDANCE! I HOPE YOU'LL STOP ACTING LIKE IDIOTS NOW!
BUT, ASTERIX, HE SAID THAT WHEN THE STORM WAS OVER THE WEATHER WOULD IMPROVE...
HE MUST BE CLEVER!
WHAT ABOUT THE FIGHT? HE FORETOLD THE FIGHT!
HE SOON REALISED THAT FIGHTS ARE TWO A SESTERTIUS HERE... ANYWAY, WHENEVER WE DISCUSS YOUR FISH THERE'S BOUND TO BE A FIGHT!
THAT'S JUST NOT TRUE!
ANYWAY, IT WOULDN'T HAPPEN IF THEY WERE FRESH.
SPLOTCH!
IF ONLY I COULD HAVE FORESEEN THAT THEY WERE SO SIMPLE-MINDED... WELL, CHANCE IS A FINE THING, AND I WAS LUCKY! JUST AS I WAS CURSING MYSELF FOR GETTING CAUGHT IN A STORM IN THE MIDDLE OF THE COUNTRYSIDE!
PAFF! BIMM!
TCHAC!
BOMMM!

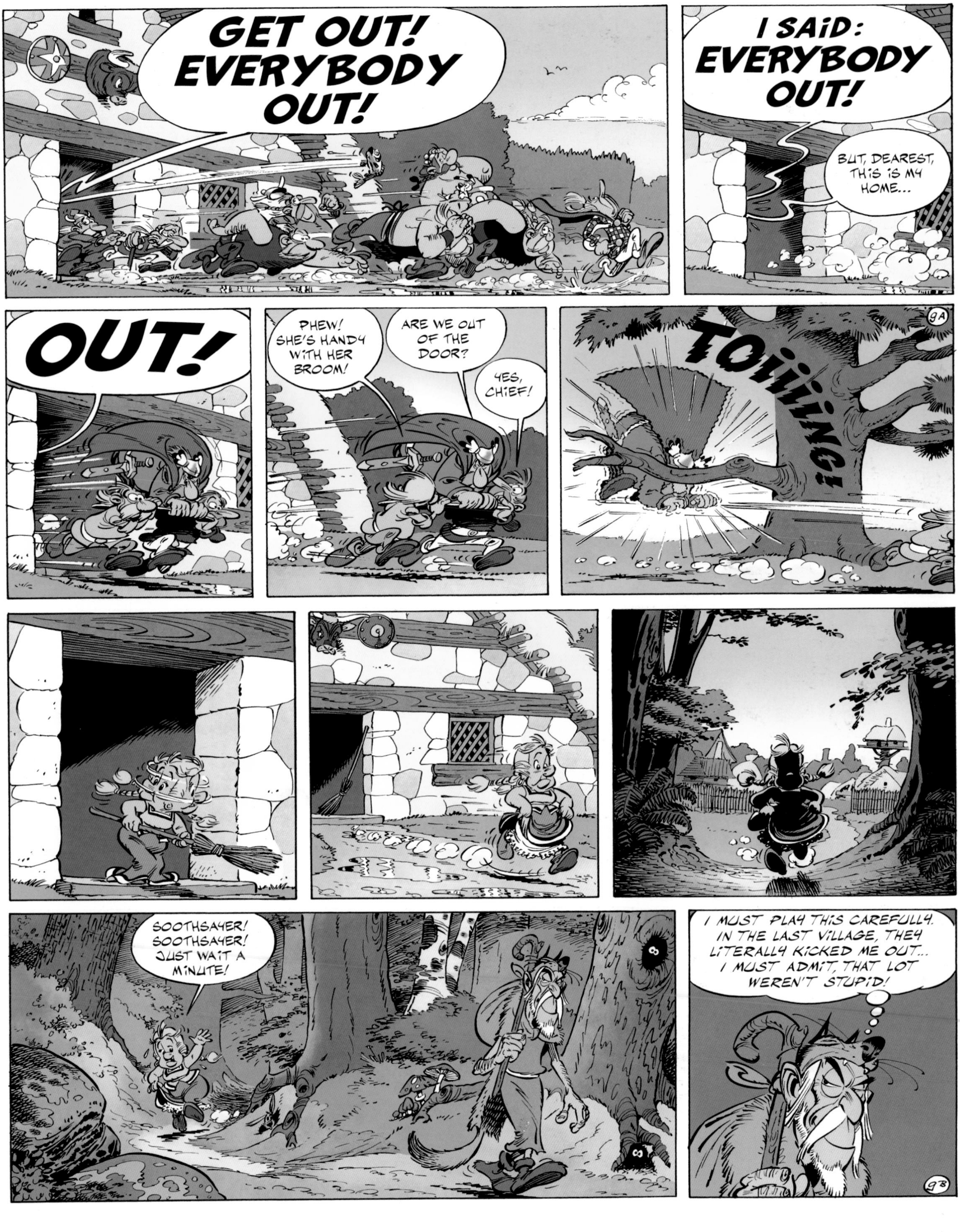

GET OUT! EVERYBODY OUT!
I SAID: EVERYBODY OUT!
BUT, DEAREST, THIS IS MY HOME...
OUT!
PHEW! SHE'S HANDY WITH HER BROOM!
ARE WE OUT OF THE DOOR?
YES, CHIEF!
TOiiiiiNG!
SOOTHSAYER! SOOTHSAYER! JUST WAIT A MINUTE!
I MUST PLAY THIS CAREFULLY. IN THE LAST VILLAGE, THEY LITERALLY KICKED ME OUT... I MUST ADMIT, THAT LOT WEREN'T STUPID!

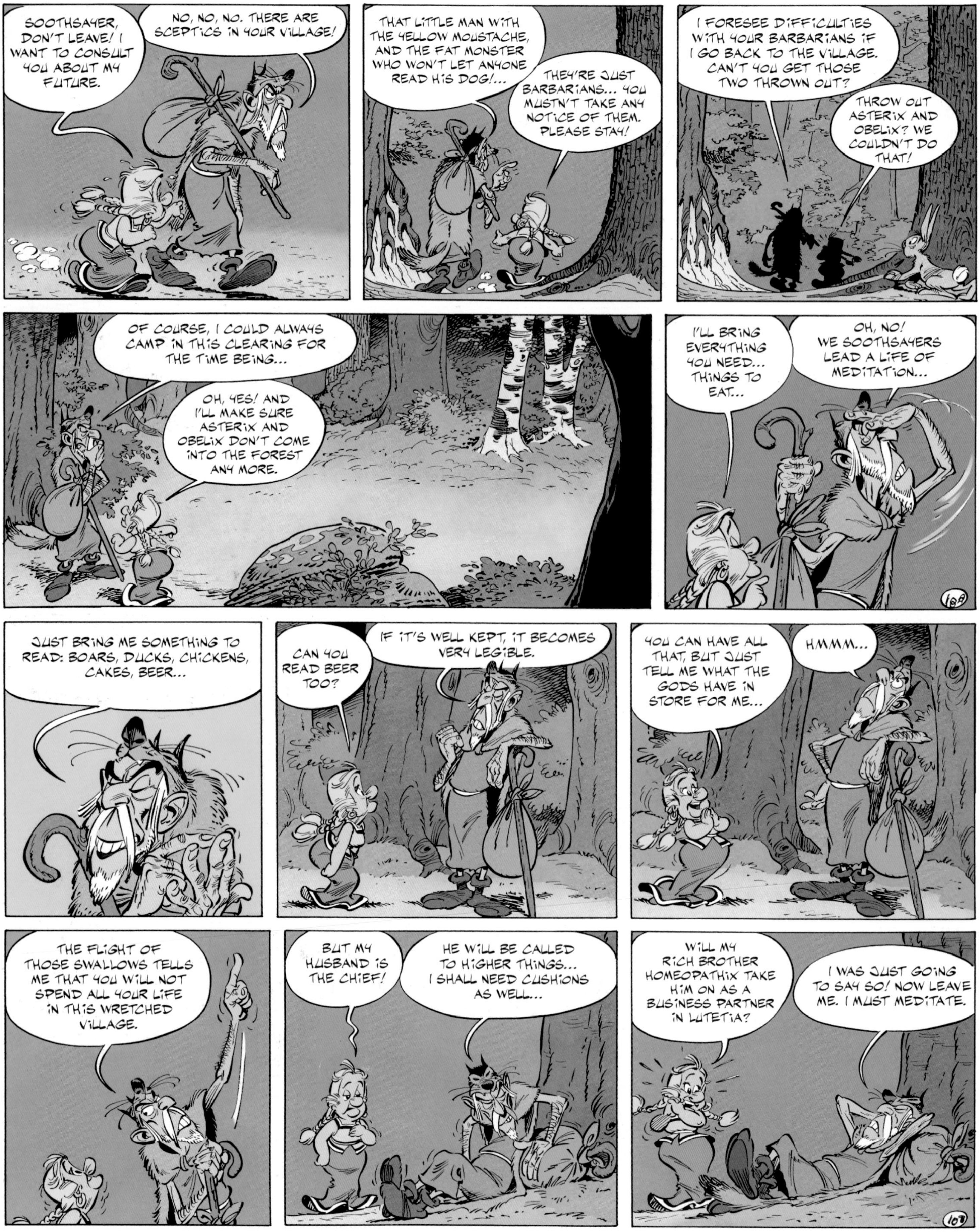
SOOTHSAYER, DON'T LEAVE! I WANT TO CONSULT YOU ABOUT MY FUTURE.
NO, NO, NO. THERE ARE SCEPTICS IN YOUR VILLAGE!
THAT LITTLE MAN WITH THE YELLOW MOUSTACHE, AND THE FAT MONSTER WHO WON'T LET ANYONE READ HIS DOG!...
THEY'RE JUST BARBARIANS... YOU MUSTN'T TAKE ANY NOTICE OF THEM. PLEASE STAY!
I FORESEE DIFFICULTIES WITH YOUR BARBARIANS IF I GO BACK TO THE VILLAGE. CAN'T YOU GET THOSE TWO THROWN OUT?
THROW OUT ASTERIX AND OBELIX? WE COULDN'T DO THAT!
OF COURSE, I COULD ALWAYS CAMP IN THIS CLEARING FOR THE TIME BEING...
OH, YES! AND I'LL MAKE SURE ASTERIX AND OBELIX DON'T COME INTO THE FOREST ANY MORE.
I'LL BRING EVERYTHING YOU NEED... THINGS TO EAT...
OH, NO! WE SOOTHSAYERS LEAD A LIFE OF MEDITATION...
JUST BRING ME SOMETHING TO READ: BOARS, DUCKS, CHICKENS, CAKES, BEER...
CAN YOU READ BEER TOO?
IF IT'S WELL KEPT, IT BECOMES VERY LEGIBLE.
YOU CAN HAVE ALL THAT, BUT JUST TELL ME WHAT THE GODS HAVE IN STORE FOR ME...
HMMM...
THE FLIGHT OF THOSE SWALLOWS TELLS ME THAT YOU WILL NOT SPEND ALL YOUR LIFE IN THIS WRETCHED VILLAGE.
BUT MY HUSBAND IS THE CHIEF!
HE WILL BE CALLED TO HIGHER THINGS... I SHALL NEED CUSHIONS AS WELL...
WILL MY RICH BROTHER HOMEOPATHIX TAKE HIM ON AS A BUSINESS PARTNER IN LUTETIA?
I WAS JUST GOING TO SAY SO! NOW LEAVE ME. I MUST MEDITATE.

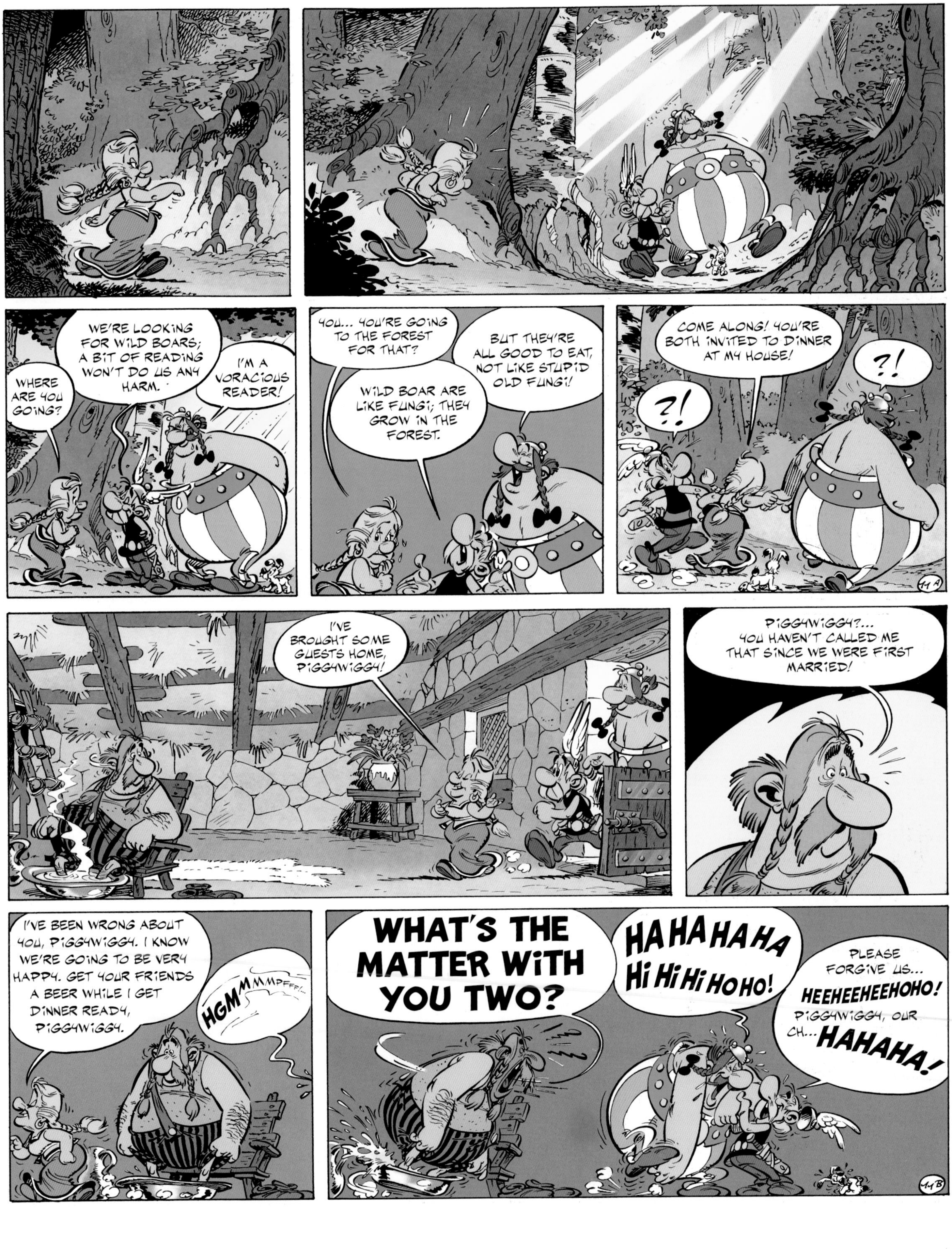

WHERE ARE YOU GOING?
WE'RE LOOKING FOR WILD BOARS; A BIT OF READING WON'T DO US ANY HARM.
I'M A VORACIOUS READER!
YOU... YOU'RE GOING TO THE FOREST FOR THAT?
WILD BOAR ARE LIKE FUNGI; THEY GROW IN THE FOREST.
BUT THEY'RE ALL GOOD TO EAT, NOT LIKE STUPID OLD FUNGI!
COME ALONG! YOU'RE BOTH INVITED TO DINNER AT MY HOUSE!
?!
?!
I'VE BROUGHT SOME GUESTS HOME, PIGGYWIGGY!
PIGGYWIGGY?... YOU HAVEN'T CALLED ME THAT SINCE WE WERE FIRST MARRIED!
I'VE BEEN WRONG ABOUT YOU, PIGGYWIGGY. I KNOW WE'RE GOING TO BE VERY HAPPY. GET YOUR FRIENDS A BEER WHILE I GET DINNER READY, PIGGYWIGGY.
HGMMMMMPFFF!...
WHAT'S THE MATTER WITH YOU TWO?
HAHAHAHAHA Hi Hi Hi HOHO!
PLEASE FORGIVE US... HEEHEEHEEHOHO! PIGGYWIGGY, OUR CH... HAHAHA!

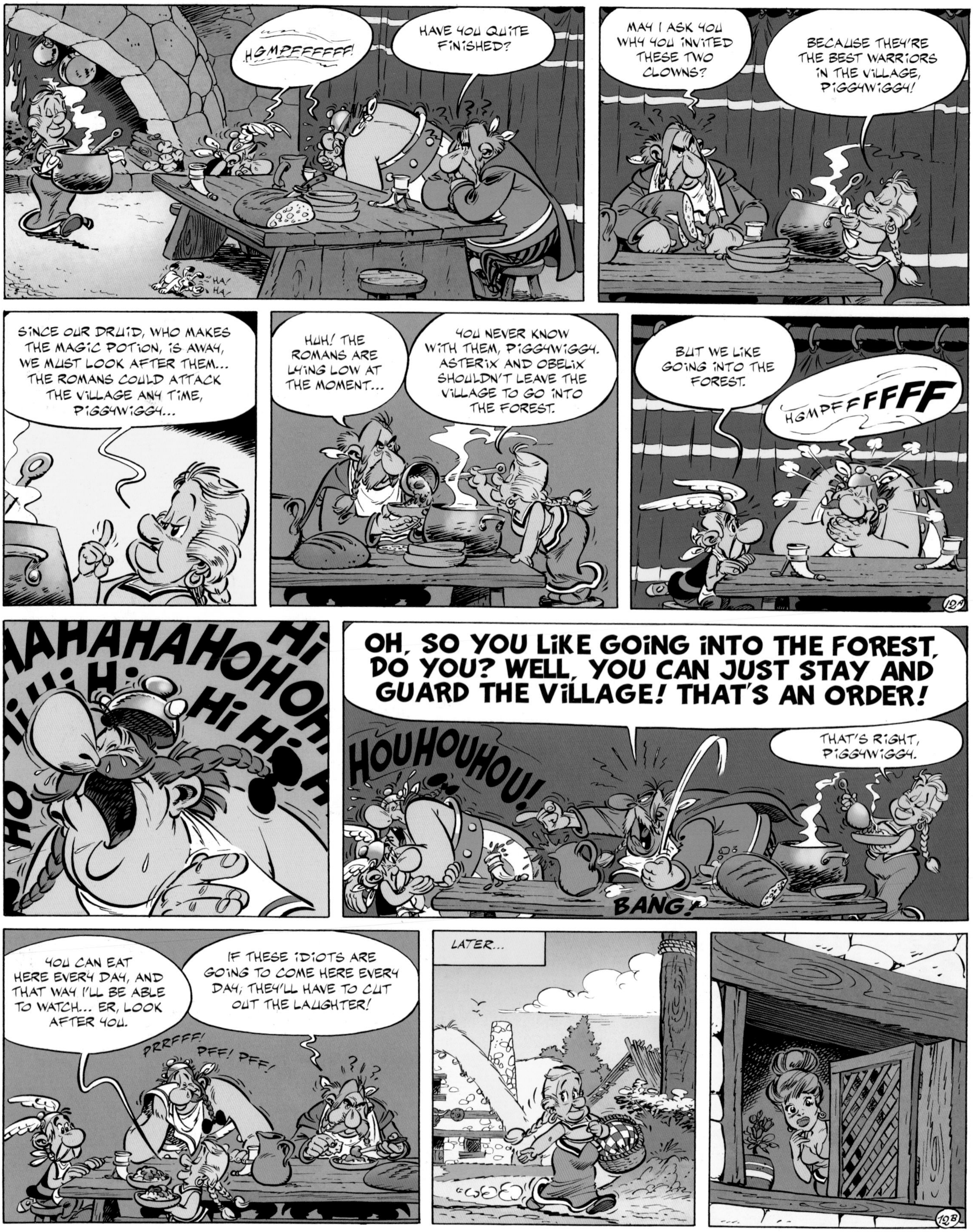
HGMPFFFFFF!
HAVE YOU QUITE FINISHED?
HA! HA!
MAY I ASK YOU WHY YOU INVITED THESE TWO CLOWNS?
BECAUSE THEY'RE THE BEST WARRIORS IN THE VILLAGE, PIGGYWIGGY!
SINCE OUR DRUID, WHO MAKES THE MAGIC POTION, IS AWAY, WE MUST LOOK AFTER THEM... THE ROMANS COULD ATTACK THE VILLAGE ANY TIME, PIGGYWIGGY...
HUH! THE ROMANS ARE LYING LOW AT THE MOMENT...
YOU NEVER KNOW WITH THEM, PIGGYWIGGY. ASTERIX AND OBELIX SHOULDN'T LEAVE THE VILLAGE TO GO INTO THE FOREST.
BUT WE LIKE GOING INTO THE FOREST.
HGMPFFFFFFF
12A
AAHAHAHAHOHOH! HI HI HI!
OH, SO YOU LIKE GOING INTO THE FOREST, DO YOU? WELL, YOU CAN JUST STAY AND GUARD THE VILLAGE! THAT'S AN ORDER!
HOUHOUHOU!
THAT'S RIGHT, PIGGYWIGGY.
BANG!
YOU CAN EAT HERE EVERY DAY, AND THAT WAY I'LL BE ABLE TO WATCH... ER, LOOK AFTER YOU.
IF THESE IDIOTS ARE GOING TO COME HERE EVERY DAY, THEY'LL HAVE TO CUT OUT THE LAUGHTER!
PRRFFF! PFF! PFF!
LATER...
12B

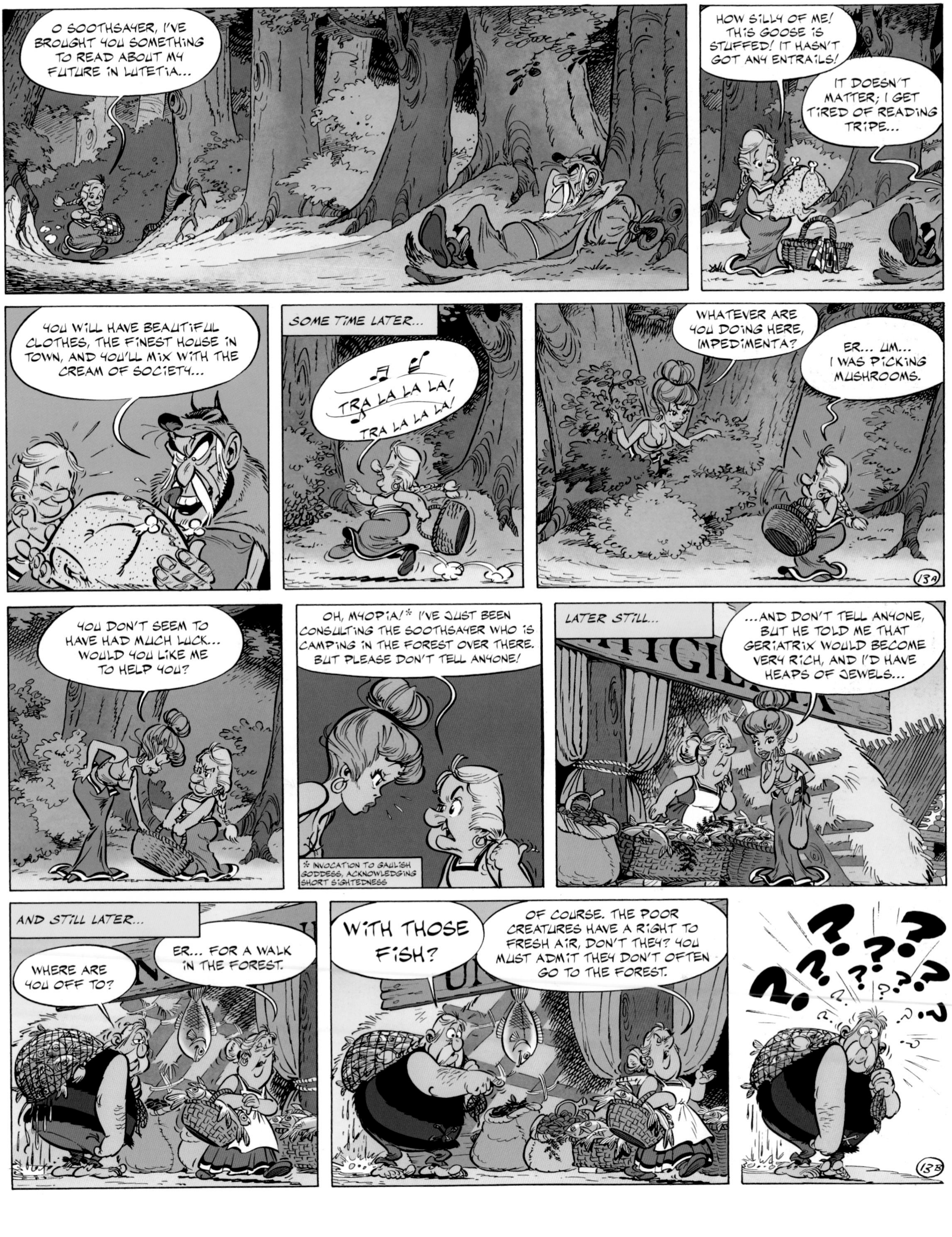
O SOOTHSAYER, I'VE BROUGHT YOU SOMETHING TO READ ABOUT MY FUTURE IN LUTETIA...
HOW SILLY OF ME! THIS GOOSE IS STUFFED! IT HASN'T GOT ANY ENTRAILS!
IT DOESN'T MATTER; I GET TIRED OF READING TRIPE...
YOU WILL HAVE BEAUTIFUL CLOTHES, THE FINEST HOUSE IN TOWN, AND YOU'LL MIX WITH THE CREAM OF SOCIETY...
SOME TIME LATER...
TRA LA LA LA! TRA LA LA LA!
WHATEVER ARE YOU DOING HERE, IMPEDIMENTA?
ER... UM... I WAS PICKING MUSHROOMS.
YOU DON'T SEEM TO HAVE HAD MUCH LUCK... WOULD YOU LIKE ME TO HELP YOU?
OH, MYOPIA!* I'VE JUST BEEN CONSULTING THE SOOTHSAYER WHO IS CAMPING IN THE FOREST OVER THERE. BUT PLEASE DON'T TELL ANYONE!
* INVOCATION TO GAULISH GODDESS, ACKNOWLEDGING SHORT SIGHTEDNESS
LATER STILL...
...AND DON'T TELL ANYONE, BUT HE TOLD ME THAT GERIATRIX WOULD BECOME VERY RICH, AND I'D HAVE HEAPS OF JEWELS...
AND STILL LATER...
WHERE ARE YOU OFF TO?
ER... FOR A WALK IN THE FOREST.
WITH THOSE FISH?
OF COURSE. THE POOR CREATURES HAVE A RIGHT TO FRESH AIR, DON'T THEY? YOU MUST ADMIT THEY DON'T OFTEN GO TO THE FOREST.
??????

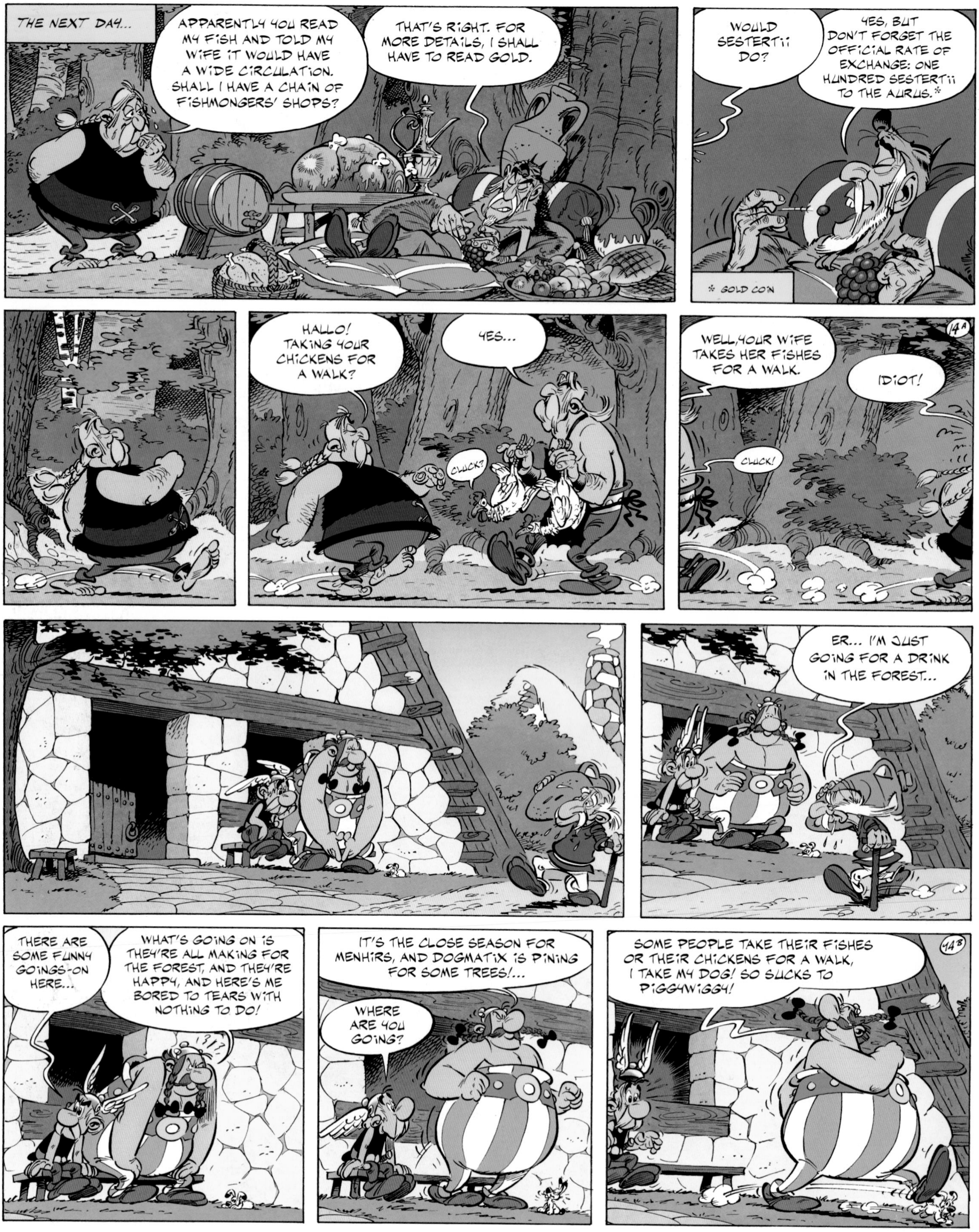
THE NEXT DAY...
APPARENTLY YOU READ MY FISH AND TOLD MY WIFE IT WOULD HAVE A WIDE CIRCULATION. SHALL I HAVE A CHAIN OF FISHMONGERS' SHOPS?
THAT'S RIGHT. FOR MORE DETAILS, I SHALL HAVE TO READ GOLD.
WOULD SESTERTII DO?
YES, BUT DON'T FORGET THE OFFICIAL RATE OF EXCHANGE: ONE HUNDRED SESTERTII TO THE AURUS.*
* GOLD COIN
HALLO! TAKING YOUR CHICKENS FOR A WALK?
YES...
CLUCK?
WELL, YOUR WIFE TAKES HER FISHES FOR A WALK.
IDIOT!
CLUCK!
ER... I'M JUST GOING FOR A DRINK IN THE FOREST...
THERE ARE SOME FUNNY GOINGS-ON HERE...
WHAT'S GOING ON IS THEY'RE ALL MAKING FOR THE FOREST, AND THEY'RE HAPPY, AND HERE'S ME BORED TO TEARS WITH NOTHING TO DO!
IT'S THE CLOSE SEASON FOR MENHIRS, AND DOGMATIX IS PINING FOR SOME TREES!...
WHERE ARE YOU GOING?
SOME PEOPLE TAKE THEIR FISHES OR THEIR CHICKENS FOR A WALK, I TAKE MY DOG! SO SUCKS TO PIGGYWIGGY!

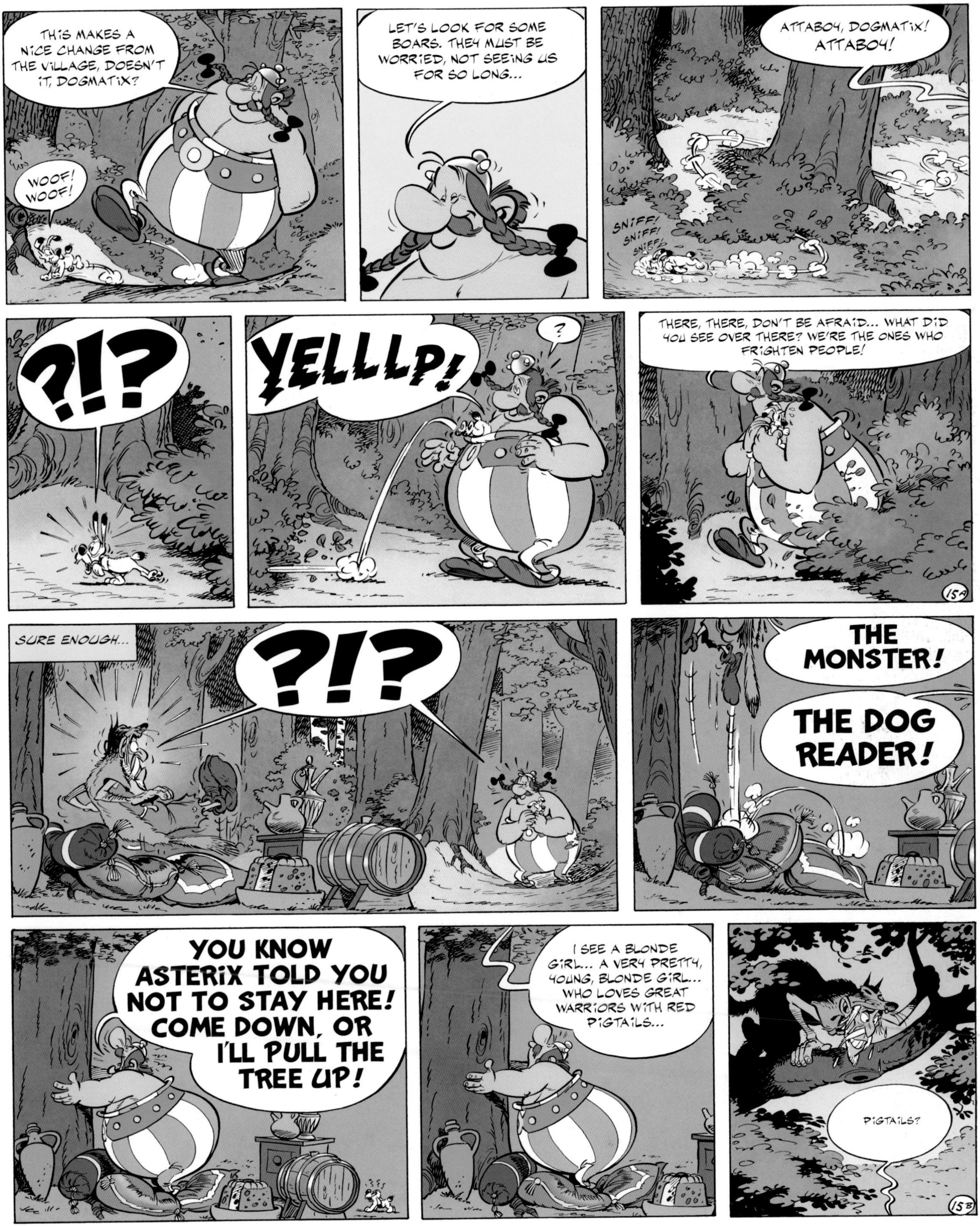
THIS MAKES A NICE CHANGE FROM THE VILLAGE, DOESN'T IT, DOGMATIX?
WOOF! WOOF!
LET'S LOOK FOR SOME BOARS. THEY MUST BE WORRIED, NOT SEEING US FOR SO LONG...
ATTABOY, DOGMATIX! ATTABOY!
SNIFF! SNIFF! SNIFF!
?!?
YELLLP!
?
THERE, THERE, DON'T BE AFRAID... WHAT DID YOU SEE OVER THERE? WE'RE THE ONES WHO FRIGHTEN PEOPLE!
15A
SURE ENOUGH...
?!?
THE MONSTER!
THE DOG READER!
YOU KNOW ASTERIX TOLD YOU NOT TO STAY HERE! COME DOWN, OR I'LL PULL THE TREE UP!
I SEE A BLONDE GIRL... A VERY PRETTY, YOUNG, BLONDE GIRL... WHO LOVES GREAT WARRIORS WITH RED PIGTAILS...
PIGTAILS?
15B

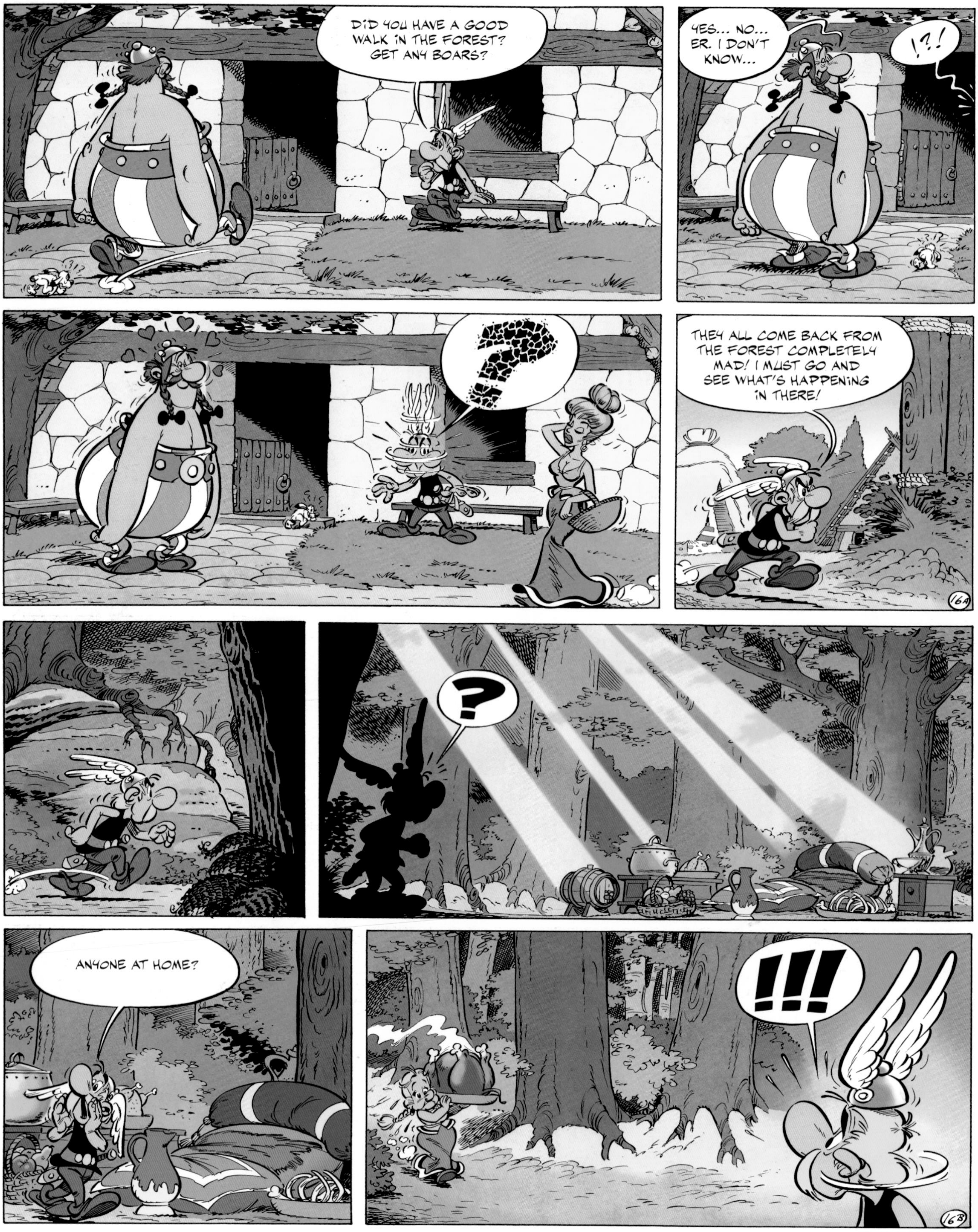
DID YOU HAVE A GOOD WALK IN THE FOREST? GET ANY BOARS?
YES... NO... ER. I DON'T KNOW...
!?!
?
THEY ALL COME BACK FROM THE FOREST COMPLETELY MAD! I MUST GO AND SEE WHAT'S HAPPENING IN THERE!
?
ANYONE AT HOME?
!!!

WHERE IS HE?

WHERE IS WHO?

YOU'VE FRIGHTENED HIM AWAY! WHEN YOUR CHIEF TOLD YOU NOT TO COME INTO THE FOREST!

THIS WILL BRING US GREAT MISFORTUNE! THE SOOTHSAYER FORETOLD IT!

THE SOOTHSAYER? IMPEDIMENTA, WAIT FOR ME!...

ASTERIX HAS DRIVEN THE SOOTHSAYER AWAY!

HE MUST BE MAD! THE SOOTHSAYER FORETOLD GREAT MISFORTUNES IF HE WAS DRIVEN AWAY!

YOU HAVE DONE A VERY FOOLISH THING, ASTERIX. THE SOOTHSAYER WARNED ME TOO...

OH, SO YOU WENT TO SEE HIM AS WELL...

WELL... ER... ONLY ONCE! FORESIGHT IS ONE OF THE ATTRIBUTES OF A CHIEFTAIN, AND...

HE TOLD ME THE MAN I LOVE WOULD BECOME STRONG AND HANDSOME!

WELL, HE WAS RIGHT THERE, ANYWAY!

NOW LISTEN: IF I'D KNOWN THE SOOTHSAYER WAS IN THE FOREST, I PROBABLY WOULD HAVE DRIVEN HIM OFF! BUT I DIDN'T KNOW AND I HAVEN'T THE FAINTEST IDEA WHAT'S GOING ON!

UNHYGIENIX

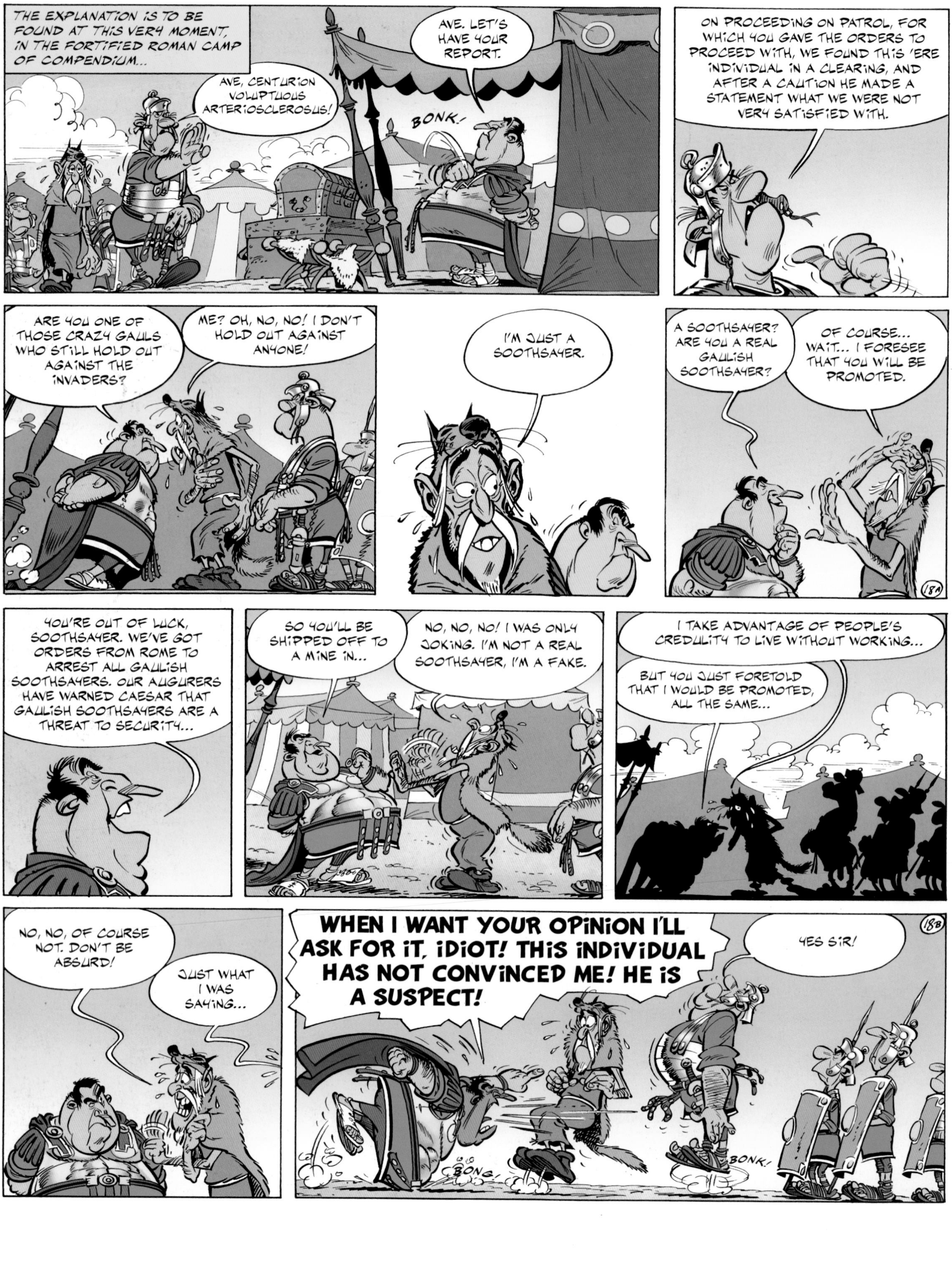
THE EXPLANATION IS TO BE FOUND AT THIS VERY MOMENT, IN THE FORTIFIED ROMAN CAMP OF COMPENDIUM...
AVE, CENTURION VOLUPTUOUS ARTERIOSCLEROSUS!
AVE. LET'S HAVE YOUR REPORT.
BONK!
ON PROCEEDING ON PATROL, FOR WHICH YOU GAVE THE ORDERS TO PROCEED WITH, WE FOUND THIS 'ERE INDIVIDUAL IN A CLEARING, AND AFTER A CAUTION HE MADE A STATEMENT WHAT WE WERE NOT VERY SATISFIED WITH.
ARE YOU ONE OF THOSE CRAZY GAULS WHO STILL HOLD OUT AGAINST THE INVADERS?
ME? OH, NO, NO! I DON'T HOLD OUT AGAINST ANYONE!
I'M JUST A SOOTHSAYER.
A SOOTHSAYER? ARE YOU A REAL GAULISH SOOTHSAYER?
OF COURSE... WAIT... I FORESEE THAT YOU WILL BE PROMOTED.
18A
YOU'RE OUT OF LUCK, SOOTHSAYER. WE'VE GOT ORDERS FROM ROME TO ARREST ALL GAULISH SOOTHSAYERS. OUR AUGURERS HAVE WARNED CAESAR THAT GAULISH SOOTHSAYERS ARE A THREAT TO SECURITY...
SO YOU'LL BE SHIPPED OFF TO A MINE IN...
NO, NO, NO! I WAS ONLY JOKING. I'M NOT A REAL SOOTHSAYER, I'M A FAKE.
I TAKE ADVANTAGE OF PEOPLE'S CREDULITY TO LIVE WITHOUT WORKING...
BUT YOU JUST FORETOLD THAT I WOULD BE PROMOTED, ALL THE SAME...
NO, NO, OF COURSE NOT. DON'T BE ABSURD!
JUST WHAT I WAS SAYING...
WHEN I WANT YOUR OPINION I'LL ASK FOR IT, IDIOT! THIS INDIVIDUAL HAS NOT CONVINCED ME! HE IS A SUSPECT!
YES SIR!
18B
BONG!
BONK!

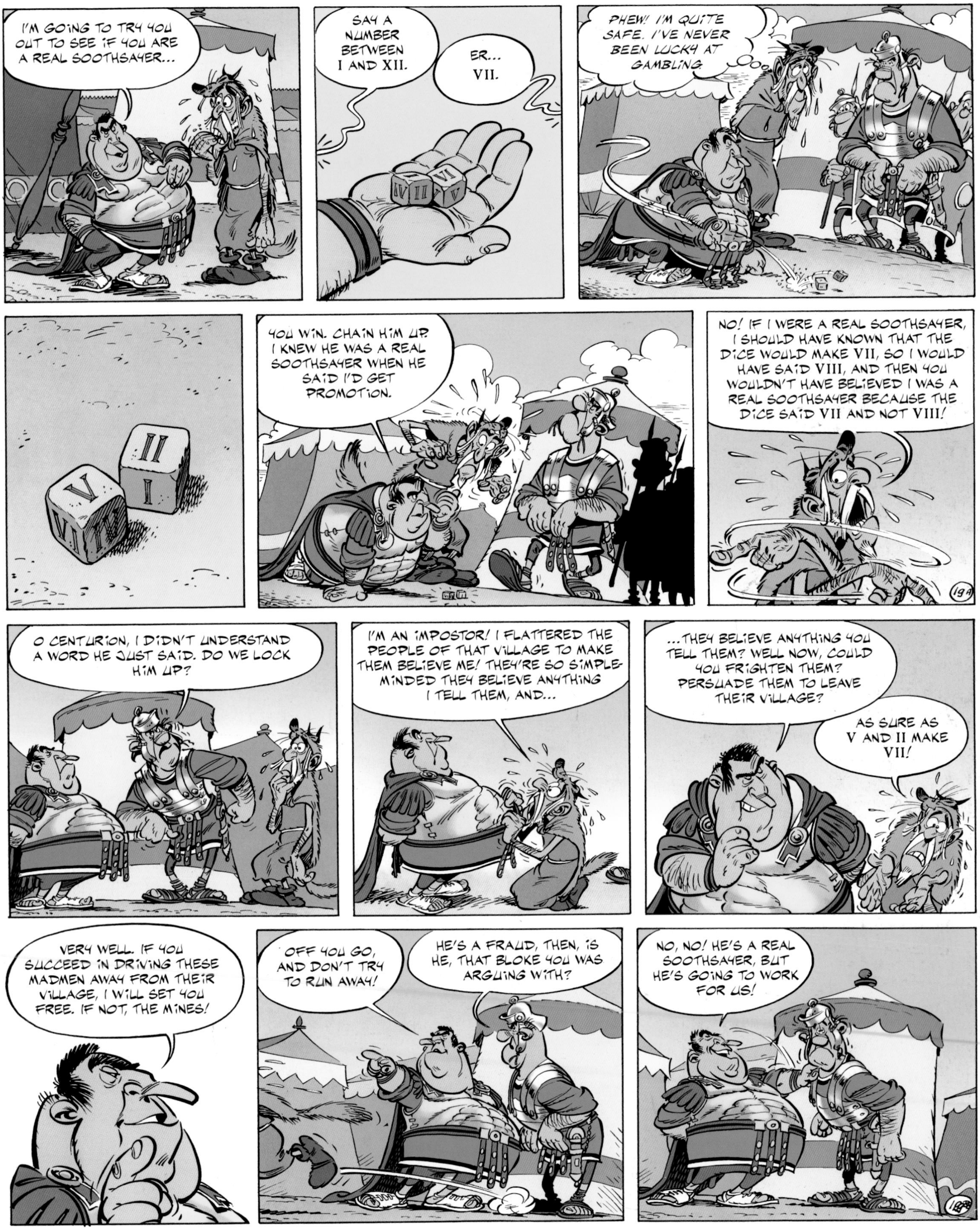
I'M GOING TO TRY YOU OUT TO SEE IF YOU ARE A REAL SOOTHSAYER...
SAY A NUMBER BETWEEN I AND XII.
ER... VII.
PHEW! I'M QUITE SAFE. I'VE NEVER BEEN LUCKY AT GAMBLING
YOU WIN. CHAIN HIM UP. I KNEW HE WAS A REAL SOOTHSAYER WHEN HE SAID I'D GET PROMOTION.
NO! IF I WERE A REAL SOOTHSAYER, I SHOULD HAVE KNOWN THAT THE DICE WOULD MAKE VII, SO I WOULD HAVE SAID VIII, AND THEN YOU WOULDN'T HAVE BELIEVED I WAS A REAL SOOTHSAYER BECAUSE THE DICE SAID VII AND NOT VIII!
O CENTURION, I DIDN'T UNDERSTAND A WORD HE JUST SAID. DO WE LOCK HIM UP?
I'M AN IMPOSTOR! I FLATTERED THE PEOPLE OF THAT VILLAGE TO MAKE THEM BELIEVE ME! THEY'RE SO SIMPLE-MINDED THEY BELIEVE ANYTHING I TELL THEM, AND...
...THEY BELIEVE ANYTHING YOU TELL THEM? WELL NOW, COULD YOU FRIGHTEN THEM? PERSUADE THEM TO LEAVE THEIR VILLAGE?
AS SURE AS V AND II MAKE VII!
VERY WELL. IF YOU SUCCEED IN DRIVING THESE MADMEN AWAY FROM THEIR VILLAGE, I WILL SET YOU FREE. IF NOT, THE MINES!
OFF YOU GO, AND DON'T TRY TO RUN AWAY!
HE'S A FRAUD, THEN, IS HE, THAT BLOKE YOU WAS ARGUING WITH?
NO, NO! HE'S A REAL SOOTHSAYER, BUT HE'S GOING TO WORK FOR US!

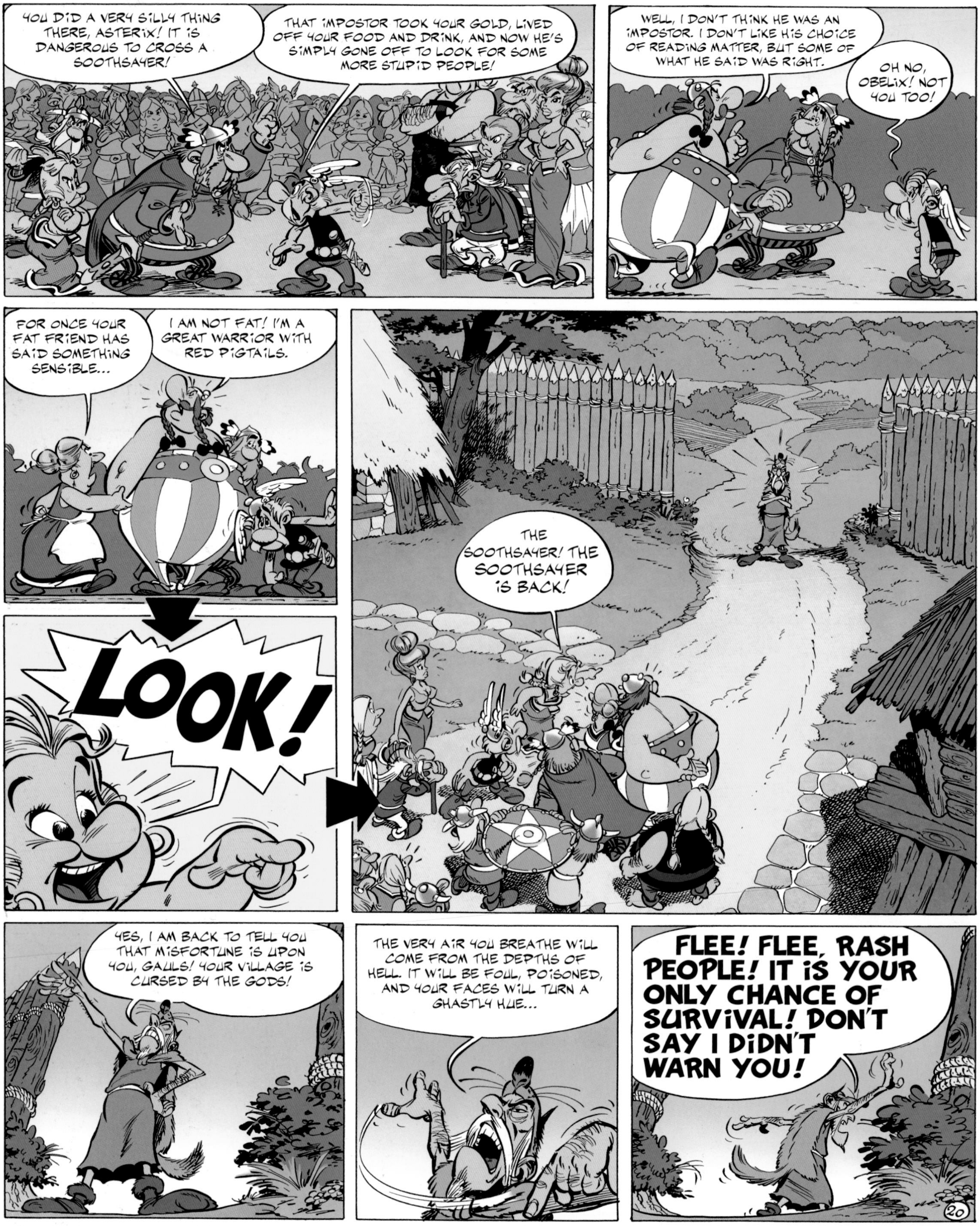
YOU DID A VERY SILLY THING THERE, ASTERIX! IT IS DANGEROUS TO CROSS A SOOTHSAYER!
THAT IMPOSTOR TOOK YOUR GOLD, LIVED OFF YOUR FOOD AND DRINK, AND NOW HE'S SIMPLY GONE OFF TO LOOK FOR SOME MORE STUPID PEOPLE!
WELL, I DON'T THINK HE WAS AN IMPOSTOR. I DON'T LIKE HIS CHOICE OF READING MATTER, BUT SOME OF WHAT HE SAID WAS RIGHT.
OH NO, OBELIX! NOT YOU TOO!
FOR ONCE YOUR FAT FRIEND HAS SAID SOMETHING SENSIBLE...
I AM NOT FAT! I'M A GREAT WARRIOR WITH RED PIGTAILS.
LOOK!
THE SOOTHSAYER! THE SOOTHSAYER IS BACK!
YES, I AM BACK TO TELL YOU THAT MISFORTUNE IS UPON YOU, GAULS! YOUR VILLAGE IS CURSED BY THE GODS!
THE VERY AIR YOU BREATHE WILL COME FROM THE DEPTHS OF HELL. IT WILL BE FOUL, POISONED, AND YOUR FACES WILL TURN A GHASTLY HUE...
FLEE! FLEE, RASH PEOPLE! IT IS YOUR ONLY CHANCE OF SURVIVAL! DON'T SAY I DIDN'T WARN YOU!
20

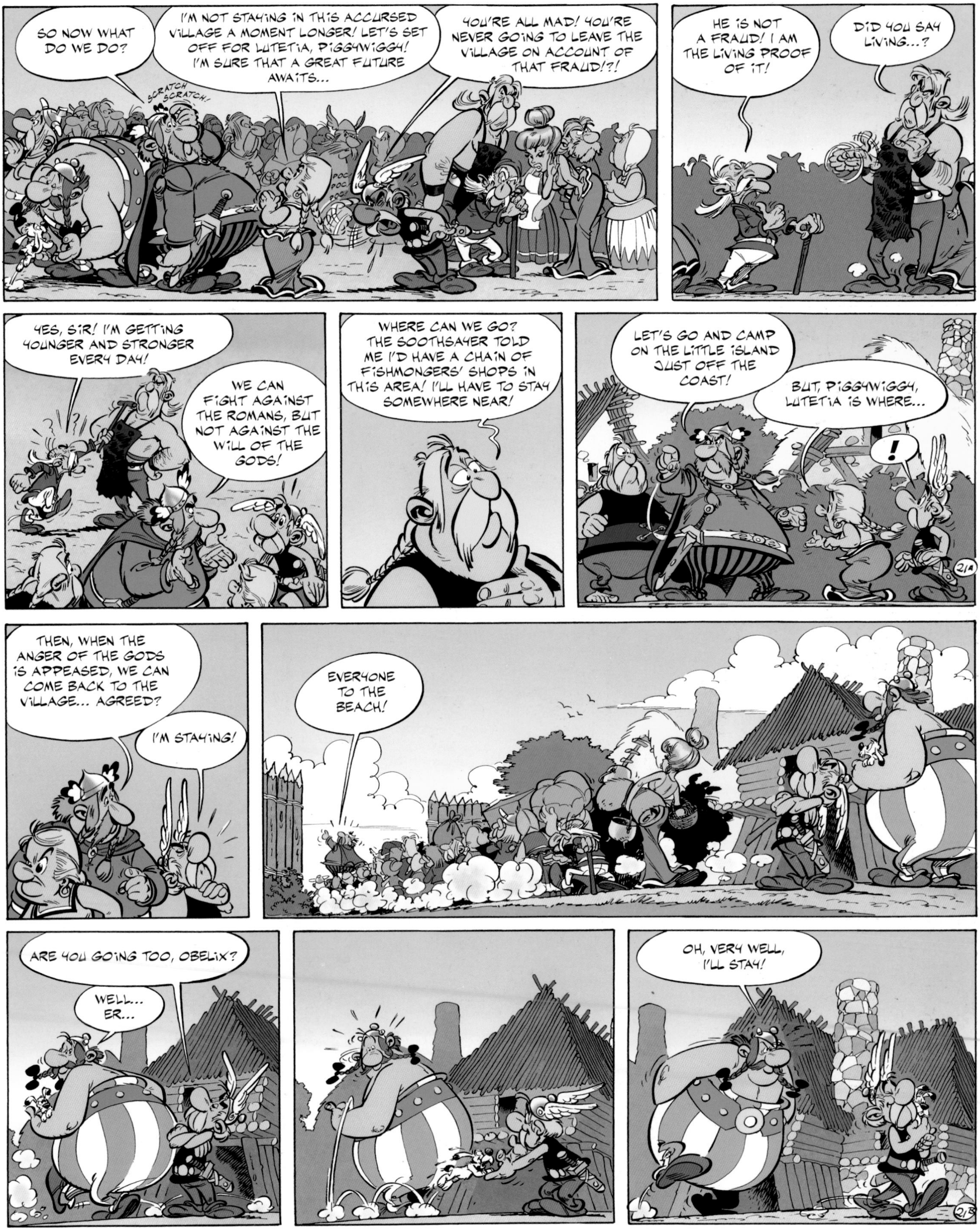
SO NOW WHAT DO WE DO?
SCRATCH SCRATCH!
I'M NOT STAYING IN THIS ACCURSED VILLAGE A MOMENT LONGER! LET'S SET OFF FOR LUTETIA, PIGGYWIGGY! I'M SURE THAT A GREAT FUTURE AWAITS...
YOU'RE ALL MAD! YOU'RE NEVER GOING TO LEAVE THE VILLAGE ON ACCOUNT OF THAT FRAUD!?!
HE IS NOT A FRAUD! I AM THE LIVING PROOF OF IT!
DID YOU SAY LIVING...?
YES, SIR! I'M GETTING YOUNGER AND STRONGER EVERY DAY!
WE CAN FIGHT AGAINST THE ROMANS, BUT NOT AGAINST THE WILL OF THE GODS!
WHERE CAN WE GO? THE SOOTHSAYER TOLD ME I'D HAVE A CHAIN OF FISHMONGERS' SHOPS IN THIS AREA! I'LL HAVE TO STAY SOMEWHERE NEAR!
LET'S GO AND CAMP ON THE LITTLE ISLAND JUST OFF THE COAST!
BUT, PIGGYWIGGY, LUTETIA IS WHERE...
!
THEN, WHEN THE ANGER OF THE GODS IS APPEASED, WE CAN COME BACK TO THE VILLAGE... AGREED?
I'M STAYING!
EVERYONE TO THE BEACH!
ARE YOU GOING TOO, OBELIX?
WELL... ER...
OH, VERY WELL, I'LL STAY!

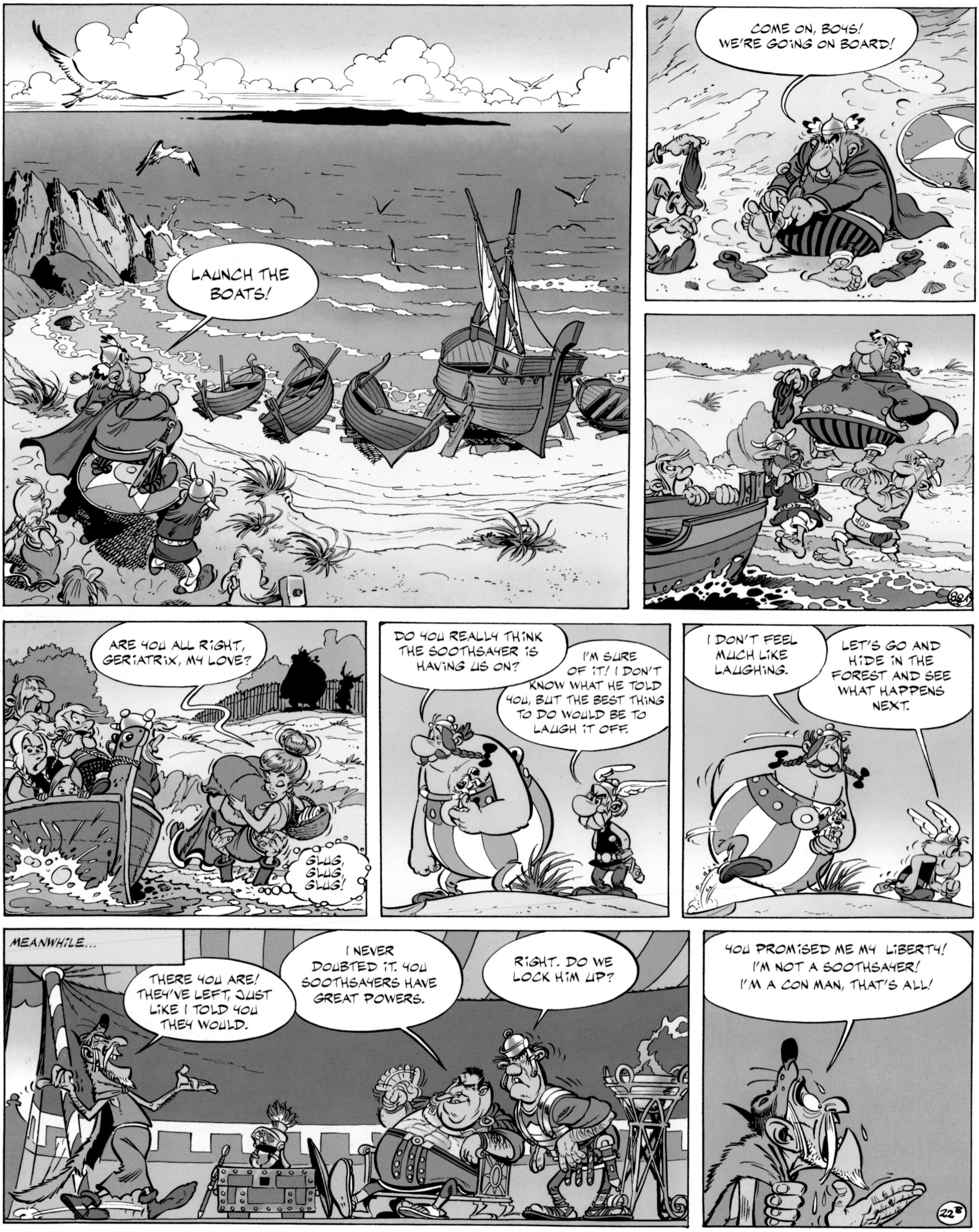
LAUNCH THE BOATS!
COME ON, BOYS! WE'RE GOING ON BOARD!
ARE YOU ALL RIGHT, GERIATRIX, MY LOVE?
GLUG, GLUG, GLUG!
DO YOU REALLY THINK THE SOOTHSAYER IS HAVING US ON?
I'M SURE OF IT! I DON'T KNOW WHAT HE TOLD YOU, BUT THE BEST THING TO DO WOULD BE TO LAUGH IT OFF.
I DON'T FEEL MUCH LIKE LAUGHING.
LET'S GO AND HIDE IN THE FOREST AND SEE WHAT HAPPENS NEXT.
MEANWHILE...
THERE YOU ARE! THEY'VE LEFT, JUST LIKE I TOLD YOU THEY WOULD.
I NEVER DOUBTED IT. YOU SOOTHSAYERS HAVE GREAT POWERS.
RIGHT. DO WE LOCK HIM UP?
YOU PROMISED ME MY LIBERTY! I'M NOT A SOOTHSAYER! I'M A CON MAN, THAT'S ALL!

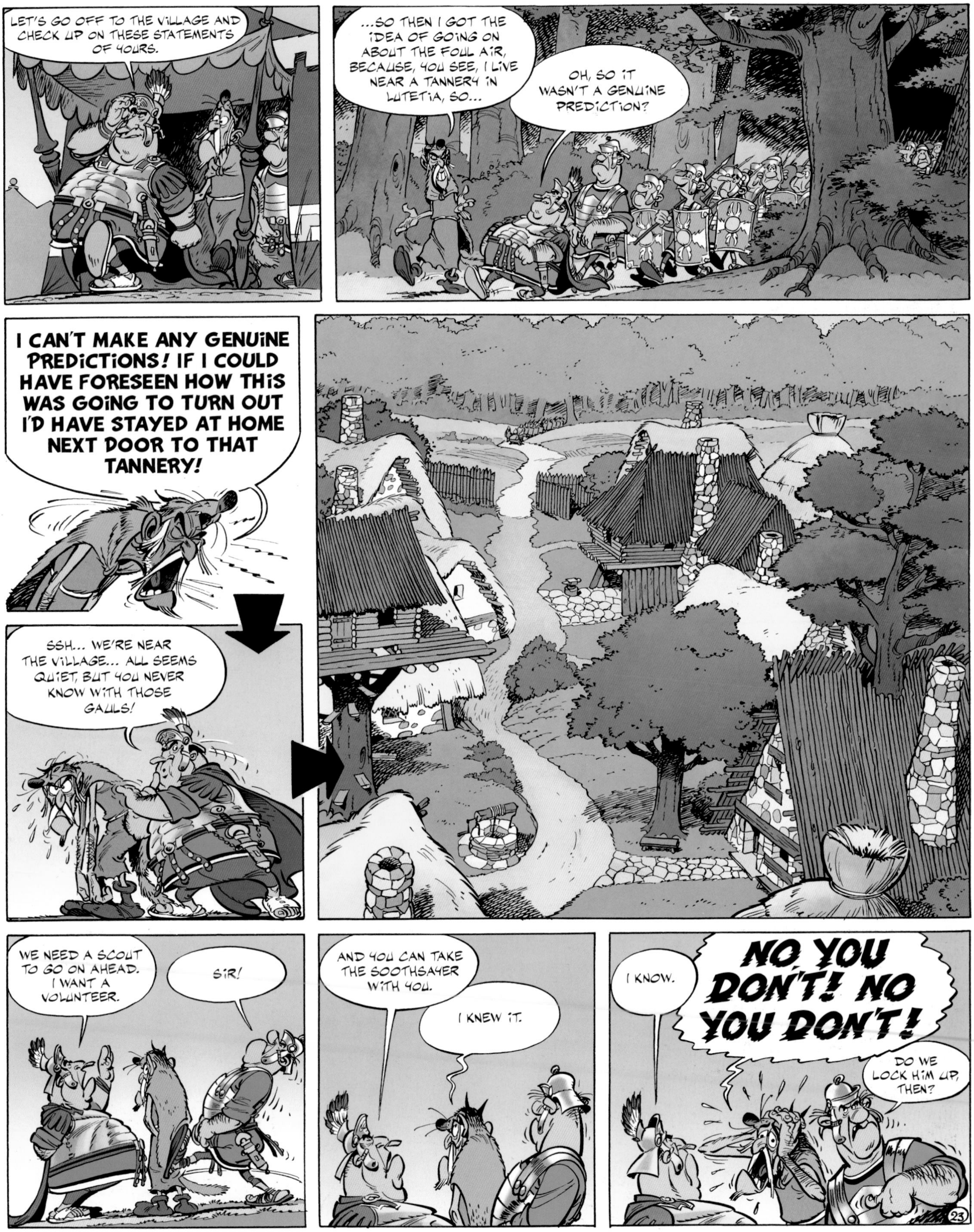
LET'S GO OFF TO THE VILLAGE AND CHECK UP ON THESE STATEMENTS OF YOURS.
...SO THEN I GOT THE IDEA OF GOING ON ABOUT THE FOUL AIR, BECAUSE, YOU SEE, I LIVE NEAR A TANNERY IN LUTETIA, SO...
OH, SO IT WASN'T A GENUINE PREDICTION?
I CAN'T MAKE ANY GENUINE PREDICTIONS! IF I COULD HAVE FORESEEN HOW THIS WAS GOING TO TURN OUT I'D HAVE STAYED AT HOME NEXT DOOR TO THAT TANNERY!
SSH... WE'RE NEAR THE VILLAGE... ALL SEEMS QUIET, BUT YOU NEVER KNOW WITH THOSE GAULS!
WE NEED A SCOUT TO GO ON AHEAD. I WANT A VOLUNTEER.
SIR!
AND YOU CAN TAKE THE SOOTHSAYER WITH YOU.
I KNEW IT.
I KNOW.
NO YOU DON'T! NO YOU DON'T!
DO WE LOCK HIM UP, THEN?
23

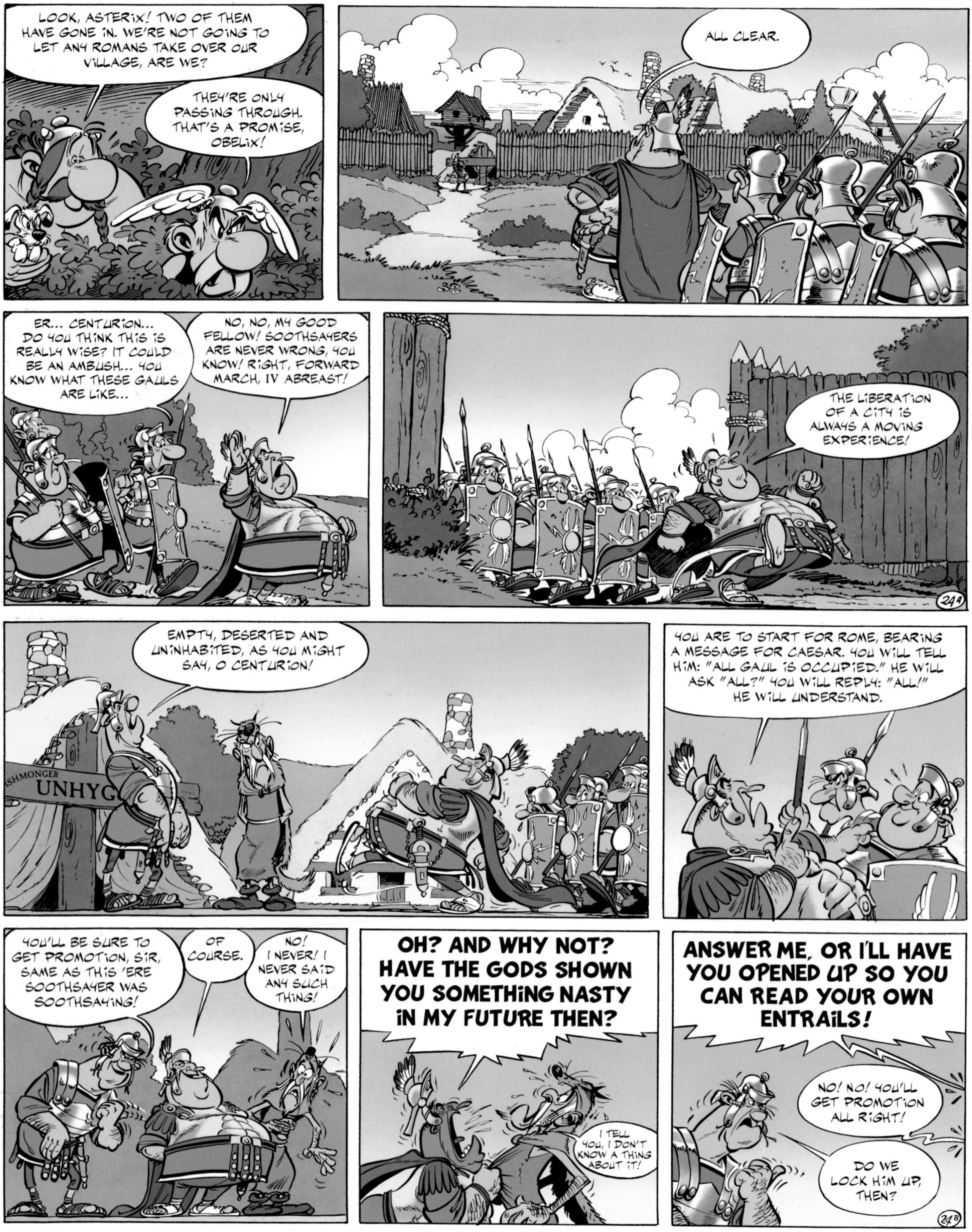
LOOK, ASTERIX! TWO OF THEM HAVE GONE IN. WE'RE NOT GOING TO LET ANY ROMANS TAKE OVER OUR VILLAGE, ARE WE?
THEY'RE ONLY PASSING THROUGH. THAT'S A PROMISE, OBELIX!
ALL CLEAR.
ER... CENTURION... DO YOU THINK THIS IS REALLY WISE? IT COULD BE AN AMBUSH... YOU KNOW WHAT THESE GAULS ARE LIKE...
NO, NO, MY GOOD FELLOW! SOOTHSAYERS ARE NEVER WRONG, YOU KNOW! RIGHT, FORWARD MARCH, IV ABREAST!
THE LIBERATION OF A CITY IS ALWAYS A MOVING EXPERIENCE!
24A
EMPTY, DESERTED AND UNINHABITED, AS YOU MIGHT SAY, O CENTURION!
ISHMONGER
UNHYG
YOU ARE TO START FOR ROME, BEARING A MESSAGE FOR CAESAR. YOU WILL TELL HIM: "ALL GAUL IS OCCUPIED." HE WILL ASK "ALL?" YOU WILL REPLY: "ALL!" HE WILL UNDERSTAND.
YOU'LL BE SURE TO GET PROMOTION, SIR, SAME AS THIS 'ERE SOOTHSAYER WAS SOOTHSAYING!
OF COURSE.
NO! I NEVER! I NEVER SAID ANY SUCH THING!
OH? AND WHY NOT? HAVE THE GODS SHOWN YOU SOMETHING NASTY IN MY FUTURE THEN?
I TELL YOU, I DON'T KNOW A THING ABOUT IT!
ANSWER ME, OR I'LL HAVE YOU OPENED UP SO YOU CAN READ YOUR OWN ENTRAILS!
NO! NO! YOU'LL GET PROMOTION ALL RIGHT!
DO WE LOCK HIM UP, THEN?
24B

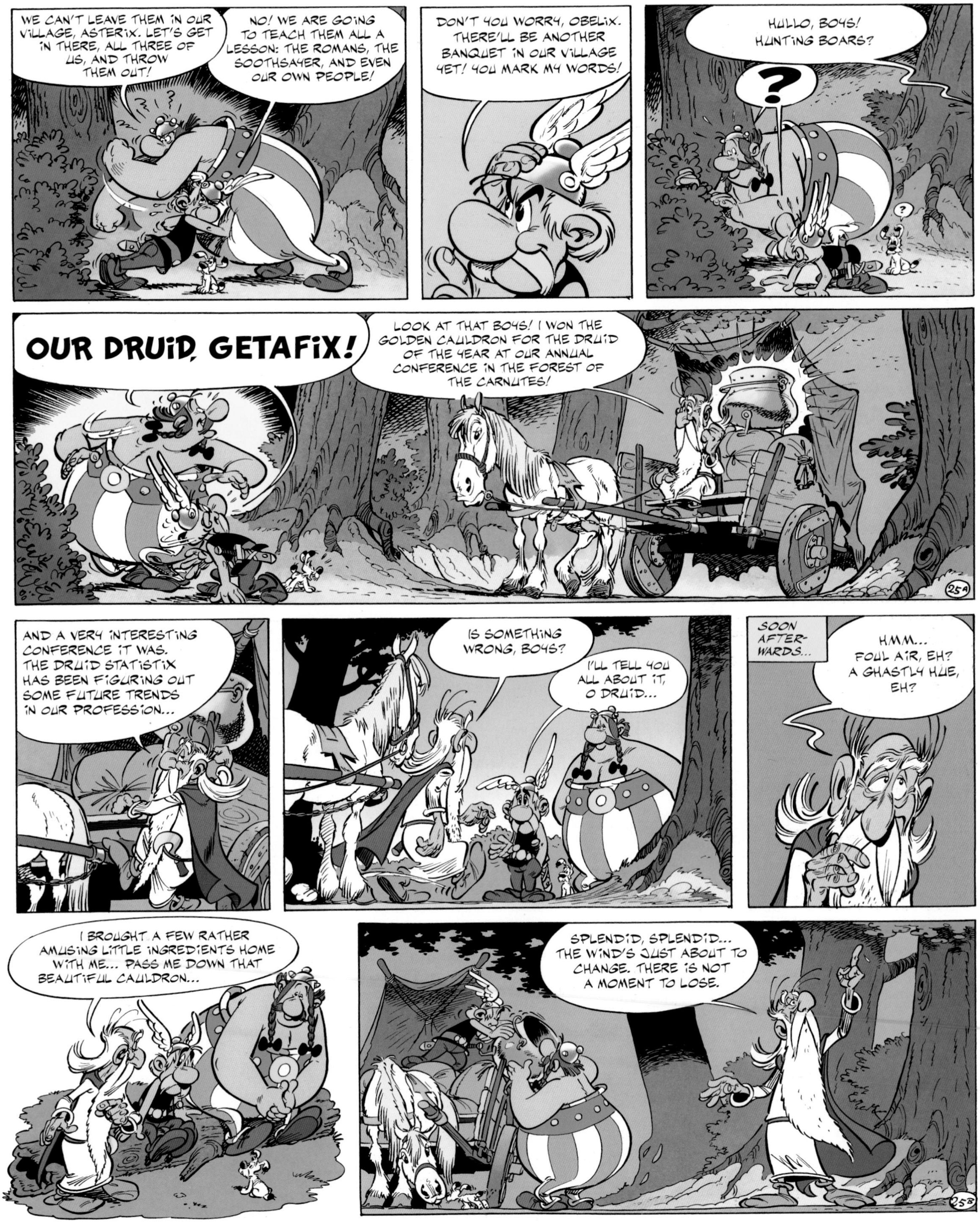

WE CAN'T LEAVE THEM IN OUR VILLAGE, ASTERIX. LET'S GET IN THERE, ALL THREE OF US, AND THROW THEM OUT!
NO! WE ARE GOING TO TEACH THEM ALL A LESSON: THE ROMANS, THE SOOTHSAYER, AND EVEN OUR OWN PEOPLE!
DON'T YOU WORRY, OBELIX. THERE'LL BE ANOTHER BANQUET IN OUR VILLAGE YET! YOU MARK MY WORDS!
HULLO, BOYS! HUNTING BOARS?
?
?
OUR DRUID, GETAFIX!
LOOK AT THAT BOYS! I WON THE GOLDEN CAULDRON FOR THE DRUID OF THE YEAR AT OUR ANNUAL CONFERENCE IN THE FOREST OF THE CARNUTES!
25A
AND A VERY INTERESTING CONFERENCE IT WAS. THE DRUID STATISTIX HAS BEEN FIGURING OUT SOME FUTURE TRENDS IN OUR PROFESSION...
IS SOMETHING WRONG, BOYS?
I'LL TELL YOU ALL ABOUT IT, O DRUID...
SOON AFTERWARDS...
HMM... FOUL AIR, EH? A GHASTLY HUE, EH?
I BROUGHT A FEW RATHER AMUSING LITTLE INGREDIENTS HOME WITH ME... PASS ME DOWN THAT BEAUTIFUL CAULDRON...
SPLENDID, SPLENDID... THE WIND'S JUST ABOUT TO CHANGE. THERE IS NOT A MOMENT TO LOSE.
25B

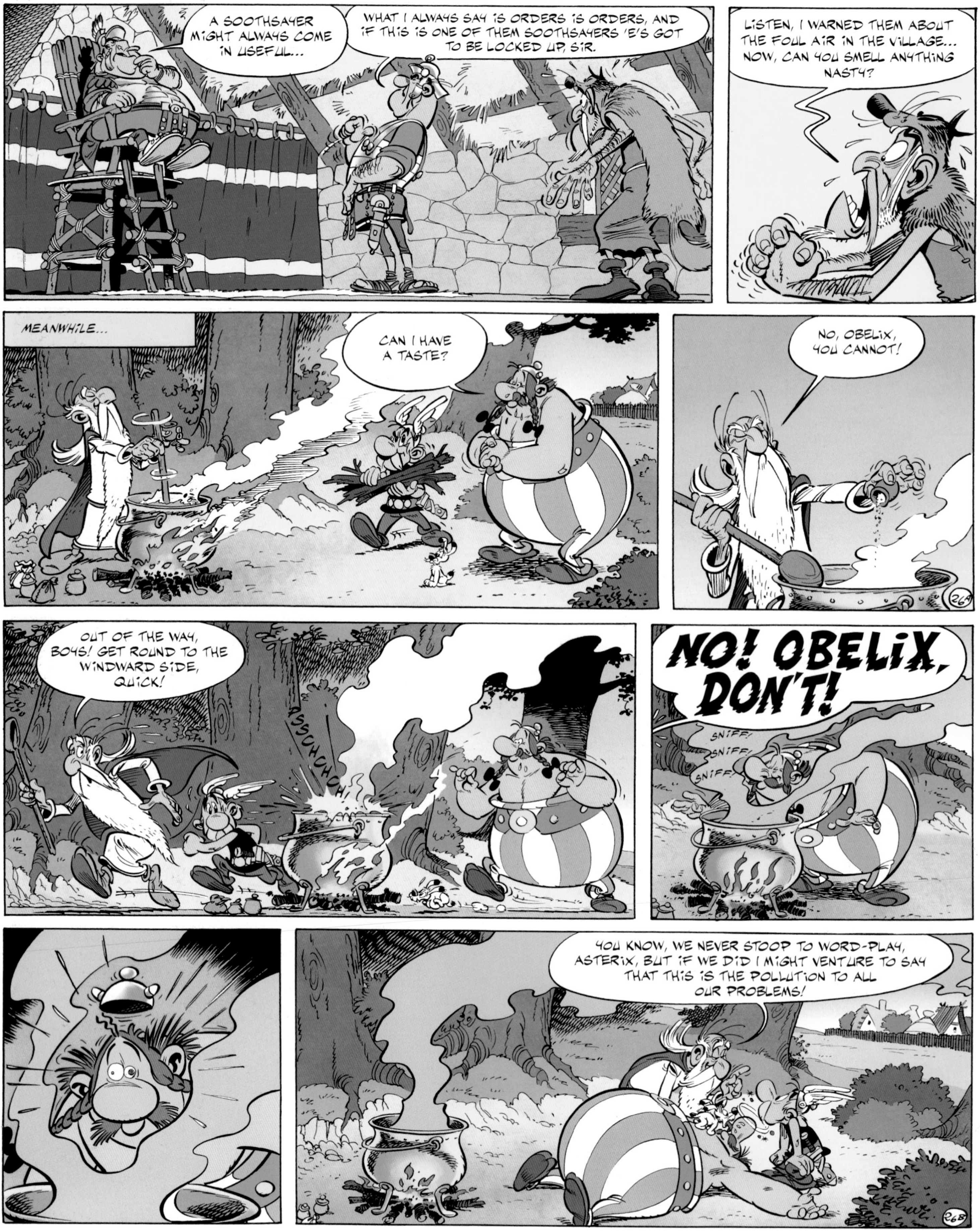
A SOOTHSAYER MIGHT ALWAYS COME IN USEFUL...
WHAT I ALWAYS SAY IS ORDERS IS ORDERS, AND IF THIS IS ONE OF THEM SOOTHSAYERS 'E'S GOT TO BE LOCKED UP, SIR.
LISTEN, I WARNED THEM ABOUT THE FOUL AIR IN THE VILLAGE... NOW, CAN YOU SMELL ANYTHING NASTY?
MEANWHILE...
CAN I HAVE A TASTE?
NO, OBELIX, YOU CANNOT!
OUT OF THE WAY, BOYS! GET ROUND TO THE WINDWARD SIDE, QUICK!
PSSCHCHCH!
NO! OBELIX, DON'T!
SNIFF! SNIFF! SNIFF!
YOU KNOW, WE NEVER STOOP TO WORD-PLAY, ASTERIX, BUT IF WE DID I MIGHT VENTURE TO SAY THAT THIS IS THE POLLUTION TO ALL OUR PROBLEMS!

TARANIS, THE GOD OF STORMS AND THUNDER, IS IN MELLOW MOOD, AND SENDS A GENTLE BREEZE, WAFTING THROUGH THE AIR A SMELL WHICH WAS STILL UNFAMILIAR IN THE YEAR 50 BC...

YUK!

I SAY, DO YOU SMELL A FUNNY KIND OF SMELL, ALL OF A SUDDEN?

SNIFF! SNIFF...

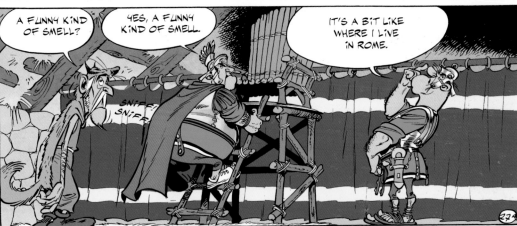

A FUNNY KIND OF SMELL?

YES, A FUNNY KIND OF SMELL.

SNIFF! SNIFF...

IT'S A BIT LIKE WHERE I LIVE IN ROME.

YOU LIVE NEAR A TANNERY, I SUPPOSE?

YES! HE GOT IT RIGHT! HE IS A SOOTHSAYER!

OOOOOH... CENTURION!

THE AIR IN THIS VILLAGE ISN'T FIT TO BREATHE... IT'S PESTILENTIAL, THAT'S WHAT IT IS!

SNIFF! SNIFF!

PES... PESTILENTIAL?

YOU TAKE MY WORD FOR IT. I'M A VETERAN, I AM. I'VE KNOWN PLENTY OF CAMPS AND BARRACKS, BUT I NEVER SMELT ANYTHING LIKE THIS BEFORE!

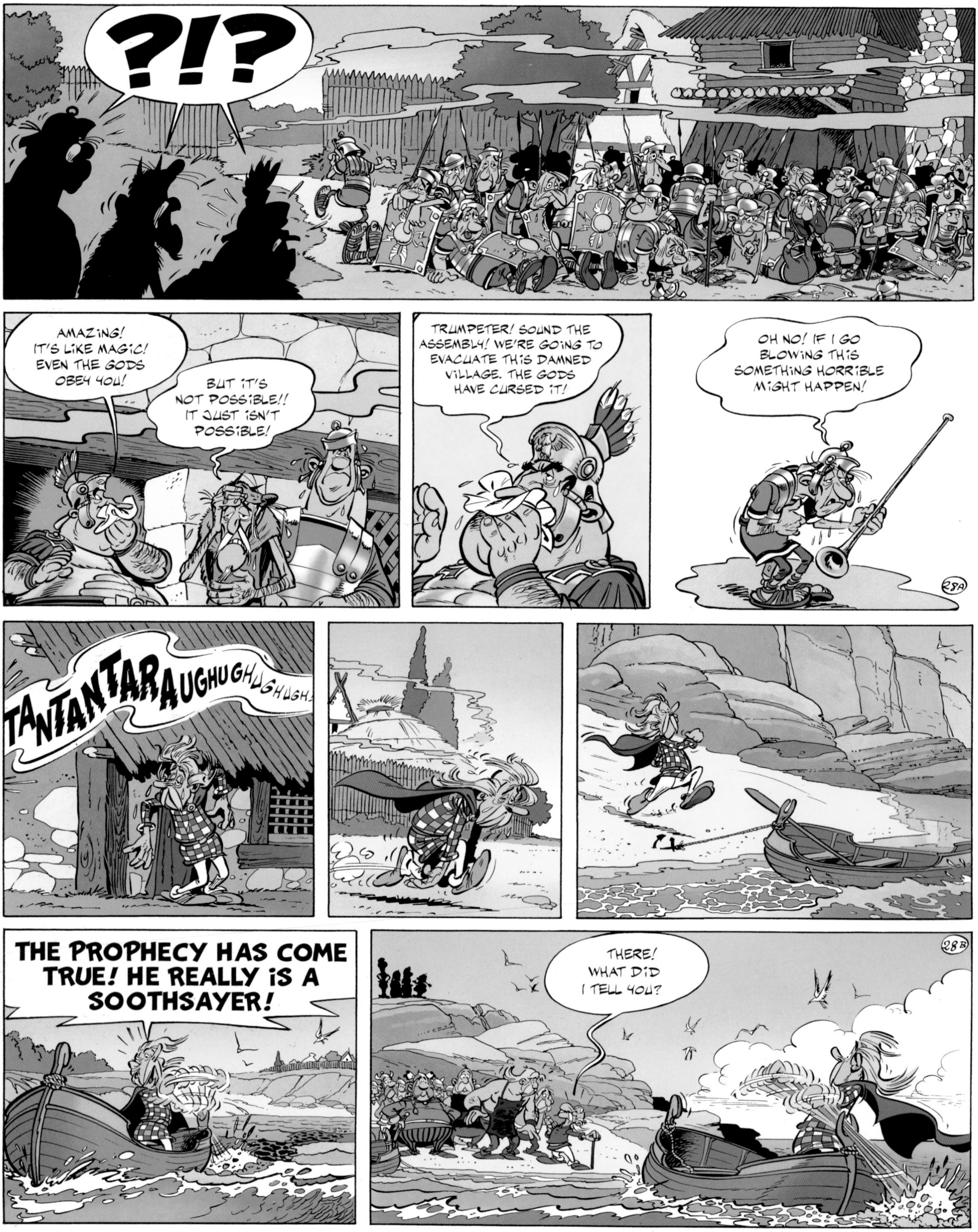
?!?
AMAZING! IT'S LIKE MAGIC! EVEN THE GODS OBEY YOU!
BUT IT'S NOT POSSIBLE!! IT JUST ISN'T POSSIBLE!
TRUMPETER! SOUND THE ASSEMBLY! WE'RE GOING TO EVACUATE THIS DAMNED VILLAGE. THE GODS HAVE CURSED IT!
OH NO! IF I GO BLOWING THIS SOMETHING HORRIBLE MIGHT HAPPEN!
28A
TANTANTARAUGHUGHUGHUGH!
THE PROPHECY HAS COME TRUE! HE REALLY IS A SOOTHSAYER!
28B
THERE! WHAT DID I TELL YOU?

I FORGOT MY LYRE, SO I WENT BACK TO THE VILLAGE TO GET IT, AND I FOUND MYSELF BREATHING FOUL AIR... AIR FROM THE DEPTHS OF HELL! EVEN THE ROMANS HAD TO RUN FOR IT!

YOU SEE? YOU SEE? WE SHOULD HAVE GONE TO LUTETIA, LIKE THE SOOTHSAYER SAID! YOU STUPID GREAT BOAR!

DARLING... AREN'T I YOUR PIGGYWIGGY ANY MORE?

WELL, I'LL JUST HAVE TO DO WITHOUT MY LYRE.

O, I DO LIKE TO BE BESIDE THE LITUS...

TCHOUF!

ARE YOU CRAZY? COME BACK!

I'D RATHER BREATHE FOUL AIR THAN LISTEN TO THAT!

WHAT ARE YOU SINGING FOR, ANYWAY?

THE SOOTHSAYER TOLD ME VOICES LIKE MINE WERE GOING TO BE VERY POPULAR IN THE FUTURE. I'M PRACTISING.

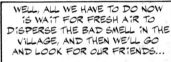

WELL, ALL WE HAVE TO DO NOW IS WAIT FOR FRESH AIR TO DISPERSE THE BAD SMELL IN THE VILLAGE, AND THEN WE'LL GO AND LOOK FOR OUR FRIENDS...

AND AS FOR THE ROMANS, I'M COUNTING ON YOU. YOU'RE SURE TO THINK OF SOMETHING.

I'VE THOUGHT OF SOMETHING ALREADY. WE GO TO THEIR CAMP AND BASH THE WHOLE PLACE UP.

WHEREVER DO YOU GET ALL THESE ORIGINAL IDEAS?

A HANDSOME WARRIOR WITH RED PIGTAILS, YES! BUT I'M NOT JUST A PRETTY FACE!

41

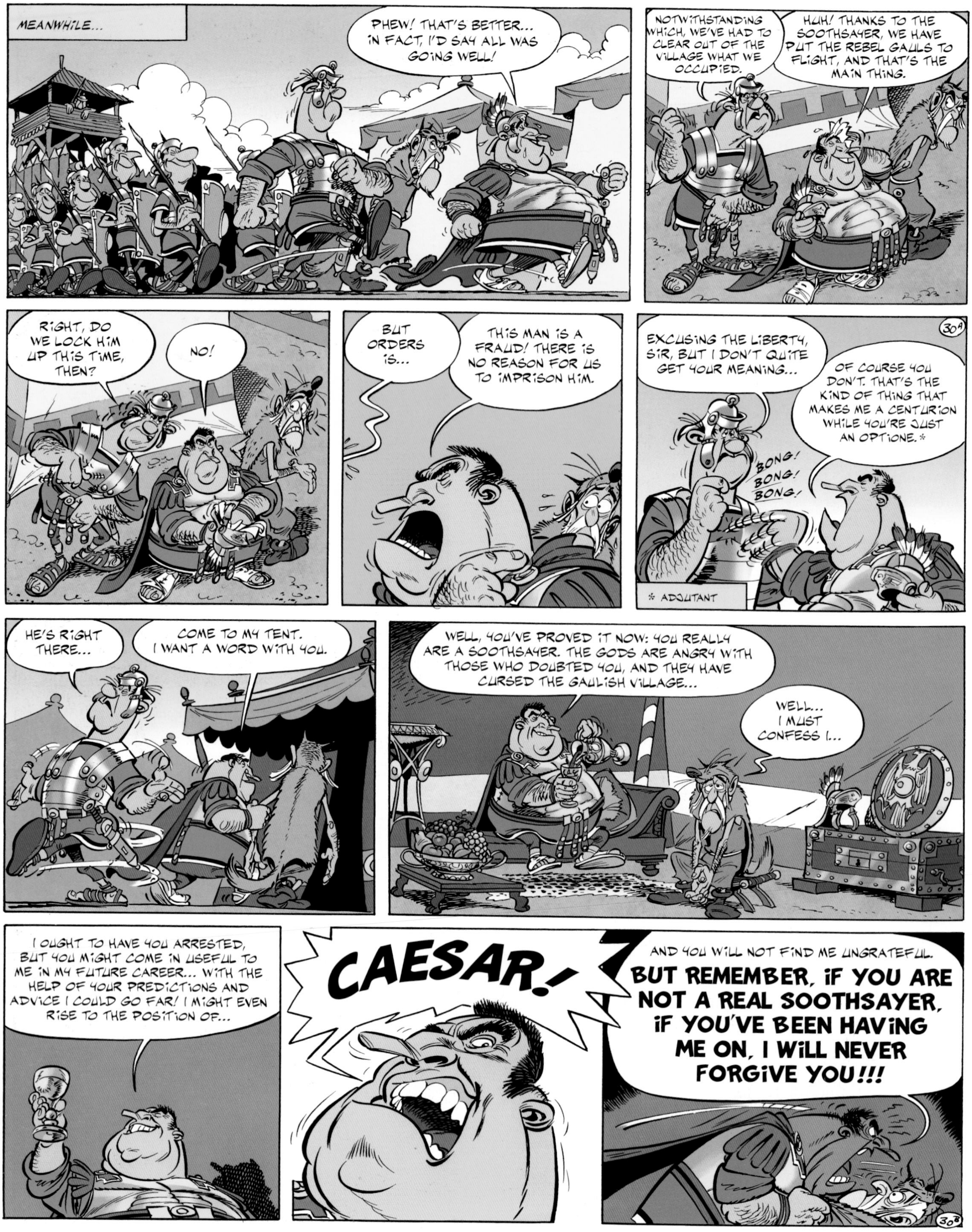
MEANWHILE...
PHEW! THAT'S BETTER... IN FACT, I'D SAY ALL WAS GOING WELL!
NOTWITHSTANDING WHICH, WE'VE HAD TO CLEAR OUT OF THE VILLAGE WHAT WE OCCUPIED.
HUH! THANKS TO THE SOOTHSAYER, WE HAVE PUT THE REBEL GAULS TO FLIGHT, AND THAT'S THE MAIN THING.
RIGHT, DO WE LOCK HIM UP THIS TIME, THEN?
NO!
BUT ORDERS IS...
THIS MAN IS A FRAUD! THERE IS NO REASON FOR US TO IMPRISON HIM.
30A
EXCUSING THE LIBERTY, SIR, BUT I DON'T QUITE GET YOUR MEANING...
OF COURSE YOU DON'T. THAT'S THE KIND OF THING THAT MAKES ME A CENTURION WHILE YOU'RE JUST AN OPTIONE.*
BONG! BONG! BONG!
* ADJUTANT
HE'S RIGHT THERE...
COME TO MY TENT. I WANT A WORD WITH YOU.
WELL, YOU'VE PROVED IT NOW: YOU REALLY ARE A SOOTHSAYER. THE GODS ARE ANGRY WITH THOSE WHO DOUBTED YOU, AND THEY HAVE CURSED THE GAULISH VILLAGE...
WELL... I MUST CONFESS I...
I OUGHT TO HAVE YOU ARRESTED, BUT YOU MIGHT COME IN USEFUL TO ME IN MY FUTURE CAREER... WITH THE HELP OF YOUR PREDICTIONS AND ADVICE I COULD GO FAR! I MIGHT EVEN RISE TO THE POSITION OF...
CAESAR!
AND YOU WILL NOT FIND ME UNGRATEFUL.
BUT REMEMBER, IF YOU ARE NOT A REAL SOOTHSAYER, IF YOU'VE BEEN HAVING ME ON, I WILL NEVER FORGIVE YOU!!!
30B

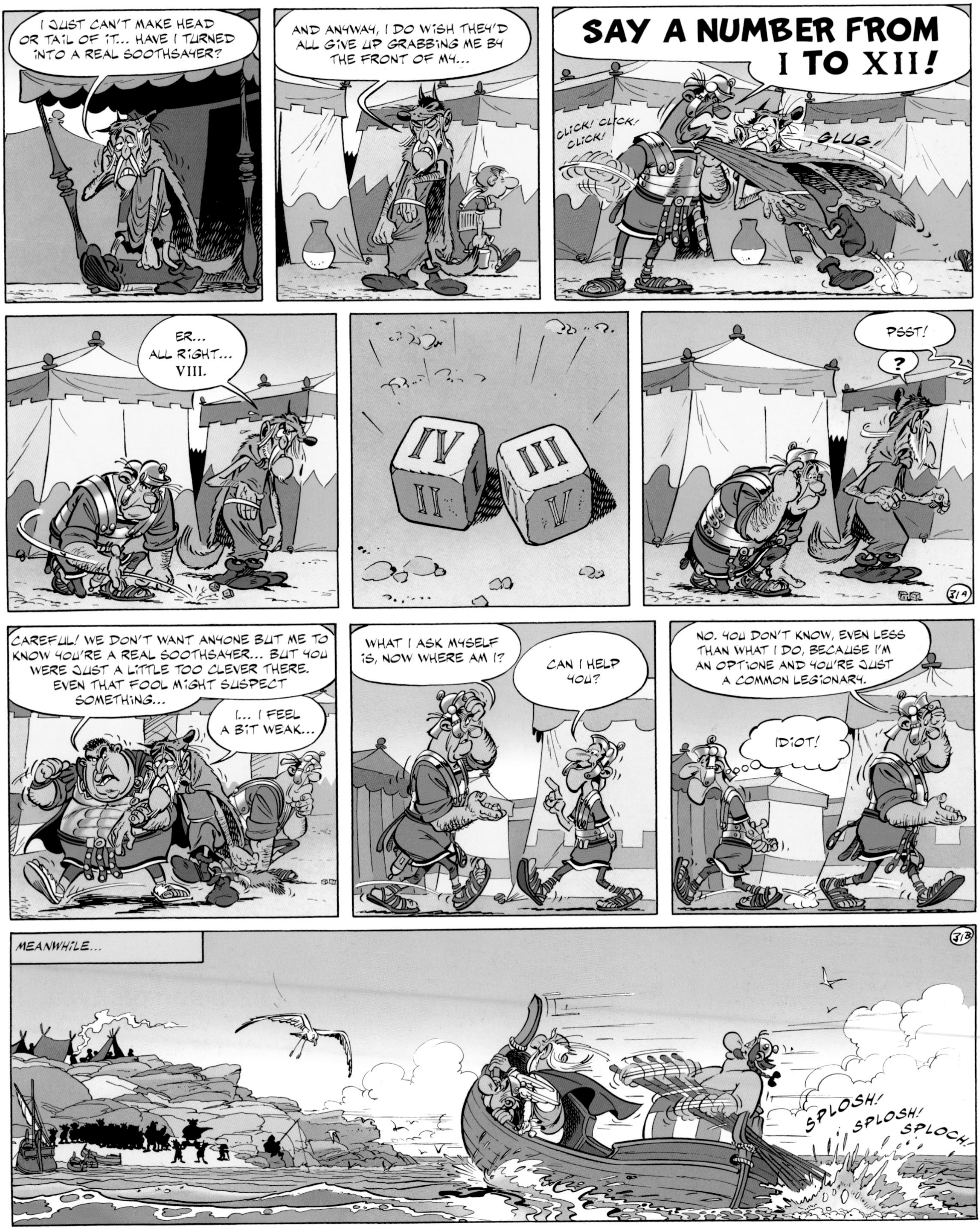
I JUST CAN'T MAKE HEAD OR TAIL OF IT... HAVE I TURNED INTO A REAL SOOTHSAYER?
AND ANYWAY, I DO WISH THEY'D ALL GIVE UP GRABBING ME BY THE FRONT OF MY...
SAY A NUMBER FROM I TO XII!
CLICK! CLICK! CLICK!
GLUG!
ER... ALL RIGHT... VIII.
IV
II
III
V
PSST!
?
CAREFUL! WE DON'T WANT ANYONE BUT ME TO KNOW YOU'RE A REAL SOOTHSAYER... BUT YOU WERE JUST A LITTLE TOO CLEVER THERE. EVEN THAT FOOL MIGHT SUSPECT SOMETHING...
I... I FEEL A BIT WEAK...
WHAT I ASK MYSELF IS, NOW WHERE AM I?
CAN I HELP YOU?
NO. YOU DON'T KNOW, EVEN LESS THAN WHAT I DO, BECAUSE I'M AN OPTIONE AND YOU'RE JUST A COMMON LEGIONARY.
IDIOT!
MEANWHILE...
SPLOSH!
SPLOSH!
SPLOCH!

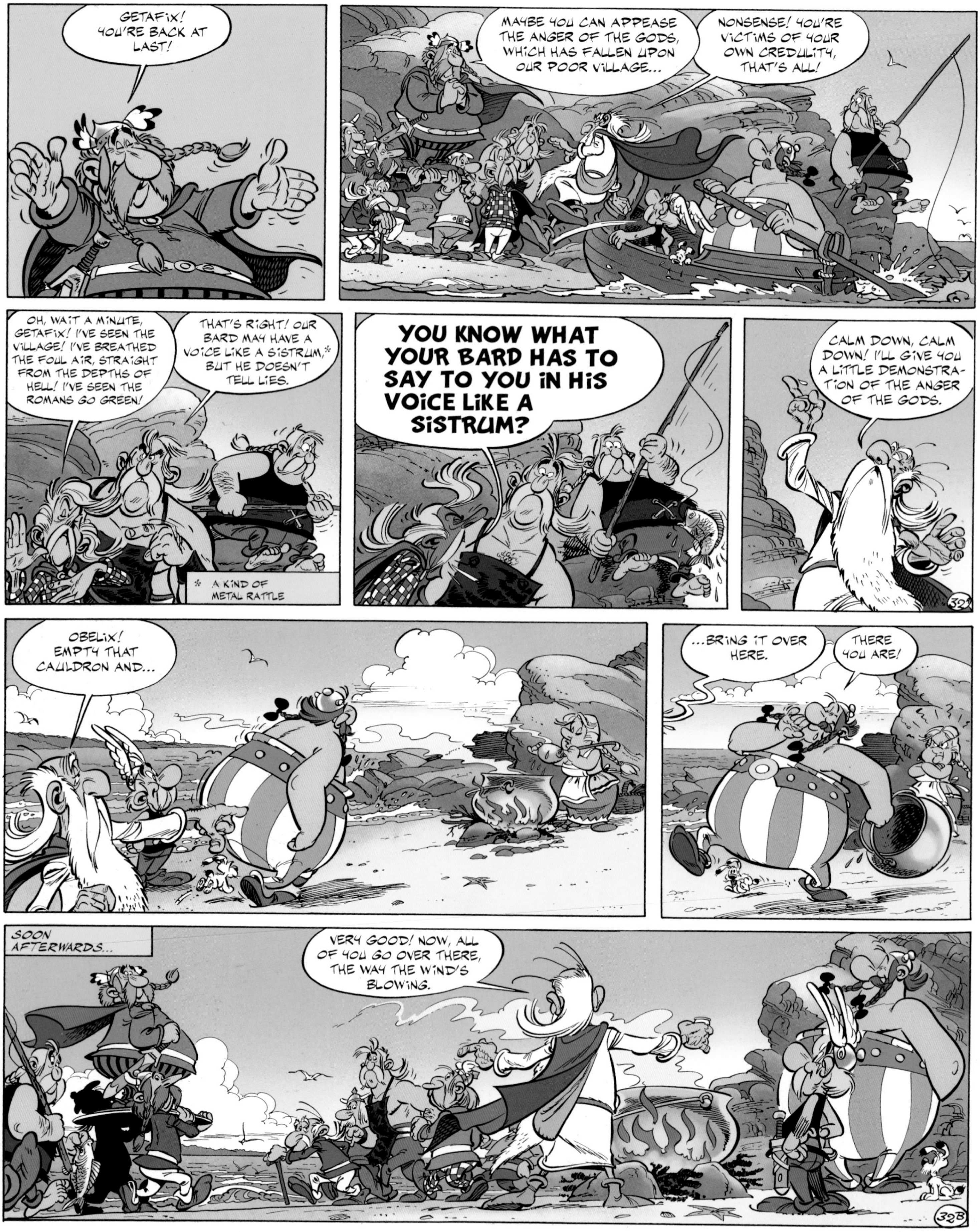
GETAFIX! YOU'RE BACK AT LAST!
MAYBE YOU CAN APPEASE THE ANGER OF THE GODS, WHICH HAS FALLEN UPON OUR POOR VILLAGE...
NONSENSE! YOU'RE VICTIMS OF YOUR OWN CREDULITY, THAT'S ALL!
OH, WAIT A MINUTE, GETAFIX! I'VE SEEN THE VILLAGE! I'VE BREATHED THE FOUL AIR, STRAIGHT FROM THE DEPTHS OF HELL! I'VE SEEN THE ROMANS GO GREEN!
THAT'S RIGHT! OUR BARD MAY HAVE A VOICE LIKE A SISTRUM,* BUT HE DOESN'T TELL LIES.
* A KIND OF METAL RATTLE
YOU KNOW WHAT YOUR BARD HAS TO SAY TO YOU IN HIS VOICE LIKE A SISTRUM?
CALM DOWN, CALM DOWN! I'LL GIVE YOU A LITTLE DEMONSTRATION OF THE ANGER OF THE GODS.
OBELIX! EMPTY THAT CAULDRON AND...
...BRING IT OVER HERE.
THERE YOU ARE!
SOON AFTERWARDS...
VERY GOOD! NOW, ALL OF YOU GO OVER THERE, THE WAY THE WIND'S BLOWING.

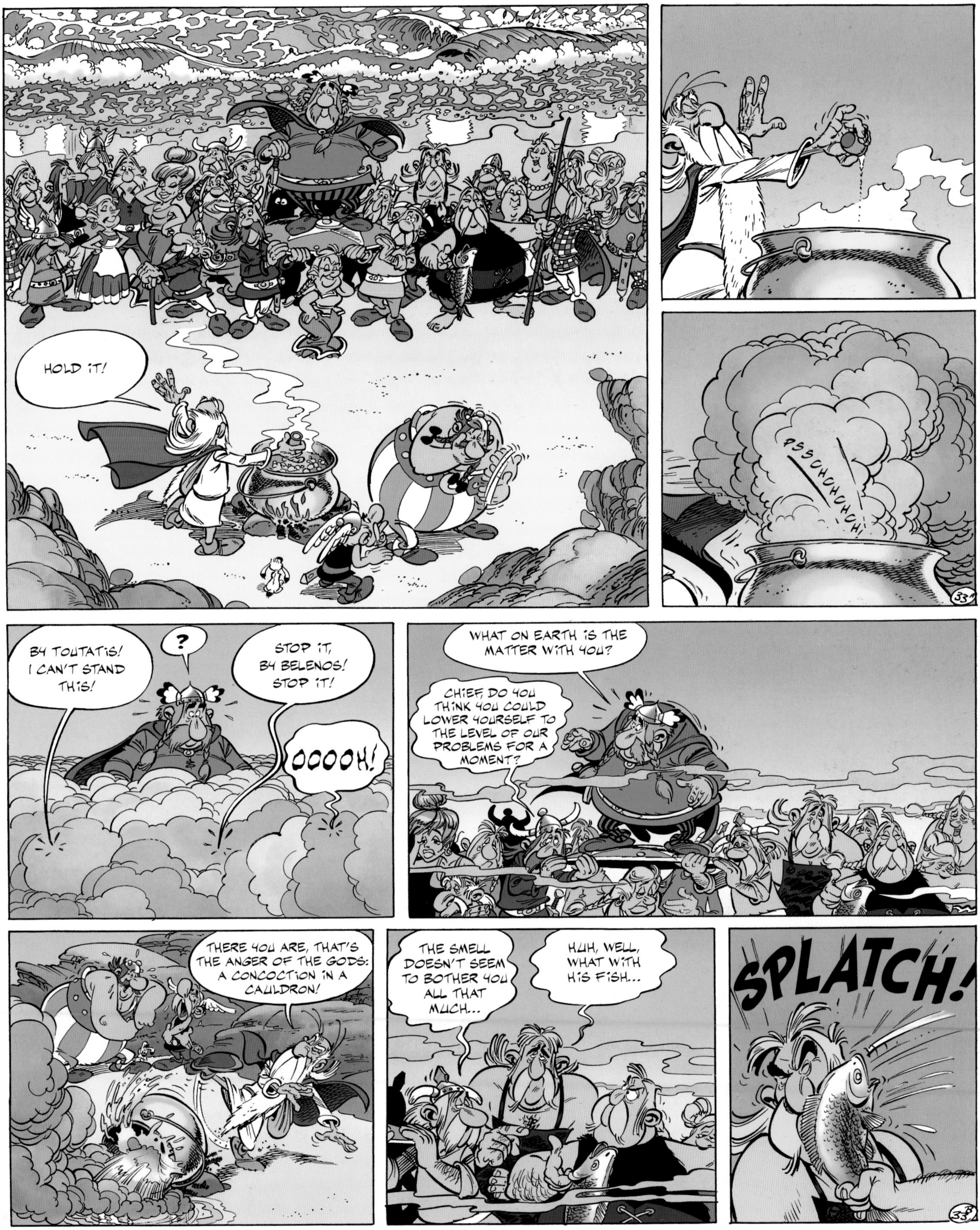

HOLD IT!
PSSOHOHOHOH!
BY TOUTATIS! I CAN'T STAND THIS!
?
STOP IT, BY BELENOS! STOP IT!
OOOOH!
WHAT ON EARTH IS THE MATTER WITH YOU?
CHIEF, DO YOU THINK YOU COULD LOWER YOURSELF TO THE LEVEL OF OUR PROBLEMS FOR A MOMENT?
THERE YOU ARE, THAT'S THE ANGER OF THE GODS: A CONCOCTION IN A CAULDRON!
THE SMELL DOESN'T SEEM TO BOTHER YOU ALL THAT MUCH...
HUH, WELL, WHAT WITH HIS FISH...
SPLATCH!

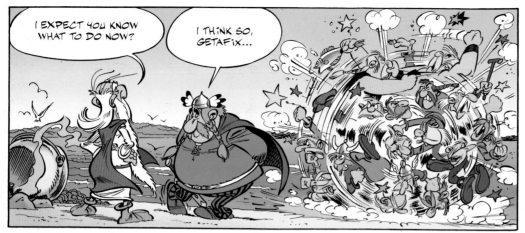

I EXPECT YOU KNOW WHAT TO DO NOW?

I THINK SO, GETAFIX...

WE GO BACK TO THE VILLAGE TONIGHT. **IN PEACE AND QUIET!**

AND THAT VERY NIGHT...

DROP ANCHOR!

DON'T YOU THINK IT'S A BIT DANGEROUS TO ANCHOR IN BETWEEN THE GAULISH COAST AND THIS UNKNOWN ISLAND, CAP'N?

SHIVER ME TIMBERS, NO! WE CONSULTED THE ENTRAILS OF A MACKEREL, AND THE ORACLE WAS ABSOLUTELY POSITIVE: IT'S SAFE AS HOUSES TO ANCHOR HERE OVERNIGHT.

NEXT MORNING...

THIS IS TERRIBLE! A SHOAL OF GAULS HAS CROSSED OUR PATH!

GLUG! GLUG! GLUG! GLUG! GLUG!

I'VE HAD A BELLYFUL OF ENTRAILS!

STOP BELLYACHING! I THOUGHT YOU HAD MORE GUTS!

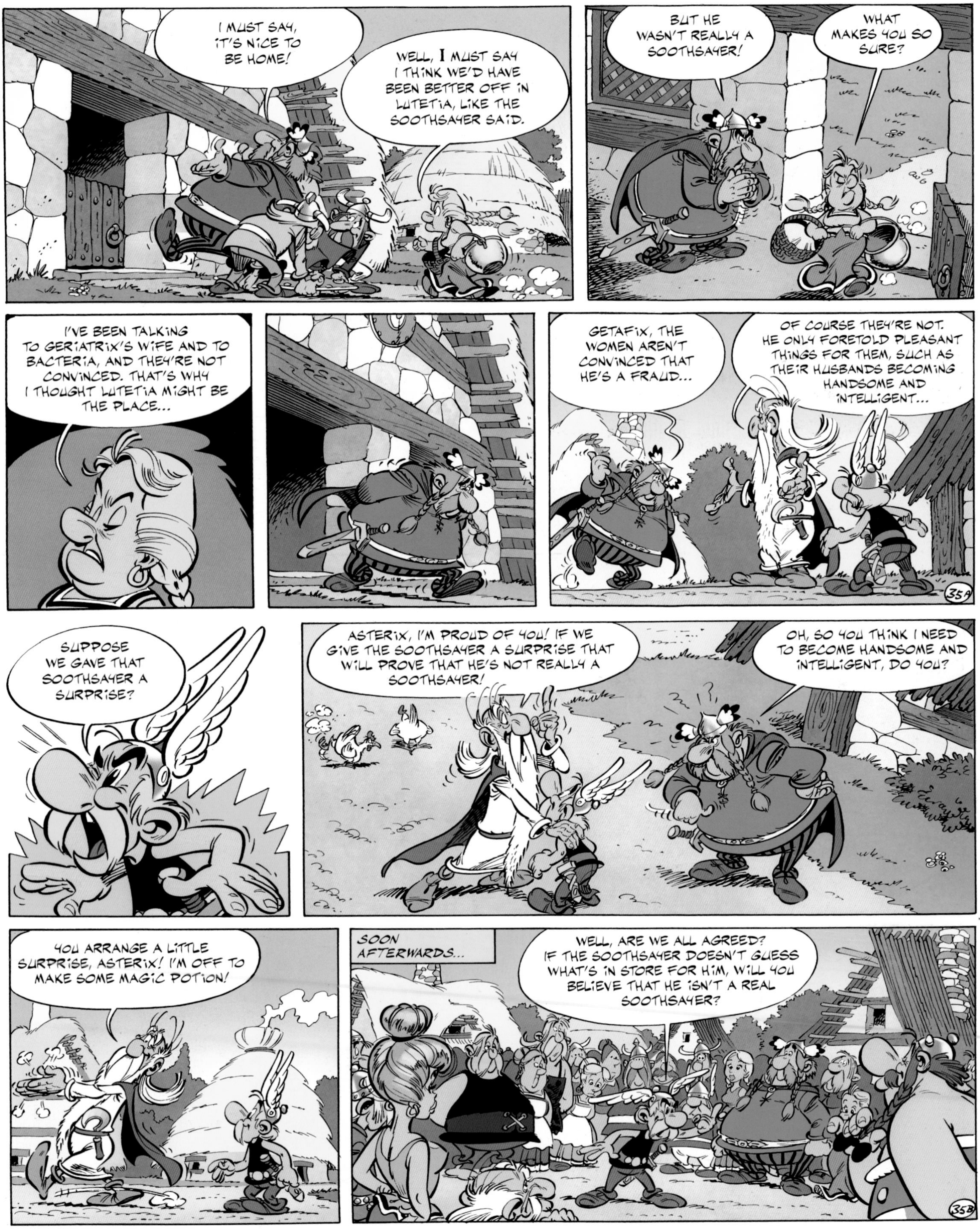
I MUST SAY, IT'S NICE TO BE HOME!
WELL, I MUST SAY I THINK WE'D HAVE BEEN BETTER OFF IN LUTETIA, LIKE THE SOOTHSAYER SAID.
BUT HE WASN'T REALLY A SOOTHSAYER!
WHAT MAKES YOU SO SURE?
I'VE BEEN TALKING TO GERIATRIX'S WIFE AND TO BACTERIA, AND THEY'RE NOT CONVINCED. THAT'S WHY I THOUGHT LUTETIA MIGHT BE THE PLACE...
GETAFIX, THE WOMEN AREN'T CONVINCED THAT HE'S A FRAUD...
OF COURSE THEY'RE NOT. HE ONLY FORETOLD PLEASANT THINGS FOR THEM, SUCH AS THEIR HUSBANDS BECOMING HANDSOME AND INTELLIGENT...
SUPPOSE WE GAVE THAT SOOTHSAYER A SURPRISE?
ASTERIX, I'M PROUD OF YOU! IF WE GIVE THE SOOTHSAYER A SURPRISE THAT WILL PROVE THAT HE'S NOT REALLY A SOOTHSAYER!
OH, SO YOU THINK I NEED TO BECOME HANDSOME AND INTELLIGENT, DO YOU?
YOU ARRANGE A LITTLE SURPRISE, ASTERIX! I'M OFF TO MAKE SOME MAGIC POTION!
SOON AFTERWARDS...
WELL, ARE WE ALL AGREED? IF THE SOOTHSAYER DOESN'T GUESS WHAT'S IN STORE FOR HIM, WILL YOU BELIEVE THAT HE ISN'T A REAL SOOTHSAYER?

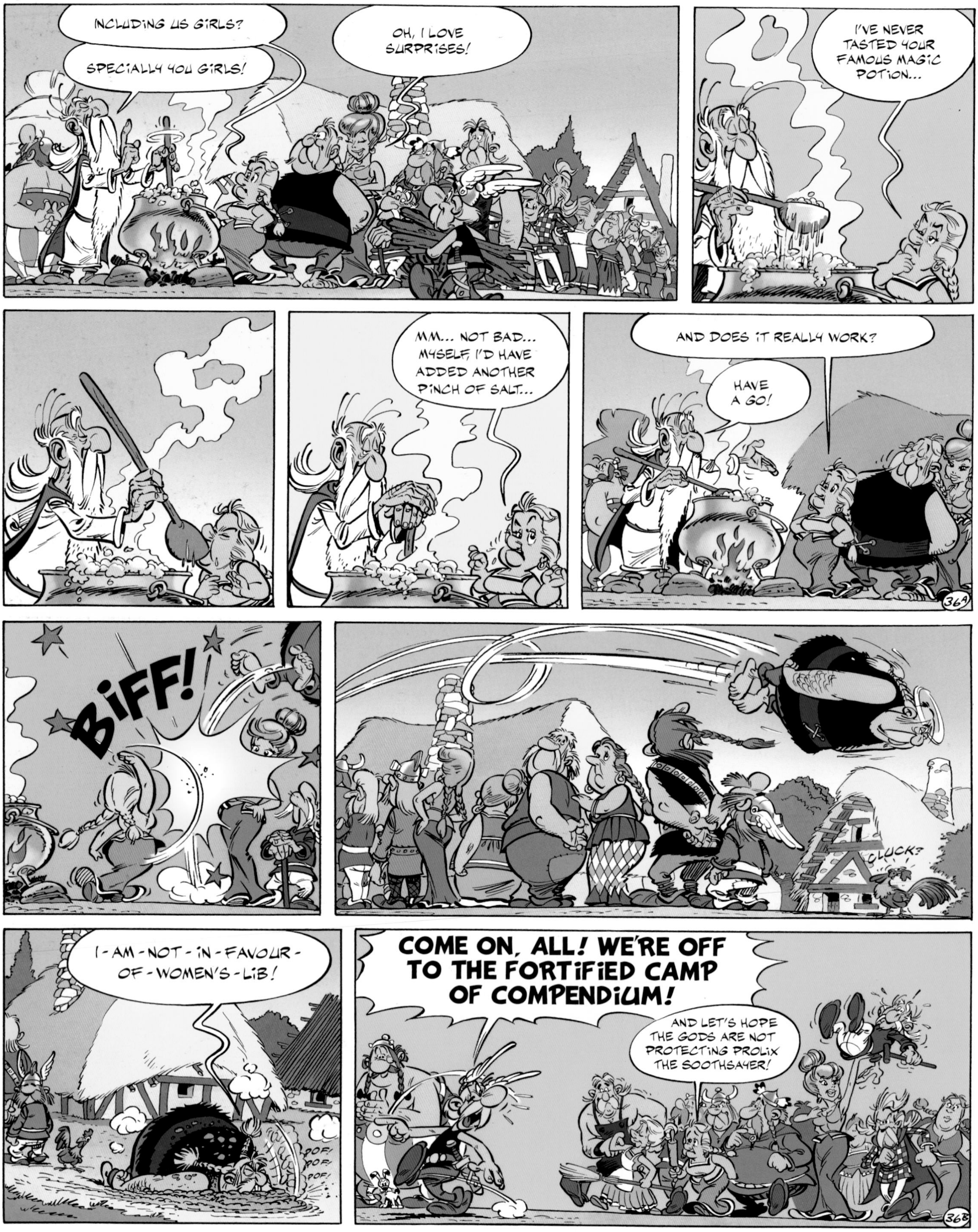
INCLUDING US GIRLS?
SPECIALLY YOU GIRLS!
OH, I LOVE SURPRISES!
I'VE NEVER TASTED YOUR FAMOUS MAGIC POTION...
MM... NOT BAD... MYSELF, I'D HAVE ADDED ANOTHER PINCH OF SALT...
AND DOES IT REALLY WORK?
HAVE A GO!
BIFF!
CLUCK?
I-AM-NOT-IN-FAVOUR-OF-WOMEN'S-LIB!
POF! POF! POF!
COME ON, ALL! WE'RE OFF TO THE FORTIFIED CAMP OF COMPENDIUM!
AND LET'S HOPE THE GODS ARE NOT PROTECTING PROLIX THE SOOTHSAYER!

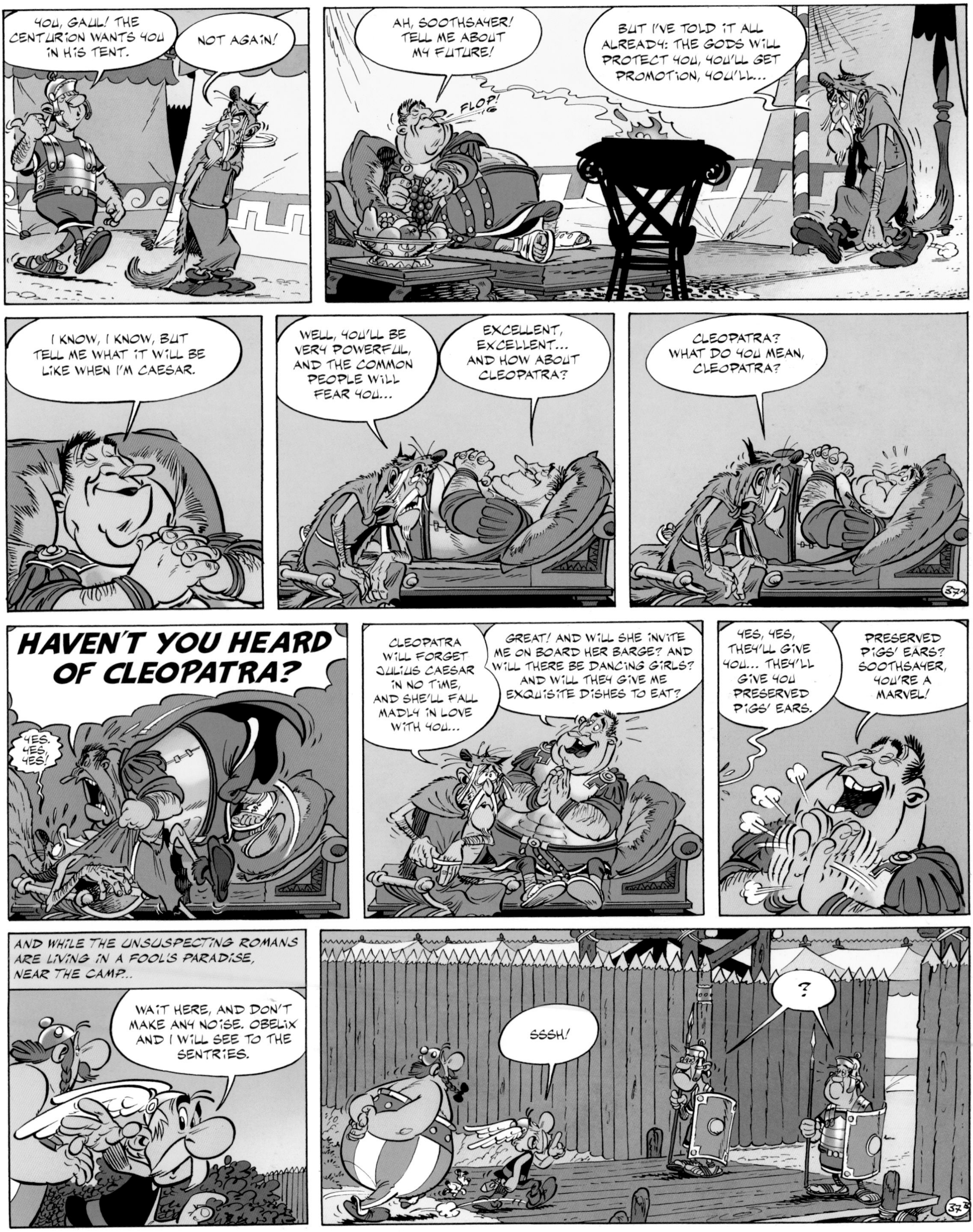
YOU, GAUL! THE CENTURION WANTS YOU IN HIS TENT.
NOT AGAIN!
AH, SOOTHSAYER! TELL ME ABOUT MY FUTURE!
FLOP!
BUT I'VE TOLD IT ALL ALREADY: THE GODS WILL PROTECT YOU, YOU'LL GET PROMOTION, YOU'LL...
I KNOW, I KNOW, BUT TELL ME WHAT IT WILL BE LIKE WHEN I'M CAESAR.
WELL, YOU'LL BE VERY POWERFUL, AND THE COMMON PEOPLE WILL FEAR YOU...
EXCELLENT, EXCELLENT... AND HOW ABOUT CLEOPATRA?
CLEOPATRA? WHAT DO YOU MEAN, CLEOPATRA?
HAVEN'T YOU HEARD OF CLEOPATRA?
YES. YES, YES!
CLEOPATRA WILL FORGET JULIUS CAESAR IN NO TIME, AND SHE'LL FALL MADLY IN LOVE WITH YOU...
GREAT! AND WILL SHE INVITE ME ON BOARD HER BARGE? AND WILL THERE BE DANCING GIRLS? AND WILL THEY GIVE ME EXQUISITE DISHES TO EAT?
YES, YES, THEY'LL GIVE YOU... THEY'LL GIVE YOU PRESERVED PIGS' EARS.
PRESERVED PIGS' EARS? SOOTHSAYER, YOU'RE A MARVEL!
AND WHILE THE UNSUSPECTING ROMANS ARE LIVING IN A FOOL'S PARADISE, NEAR THE CAMP...
WAIT HERE, AND DON'T MAKE ANY NOISE. OBELIX AND I WILL SEE TO THE SENTRIES.
SSSH!
?

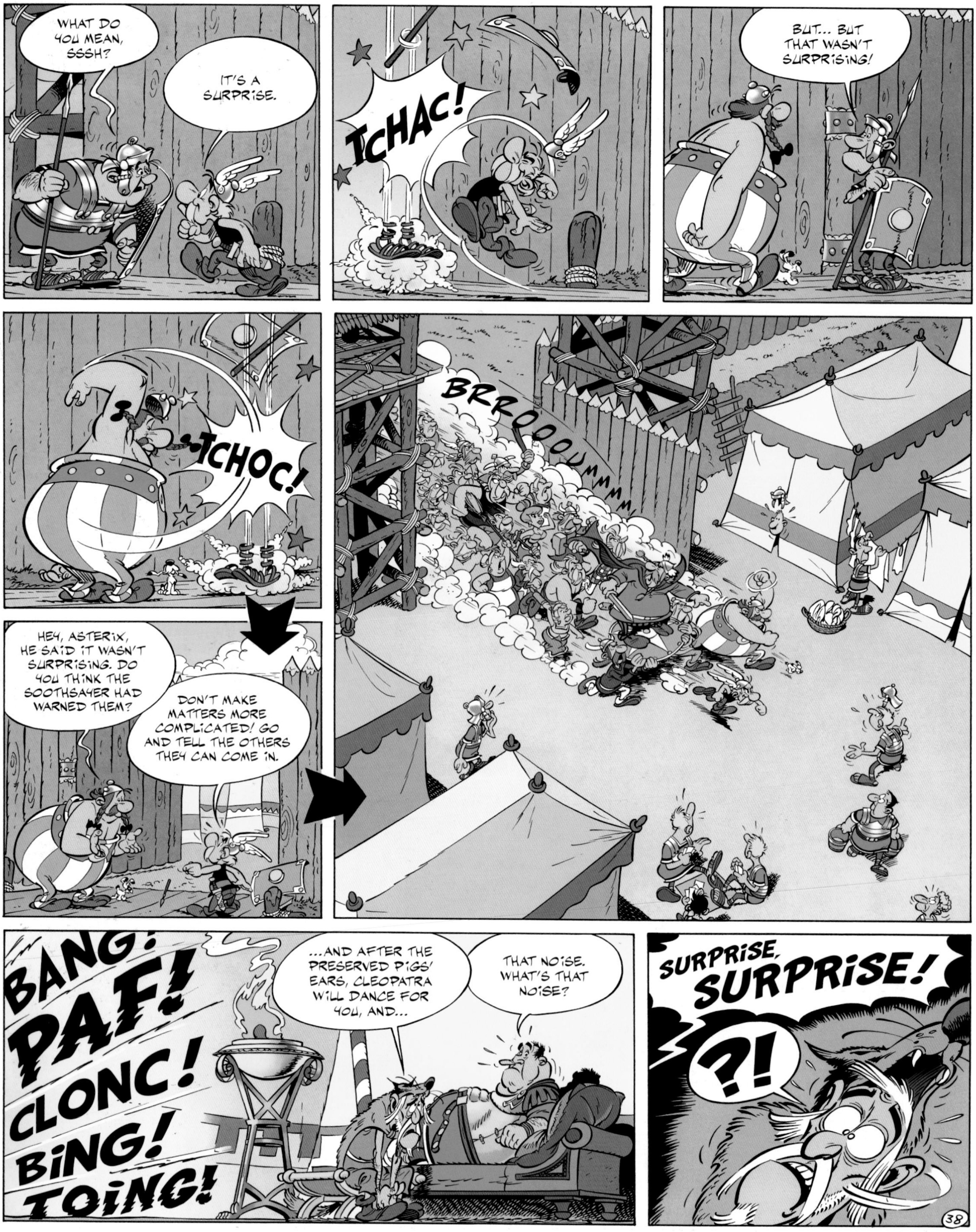

WHAT DO YOU MEAN, SSSH?
IT'S A SURPRISE.
TCHAC!
BUT... BUT THAT WASN'T SURPRISING!
TCHOC!
BRROOOOUMMMM
HEY, ASTERIX, HE SAID IT WASN'T SURPRISING. DO YOU THINK THE SOOTHSAYER HAD WARNED THEM?
DON'T MAKE MATTERS MORE COMPLICATED! GO AND TELL THE OTHERS THEY CAN COME IN.
BANG! PAF! CLONC! BING! TOING!
...AND AFTER THE PRESERVED PIGS' EARS, CLEOPATRA WILL DANCE FOR YOU, AND...
THAT NOISE. WHAT'S THAT NOISE?
SURPRISE, SURPRISE!
?!
38

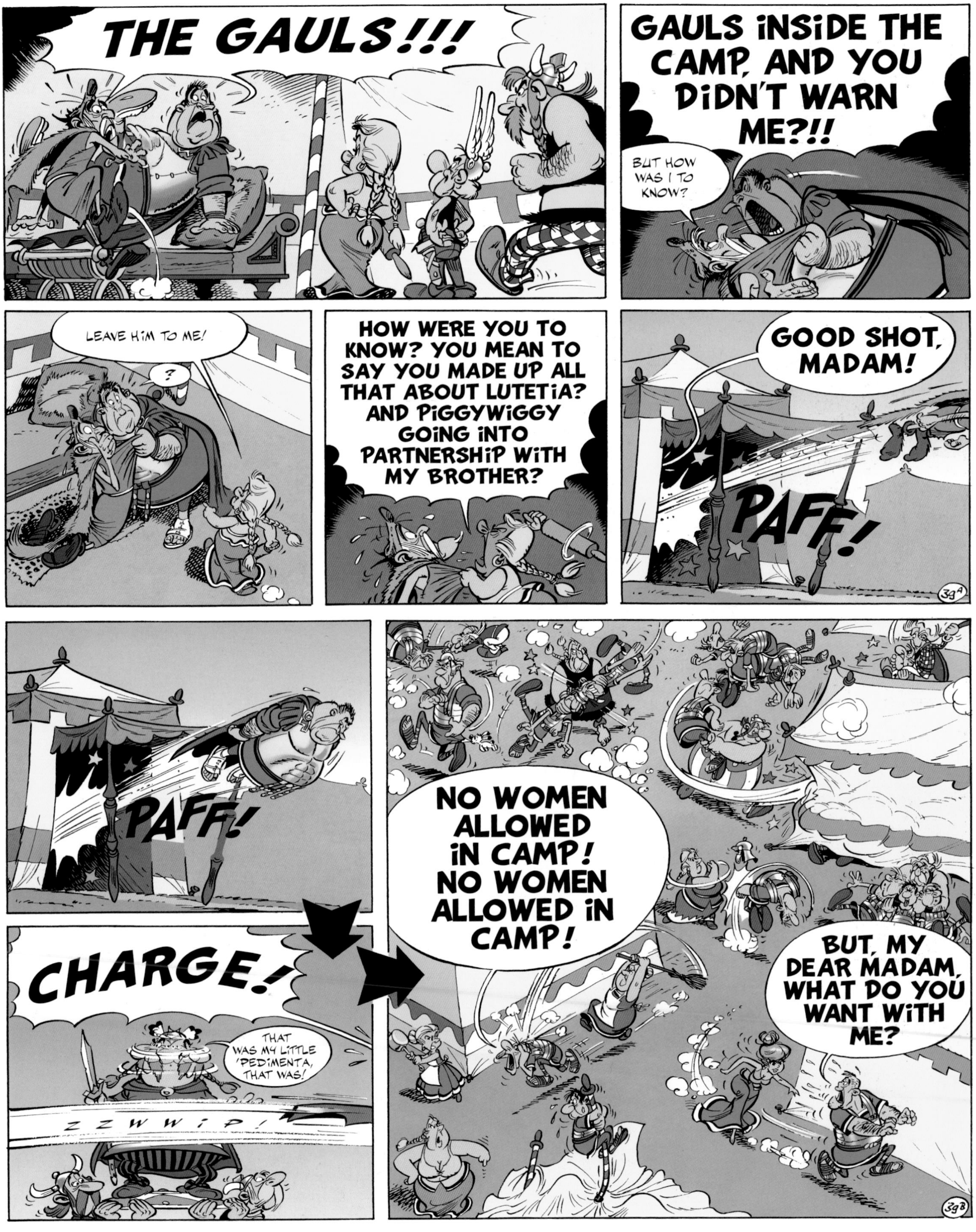
THE GAULS!!!
GAULS INSIDE THE CAMP, AND YOU DIDN'T WARN ME?!!
BUT HOW WAS I TO KNOW?
LEAVE HIM TO ME!
?
HOW WERE YOU TO KNOW? YOU MEAN TO SAY YOU MADE UP ALL THAT ABOUT LUTETIA? AND PIGGYWIGGY GOING INTO PARTNERSHIP WITH MY BROTHER?
GOOD SHOT, MADAM!
PAFF!
39A
PAFF!
CHARGE!
THAT WAS MY LITTLE 'PEDIMENTA, THAT WAS!
ZZWWIP!
NO WOMEN ALLOWED IN CAMP! NO WOMEN ALLOWED IN CAMP!
BUT, MY DEAR MADAM, WHAT DO YOU WANT WITH ME?
39B

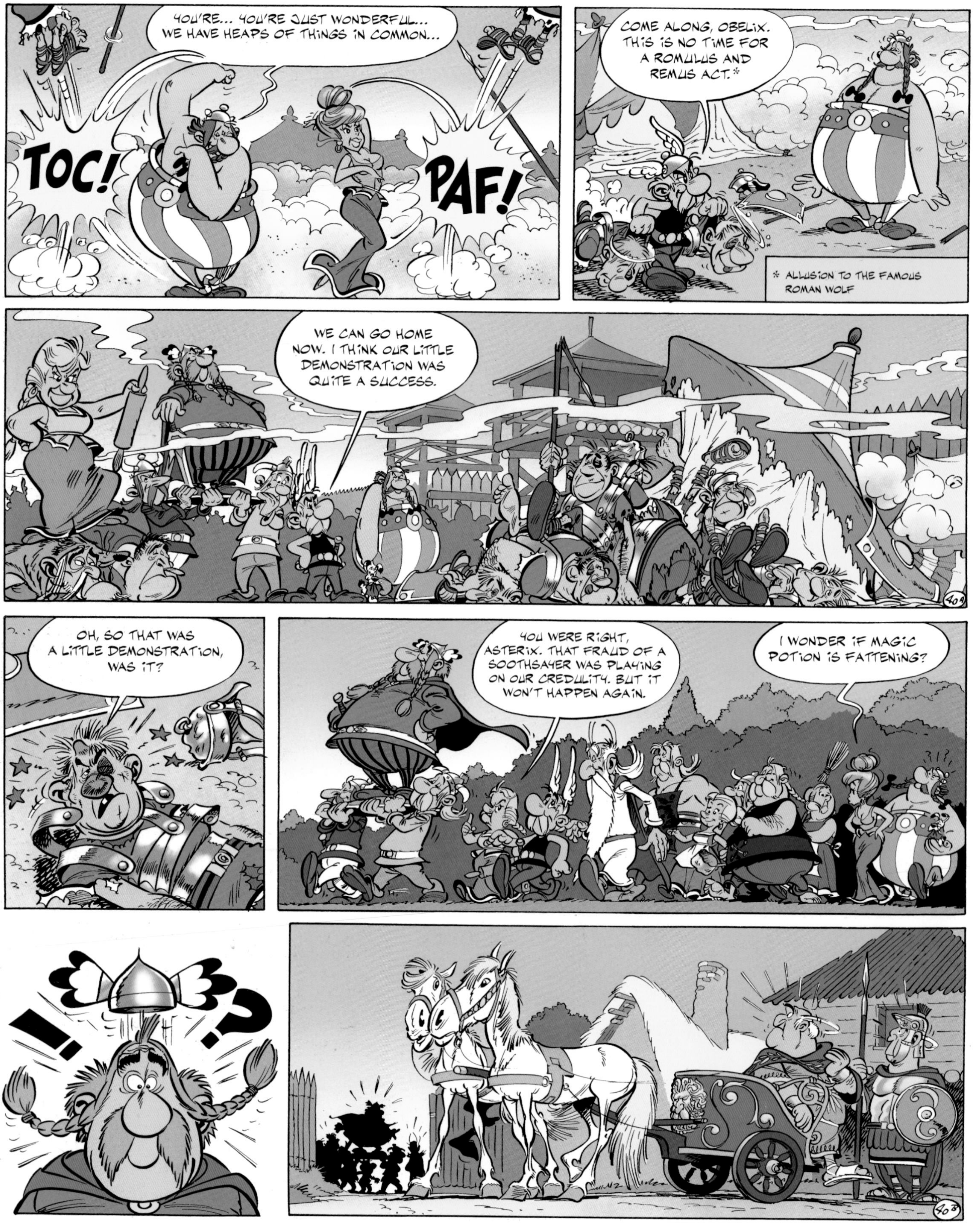
YOU'RE... YOU'RE JUST WONDERFUL... WE HAVE HEAPS OF THINGS IN COMMON...
TOC!
PAF!
COME ALONG, OBELIX. THIS IS NO TIME FOR A ROMULUS AND REMUS ACT.*
* ALLUSION TO THE FAMOUS ROMAN WOLF
WE CAN GO HOME NOW. I THINK OUR LITTLE DEMONSTRATION WAS QUITE A SUCCESS.
OH, SO THAT WAS A LITTLE DEMONSTRATION, WAS IT?
YOU WERE RIGHT, ASTERIX. THAT FRAUD OF A SOOTHSAYER WAS PLAYING ON OUR CREDULITY. BUT IT WON'T HAPPEN AGAIN.
I WONDER IF MAGIC POTION IS FATTENING?
!!
?

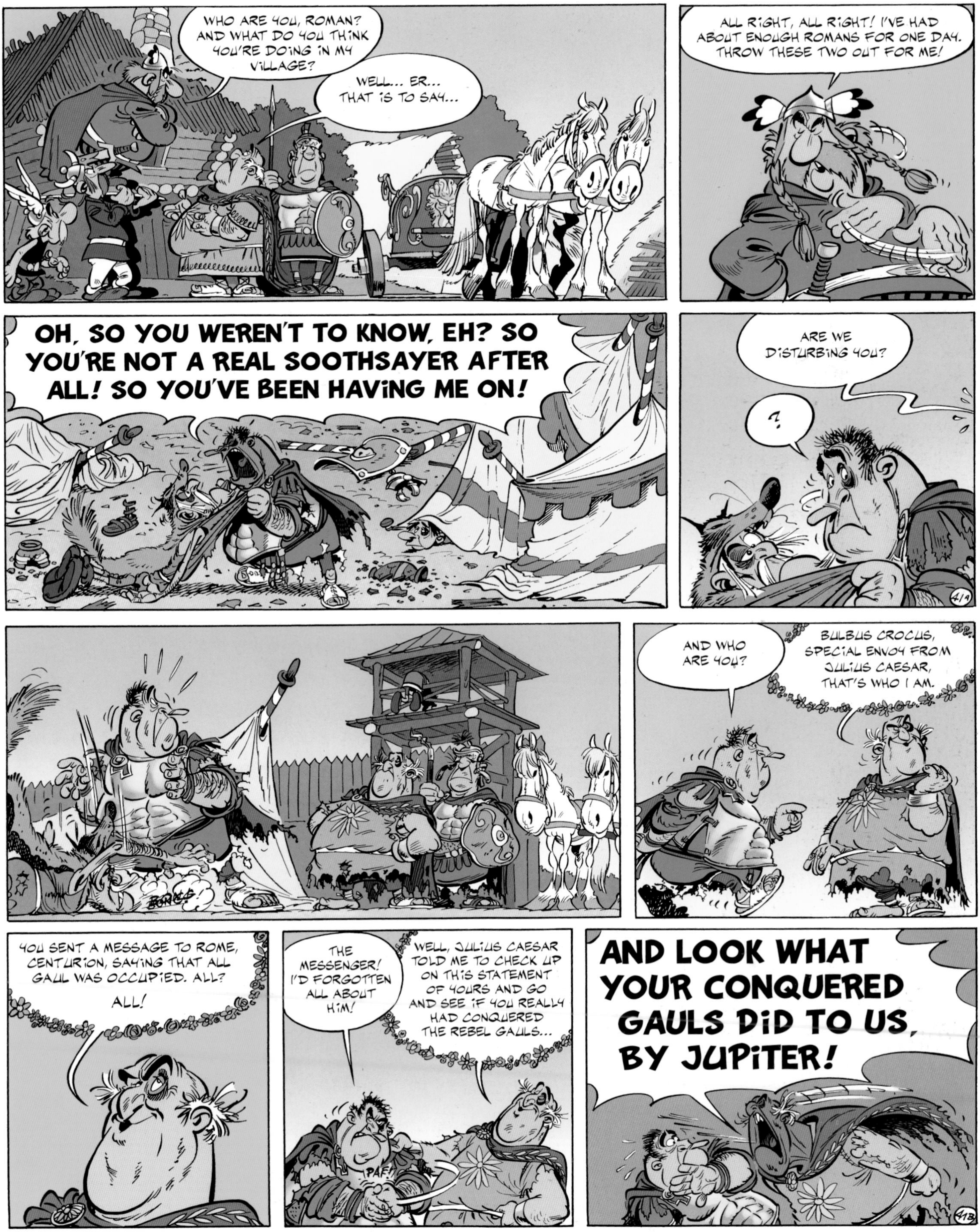
WHO ARE YOU, ROMAN? AND WHAT DO YOU THINK YOU'RE DOING IN MY VILLAGE?
WELL... ER... THAT IS TO SAY...
ALL RIGHT, ALL RIGHT! I'VE HAD ABOUT ENOUGH ROMANS FOR ONE DAY. THROW THESE TWO OUT FOR ME!
OH, SO YOU WEREN'T TO KNOW, EH? SO YOU'RE NOT A REAL SOOTHSAYER AFTER ALL! SO YOU'VE BEEN HAVING ME ON!
ARE WE DISTURBING YOU?
?
41A
AND WHO ARE YOU?
BULBUS CROCUS, SPECIAL ENVOY FROM JULIUS CAESAR, THAT'S WHO I AM.
YOU SENT A MESSAGE TO ROME, CENTURION, SAYING THAT ALL GAUL WAS OCCUPIED. ALL? ALL!
THE MESSENGER! I'D FORGOTTEN ALL ABOUT HIM!
WELL, JULIUS CAESAR TOLD ME TO CHECK UP ON THIS STATEMENT OF YOURS AND GO AND SEE IF YOU REALLY HAD CONQUERED THE REBEL GAULS...
PAF!
AND LOOK WHAT YOUR CONQUERED GAULS DID TO US, BY JUPITER!
41B

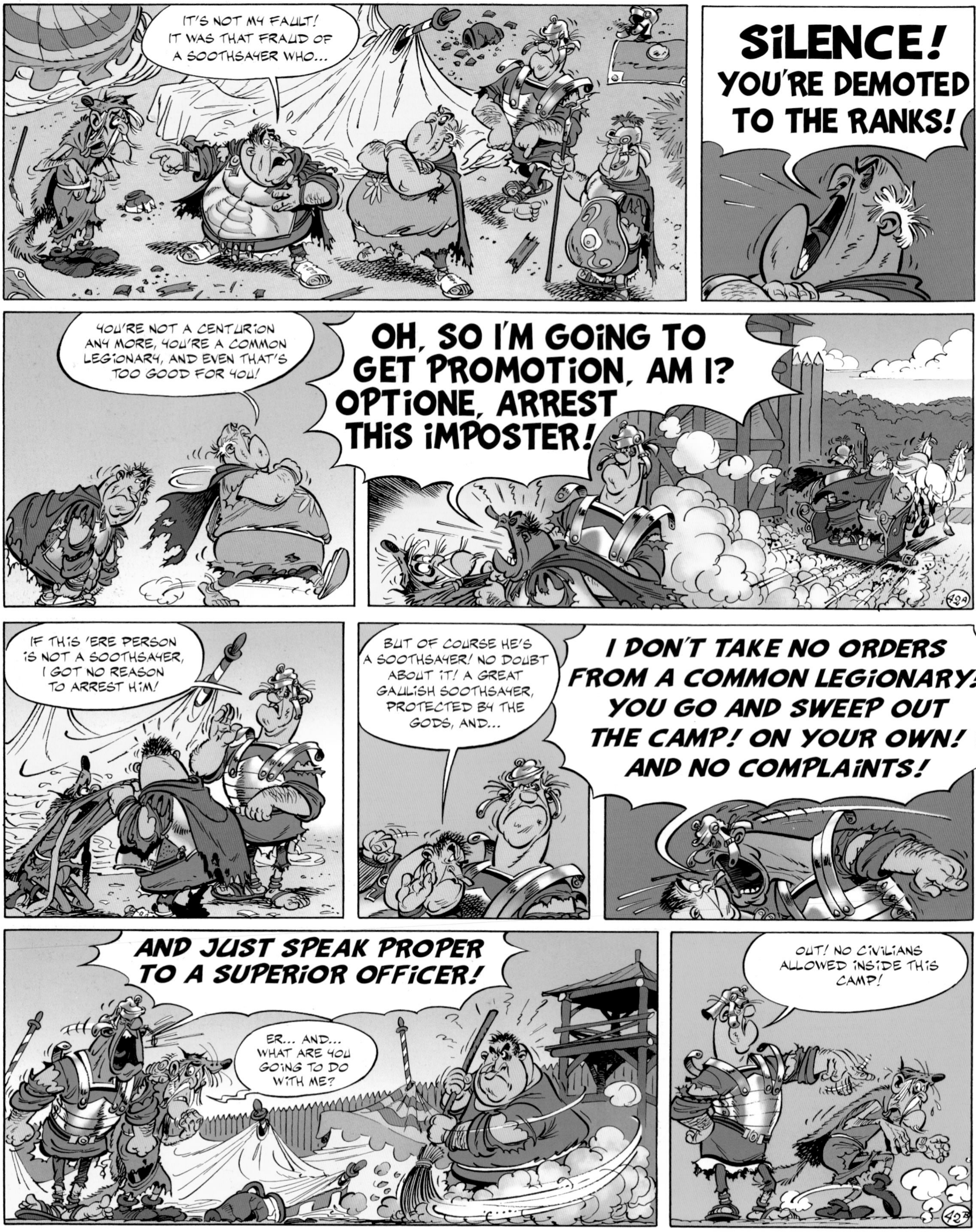
IT'S NOT MY FAULT! IT WAS THAT FRAUD OF A SOOTHSAYER WHO...
SILENCE! YOU'RE DEMOTED TO THE RANKS!
YOU'RE NOT A CENTURION ANY MORE, YOU'RE A COMMON LEGIONARY, AND EVEN THAT'S TOO GOOD FOR YOU!
OH, SO I'M GOING TO GET PROMOTION, AM I? OPTIONE, ARREST THIS IMPOSTER!
42A
IF THIS 'ERE PERSON IS NOT A SOOTHSAYER, I GOT NO REASON TO ARREST HIM!
BUT OF COURSE HE'S A SOOTHSAYER! NO DOUBT ABOUT IT! A GREAT GAULISH SOOTHSAYER, PROTECTED BY THE GODS, AND...
I DON'T TAKE NO ORDERS FROM A COMMON LEGIONARY! YOU GO AND SWEEP OUT THE CAMP! ON YOUR OWN! AND NO COMPLAINTS!
AND JUST SPEAK PROPER TO A SUPERIOR OFFICER!
ER... AND... WHAT ARE YOU GOING TO DO WITH ME?
OUT! NO CIVILIANS ALLOWED INSIDE THIS CAMP!
42B

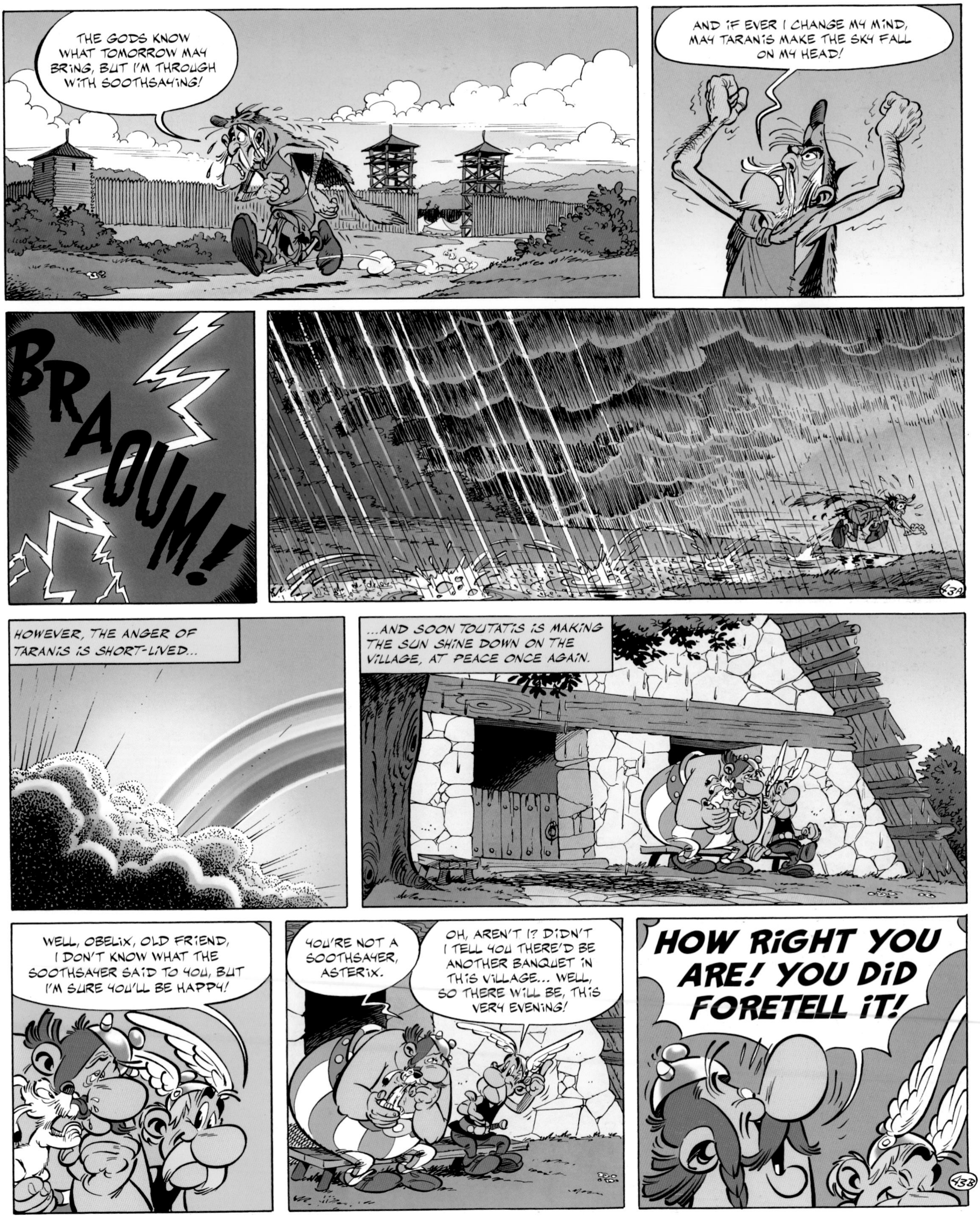
THE GODS KNOW WHAT TOMORROW MAY BRING, BUT I'M THROUGH WITH SOOTHSAYING!
AND IF EVER I CHANGE MY MIND, MAY TARANIS MAKE THE SKY FALL ON MY HEAD!
BRAAOUM!
HOWEVER, THE ANGER OF TARANIS IS SHORT-LIVED...
...AND SOON TOUTATIS IS MAKING THE SUN SHINE DOWN ON THE VILLAGE, AT PEACE ONCE AGAIN.
WELL, OBELIX, OLD FRIEND, I DON'T KNOW WHAT THE SOOTHSAYER SAID TO YOU, BUT I'M SURE YOU'LL BE HAPPY!
YOU'RE NOT A SOOTHSAYER, ASTERIX.
OH, AREN'T I? DIDN'T I TELL YOU THERE'D BE ANOTHER BANQUET IN THIS VILLAGE... WELL, SO THERE WILL BE, THIS VERY EVENING!
HOW RIGHT YOU ARE! YOU DID FORETELL IT!

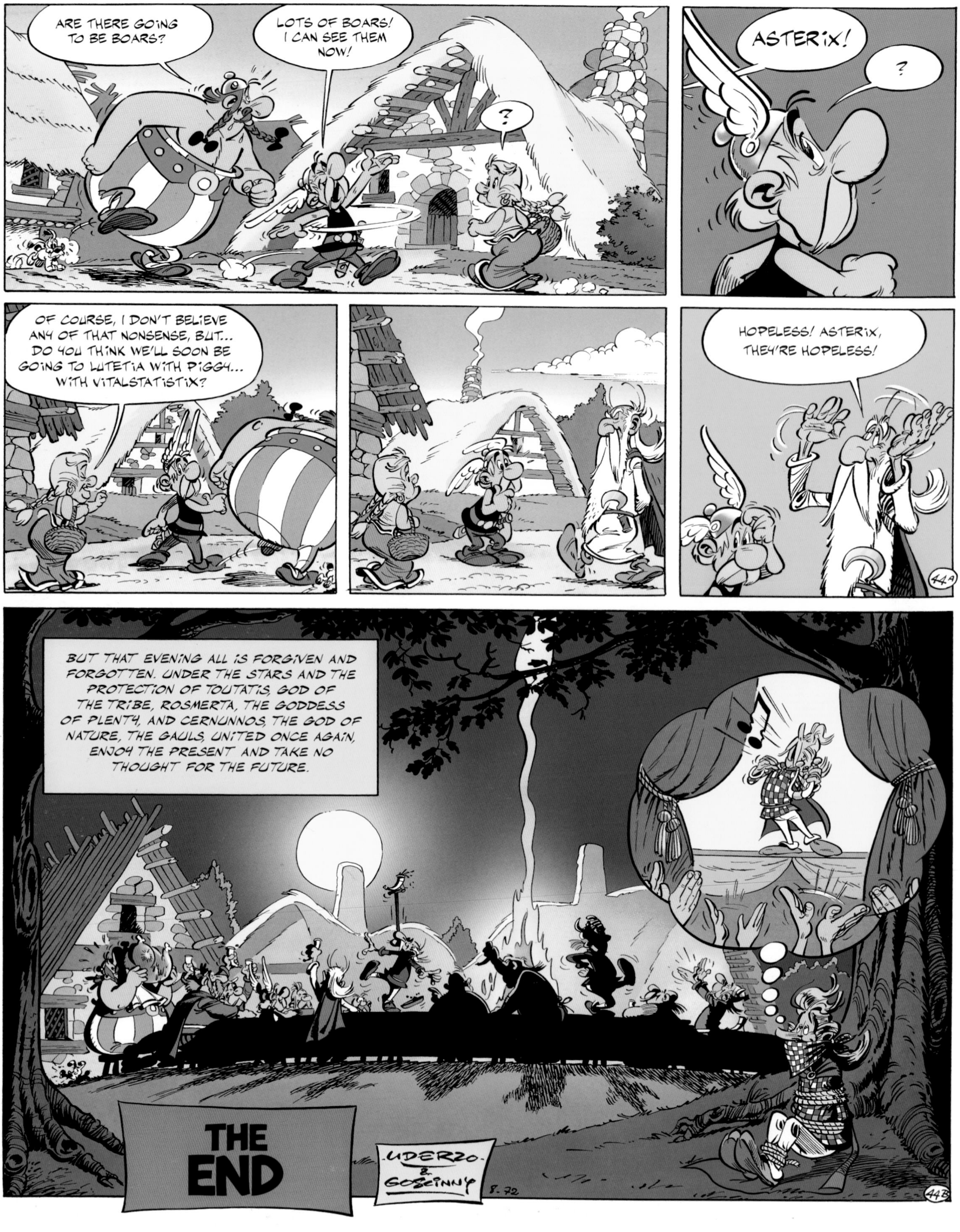
ARE THERE GOING TO BE BOARS?
LOTS OF BOARS! I CAN SEE THEM NOW!
?
ASTERIX!
?
OF COURSE, I DON'T BELIEVE ANY OF THAT NONSENSE, BUT... DO YOU THINK WE'LL SOON BE GOING TO LUTETIA WITH PIGGY... WITH VITALSTATISTIX?
HOPELESS! ASTERIX, THEY'RE HOPELESS!
44A
BUT THAT EVENING ALL IS FORGIVEN AND FORGOTTEN. UNDER THE STARS AND THE PROTECTION OF TOUTATIS, GOD OF THE TRIBE, ROSMERTA, THE GODDESS OF PLENTY, AND CERNUNNOS, THE GOD OF NATURE, THE GAULS, UNITED ONCE AGAIN, ENJOY THE PRESENT AND TAKE NO THOUGHT FOR THE FUTURE.
THE END
UDERZO & GOSCINNY
8.72
44B

R. GOSCINNY ASTERIX A. UDERZO

ASTERIX IN CORSICA

Written by René GOSCINNY

Illustrated by Albert UDERZO

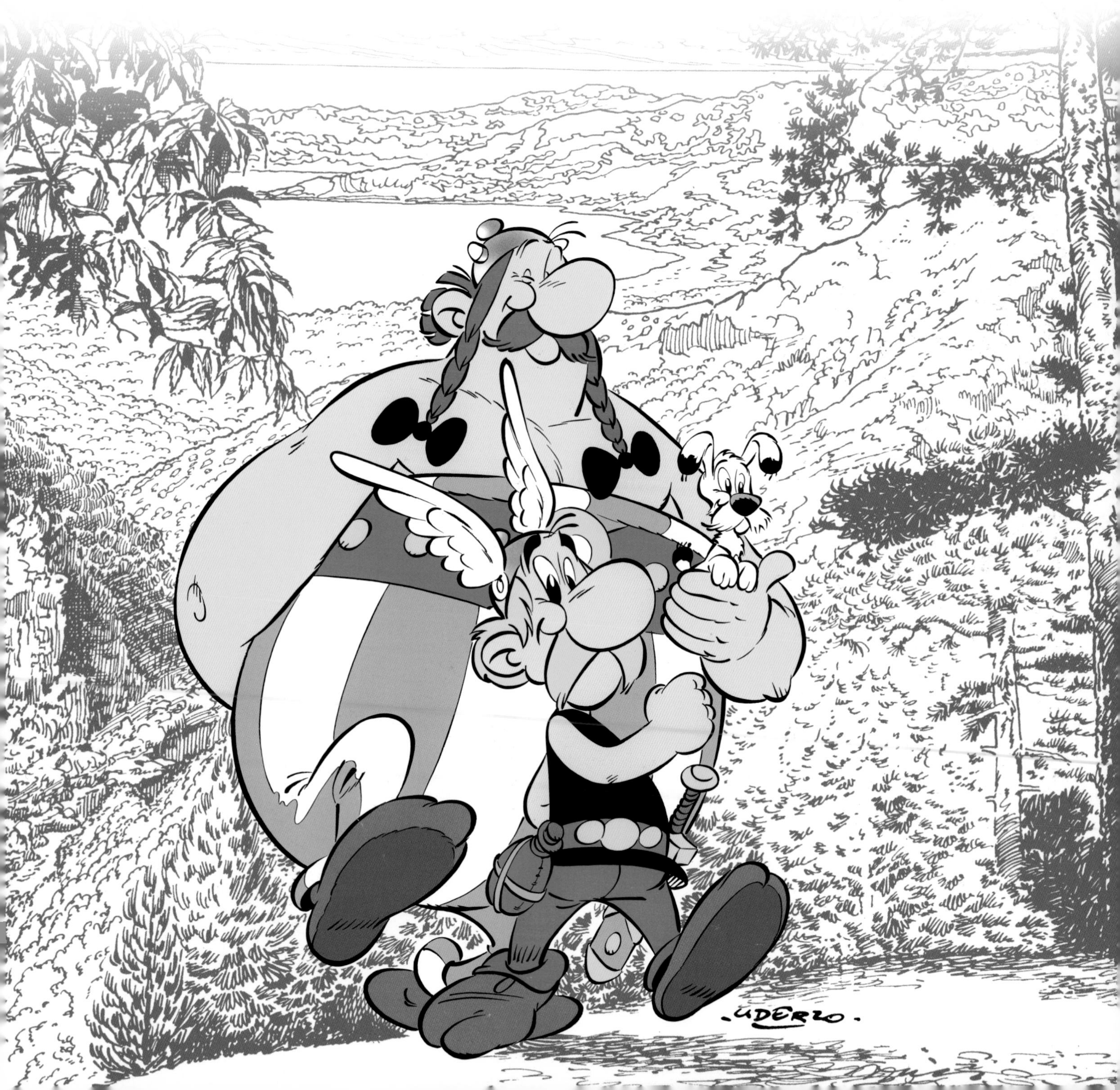
UDERZO

PREAMBLE

For most people, Corsica is the homeland of an emperor who has left pages in history as indelible as those inspired by our old friend Julius Caesar. It is also the birthplace of Tino Rossi, a singer with a long and prestigious career whose songs about Marinella and Bella Catarineta have toured the world. It is a country of vendettas, siestas, complicated political games, strong cheeses, wild pigs, chestnuts, succulent blackbirds, and spry old men watching the world go by.

But Corsica is more than all that. It is one of those privileged places in the world with a character, a strong personality that neither time nor man has ever tamed. It is one of the most beautiful places in the world – no wonder people call it the Isle of Beauty.

But why this preamble, you may ask. Because the Corsicans, who are described as individualists – having both exuberance and self-control – nonchalant, hospitable, loyal, faithful in friendship, attached to their homeland, eloquent and courageous, are also more than all that.

They are sensitive.

The Authors

GOSCINNY AND UDERZO
PRESENT
An Asterix Adventure

ASTERIX
IN
CORSICA

Written by RENÉ GOSCINNY *and Illustrated by* ALBERT UDERZO

Translated by Anthea Bell *and* Derek Hockridge

Orion
Children's Books

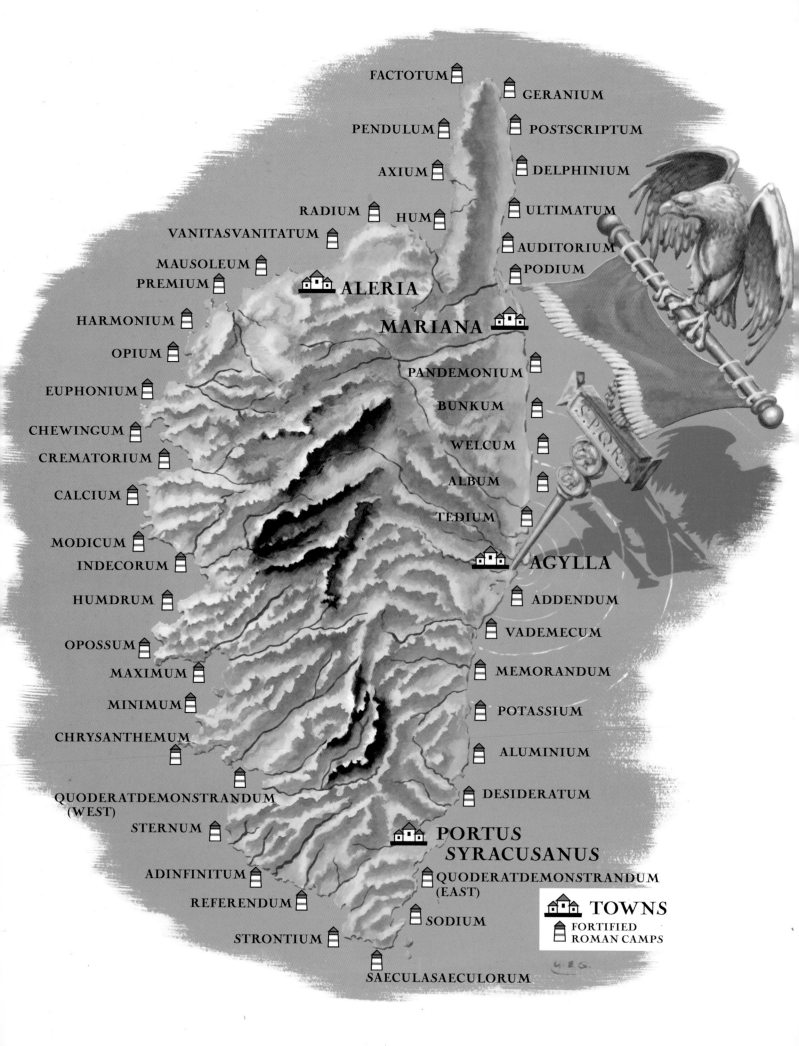

FACTOTUM

GERANIUM

PENDULUM

POSTSCRIPTUM

AXIUM

DELPHINIUM

RADIUM

HUM

ULTIMATUM

VANITASVANITATUM

AUDITORIUM

MAUSOLEUM

PODIUM

PREMIUM

ALERIA

HARMONIUM

MARIANA

OPIUM

PANDEMONIUM

EUPHONIUM

BUNKUM

CHEWINGUM

WELCUM

CREMATORIUM

ALBUM

CALCIUM

TEDIUM

MODICUM

INDECORUM

AGYLLA

HUMDRUM

ADDENDUM

OPOSSUM

VADEMECUM

MAXIMUM

MEMORANDUM

MINIMUM

POTASSIUM

CHRYSANTHEMUM

ALUMINIUM

QUODERATDEMONSTRANDUM
(WEST)

DESIDERATUM

STERNUM

PORTUS
SYRACUSANUS

ADINFINITUM

QUODERATDEMONSTRANDUM
(EAST)

REFERENDUM

SODIUM

STRONTIUM

TOWNS

FORTIFIED
ROMAN CAMPS

SAECULASAECULORUM

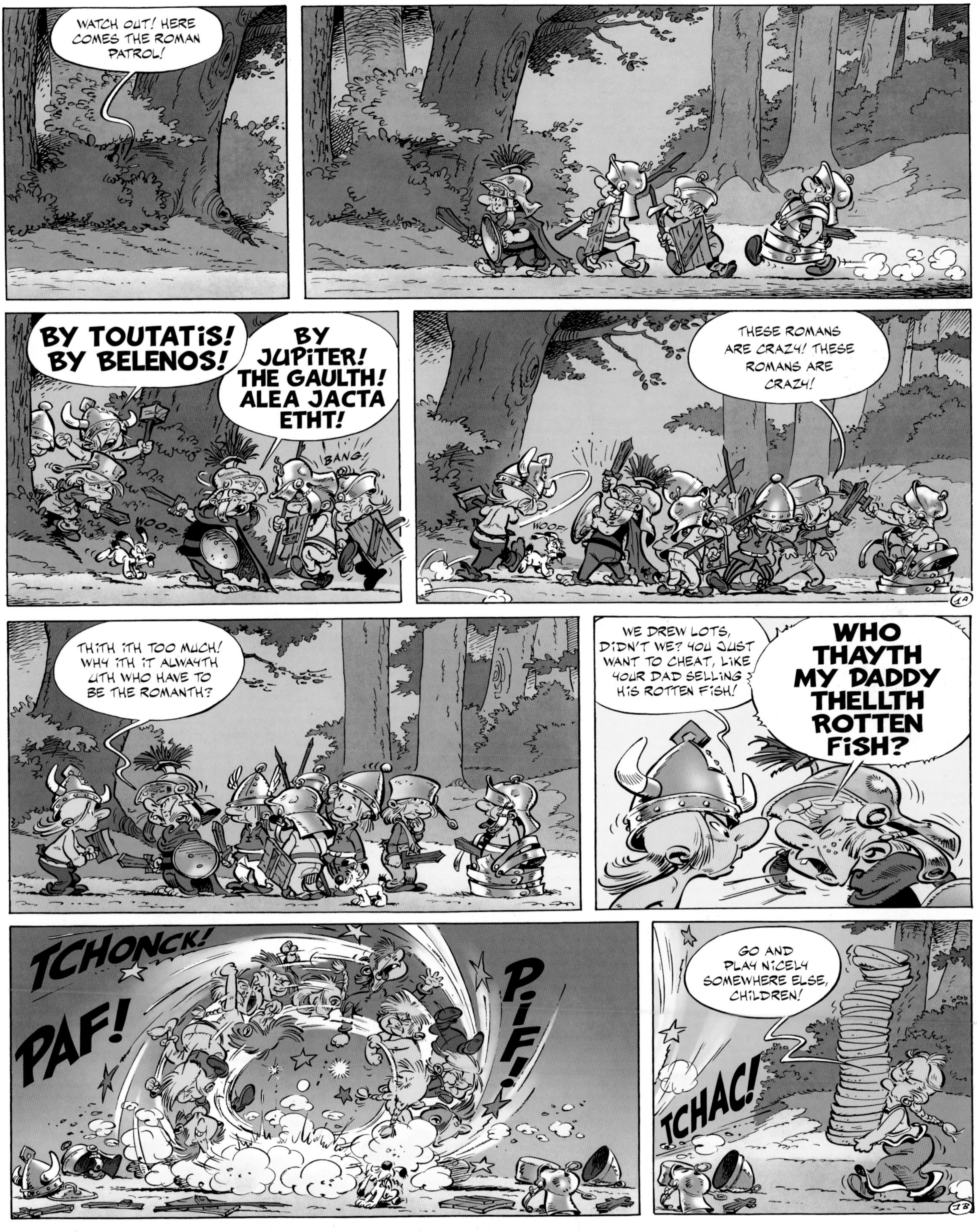
WATCH OUT! HERE COMES THE ROMAN PATROL!
BY TOUTATIS! BY BELENOS!
BY JUPITER! THE GAULTH! ALEA JACTA ETHT!
BANG!
WOOF!
THESE ROMANS ARE CRAZY! THESE ROMANS ARE CRAZY!
WOOF!
THITH ITH TOO MUCH! WHY ITH IT ALWAYTH UTH WHO HAVE TO BE THE ROMANTH?
WE DREW LOTS, DIDN'T WE? YOU JUST WANT TO CHEAT, LIKE YOUR DAD SELLING HIS ROTTEN FISH!
WHO THAYTH MY DADDY THELLTH ROTTEN FISH?
TCHONCK!
PAF!
PIF!
GO AND PLAY NICELY SOMEWHERE ELSE, CHILDREN!
TCHAC!

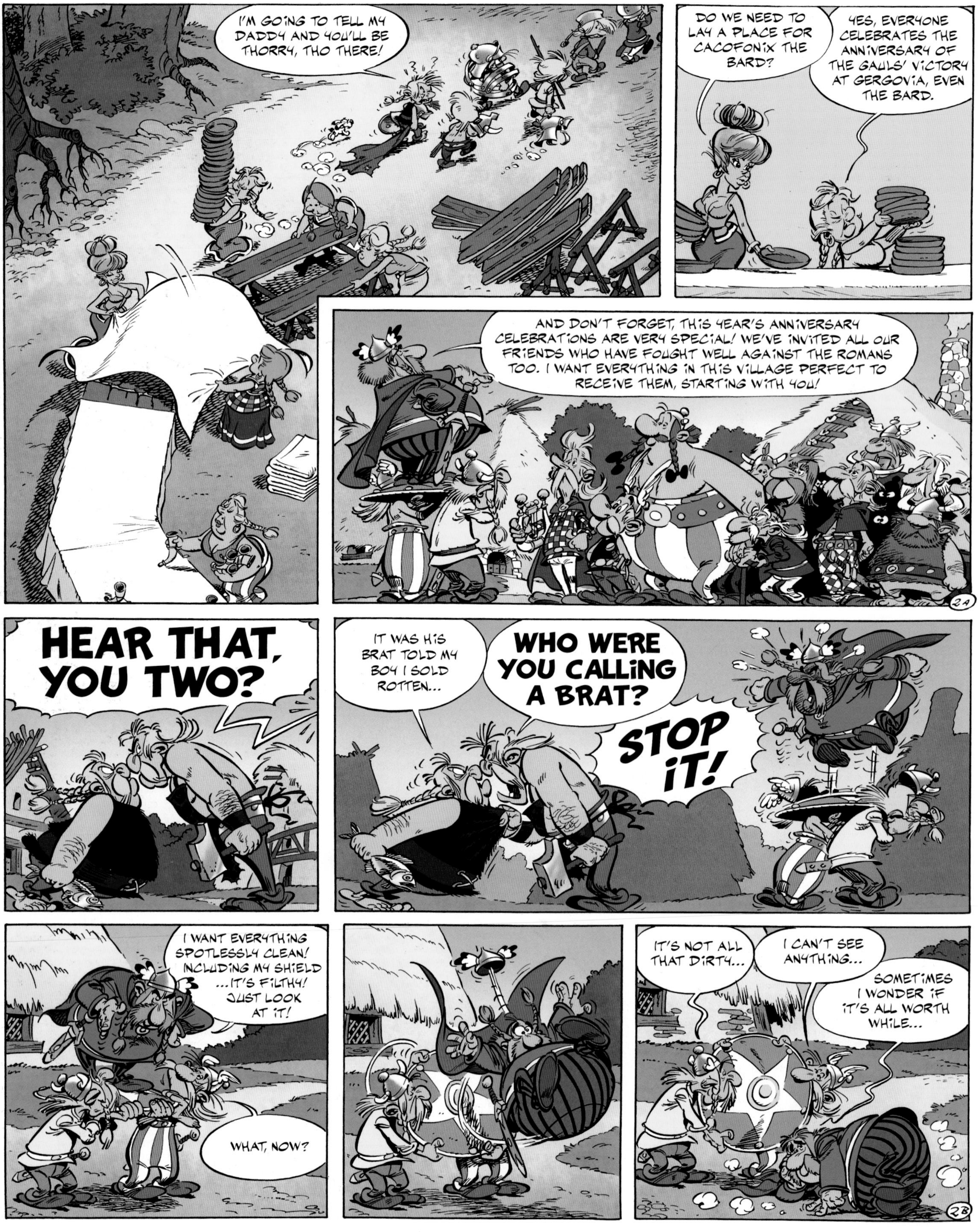
I'M GOING TO TELL MY DADDY AND YOU'LL BE THORRY, THO THERE!
DO WE NEED TO LAY A PLACE FOR CACOFONIX THE BARD?
YES, EVERYONE CELEBRATES THE ANNIVERSARY OF THE GAULS' VICTORY AT GERGOVIA, EVEN THE BARD.
AND DON'T FORGET, THIS YEAR'S ANNIVERSARY CELEBRATIONS ARE VERY SPECIAL! WE'VE INVITED ALL OUR FRIENDS WHO HAVE FOUGHT WELL AGAINST THE ROMANS TOO. I WANT EVERYTHING IN THIS VILLAGE PERFECT TO RECEIVE THEM, STARTING WITH YOU!
2A
HEAR THAT, YOU TWO?
IT WAS HIS BRAT TOLD MY BOY I SOLD ROTTEN...
WHO WERE YOU CALLING A BRAT?
STOP IT!
I WANT EVERYTHING SPOTLESSLY CLEAN! INCLUDING MY SHIELD ...IT'S FILTHY! JUST LOOK AT IT!
WHAT, NOW?
IT'S NOT ALL THAT DIRTY...
I CAN'T SEE ANYTHING...
SOMETIMES I WONDER IF IT'S ALL WORTH WHILE...
2B

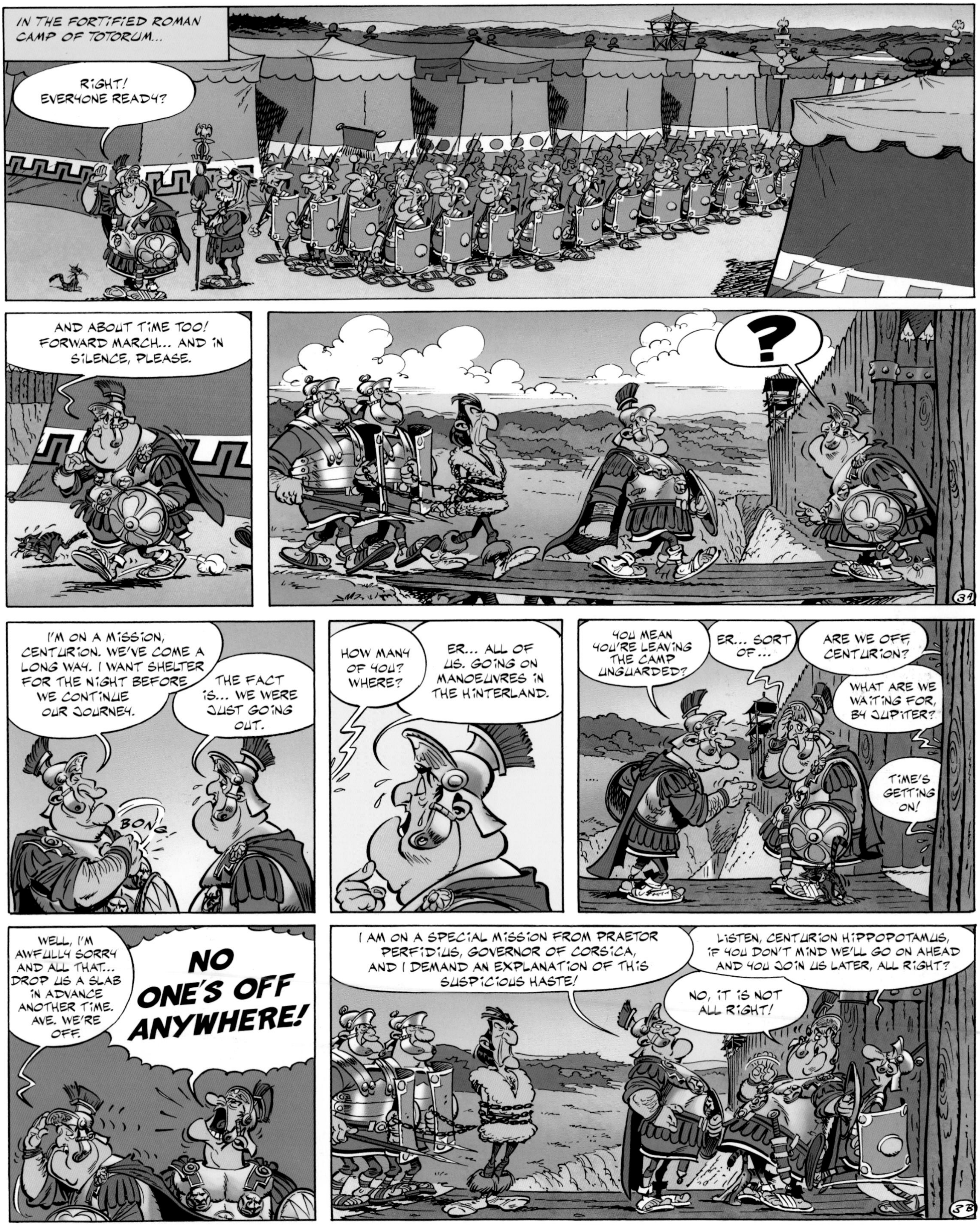
IN THE FORTIFIED ROMAN CAMP OF TOTORUM...
RIGHT! EVERYONE READY?
AND ABOUT TIME TOO! FORWARD MARCH... AND IN SILENCE, PLEASE.
?
I'M ON A MISSION, CENTURION. WE'VE COME A LONG WAY. I WANT SHELTER FOR THE NIGHT BEFORE WE CONTINUE OUR JOURNEY.
THE FACT IS... WE WERE JUST GOING OUT.
BONG
HOW MANY OF YOU? WHERE?
ER... ALL OF US. GOING ON MANOEUVRES IN THE HINTERLAND.
YOU MEAN YOU'RE LEAVING THE CAMP UNGUARDED?
ER... SORT OF...
ARE WE OFF, CENTURION?
WHAT ARE WE WAITING FOR, BY JUPITER?
TIME'S GETTING ON!
WELL, I'M AWFULLY SORRY AND ALL THAT... DROP US A SLAB IN ADVANCE ANOTHER TIME. AVE. WE'RE OFF.
NO ONE'S OFF ANYWHERE!
I AM ON A SPECIAL MISSION FROM PRAETOR PERFIDIUS, GOVERNOR OF CORSICA, AND I DEMAND AN EXPLANATION OF THIS SUSPICIOUS HASTE!
LISTEN, CENTURION HIPPOPOTAMUS, IF YOU DON'T MIND WE'LL GO ON AHEAD AND YOU JOIN US LATER, ALL RIGHT?
NO, IT IS NOT ALL RIGHT!

HERE, COME INTO MY TENT... DON'T START WITHOUT ME, YOU LOT. THIS WON'T TAKE LONG.

?

TODAY IS THE ANNIVERSARY OF THE BATTLE OF GERGOVIA. THE PEOPLE OF THE NEARBY GAULISH VILLAGE HAVE A WAY OF CELEBRATING THE OCCASION BY ATTACKING THE NEIGHBOURING ROMAN GARRISONS.

AND YOU DON'T ATTEMPT TO STOP THIS LOCAL CUSTOM?

WE CERTAINLY DO! WE STOP IT BY LEAVING CAMP AND GOING ON MANOEUVRES!

ARE YOU READY, CENTURION HIPPOPOTAMUS? THE BOYS ARE GETTING A BIT IMPATIENT, AND...

ARE THESE GAULS REALLY SO FEROCIOUS?

WELL, TOO BAD. I'M ESCORTING A CORSICAN EXILE, AND HE'S SPENDING THE NIGHT IN THIS CAMP. YOU AND YOUR GARRISON ARE RESPONSIBLE TO CAESAR FOR HIS SAFE KEEPING. I'LL BE BACK TO PICK HIM UP TOMORROW.

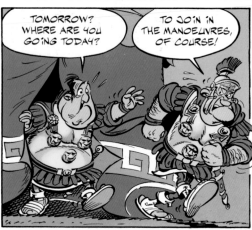

TOMORROW? WHERE ARE YOU GOING TODAY?

TO JOIN IN THE MANOEUVRES, OF COURSE!

BUT... BUT YOU CAN'T DO THIS TO US! THE GAULS WILL SLAUGHTER US! WHAT'S MORE, IF THEY SEE WE'VE GOT A PRISONER HERE, THEY'LL...

BRING THE EXILE ALONG!

AVE, CENTURION, AND DON'T FORGET, CAESAR WILL HOLD YOU RESPONSIBLE!

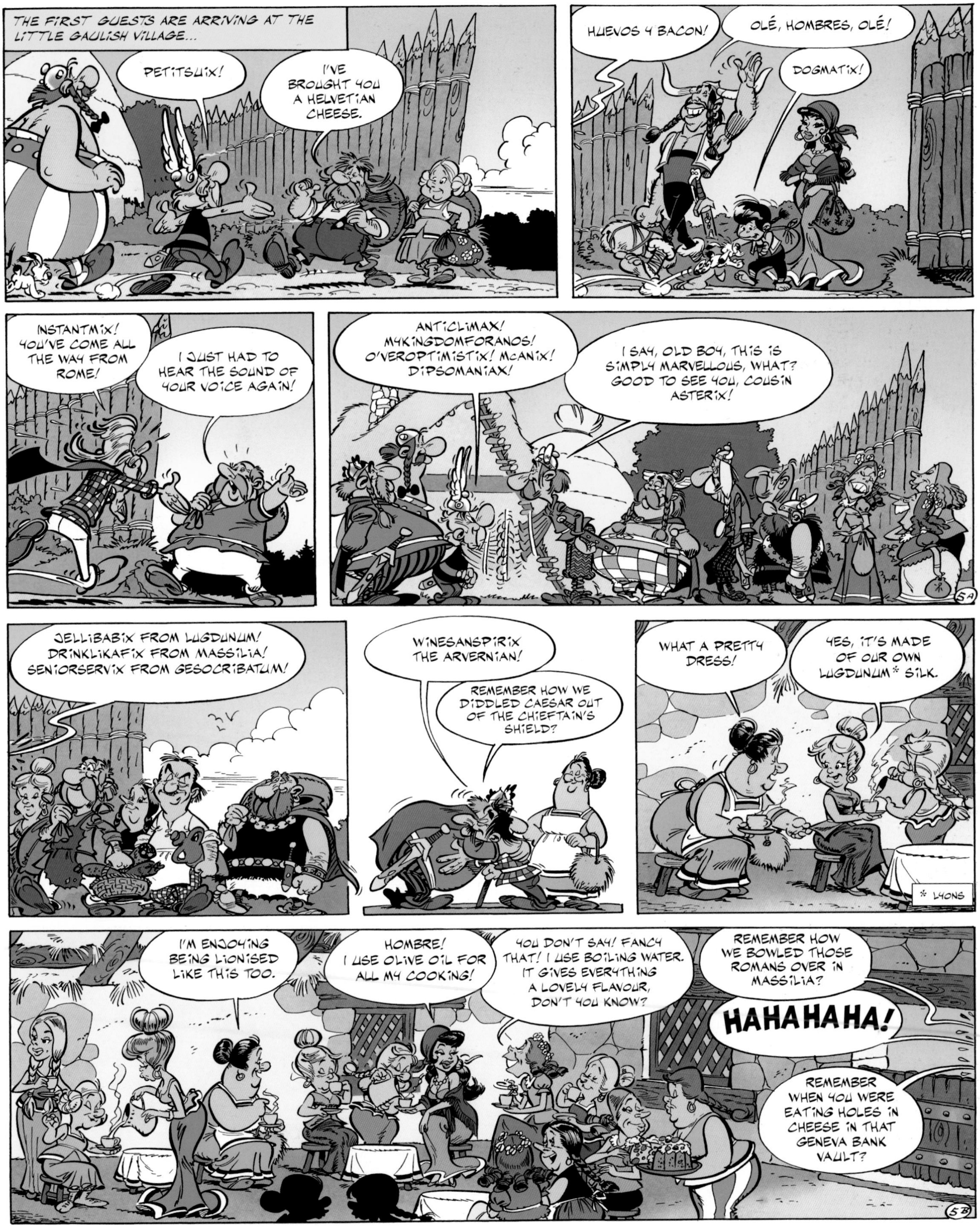
THE FIRST GUESTS ARE ARRIVING AT THE LITTLE GAULISH VILLAGE...
PETITSUIX!
I'VE BROUGHT YOU A HELVETIAN CHEESE.
HUEVOS Y BACON!
OLÉ, HOMBRES, OLÉ!
DOGMATIX!
INSTANTMIX! YOU'VE COME ALL THE WAY FROM ROME!
I JUST HAD TO HEAR THE SOUND OF YOUR VOICE AGAIN!
ANTICLIMAX! MYKINGDOMFORANOS! O'VEROPTIMISTIX! McANIX! DIPSOMANIAX!
I SAY, OLD BOY, THIS IS SIMPLY MARVELLOUS, WHAT? GOOD TO SEE YOU, COUSIN ASTERIX!
JELLIBABIX FROM LUGDUNUM! DRINKLIKAFIX FROM MASSILIA! SENIORSERVIX FROM GESOCRIBATUM!
WINESANSPIRIX THE ARVERNIAN!
REMEMBER HOW WE DIDDLED CAESAR OUT OF THE CHIEFTAIN'S SHIELD?
WHAT A PRETTY DRESS!
YES, IT'S MADE OF OUR OWN LUGDUNUM* SILK.
* LYONS
I'M ENJOYING BEING LIONISED LIKE THIS TOO.
HOMBRE! I USE OLIVE OIL FOR ALL MY COOKING!
YOU DON'T SAY! FANCY THAT! I USE BOILING WATER. IT GIVES EVERYTHING A LOVELY FLAVOUR, DON'T YOU KNOW?
REMEMBER HOW WE BOWLED THOSE ROMANS OVER IN MASSILIA?
HAHAHAHA!
REMEMBER WHEN YOU WERE EATING HOLES IN CHEESE IN THAT GENEVA BANK VAULT?

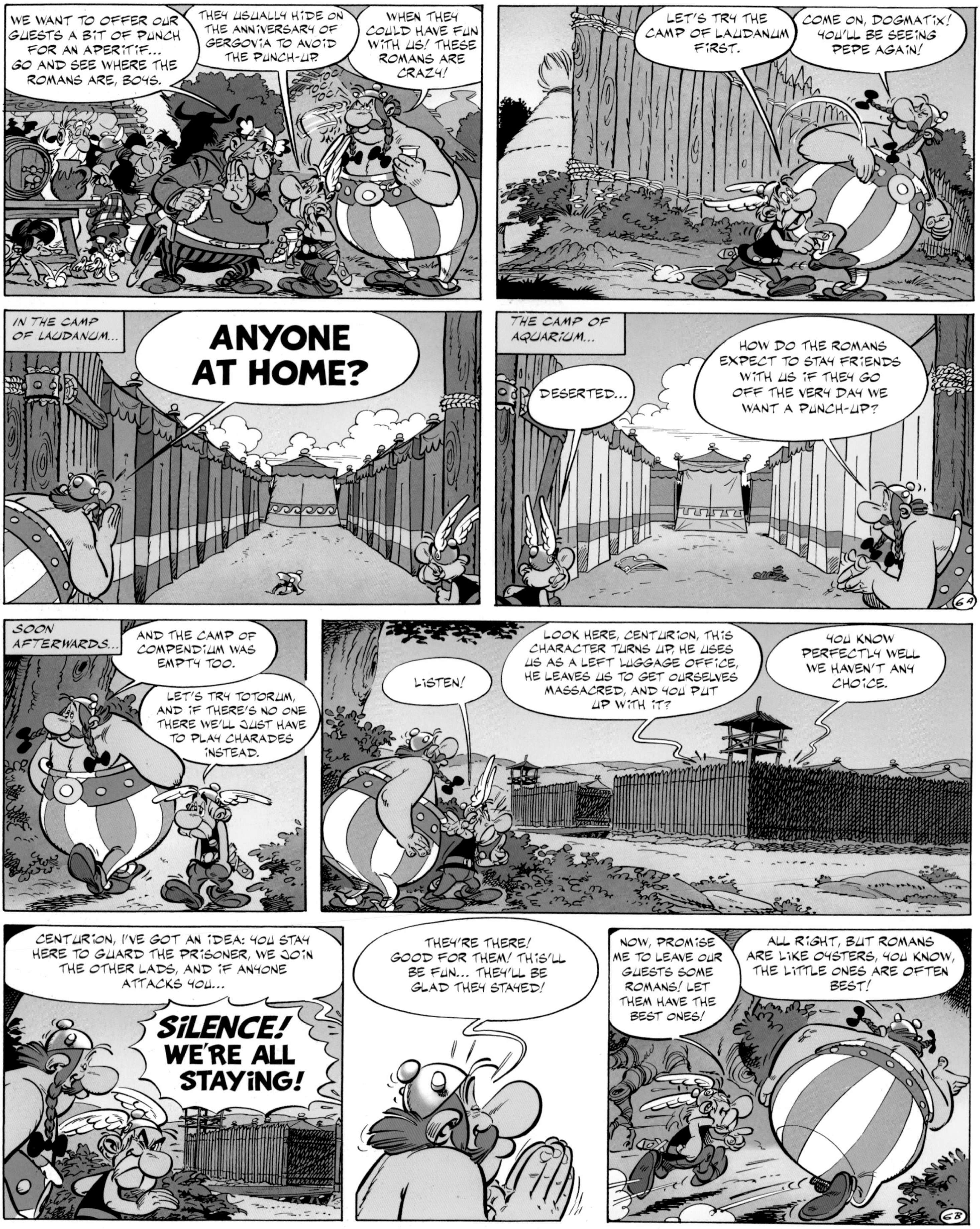

WE WANT TO OFFER OUR GUESTS A BIT OF PUNCH FOR AN APERITIF... GO AND SEE WHERE THE ROMANS ARE, BOYS.
THEY USUALLY HIDE ON THE ANNIVERSARY OF GERGOVIA TO AVOID THE PUNCH-UP.
WHEN THEY COULD HAVE FUN WITH US! THESE ROMANS ARE CRAZY!
LET'S TRY THE CAMP OF LAUDANUM FIRST.
COME ON, DOGMATIX! YOU'LL BE SEEING PEPE AGAIN!
IN THE CAMP OF LAUDANUM...
ANYONE AT HOME?
THE CAMP OF AQUARIUM...
DESERTED...
HOW DO THE ROMANS EXPECT TO STAY FRIENDS WITH US IF THEY GO OFF THE VERY DAY WE WANT A PUNCH-UP?
SOON AFTERWARDS...
AND THE CAMP OF COMPENDIUM WAS EMPTY TOO.
LET'S TRY TOTORUM, AND IF THERE'S NO ONE THERE WE'LL JUST HAVE TO PLAY CHARADES INSTEAD.
LISTEN!
LOOK HERE, CENTURION, THIS CHARACTER TURNS UP, HE USES US AS A LEFT LUGGAGE OFFICE, HE LEAVES US TO GET OURSELVES MASSACRED, AND YOU PUT UP WITH IT?
YOU KNOW PERFECTLY WELL WE HAVEN'T ANY CHOICE.
CENTURION, I'VE GOT AN IDEA: YOU STAY HERE TO GUARD THE PRISONER, WE JOIN THE OTHER LADS, AND IF ANYONE ATTACKS YOU...
SILENCE! WE'RE ALL STAYING!
THEY'RE THERE! GOOD FOR THEM! THIS'LL BE FUN... THEY'LL BE GLAD THEY STAYED!
NOW, PROMISE ME TO LEAVE OUR GUESTS SOME ROMANS! LET THEM HAVE THE BEST ONES!
ALL RIGHT, BUT ROMANS ARE LIKE OYSTERS, YOU KNOW, THE LITTLE ONES ARE OFTEN BEST!

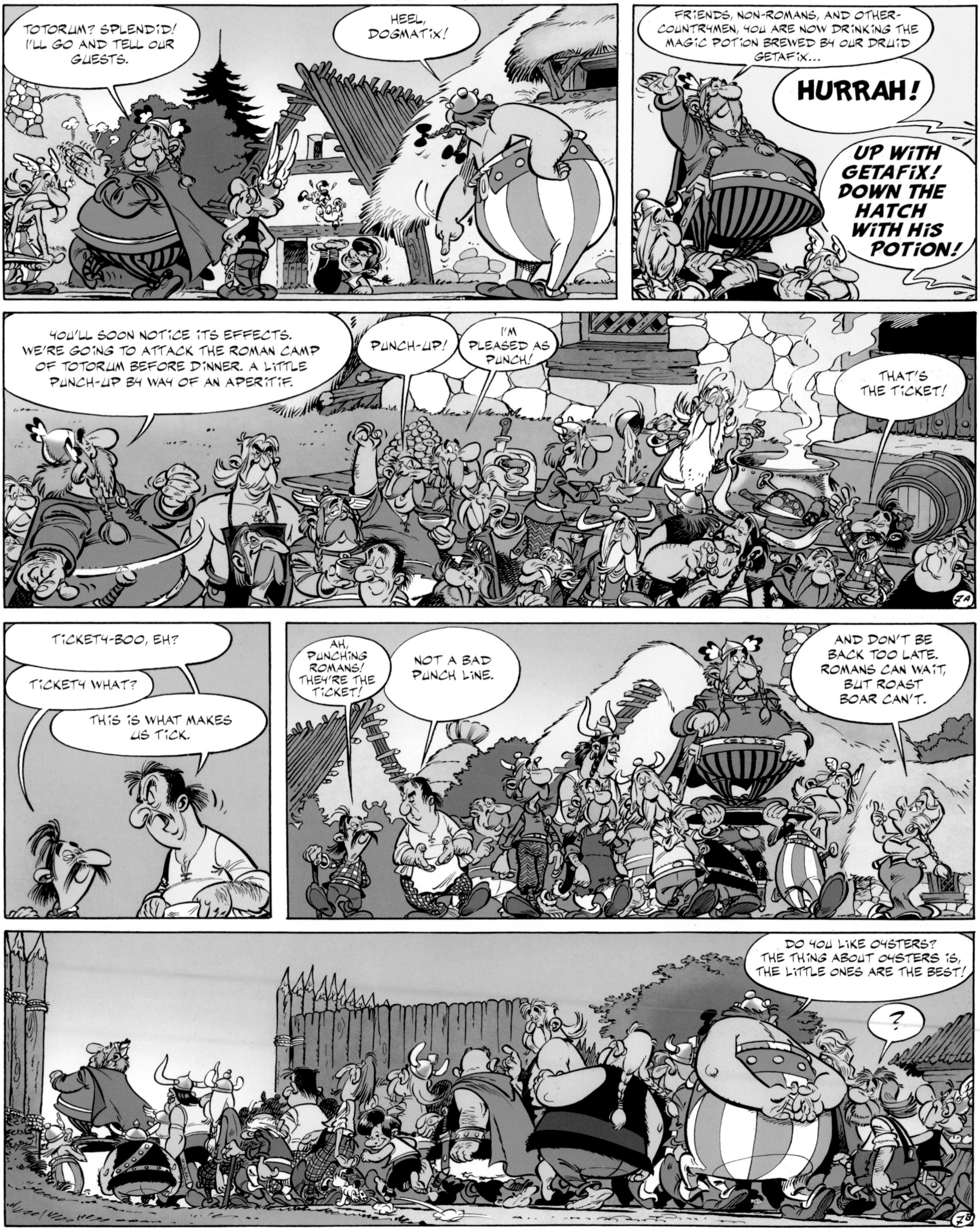

TOTORUM? SPLENDID! I'LL GO AND TELL OUR GUESTS.
HEEL, DOGMATIX!
FRIENDS, NON-ROMANS, AND OTHER-COUNTRYMEN, YOU ARE NOW DRINKING THE MAGIC POTION BREWED BY OUR DRUID GETAFIX...
HURRAH!
UP WITH GETAFIX! DOWN THE HATCH WITH HIS POTION!
YOU'LL SOON NOTICE ITS EFFECTS. WE'RE GOING TO ATTACK THE ROMAN CAMP OF TOTORUM BEFORE DINNER. A LITTLE PUNCH-UP BY WAY OF AN APERITIF.
PUNCH-UP!
I'M PLEASED AS PUNCH!
THAT'S THE TICKET!
TICKETY-BOO, EH?
TICKETY WHAT?
THIS IS WHAT MAKES US TICK.
AH, PUNCHING ROMANS! THEY'RE THE TICKET!
NOT A BAD PUNCH LINE.
AND DON'T BE BACK TOO LATE. ROMANS CAN WAIT, BUT ROAST BOAR CAN'T.
DO YOU LIKE OYSTERS? THE THING ABOUT OYSTERS IS, THE LITTLE ONES ARE THE BEST!
?

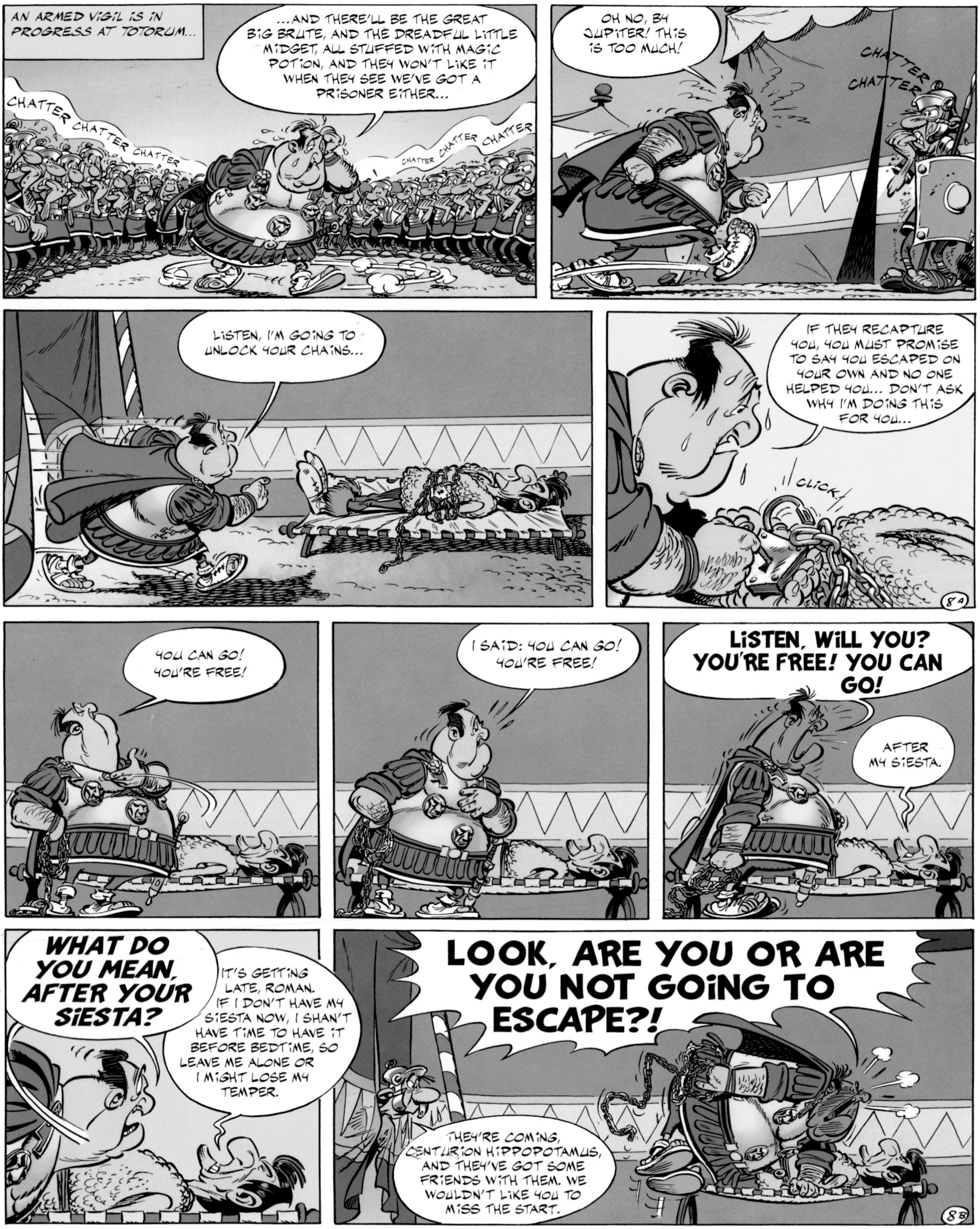
AN ARMED VIGIL IS IN PROGRESS AT TOTORUM...
...AND THERE'LL BE THE GREAT BIG BRUTE, AND THE DREADFUL LITTLE MIDGET, ALL STUFFED WITH MAGIC POTION, AND THEY WON'T LIKE IT WHEN THEY SEE WE'VE GOT A PRISONER EITHER...
CHATTER CHATTER CHATTER
CHATTER CHATTER CHATTER
OH NO, BY JUPITER! THIS IS TOO MUCH!
CHATTER CHATTER
LISTEN, I'M GOING TO UNLOCK YOUR CHAINS...
IF THEY RECAPTURE YOU, YOU MUST PROMISE TO SAY YOU ESCAPED ON YOUR OWN AND NO ONE HELPED YOU... DON'T ASK WHY I'M DOING THIS FOR YOU...
CLICK
YOU CAN GO! YOU'RE FREE!
I SAID: YOU CAN GO! YOU'RE FREE!
LISTEN, WILL YOU? YOU'RE FREE! YOU CAN GO!
AFTER MY SIESTA.
WHAT DO YOU MEAN, AFTER YOUR SIESTA?
IT'S GETTING LATE, ROMAN. IF I DON'T HAVE MY SIESTA NOW, I SHAN'T HAVE TIME TO HAVE IT BEFORE BEDTIME, SO LEAVE ME ALONE OR I MIGHT LOSE MY TEMPER.
LOOK, ARE YOU OR ARE YOU NOT GOING TO ESCAPE?!
THEY'RE COMING, CENTURION HIPPOPOTAMUS, AND THEY'VE GOT SOME FRIENDS WITH THEM. WE WOULDN'T LIKE YOU TO MISS THE START.

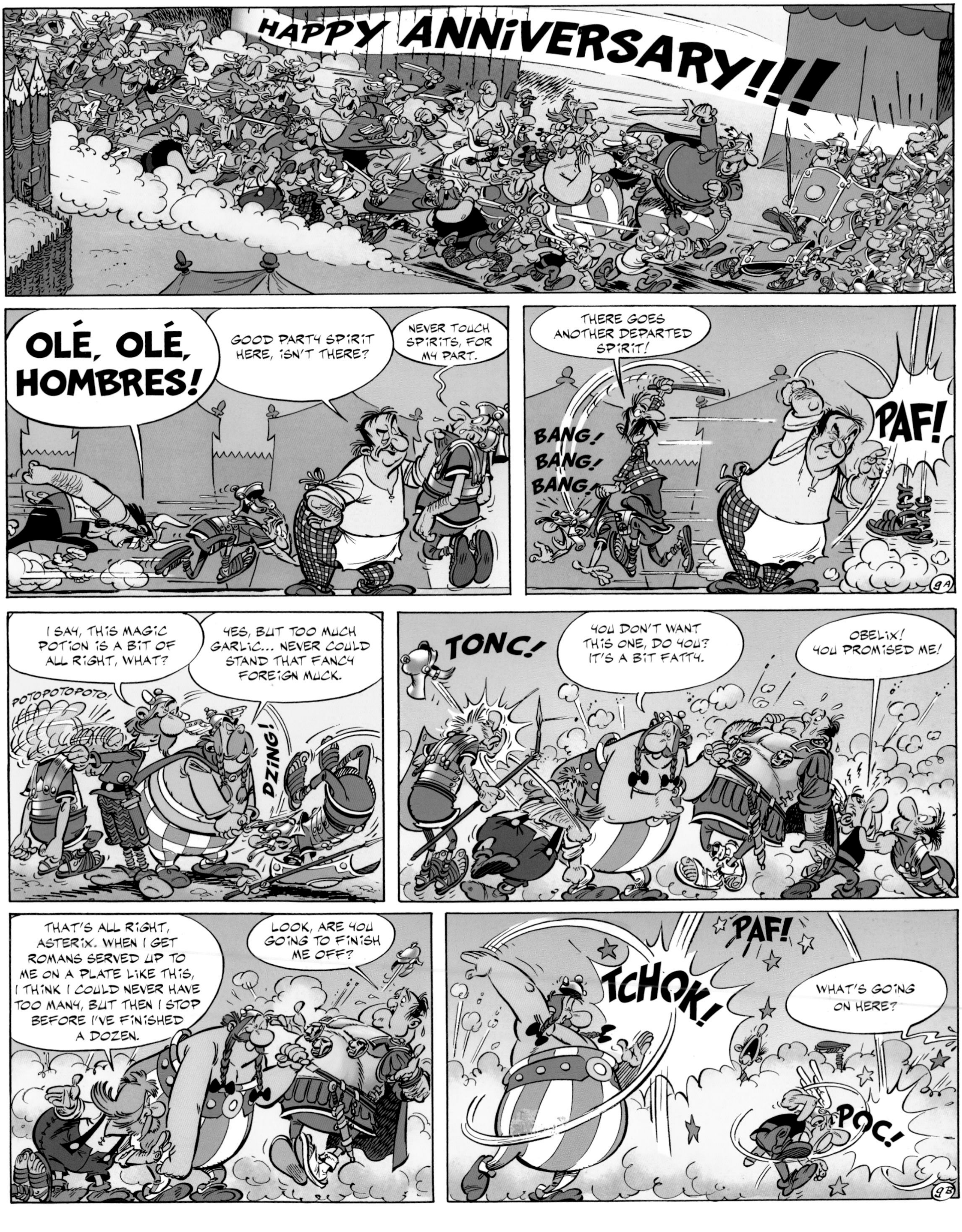
HAPPY ANNIVERSARY!!!!
OLÉ, OLÉ, HOMBRES!
GOOD PARTY SPIRIT HERE, ISN'T THERE?
NEVER TOUCH SPIRITS, FOR MY PART.
THERE GOES ANOTHER DEPARTED SPIRIT!
BANG! BANG! BANG!
PAF!
I SAY, THIS MAGIC POTION IS A BIT OF ALL RIGHT, WHAT?
YES, BUT TOO MUCH GARLIC... NEVER COULD STAND THAT FANCY FOREIGN MUCK.
POTOPOTOPOTO!
DZING!
TONC!
YOU DON'T WANT THIS ONE, DO YOU? IT'S A BIT FATTY.
OBELIX! YOU PROMISED ME!
THAT'S ALL RIGHT, ASTERIX. WHEN I GET ROMANS SERVED UP TO ME ON A PLATE LIKE THIS, I THINK I COULD NEVER HAVE TOO MANY, BUT THEN I STOP BEFORE I'VE FINISHED A DOZEN.
LOOK, ARE YOU GOING TO FINISH ME OFF?
PAF!
TCHOK!
WHAT'S GOING ON HERE?
POC!

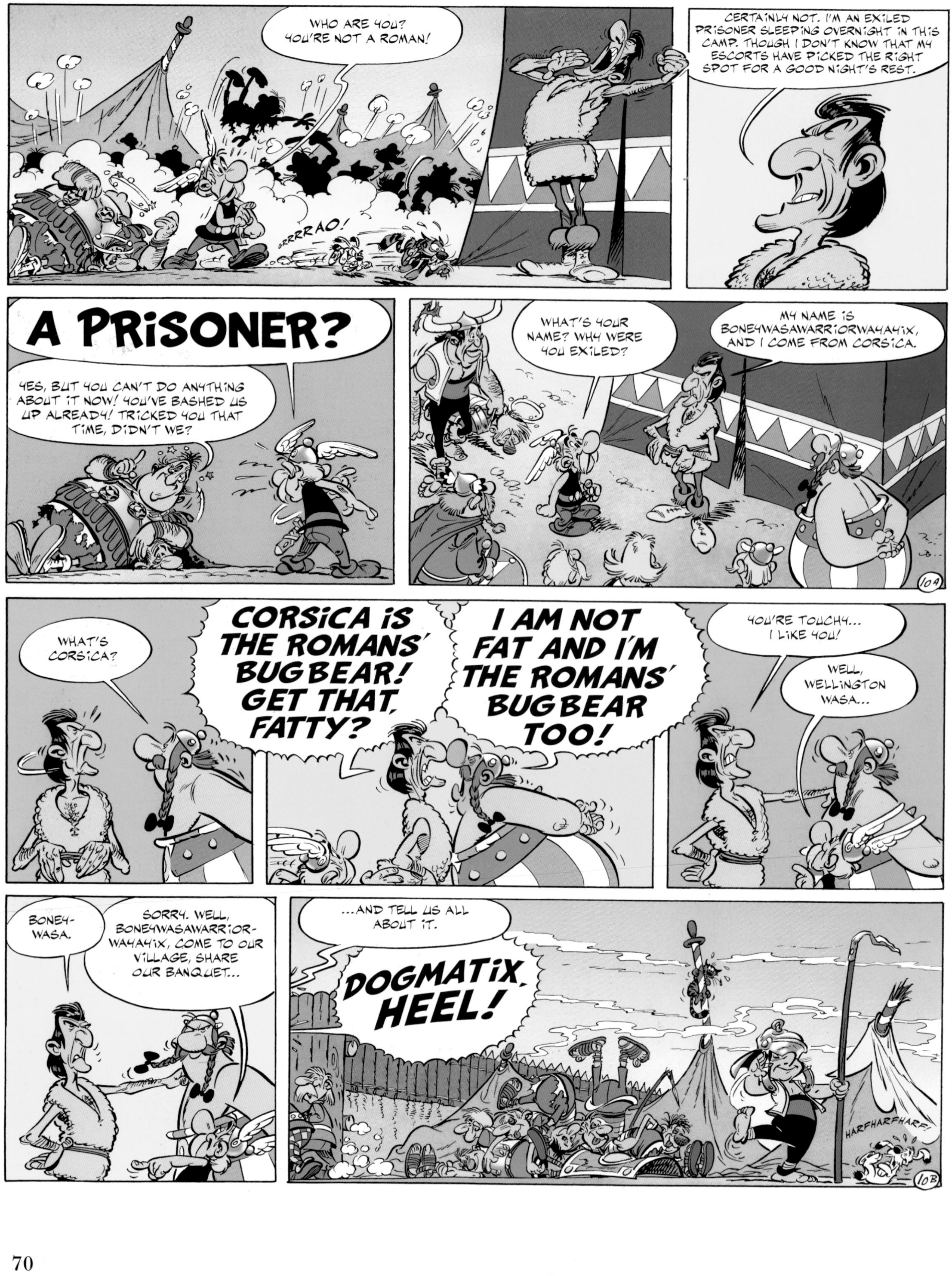
WHO ARE YOU? YOU'RE NOT A ROMAN!
GRRRRAO!
CERTAINLY NOT. I'M AN EXILED PRISONER SLEEPING OVERNIGHT IN THIS CAMP. THOUGH I DON'T KNOW THAT MY ESCORTS HAVE PICKED THE RIGHT SPOT FOR A GOOD NIGHT'S REST.
A PRISONER?
YES, BUT YOU CAN'T DO ANYTHING ABOUT IT NOW! YOU'VE BASHED US UP ALREADY! TRICKED YOU THAT TIME, DIDN'T WE?
WHAT'S YOUR NAME? WHY WERE YOU EXILED?
MY NAME IS BONEYWASAWARRIORWAYAYIX, AND I COME FROM CORSICA.
10A
WHAT'S CORSICA?
CORSICA IS THE ROMANS' BUGBEAR! GET THAT, FATTY?
I AM NOT FAT AND I'M THE ROMANS' BUGBEAR TOO!
YOU'RE TOUCHY... I LIKE YOU!
WELL, WELLINGTON WASA...
BONEY-WASA.
SORRY. WELL, BONEYWASAWARRIOR-WAYAYIX, COME TO OUR VILLAGE, SHARE OUR BANQUET...
...AND TELL US ALL ABOUT IT.
DOGMATIX, HEEL!
HARFHARFHARF!
10B

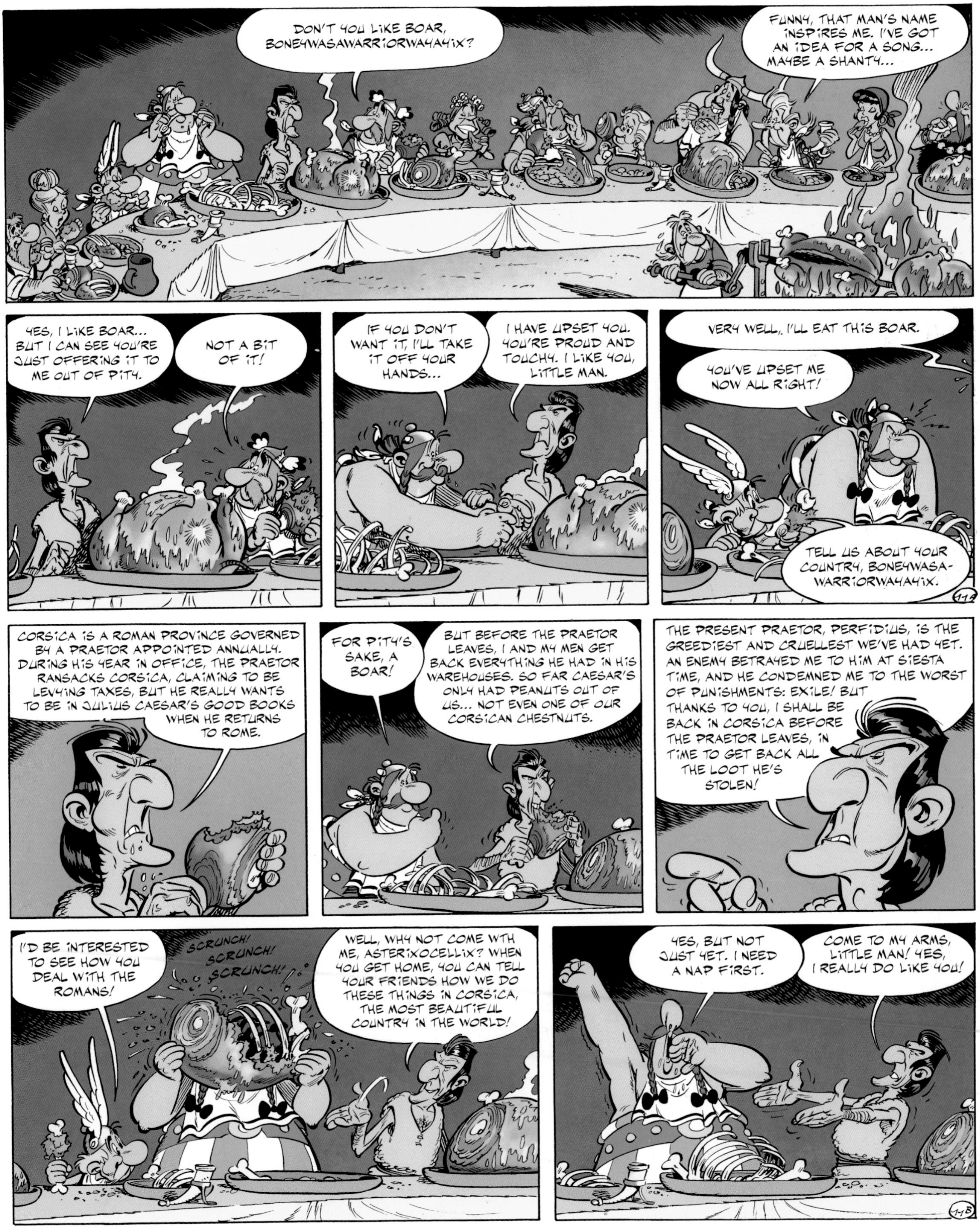
DON'T YOU LIKE BOAR, BONEYWASAWARRIORWAYAYIX?
FUNNY, THAT MAN'S NAME INSPIRES ME. I'VE GOT AN IDEA FOR A SONG... MAYBE A SHANTY...
YES, I LIKE BOAR... BUT I CAN SEE YOU'RE JUST OFFERING IT TO ME OUT OF PITY.
NOT A BIT OF IT!
IF YOU DON'T WANT IT, I'LL TAKE IT OFF YOUR HANDS...
I HAVE UPSET YOU. YOU'RE PROUD AND TOUCHY. I LIKE YOU, LITTLE MAN.
VERY WELL, I'LL EAT THIS BOAR.
YOU'VE UPSET ME NOW ALL RIGHT!
TELL US ABOUT YOUR COUNTRY, BONEYWASA-WARRIORWAYAYIX.
CORSICA IS A ROMAN PROVINCE GOVERNED BY A PRAETOR APPOINTED ANNUALLY. DURING HIS YEAR IN OFFICE, THE PRAETOR RANSACKS CORSICA, CLAIMING TO BE LEVYING TAXES, BUT HE REALLY WANTS TO BE IN JULIUS CAESAR'S GOOD BOOKS WHEN HE RETURNS TO ROME.
FOR PITY'S SAKE, A BOAR!
BUT BEFORE THE PRAETOR LEAVES, I AND MY MEN GET BACK EVERYTHING HE HAD IN HIS WAREHOUSES. SO FAR CAESAR'S ONLY HAD PEANUTS OUT OF US... NOT EVEN ONE OF OUR CORSICAN CHESTNUTS.
THE PRESENT PRAETOR, PERFIDIUS, IS THE GREEDIEST AND CRUELLEST WE'VE HAD YET. AN ENEMY BETRAYED ME TO HIM AT SIESTA TIME, AND HE CONDEMNED ME TO THE WORST OF PUNISHMENTS: EXILE! BUT THANKS TO YOU, I SHALL BE BACK IN CORSICA BEFORE THE PRAETOR LEAVES, IN TIME TO GET BACK ALL THE LOOT HE'S STOLEN!
I'D BE INTERESTED TO SEE HOW YOU DEAL WITH THE ROMANS!
SCRUNCH! SCRUNCH! SCRUNCH!
WELL, WHY NOT COME WITH ME, ASTERIXOCELLIX? WHEN YOU GET HOME, YOU CAN TELL YOUR FRIENDS HOW WE DO THESE THINGS IN CORSICA, THE MOST BEAUTIFUL COUNTRY IN THE WORLD!
YES, BUT NOT JUST YET. I NEED A NAP FIRST.
COME TO MY ARMS, LITTLE MAN! YES, I REALLY DO LIKE YOU!

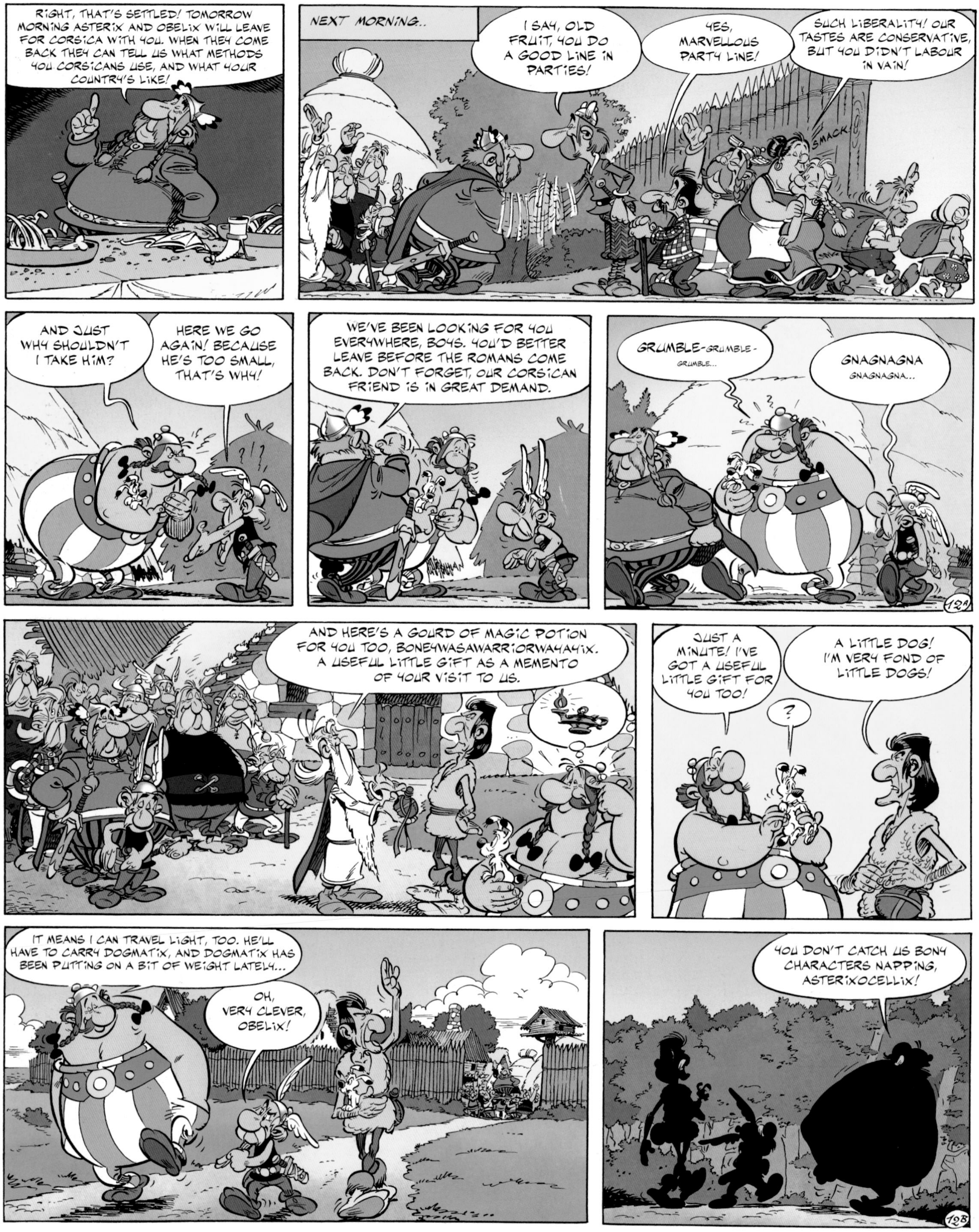

RIGHT, THAT'S SETTLED! TOMORROW MORNING ASTERIX AND OBELIX WILL LEAVE FOR CORSICA WITH YOU. WHEN THEY COME BACK THEY CAN TELL US WHAT METHODS YOU CORSICANS USE, AND WHAT YOUR COUNTRY'S LIKE!
NEXT MORNING...
I SAY, OLD FRUIT, YOU DO A GOOD LINE IN PARTIES!
YES, MARVELLOUS PARTY LINE!
SUCH LIBERALITY! OUR TASTES ARE CONSERVATIVE, BUT YOU DIDN'T LABOUR IN VAIN!
SMACK
AND JUST WHY SHOULDN'T I TAKE HIM?
HERE WE GO AGAIN! BECAUSE HE'S TOO SMALL, THAT'S WHY!
WE'VE BEEN LOOKING FOR YOU EVERYWHERE, BOYS. YOU'D BETTER LEAVE BEFORE THE ROMANS COME BACK. DON'T FORGET, OUR CORSICAN FRIEND IS IN GREAT DEMAND.
GRUMBLE-GRUMBLE-GRUMBLE...
GNAGNAGNA GNAGNAGNA...
12A
AND HERE'S A GOURD OF MAGIC POTION FOR YOU TOO, BONEYWASAWARRIORWAYAYIX. A USEFUL LITTLE GIFT AS A MEMENTO OF YOUR VISIT TO US.
JUST A MINUTE! I'VE GOT A USEFUL LITTLE GIFT FOR YOU TOO!
?
A LITTLE DOG! I'M VERY FOND OF LITTLE DOGS!
IT MEANS I CAN TRAVEL LIGHT, TOO. HE'LL HAVE TO CARRY DOGMATIX, AND DOGMATIX HAS BEEN PUTTING ON A BIT OF WEIGHT LATELY...
OH, VERY CLEVER, OBELIX!
YOU DON'T CATCH US BONY CHARACTERS NAPPING, ASTERIXOCELLIX!
12B

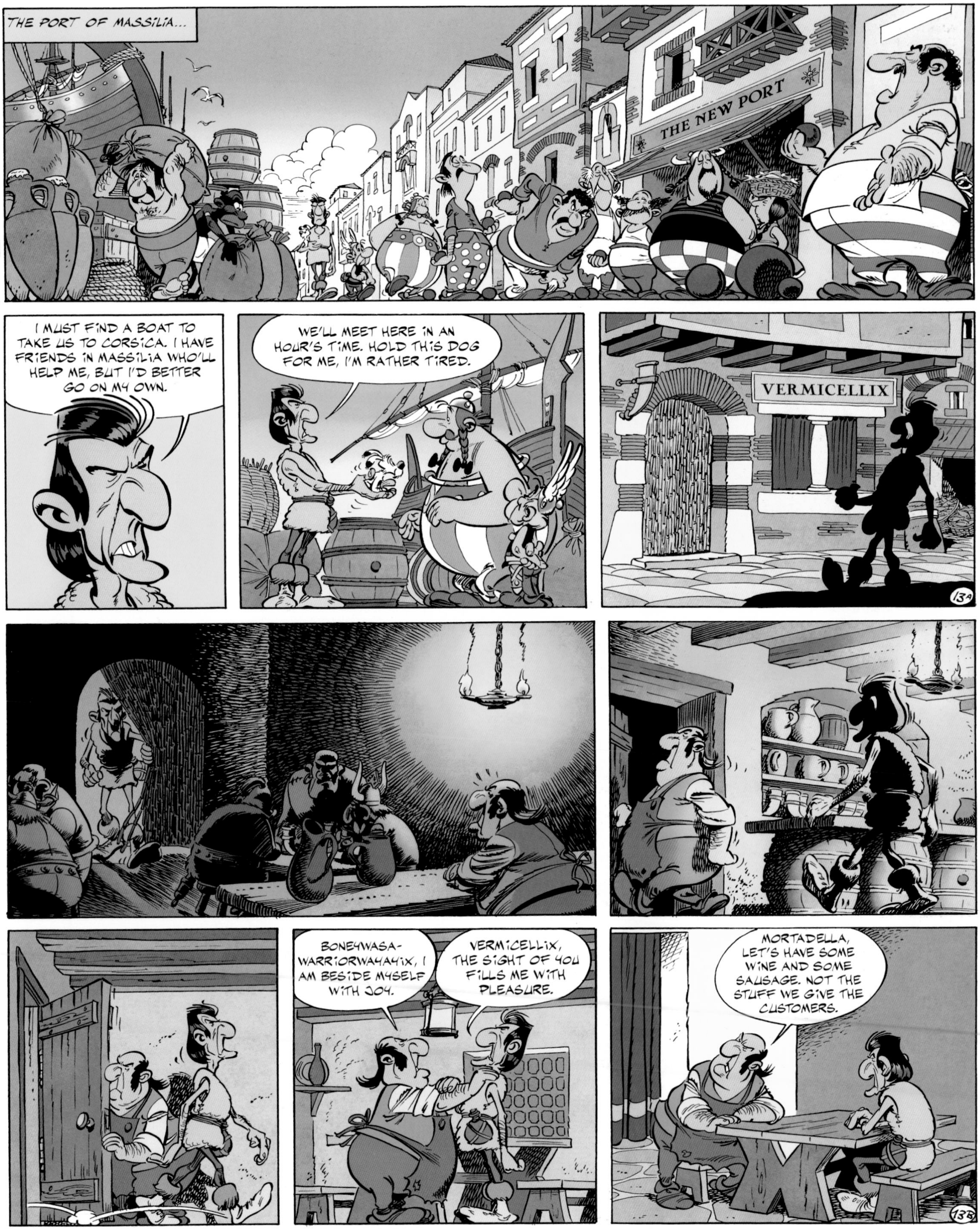
THE PORT OF MASSILIA...
THE NEW PORT
I MUST FIND A BOAT TO TAKE US TO CORSICA. I HAVE FRIENDS IN MASSILIA WHO'LL HELP ME, BUT I'D BETTER GO ON MY OWN.
WE'LL MEET HERE IN AN HOUR'S TIME. HOLD THIS DOG FOR ME, I'M RATHER TIRED.
VERMICELLIX
13A
BONEYWASAWARRIORWAYAYIX, I AM BESIDE MYSELF WITH JOY.
VERMICELLIX, THE SIGHT OF YOU FILLS ME WITH PLEASURE.
MORTADELLA, LET'S HAVE SOME WINE AND SOME SAUSAGE. NOT THE STUFF WE GIVE THE CUSTOMERS.
13B

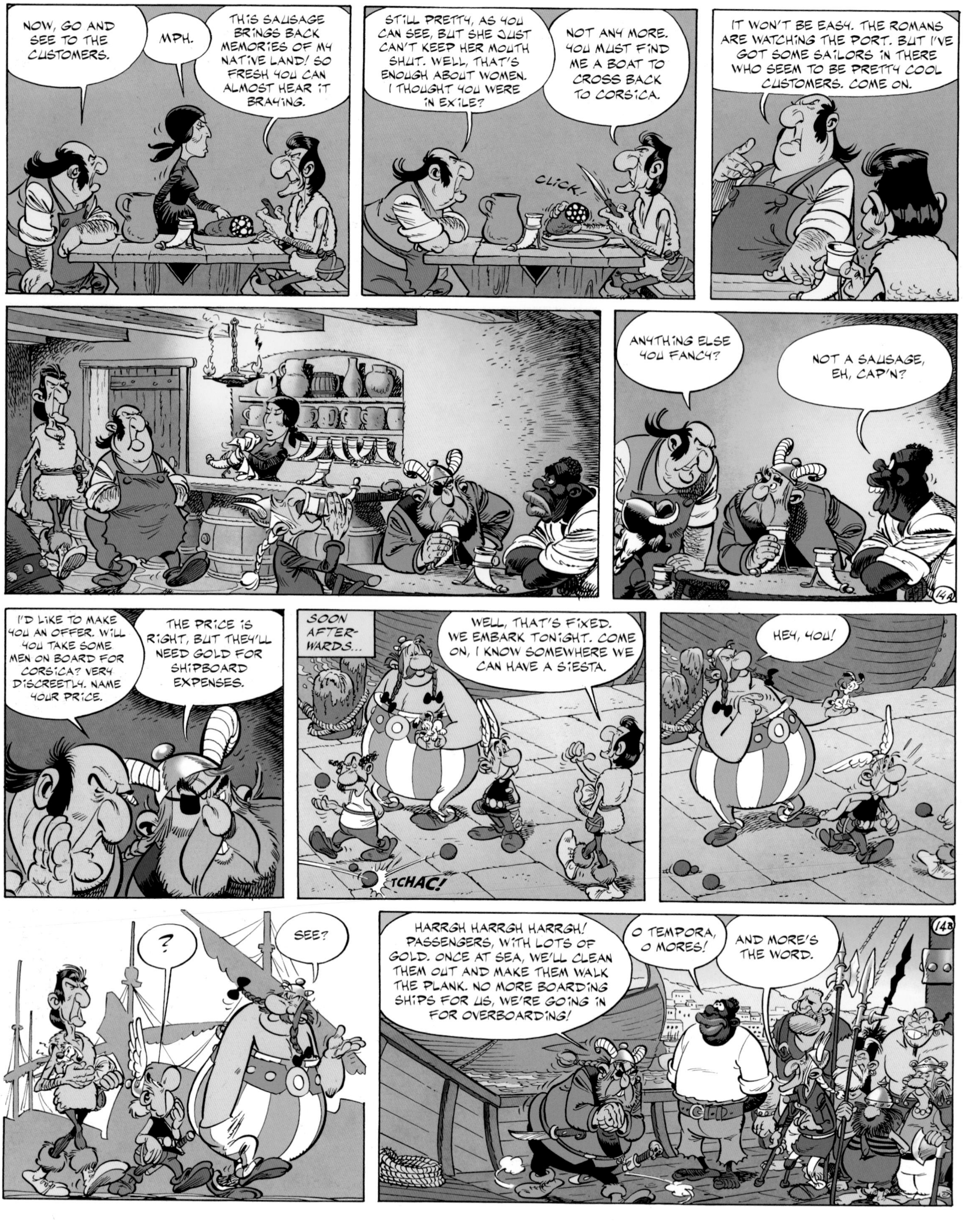
NOW, GO AND SEE TO THE CUSTOMERS.
MPH.
THIS SAUSAGE BRINGS BACK MEMORIES OF MY NATIVE LAND! SO FRESH YOU CAN ALMOST HEAR IT BRAYING.
STILL PRETTY, AS YOU CAN SEE, BUT SHE JUST CAN'T KEEP HER MOUTH SHUT. WELL, THAT'S ENOUGH ABOUT WOMEN. I THOUGHT YOU WERE IN EXILE?
NOT ANY MORE. YOU MUST FIND ME A BOAT TO CROSS BACK TO CORSICA.
CLICK!
IT WON'T BE EASY. THE ROMANS ARE WATCHING THE PORT. BUT I'VE GOT SOME SAILORS IN THERE WHO SEEM TO BE PRETTY COOL CUSTOMERS. COME ON.
ANYTHING ELSE YOU FANCY?
NOT A SAUSAGE, EH, CAP'N?
I'D LIKE TO MAKE YOU AN OFFER. WILL YOU TAKE SOME MEN ON BOARD FOR CORSICA? VERY DISCREETLY. NAME YOUR PRICE.
THE PRICE IS RIGHT, BUT THEY'LL NEED GOLD FOR SHIPBOARD EXPENSES.
SOON AFTERWARDS...
WELL, THAT'S FIXED. WE EMBARK TONIGHT. COME ON, I KNOW SOMEWHERE WE CAN HAVE A SIESTA.
TCHAC!
HEY, YOU!
?
SEE?
HARRGH HARRGH HARRGH! PASSENGERS, WITH LOTS OF GOLD. ONCE AT SEA, WE'LL CLEAN THEM OUT AND MAKE THEM WALK THE PLANK. NO MORE BOARDING SHIPS FOR US, WE'RE GOING IN FOR OVERBOARDING!
O TEMPORA, O MORES!
AND MORE'S THE WORD.

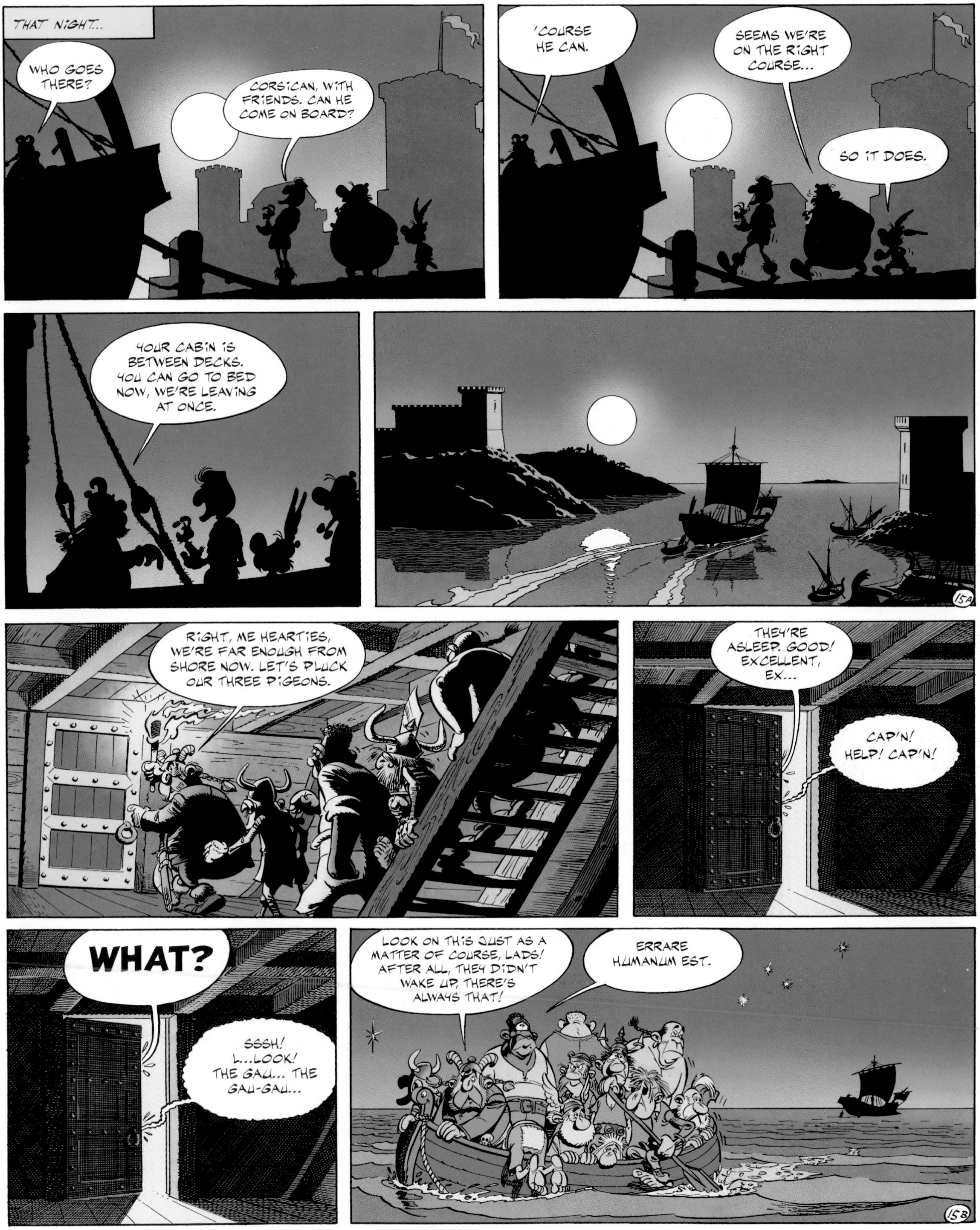
THAT NIGHT...
WHO GOES THERE?
CORSICAN, WITH FRIENDS. CAN HE COME ON BOARD?
'COURSE HE CAN.
SEEMS WE'RE ON THE RIGHT COURSE...
SO IT DOES.
YOUR CABIN IS BETWEEN DECKS. YOU CAN GO TO BED NOW, WE'RE LEAVING AT ONCE.
RIGHT, ME HEARTIES, WE'RE FAR ENOUGH FROM SHORE NOW. LET'S PLUCK OUR THREE PIGEONS.
THEY'RE ASLEEP. GOOD! EXCELLENT, EX...
CAP'N! HELP! CAP'N!
WHAT?
SSSH! L...LOOK! THE GAU... THE GAU-GAU...
LOOK ON THIS JUST AS A MATTER OF COURSE, LADS! AFTER ALL, THEY DIDN'T WAKE UP, THERE'S ALWAYS THAT!
ERRARE HUMANUM EST.

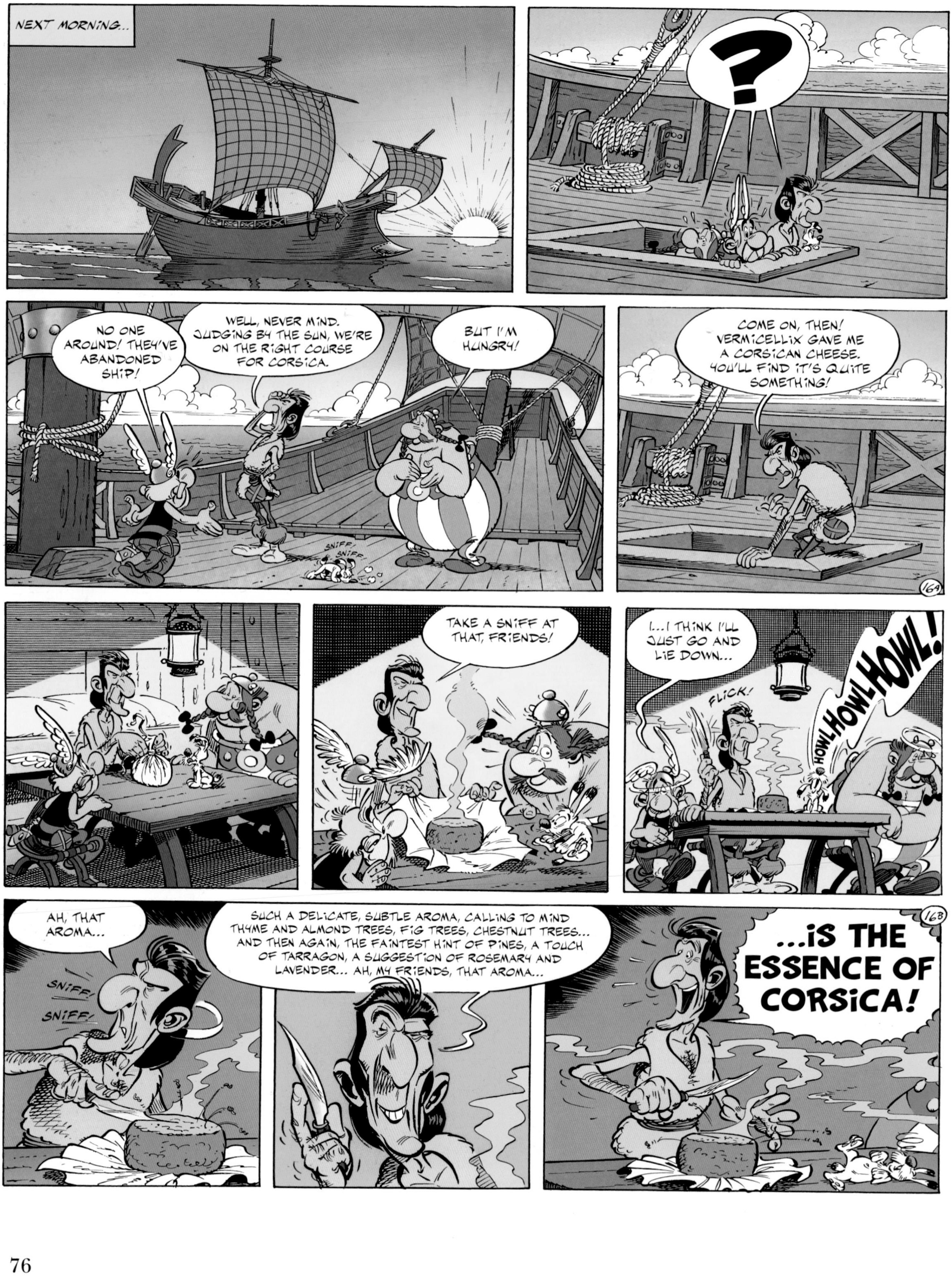
NEXT MORNING...
?
NO ONE AROUND! THEY'VE ABANDONED SHIP!
WELL, NEVER MIND. JUDGING BY THE SUN, WE'RE ON THE RIGHT COURSE FOR CORSICA.
BUT I'M HUNGRY!
SNIFF! SNIFF!
COME ON, THEN! VERMICELLIX GAVE ME A CORSICAN CHEESE. YOU'LL FIND IT'S QUITE SOMETHING!
TAKE A SNIFF AT THAT, FRIENDS!
I...I THINK I'LL JUST GO AND LIE DOWN...
FLICK!
HOWL! HOWL! HOWL!
AH, THAT AROMA...
SNIFF! SNIFF!
SUCH A DELICATE, SUBTLE AROMA, CALLING TO MIND THYME AND ALMOND TREES, FIG TREES, CHESTNUT TREES... AND THEN AGAIN, THE FAINTEST HINT OF PINES, A TOUCH OF TARRAGON, A SUGGESTION OF ROSEMARY AND LAVENDER... AH, MY FRIENDS, THAT AROMA...
...IS THE ESSENCE OF CORSICA!

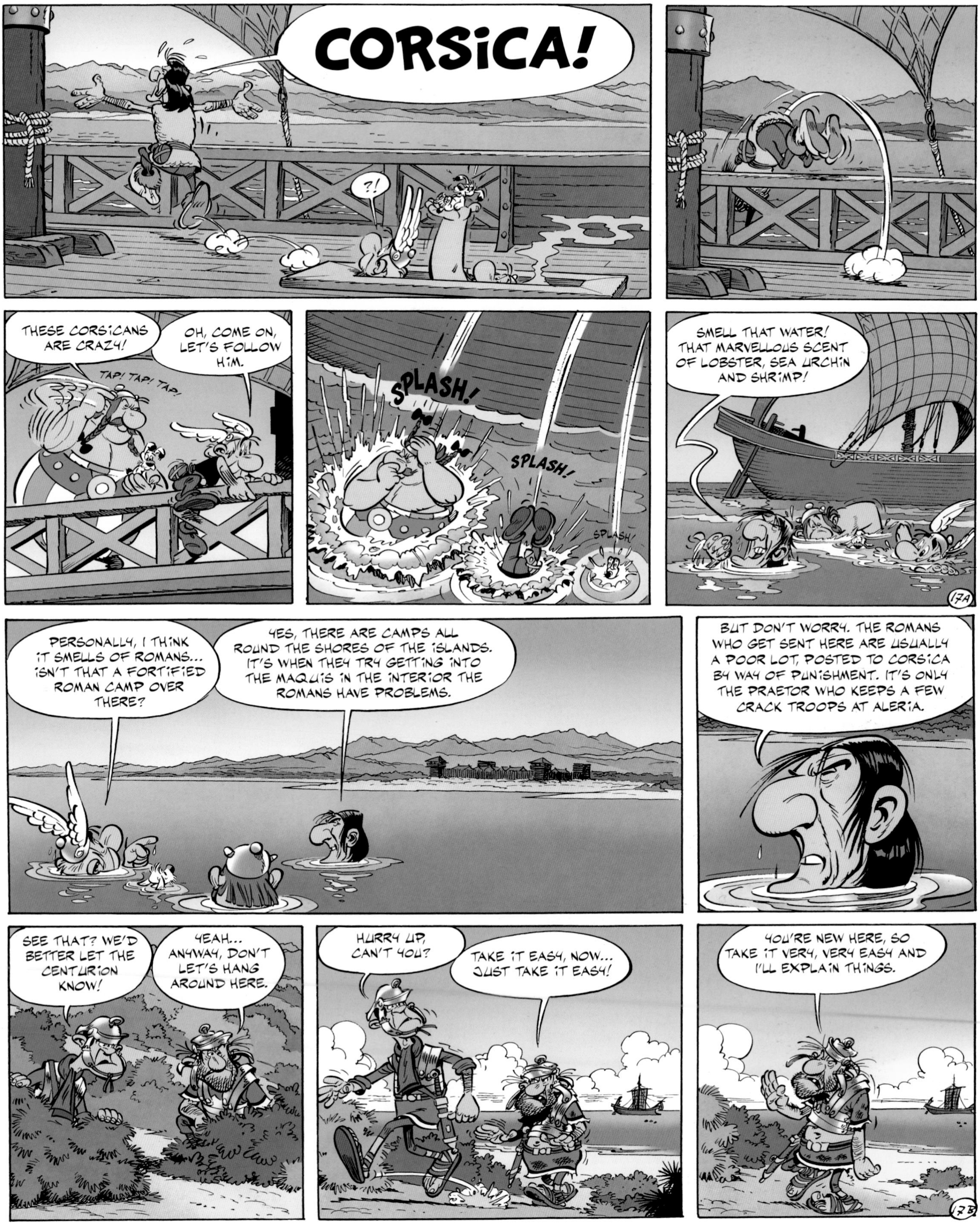
CORSICA!
?!
THESE CORSICANS ARE CRAZY!
TAP! TAP! TAP!
OH, COME ON, LET'S FOLLOW HIM.
SPLASH!
SPLASH!
SPLASH!
SMELL THAT WATER! THAT MARVELLOUS SCENT OF LOBSTER, SEA URCHIN AND SHRIMP!
17A
PERSONALLY, I THINK IT SMELLS OF ROMANS... ISN'T THAT A FORTIFIED ROMAN CAMP OVER THERE?
YES, THERE ARE CAMPS ALL ROUND THE SHORES OF THE ISLANDS. IT'S WHEN THEY TRY GETTING INTO THE MAQUIS IN THE INTERIOR THE ROMANS HAVE PROBLEMS.
BUT DON'T WORRY. THE ROMANS WHO GET SENT HERE ARE USUALLY A POOR LOT, POSTED TO CORSICA BY WAY OF PUNISHMENT. IT'S ONLY THE PRAETOR WHO KEEPS A FEW CRACK TROOPS AT ALERIA.
SEE THAT? WE'D BETTER LET THE CENTURION KNOW!
YEAH... ANYWAY, DON'T LET'S HANG AROUND HERE.
HURRY UP, CAN'T YOU?
TAKE IT EASY, NOW... JUST TAKE IT EASY!
YOU'RE NEW HERE, SO TAKE IT VERY, VERY EASY AND I'LL EXPLAIN THINGS.
17B

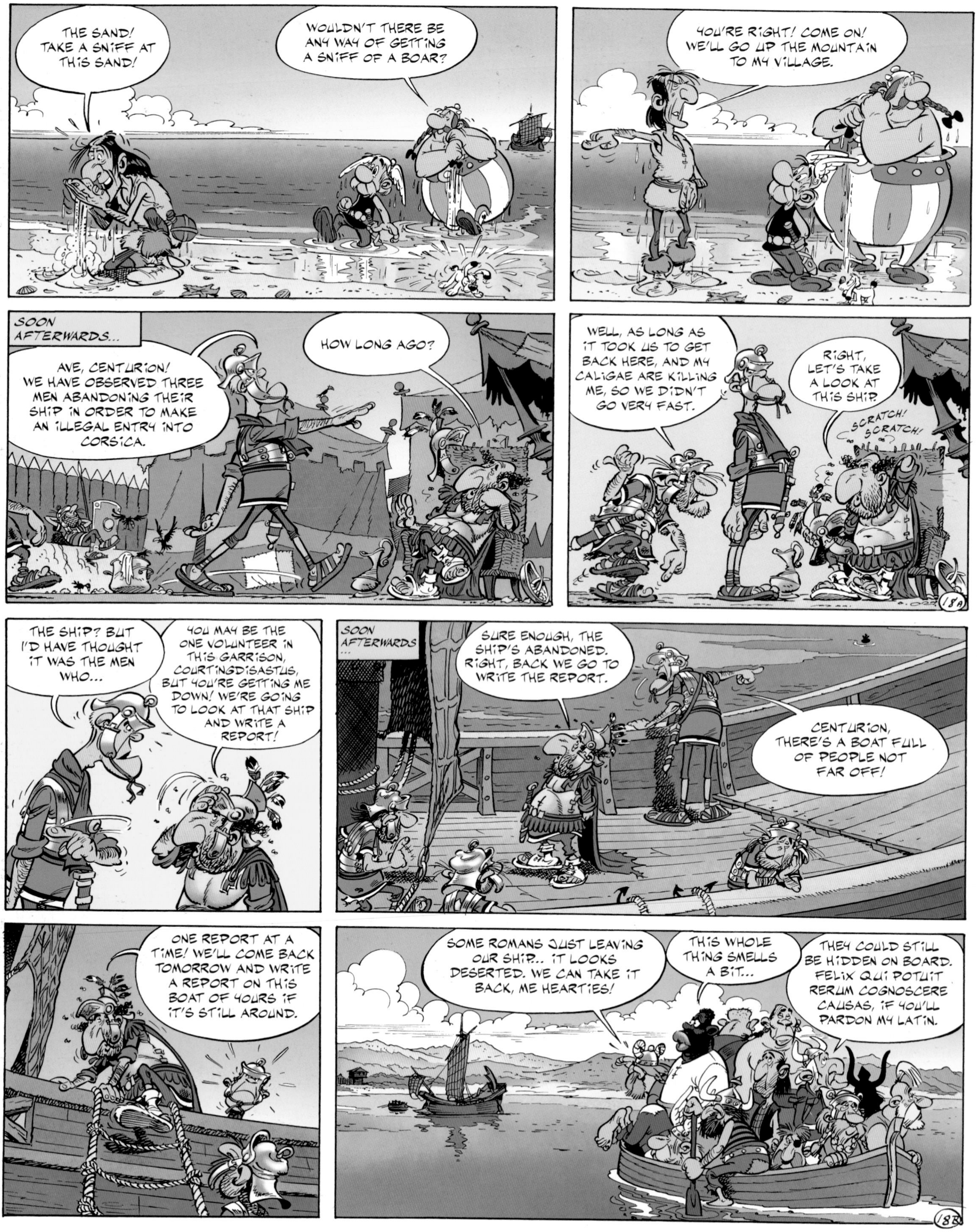
THE SAND! TAKE A SNIFF AT THIS SAND!
WOULDN'T THERE BE ANY WAY OF GETTING A SNIFF OF A BOAR?
YOU'RE RIGHT! COME ON! WE'LL GO UP THE MOUNTAIN TO MY VILLAGE.
SOON AFTERWARDS...
AVE, CENTURION! WE HAVE OBSERVED THREE MEN ABANDONING THEIR SHIP IN ORDER TO MAKE AN ILLEGAL ENTRY INTO CORSICA.
HOW LONG AGO?
WELL, AS LONG AS IT TOOK US TO GET BACK HERE, AND MY CALIGAE ARE KILLING ME, SO WE DIDN'T GO VERY FAST.
RIGHT, LET'S TAKE A LOOK AT THIS SHIP.
SCRATCH! SCRATCH!
18A
THE SHIP? BUT I'D HAVE THOUGHT IT WAS THE MEN WHO...
YOU MAY BE THE ONE VOLUNTEER IN THIS GARRISON, COURTINGDISASTUS, BUT YOU'RE GETTING ME DOWN! WE'RE GOING TO LOOK AT THAT SHIP AND WRITE A REPORT!
SOON AFTERWARDS...
SURE ENOUGH, THE SHIP'S ABANDONED. RIGHT, BACK WE GO TO WRITE THE REPORT.
CENTURION, THERE'S A BOAT FULL OF PEOPLE NOT FAR OFF!
ONE REPORT AT A TIME! WE'LL COME BACK TOMORROW AND WRITE A REPORT ON THIS BOAT OF YOURS IF IT'S STILL AROUND.
SOME ROMANS JUST LEAVING OUR SHIP.. IT LOOKS DESERTED. WE CAN TAKE IT BACK, ME HEARTIES!
THIS WHOLE THING SMELLS A BIT...
THEY COULD STILL BE HIDDEN ON BOARD. FELIX QUI POTUIT RERUM COGNOSCERE CAUSAS, IF YOU'LL PARDON MY LATIN.
18B

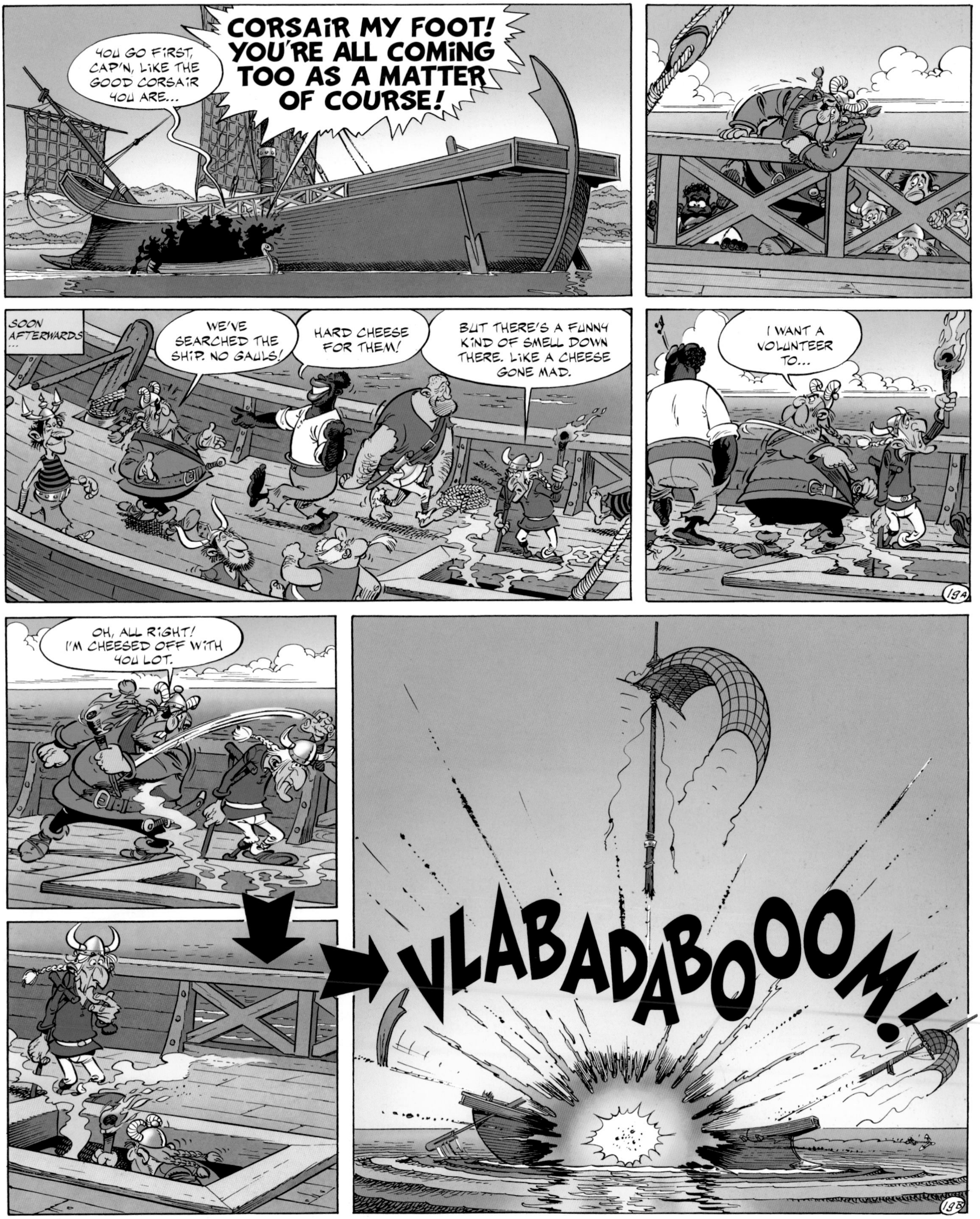
YOU GO FIRST, CAP'N, LIKE THE GOOD CORSAIR YOU ARE...
CORSAIR MY FOOT! YOU'RE ALL COMING TOO AS A MATTER OF COURSE!
SOON AFTERWARDS ...
WE'VE SEARCHED THE SHIP. NO GAULS!
HARD CHEESE FOR THEM!
BUT THERE'S A FUNNY KIND OF SMELL DOWN THERE. LIKE A CHEESE GONE MAD.
SNIFF
SNIFF
I WANT A VOLUNTEER TO...
19A
OH, ALL RIGHT! I'M CHEESED OFF WITH YOU LOT.
VLABADABOOOM!
19B

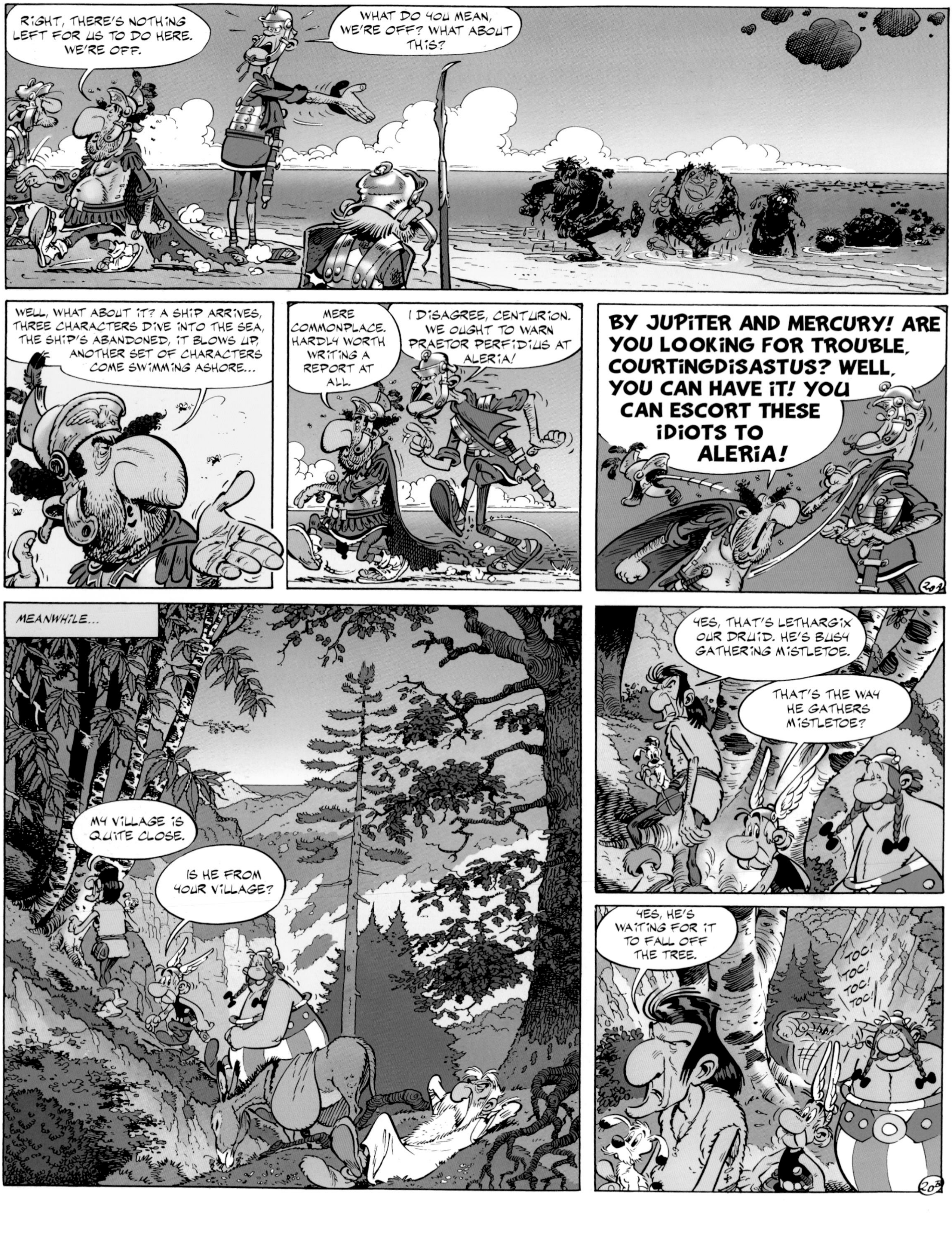
RIGHT, THERE'S NOTHING LEFT FOR US TO DO HERE. WE'RE OFF.
WHAT DO YOU MEAN, WE'RE OFF? WHAT ABOUT THIS?
WELL, WHAT ABOUT IT? A SHIP ARRIVES, THREE CHARACTERS DIVE INTO THE SEA, THE SHIP'S ABANDONED, IT BLOWS UP, ANOTHER SET OF CHARACTERS COME SWIMMING ASHORE...
MERE COMMONPLACE. HARDLY WORTH WRITING A REPORT AT ALL.
I DISAGREE, CENTURION. WE OUGHT TO WARN PRAETOR PERFIDIUS AT ALERIA!
BY JUPITER AND MERCURY! ARE YOU LOOKING FOR TROUBLE, COURTINGDISASTUS? WELL, YOU CAN HAVE IT! YOU CAN ESCORT THESE IDIOTS TO ALERIA!
MEANWHILE...
MY VILLAGE IS QUITE CLOSE.
IS HE FROM YOUR VILLAGE?
YES, THAT'S LETHARGIX OUR DRUID. HE'S BUSY GATHERING MISTLETOE.
THAT'S THE WAY HE GATHERS MISTLETOE?
YES, HE'S WAITING FOR IT TO FALL OFF THE TREE.
TOC! TOC! TOC! TOC!

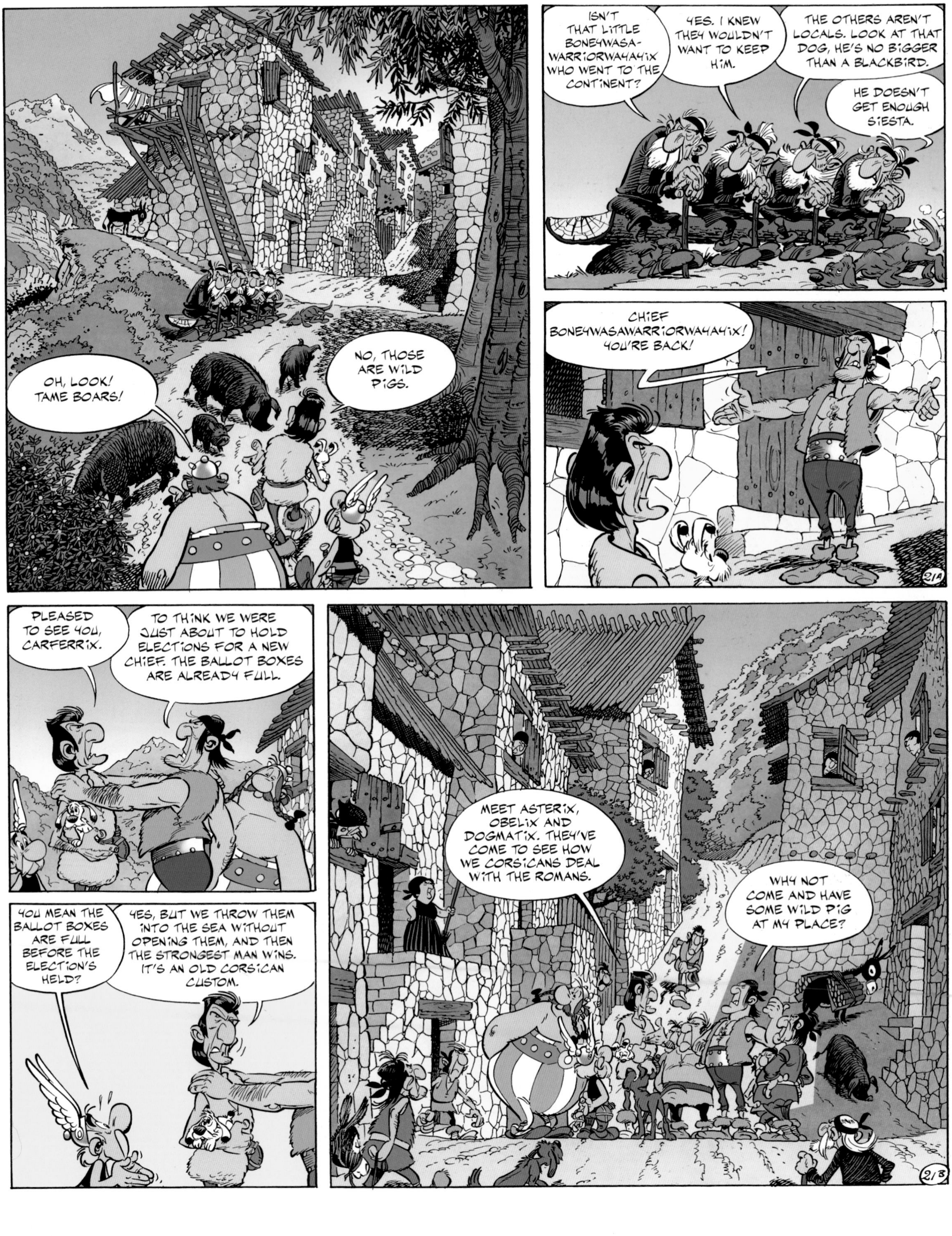
OH, LOOK! TAME BOARS!
NO, THOSE ARE WILD PIGS.
ISN'T THAT LITTLE BONEYWASA-WARRIORWAYAYIX WHO WENT TO THE CONTINENT?
YES. I KNEW THEY WOULDN'T WANT TO KEEP HIM.
THE OTHERS AREN'T LOCALS. LOOK AT THAT DOG, HE'S NO BIGGER THAN A BLACKBIRD.
HE DOESN'T GET ENOUGH SIESTA.
CHIEF BONEYWASAWARRIORWAYAYIX! YOU'RE BACK!
21A
PLEASED TO SEE YOU, CARFERRIX.
TO THINK WE WERE JUST ABOUT TO HOLD ELECTIONS FOR A NEW CHIEF. THE BALLOT BOXES ARE ALREADY FULL.
YOU MEAN THE BALLOT BOXES ARE FULL BEFORE THE ELECTION'S HELD?
YES, BUT WE THROW THEM INTO THE SEA WITHOUT OPENING THEM, AND THEN THE STRONGEST MAN WINS. IT'S AN OLD CORSICAN CUSTOM.
MEET ASTERIX, OBELIX AND DOGMATIX. THEY'VE COME TO SEE HOW WE CORSICANS DEAL WITH THE ROMANS.
WHY NOT COME AND HAVE SOME WILD PIG AT MY PLACE?
21B

LOOK, NO BIGGER THAN A CHESTNUT, BUT HE EATS AS IF HIS SIESTA DEPENDED ON IT!

SCRUNCH! SCRUNCH!

WELL, HOW ARE THINGS GOING?

THE WAREHOUSES OF ALERIA ARE FULL OF THE LOOT PRAETOR PERFIDIUS HAS TAKEN. THERE ISN'T MUCH TIME LEFT, THE PRAETOR WILL SOON BE RECALLED TO ROME.

THEN WHY NOT ATTACK NOW?

ALERIA IS WELL DEFENDED. WE NEED TIME TO SUMMON EVERYONE FROM THE OTHER VILLAGES. THAT'S WHAT I WAS DOING WHEN I WAS CAPTURED IN OLABELLAMARGARITIX'S VILLAGE.

OLABELLA-MARGARITIX?

MY CLAN AND OLABELLAMARGARITIX'S CLAN HAVE A VENDETTA GOING, BUT I NEVER THOUGHT HE'D BETRAY ME TO THE ROMANS.

THERE'S NO PROOF HE DID...

THE OLABELLAMARGARITIX CLAN ARE CAPABLE OF ANYTHING!

WHAT'S THE VENDETTA ABOUT?

NO ONE'S TOO SURE ANY MORE...

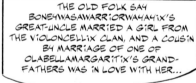

THE OLD FOLK SAY BONEYWASAWARRIORWAYAYIX'S GREAT-UNCLE MARRIED A GIRL FROM THE VIOLONCELLIX CLAN, AND A COUSIN BY MARRIAGE OF ONE OF OLABELLAMARGARITIX'S GRAND-FATHERS WAS IN LOVE WITH HER...

BUT OTHERS SAY IT WAS BECAUSE OF A DONKEY WHICH OLABELLAMARGARITIX'S GREAT-GRANDFATHER REFUSED TO PAY FOR WHEN HE GOT HIM FROM THE BROTHER-IN-LAW OF A CLOSE FRIEND OF THE BONEYWASAWARRIORWAYAYIX CLAN, CLAIMING THAT HE WAS LAME (THE DONKEY, NOT THE BONEYWASAWARRIORWAYAYIXES' FRIEND'S BROTHER-IN-LAW)...

...ANYWAY, IT'S VERY SERIOUS.

?

TAP! TAP! TAP!

22

82

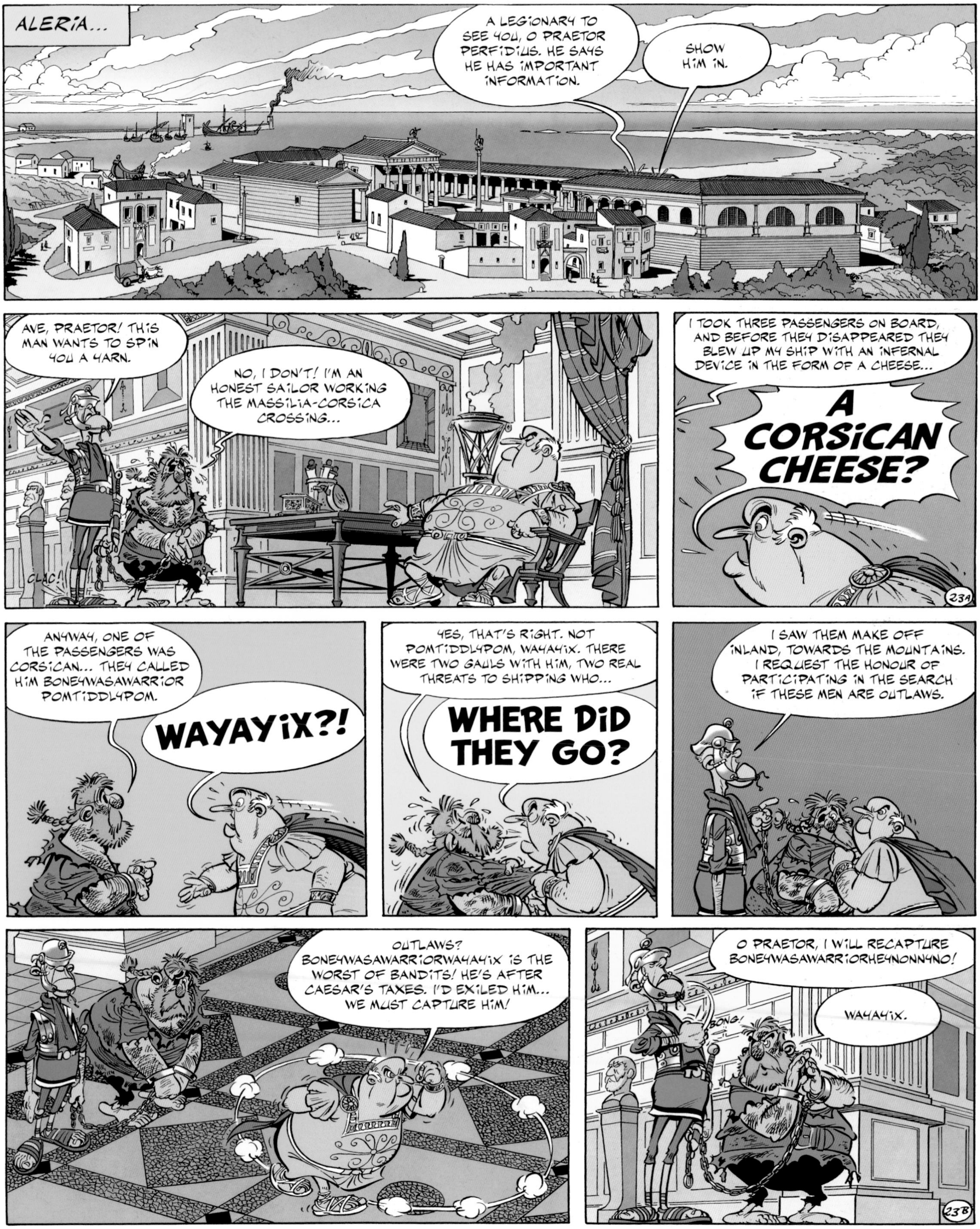

ALERIA...
A LEGIONARY TO SEE YOU, O PRAETOR PERFIDIUS. HE SAYS HE HAS IMPORTANT INFORMATION.
SHOW HIM IN.
AVE, PRAETOR! THIS MAN WANTS TO SPIN YOU A YARN.
NO, I DON'T! I'M AN HONEST SAILOR WORKING THE MASSILIA-CORSICA CROSSING...
CLAC!
I TOOK THREE PASSENGERS ON BOARD, AND BEFORE THEY DISAPPEARED THEY BLEW UP MY SHIP WITH AN INFERNAL DEVICE IN THE FORM OF A CHEESE...
A CORSICAN CHEESE?
23A
ANYWAY, ONE OF THE PASSENGERS WAS CORSICAN... THEY CALLED HIM BONEYWASAWARRIOR POMTIDDLYPOM.
WAYAYIX?!
YES, THAT'S RIGHT. NOT POMTIDDLYPOM, WAYAYIX. THERE WERE TWO GAULS WITH HIM, TWO REAL THREATS TO SHIPPING WHO...
WHERE DID THEY GO?
I SAW THEM MAKE OFF INLAND, TOWARDS THE MOUNTAINS. I REQUEST THE HONOUR OF PARTICIPATING IN THE SEARCH IF THESE MEN ARE OUTLAWS.
OUTLAWS? BONEYWASAWARRIORWAYAYIX IS THE WORST OF BANDITS! HE'S AFTER CAESAR'S TAXES. I'D EXILED HIM... WE MUST CAPTURE HIM!
O PRAETOR, I WILL RECAPTURE BONEYWASAWARRIORHEYNONNYNO!
BONG!
WAYAYIX.
23B

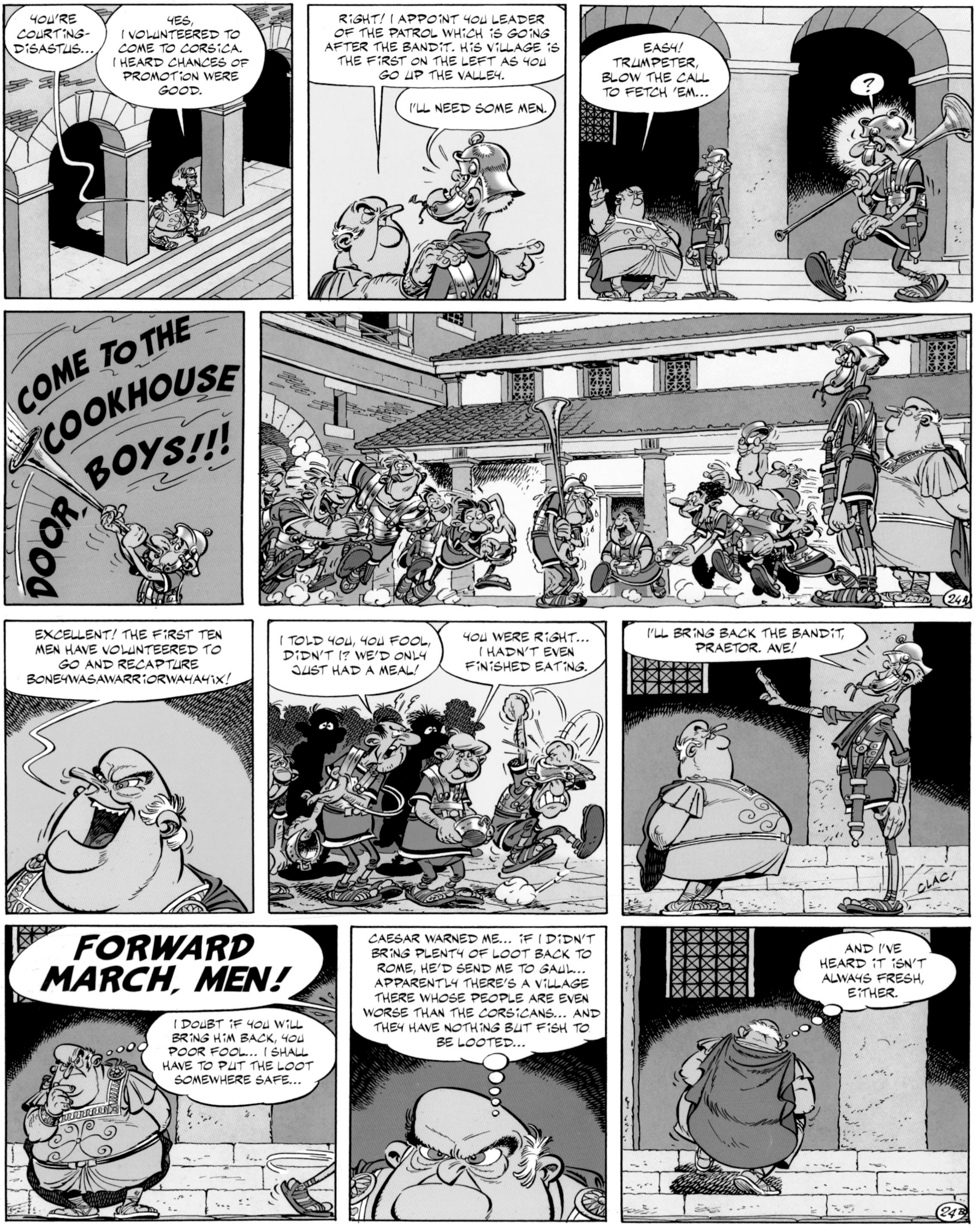

YOU'RE COURTING-DISASTUS...
YES, I VOLUNTEERED TO COME TO CORSICA. I HEARD CHANCES OF PROMOTION WERE GOOD.
RIGHT! I APPOINT YOU LEADER OF THE PATROL WHICH IS GOING AFTER THE BANDIT. HIS VILLAGE IS THE FIRST ON THE LEFT AS YOU GO UP THE VALLEY.
I'LL NEED SOME MEN.
EASY! TRUMPETER, BLOW THE CALL TO FETCH 'EM...
?
COME TO THE COOKHOUSE DOOR, BOYS!!!
24A
EXCELLENT! THE FIRST TEN MEN HAVE VOLUNTEERED TO GO AND RECAPTURE BONEYWASAWARRIORWAYAYIX!
I TOLD YOU, YOU FOOL, DIDN'T I? WE'D ONLY JUST HAD A MEAL!
YOU WERE RIGHT... I HADN'T EVEN FINISHED EATING.
I'LL BRING BACK THE BANDIT, PRAETOR. AVE!
CLAC!
FORWARD MARCH, MEN!
I DOUBT IF YOU WILL BRING HIM BACK, YOU POOR FOOL... I SHALL HAVE TO PUT THE LOOT SOMEWHERE SAFE...
CAESAR WARNED ME... IF I DIDN'T BRING PLENTY OF LOOT BACK TO ROME, HE'D SEND ME TO GAUL... APPARENTLY THERE'S A VILLAGE THERE WHOSE PEOPLE ARE EVEN WORSE THAN THE CORSICANS... AND THEY HAVE NOTHING BUT FISH TO BE LOOTED...
AND I'VE HEARD IT ISN'T ALWAYS FRESH, EITHER.
24B

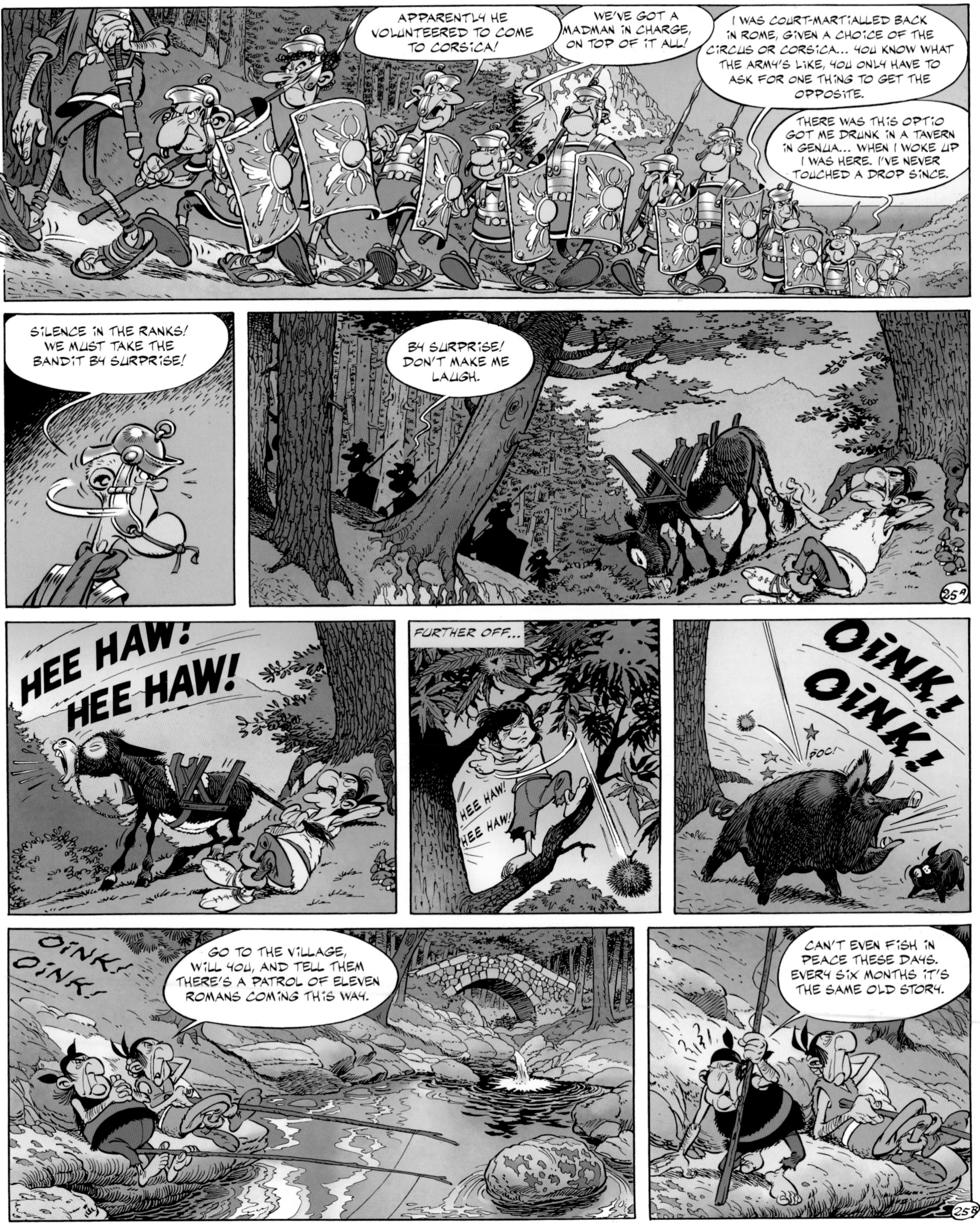
APPARENTLY HE VOLUNTEERED TO COME TO CORSICA!
WE'VE GOT A MADMAN IN CHARGE, ON TOP OF IT ALL!
I WAS COURT-MARTIALLED BACK IN ROME, GIVEN A CHOICE OF THE CIRCUS OR CORSICA... YOU KNOW WHAT THE ARMY'S LIKE, YOU ONLY HAVE TO ASK FOR ONE THING TO GET THE OPPOSITE.
THERE WAS THIS OPTIO GOT ME DRUNK IN A TAVERN IN GENUA... WHEN I WOKE UP I WAS HERE. I'VE NEVER TOUCHED A DROP SINCE.
SILENCE IN THE RANKS! WE MUST TAKE THE BANDIT BY SURPRISE!
BY SURPRISE! DON'T MAKE ME LAUGH.
25A
HEE HAW! HEE HAW!
FURTHER OFF...
HEE HAW! HEE HAW!
OINK! OINK!
POC!
OINK! OINK!
GO TO THE VILLAGE, WILL YOU, AND TELL THEM THERE'S A PATROL OF ELEVEN ROMANS COMING THIS WAY.
CAN'T EVEN FISH IN PEACE THESE DAYS. EVERY SIX MONTHS IT'S THE SAME OLD STORY.
25B

CHIPOLATA! POUR US SOME MORE WINE!

COMING!

CARFERRIX!

THANK YOU.

TELL YOUR FRIEND TO WATCH OUT. CARFERRIX DOESN'T LIKE PEOPLE BEING DISRESPECTFUL TO HIS SISTER.

BUT HE DIDN'T DO ANYTHING DISRESPECTFUL.

YES, HE DID. HE SPOKE TO HER. HE SMILED, TOO. SO WATCH OUT!

!?!

BONEYWASAWARRIORWAYAYYIX, THERE ARE SOME ROMANS COMING.

RIGHT! WE'LL BE OFF TO THE MAQUIS.

26A

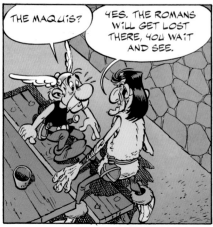

THE MAQUIS?

YES. THE ROMANS WILL GET LOST THERE, YOU WAIT AND SEE.

HE CERTAINLY WON'T!

I TAKE NO FURTHER INTEREST IN THE MATTER.

SAME HERE. IT'S NONE OF MY BUSINESS.

GET READY TO PICK HIM UP, HE WON'T BE EXPECTING THIS!

SEE THAT? THE VILLAGE IS PEACEFUL... WE'LL START WITH THE FIRST HOUSE, OVER THERE...

THEIR LEADER MUST BE NEW.

HE REMINDS ME OF SALAMIX, WHO FELL OUT OF A CHESTNUT TREE AND LANDED ON HIS HEAD.

I HEARD HE JOINED THE ROMAN ARMY AFTER THAT.

YES, HE'D GONE SO HALF-WITTED YOU HAD TIME TO STONE HIS DONKEY TO DEATH WITH RIPE FIGS BEFORE YOU COULD GET THROUGH TO HIM.

26B

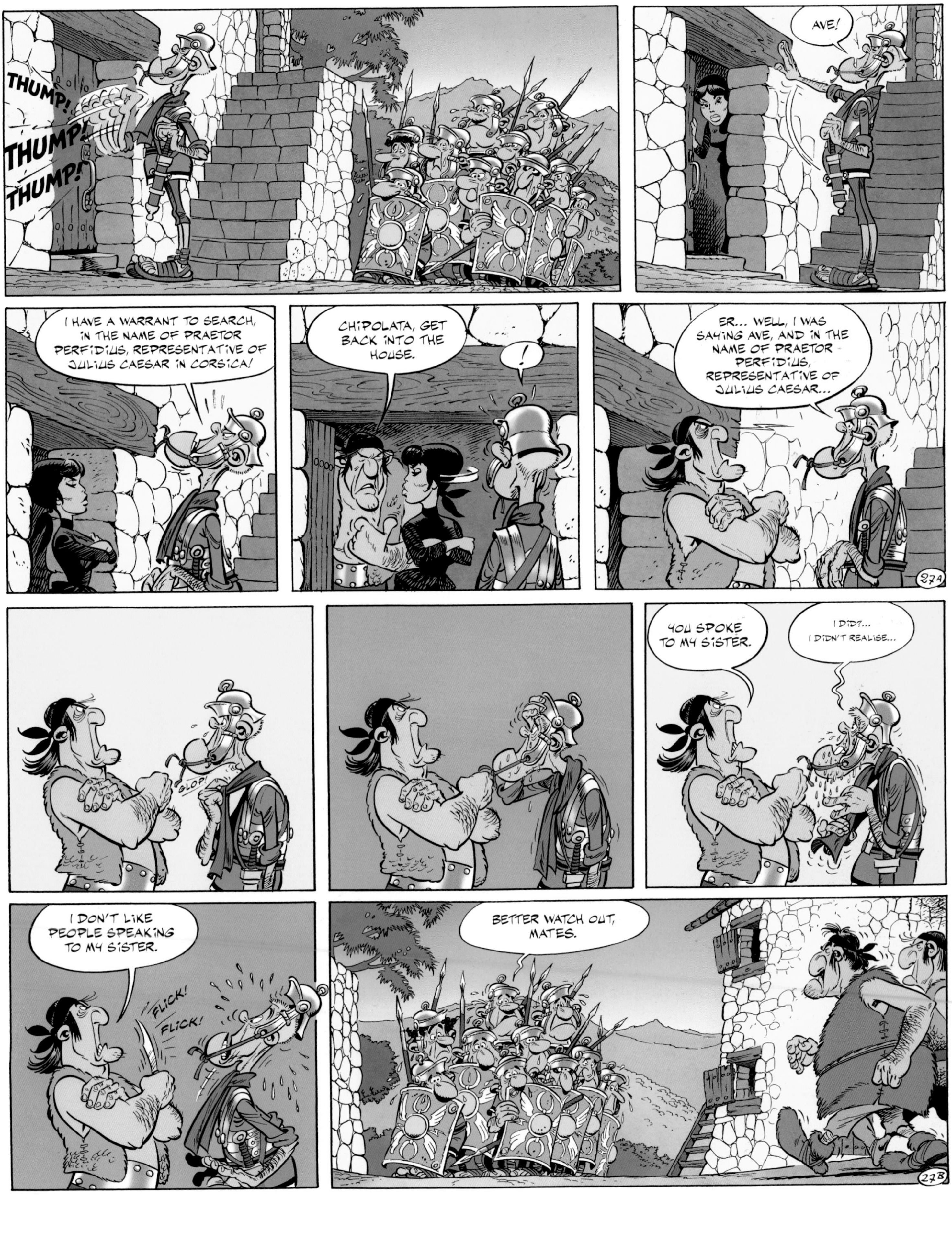
THUMP!
THUMP!
THUMP!
AVE!
I HAVE A WARRANT TO SEARCH, IN THE NAME OF PRAETOR PERFIDIUS, REPRESENTATIVE OF JULIUS CAESAR IN CORSICA!
CHIPOLATA, GET BACK INTO THE HOUSE.
!
ER... WELL, I WAS SAYING AVE, AND IN THE NAME OF PRAETOR PERFIDIUS, REPRESENTATIVE OF JULIUS CAESAR...
27A
GLOP!
YOU SPOKE TO MY SISTER.
I DID?... I DIDN'T REALISE...
I DON'T LIKE PEOPLE SPEAKING TO MY SISTER.
FLICK!
FLICK!
BETTER WATCH OUT, MATES.
27B

BUT... BUT I'M NOT INTERESTED IN YOUR SISTER. I ONLY WANTED TO...

YOU DON'T LIKE MY SISTER?

YES, YES, OF COURSE I LIKE YOUR SISTER...

OH, SO YOU LIKE MY SISTER, DO YOU? HOLD ME BACK OR I'LL MURDER HIM... HIM AND THE REST OF THEM!

RUN FOR IT! WE'LL DO OUR BEST TO HOLD HIM...

...JUST LONG ENOUGH FOR A CHESTNUT TO FALL!

ALL RIGHT, I'M OFF!

CHIPOLATA, DON'T LET ME CATCH YOU COURTING DISASTER BY FLIRTING WITH ANY ROMANS AGAIN!

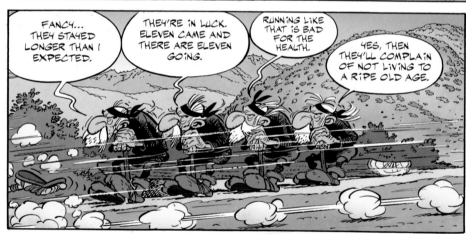

FANCY... THEY STAYED LONGER THAN I EXPECTED.

THEY'RE IN LUCK. ELEVEN CAME AND THERE ARE ELEVEN GOING.

RUNNING LIKE THAT IS BAD FOR THE HEALTH.

YES, THEN THEY'LL COMPLAIN OF NOT LIVING TO A RIPE OLD AGE.

PUFF! PUFF! PUFF!

YOU KNOW, THERE'S NOTHING TO FEEL BAD ABOUT. THE BANDIT WILL HAVE MADE IT TO THE MAQUIS BY NOW.

THE MAQUIS? WHY DIDN'T YOU SAY SO BEFORE? WE'RE GOING TO SEARCH THE MAQUIS!

SEARCH THE MAQUIS? HE'S AS CRAZY AS THAT NUT SALAMIX!

TOC! TOC! TOC!

AND ANY DESERTERS WILL BE TREATED AS THEY DESERVE!

WHAT DO DESERTERS DESERVE?

THEIR JUST DESERTS.

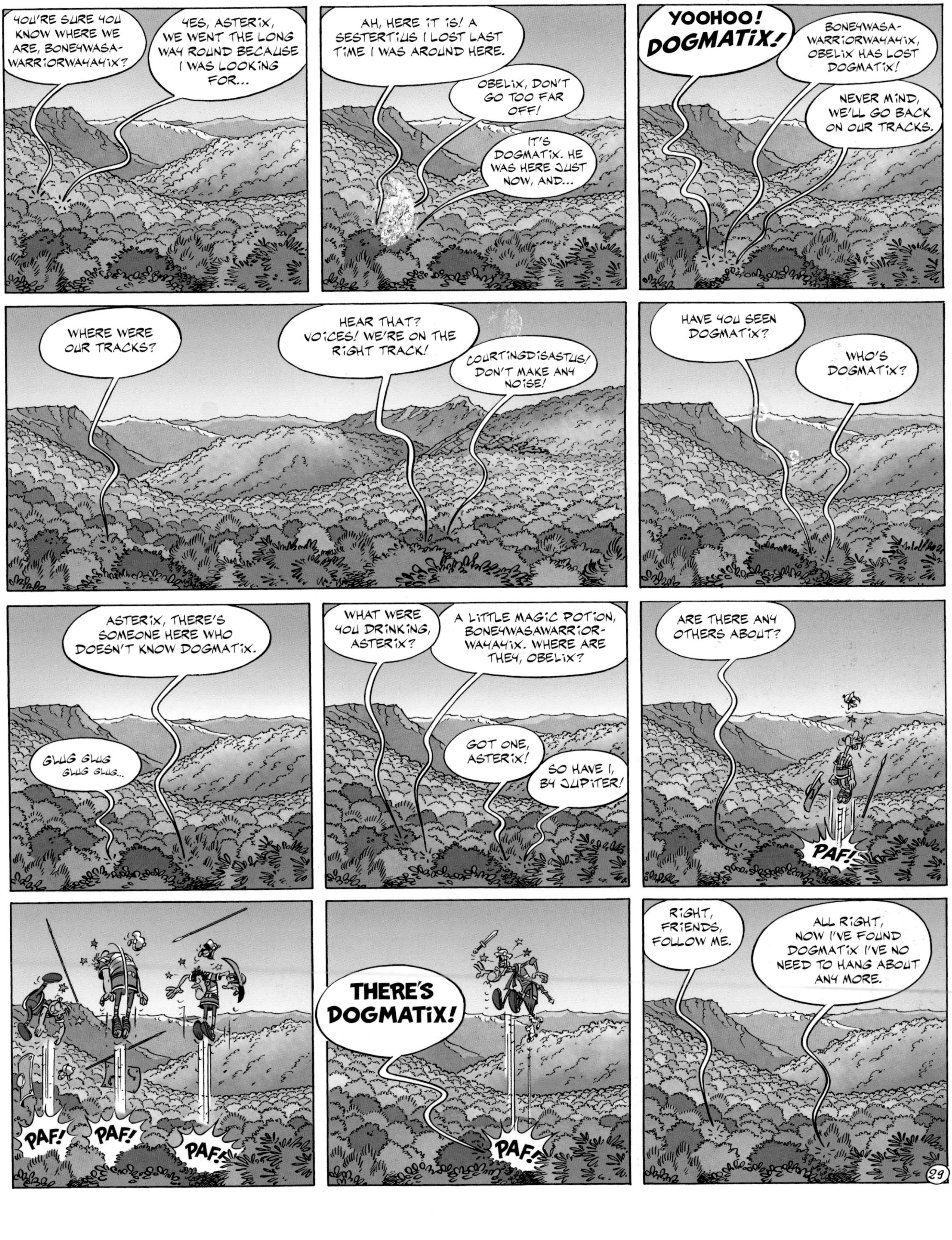
YOU'RE SURE YOU KNOW WHERE WE ARE, BONEYWASAWARRIORWAYAYIX?
YES, ASTERIX, WE WENT THE LONG WAY ROUND BECAUSE I WAS LOOKING FOR...
AH, HERE IT IS! A SESTERTIUS I LOST LAST TIME I WAS AROUND HERE.
OBELIX, DON'T GO TOO FAR OFF!
IT'S DOGMATIX. HE WAS HERE JUST NOW, AND...
YOOHOO! DOGMATIX!
BONEYWASAWARRIORWAYAYIX, OBELIX HAS LOST DOGMATIX!
NEVER MIND, WE'LL GO BACK ON OUR TRACKS.
WHERE WERE OUR TRACKS?
HEAR THAT? VOICES! WE'RE ON THE RIGHT TRACK!
COURTINGDISASTUS! DON'T MAKE ANY NOISE!
HAVE YOU SEEN DOGMATIX?
WHO'S DOGMATIX?
ASTERIX, THERE'S SOMEONE HERE WHO DOESN'T KNOW DOGMATIX.
GLUG GLUG GLUG GLUG...
WHAT WERE YOU DRINKING, ASTERIX?
A LITTLE MAGIC POTION, BONEYWASAWARRIORWAYAYIX. WHERE ARE THEY, OBELIX?
GOT ONE, ASTERIX!
SO HAVE I, BY JUPITER!
ARE THERE ANY OTHERS ABOUT?
PAF!
PAF!
PAF!
PAF!
THERE'S DOGMATIX!
PAF!
RIGHT, FRIENDS, FOLLOW ME.
ALL RIGHT, NOW I'VE FOUND DOGMATIX I'VE NO NEED TO HANG ABOUT ANY MORE.
29

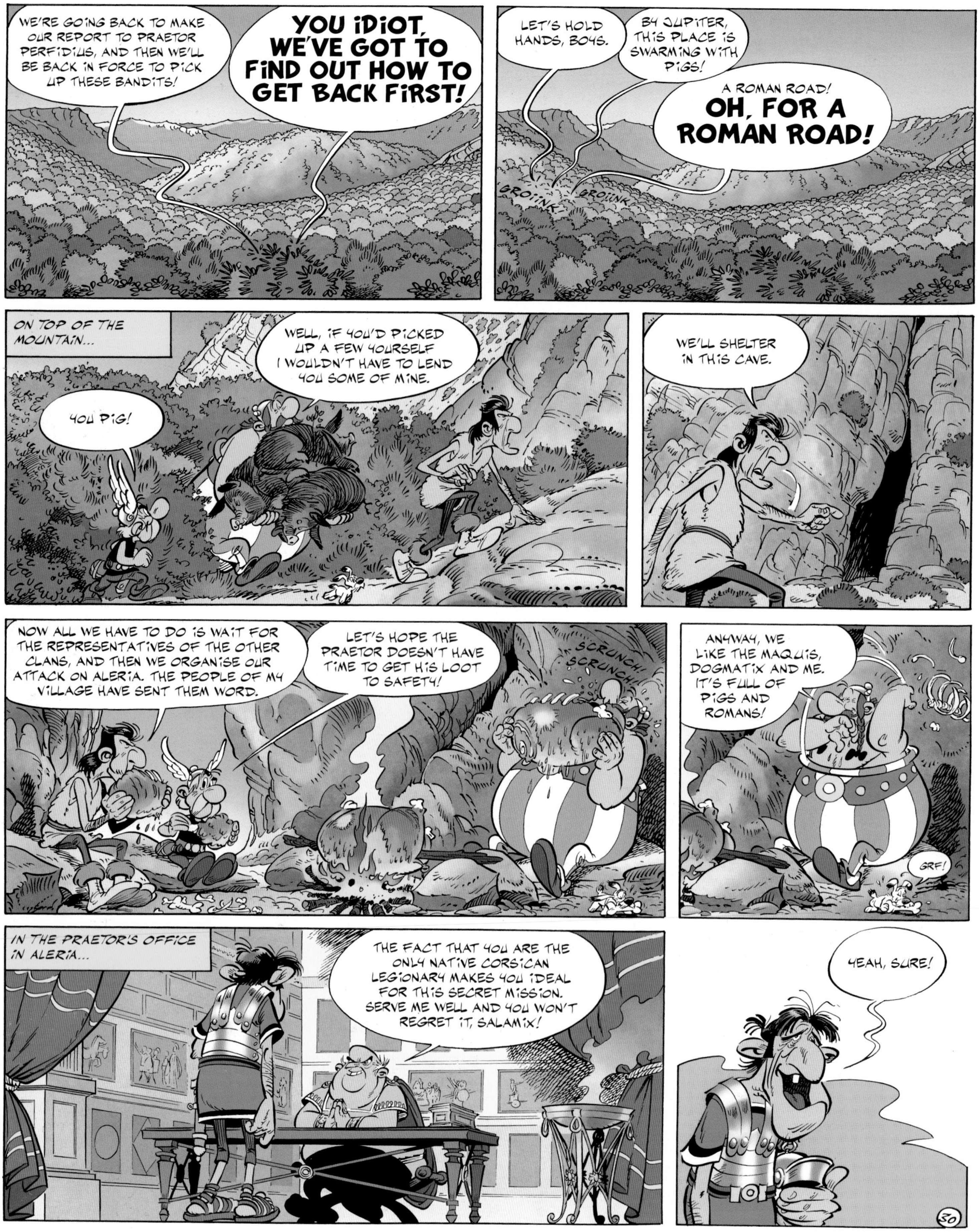
WE'RE GOING BACK TO MAKE OUR REPORT TO PRAETOR PERFIDIUS, AND THEN WE'LL BE BACK IN FORCE TO PICK UP THESE BANDITS!
YOU IDIOT, WE'VE GOT TO FIND OUT HOW TO GET BACK FIRST!
LET'S HOLD HANDS, BOYS.
BY JUPITER, THIS PLACE IS SWARMING WITH PIGS!
A ROMAN ROAD! OH, FOR A ROMAN ROAD!
GROINK
GROINK
ON TOP OF THE MOUNTAIN...
WELL, IF YOU'D PICKED UP A FEW YOURSELF I WOULDN'T HAVE TO LEND YOU SOME OF MINE.
YOU PIG!
WE'LL SHELTER IN THIS CAVE.
NOW ALL WE HAVE TO DO IS WAIT FOR THE REPRESENTATIVES OF THE OTHER CLANS, AND THEN WE ORGANISE OUR ATTACK ON ALERIA. THE PEOPLE OF MY VILLAGE HAVE SENT THEM WORD.
LET'S HOPE THE PRAETOR DOESN'T HAVE TIME TO GET HIS LOOT TO SAFETY!
SCRUNCH! SCRUNCH!
ANYWAY, WE LIKE THE MAQUIS, DOGMATIX AND ME. IT'S FULL OF PIGS AND ROMANS!
GRF!
IN THE PRAETOR'S OFFICE IN ALERIA...
THE FACT THAT YOU ARE THE ONLY NATIVE CORSICAN LEGIONARY MAKES YOU IDEAL FOR THIS SECRET MISSION. SERVE ME WELL AND YOU WON'T REGRET IT, SALAMIX!
YEAH, SURE!
30

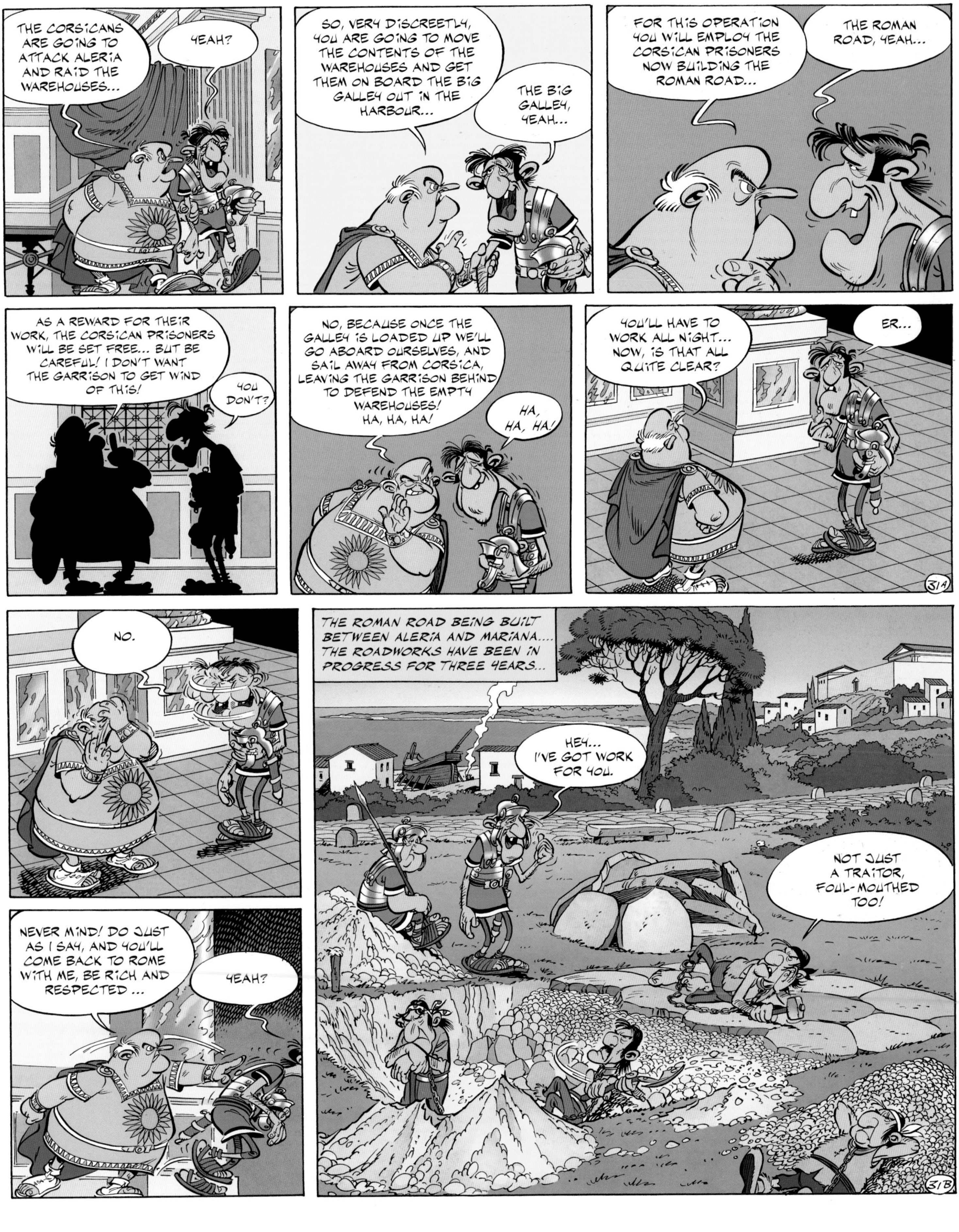
THE CORSICANS ARE GOING TO ATTACK ALERIA AND RAID THE WAREHOUSES...
YEAH?
SO, VERY DISCREETLY, YOU ARE GOING TO MOVE THE CONTENTS OF THE WAREHOUSES AND GET THEM ON BOARD THE BIG GALLEY OUT IN THE HARBOUR...
THE BIG GALLEY, YEAH...
FOR THIS OPERATION YOU WILL EMPLOY THE CORSICAN PRISONERS NOW BUILDING THE ROMAN ROAD...
THE ROMAN ROAD, YEAH...
AS A REWARD FOR THEIR WORK, THE CORSICAN PRISONERS WILL BE SET FREE... BUT BE CAREFUL! I DON'T WANT THE GARRISON TO GET WIND OF THIS!
YOU DON'T?
NO, BECAUSE ONCE THE GALLEY IS LOADED UP WE'LL GO ABOARD OURSELVES, AND SAIL AWAY FROM CORSICA, LEAVING THE GARRISON BEHIND TO DEFEND THE EMPTY WAREHOUSES! HA, HA, HA!
HA, HA, HA!
YOU'LL HAVE TO WORK ALL NIGHT... NOW, IS THAT ALL QUITE CLEAR?
ER...
31A
NO.
NEVER MIND! DO JUST AS I SAY, AND YOU'LL COME BACK TO ROME WITH ME, BE RICH AND RESPECTED ...
YEAH?
THE ROMAN ROAD BEING BUILT BETWEEN ALERIA AND MARIANA.... THE ROADWORKS HAVE BEEN IN PROGRESS FOR THREE YEARS...
HEY... I'VE GOT WORK FOR YOU.
NOT JUST A TRAITOR, FOUL-MOUTHED TOO!
31B

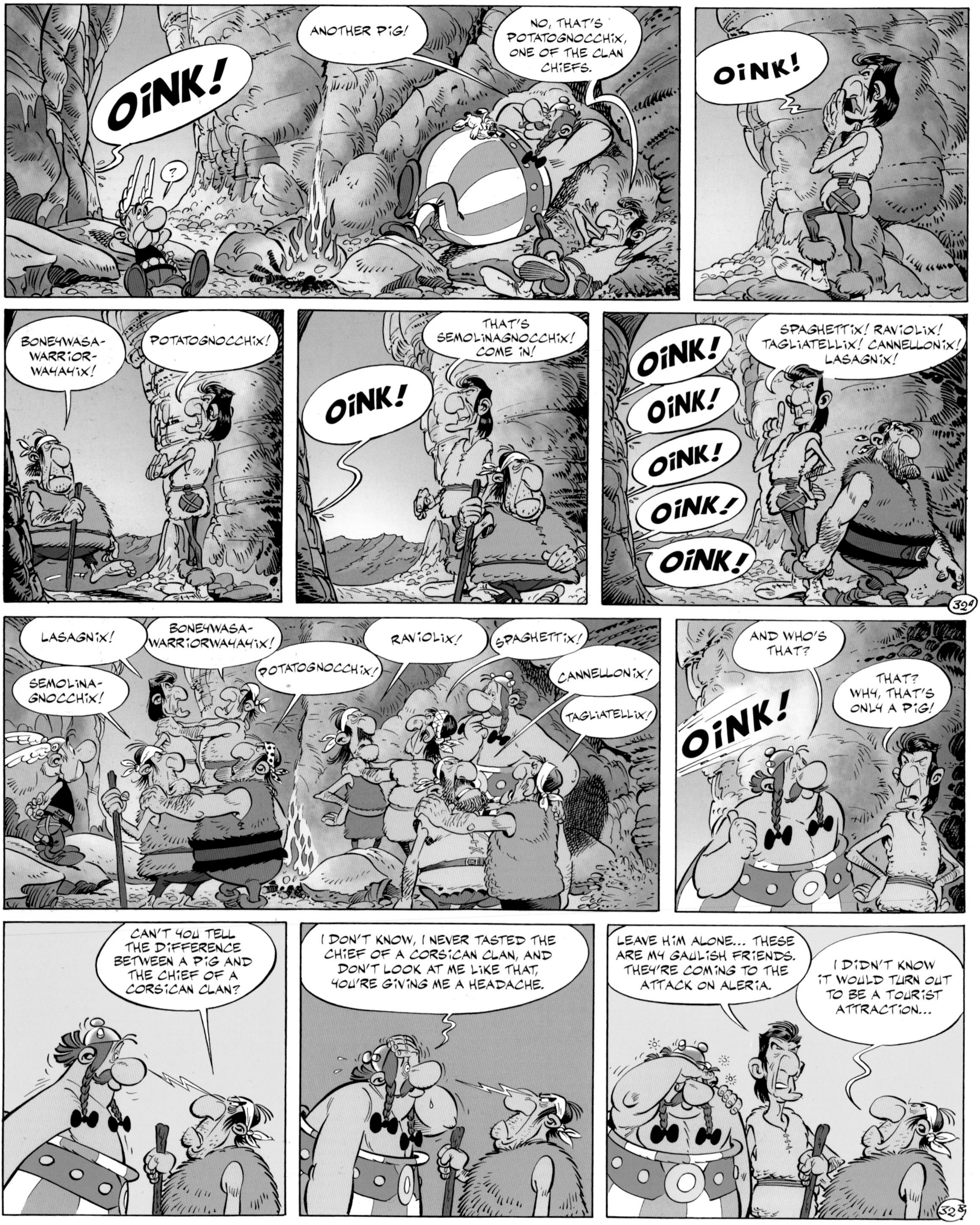
ANOTHER PIG!
NO, THAT'S POTATOGNOCCHIX, ONE OF THE CLAN CHIEFS.
OINK!
?
OINK!
BONEYWASA-WARRIOR-WAYAYIX!
POTATOGNOCCHIX!
THAT'S SEMOLINAGNOCCHIX! COME IN!
OINK!
SPAGHETTIX! RAVIOLIX! TAGLIATELLIX! CANNELLONIX! LASAGNIX!
OINK!
OINK!
OINK!
OINK!
OINK!
LASAGNIX!
BONEYWASA-WARRIORWAYAYIX!
SEMOLINA-GNOCCHIX!
POTATOGNOCCHIX!
RAVIOLIX!
SPAGHETTIX!
CANNELLONIX!
TAGLIATELLIX!
AND WHO'S THAT?
OINK!
THAT? WHY, THAT'S ONLY A PIG!
CAN'T YOU TELL THE DIFFERENCE BETWEEN A PIG AND THE CHIEF OF A CORSICAN CLAN?
I DON'T KNOW, I NEVER TASTED THE CHIEF OF A CORSICAN CLAN, AND DON'T LOOK AT ME LIKE THAT, YOU'RE GIVING ME A HEADACHE.
LEAVE HIM ALONE... THESE ARE MY GAULISH FRIENDS. THEY'RE COMING TO THE ATTACK ON ALERIA.
I DIDN'T KNOW IT WOULD TURN OUT TO BE A TOURIST ATTRACTION...

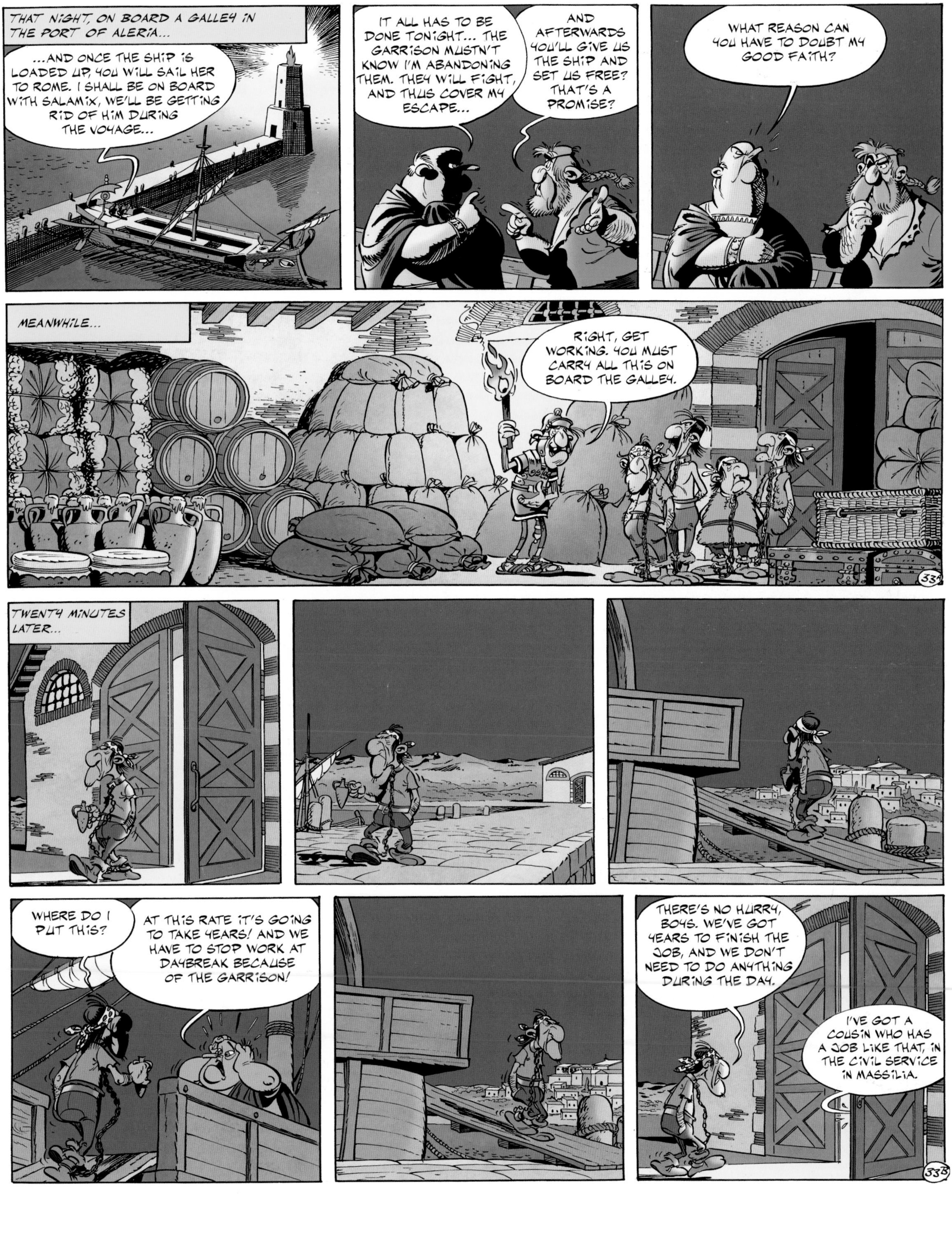
THAT NIGHT, ON BOARD A GALLEY IN THE PORT OF ALERIA...
...AND ONCE THE SHIP IS LOADED UP, YOU WILL SAIL HER TO ROME. I SHALL BE ON BOARD WITH SALAMIX, WE'LL BE GETTING RID OF HIM DURING THE VOYAGE...
IT ALL HAS TO BE DONE TONIGHT... THE GARRISON MUSTN'T KNOW I'M ABANDONING THEM. THEY WILL FIGHT, AND THUS COVER MY ESCAPE...
AND AFTERWARDS YOU'LL GIVE US THE SHIP AND SET US FREE? THAT'S A PROMISE?
WHAT REASON CAN YOU HAVE TO DOUBT MY GOOD FAITH?
MEANWHILE...
RIGHT, GET WORKING. YOU MUST CARRY ALL THIS ON BOARD THE GALLEY.
33A
TWENTY MINUTES LATER...
WHERE DO I PUT THIS?
AT THIS RATE IT'S GOING TO TAKE YEARS! AND WE HAVE TO STOP WORK AT DAYBREAK BECAUSE OF THE GARRISON!
THERE'S NO HURRY, BOYS. WE'VE GOT YEARS TO FINISH THE JOB, AND WE DON'T NEED TO DO ANYTHING DURING THE DAY.
I'VE GOT A COUSIN WHO HAS A JOB LIKE THAT, IN THE CIVIL SERVICE IN MASSILIA.
33B

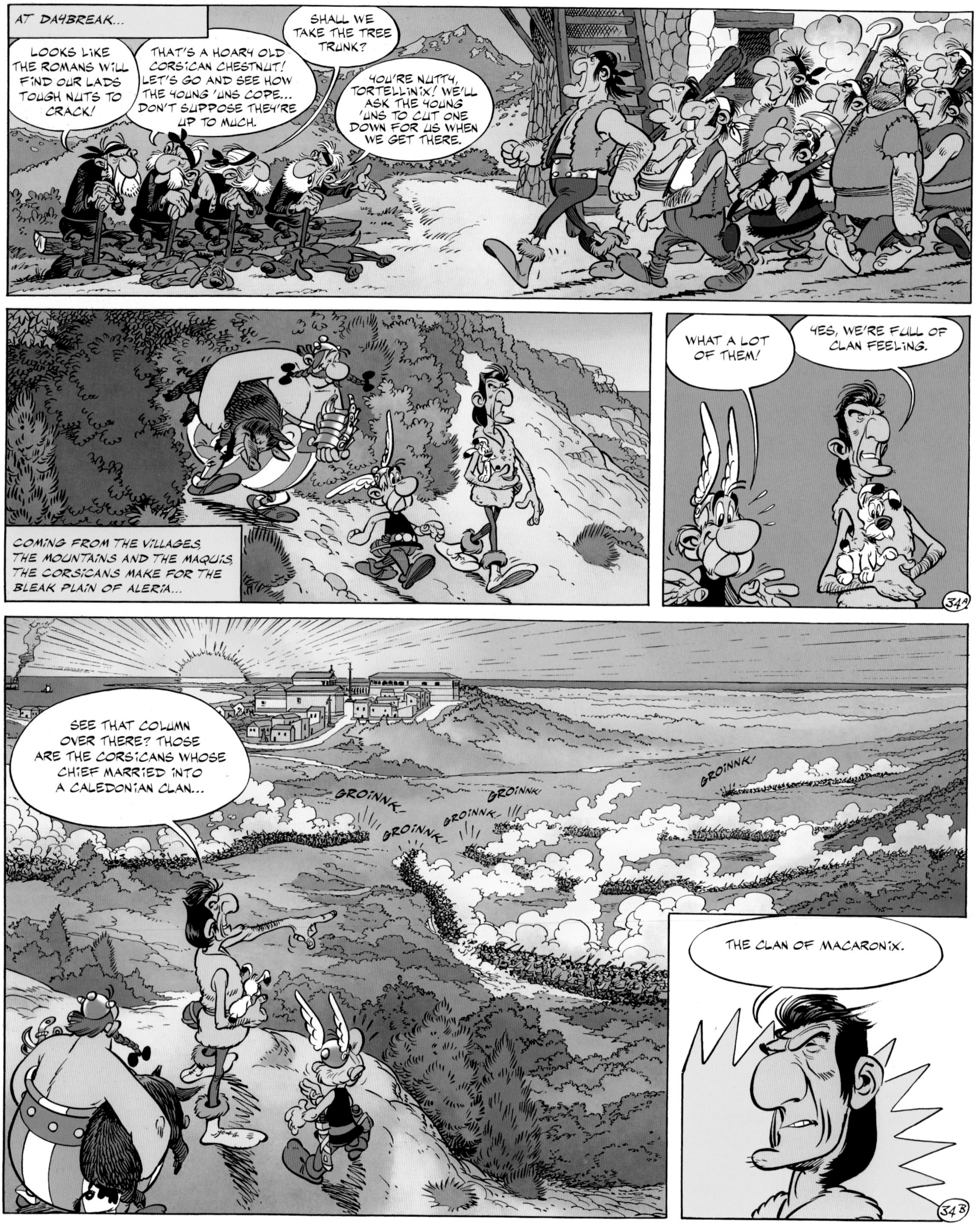

AT DAYBREAK...
LOOKS LIKE THE ROMANS WILL FIND OUR LADS TOUGH NUTS TO CRACK!
THAT'S A HOARY OLD CORSICAN CHESTNUT! LET'S GO AND SEE HOW THE YOUNG 'UNS COPE... DON'T SUPPOSE THEY'RE UP TO MUCH.
SHALL WE TAKE THE TREE TRUNK?
YOU'RE NUTTY, TORTELLINIX! WE'LL ASK THE YOUNG 'UNS TO CUT ONE DOWN FOR US WHEN WE GET THERE.
COMING FROM THE VILLAGES, THE MOUNTAINS AND THE MAQUIS, THE CORSICANS MAKE FOR THE BLEAK PLAIN OF ALERIA...
WHAT A LOT OF THEM!
YES, WE'RE FULL OF CLAN FEELING.
34A
SEE THAT COLUMN OVER THERE? THOSE ARE THE CORSICANS WHOSE CHIEF MARRIED INTO A CALEDONIAN CLAN...
GROINNK!
GROINNK!
GROINNK!
GROINNK!
GROINNK!
THE CLAN OF MACARONIX.
34B

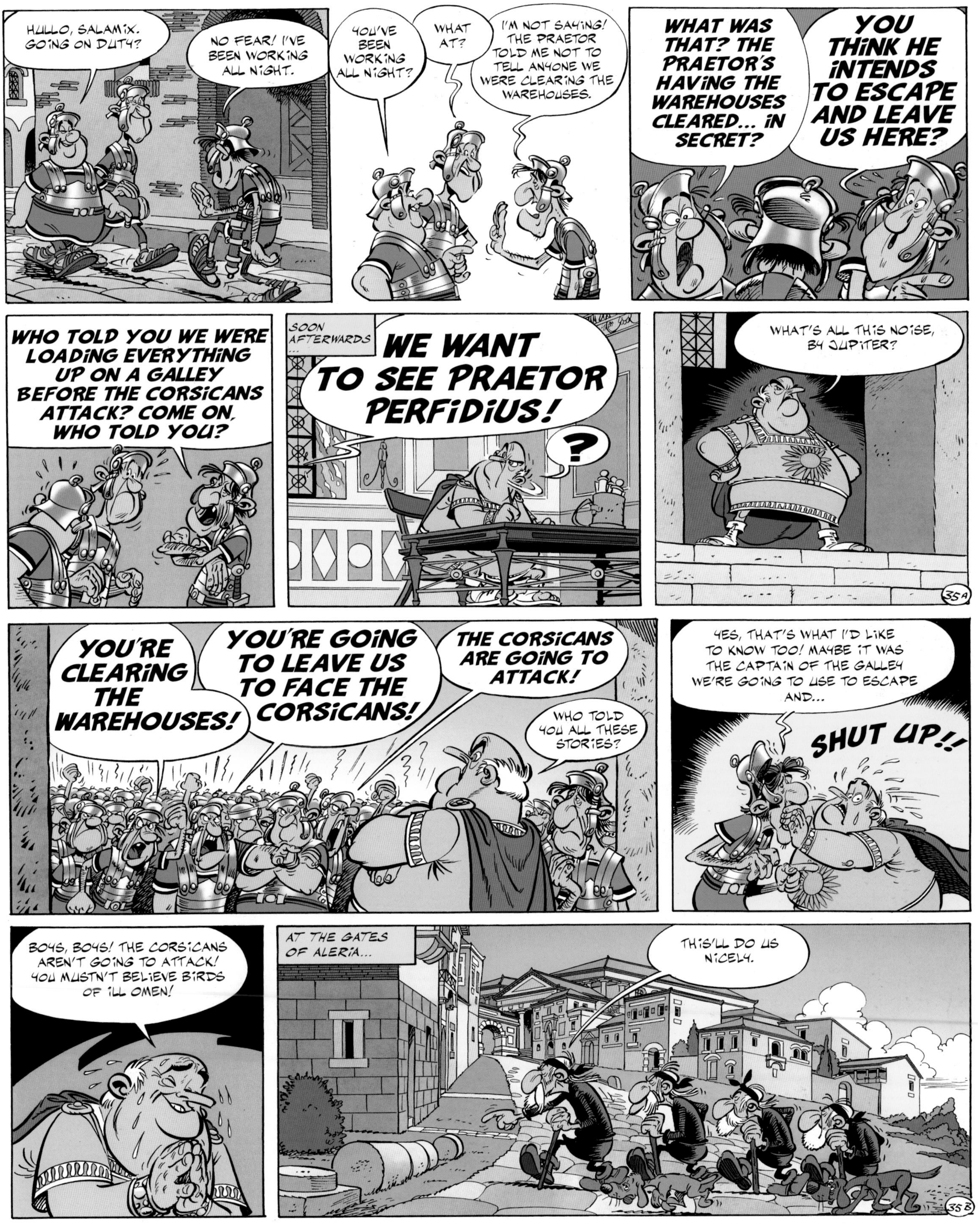
HULLO, SALAMIX. GOING ON DUTY?
NO FEAR! I'VE BEEN WORKING ALL NIGHT.
YOU'VE BEEN WORKING ALL NIGHT?
WHAT AT?
I'M NOT SAYING! THE PRAETOR TOLD ME NOT TO TELL ANYONE WE WERE CLEARING THE WAREHOUSES.
WHAT WAS THAT? THE PRAETOR'S HAVING THE WAREHOUSES CLEARED... IN SECRET?
YOU THINK HE INTENDS TO ESCAPE AND LEAVE US HERE?
WHO TOLD YOU WE WERE LOADING EVERYTHING UP ON A GALLEY BEFORE THE CORSICANS ATTACK? COME ON, WHO TOLD YOU?
SOON AFTERWARDS ...
WE WANT TO SEE PRAETOR PERFIDIUS!
?
WHAT'S ALL THIS NOISE, BY JUPITER?
35A
YOU'RE CLEARING THE WAREHOUSES!
YOU'RE GOING TO LEAVE US TO FACE THE CORSICANS!
THE CORSICANS ARE GOING TO ATTACK!
WHO TOLD YOU ALL THESE STORIES?
YES, THAT'S WHAT I'D LIKE TO KNOW TOO! MAYBE IT WAS THE CAPTAIN OF THE GALLEY WE'RE GOING TO USE TO ESCAPE AND...
SHUT UP!!
BOYS, BOYS! THE CORSICANS AREN'T GOING TO ATTACK! YOU MUSTN'T BELIEVE BIRDS OF ILL OMEN!
AT THE GATES OF ALERIA...
THIS'LL DO US NICELY.
35B

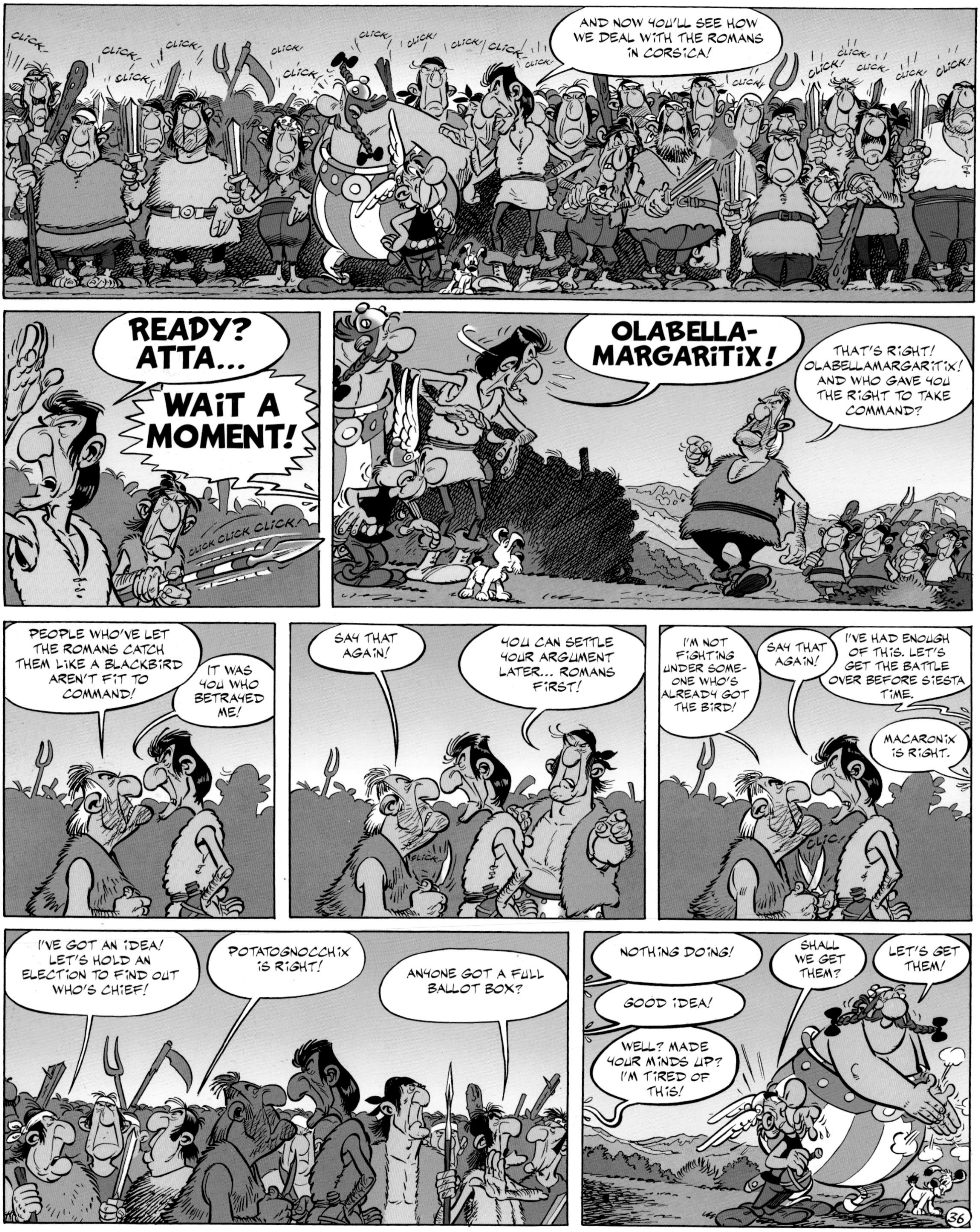
CLICK
CLICK
CLICK
CLICK!
CLICK!
CLICK!
CLICK!
CLICK!
CLICK!
CLICK
AND NOW YOU'LL SEE HOW WE DEAL WITH THE ROMANS IN CORSICA!
CLICK!
CLICK!
CLICK!
CLICK!
CLICK!
CLICK!
READY? ATTA...
WAIT A MOMENT!
CLICK CLICK CLICK!
OLABELLA-MARGARITIX!
THAT'S RIGHT! OLABELLAMARGARITIX! AND WHO GAVE YOU THE RIGHT TO TAKE COMMAND?
PEOPLE WHO'VE LET THE ROMANS CATCH THEM LIKE A BLACKBIRD AREN'T FIT TO COMMAND!
IT WAS YOU WHO BETRAYED ME!
SAY THAT AGAIN!
YOU CAN SETTLE YOUR ARGUMENT LATER... ROMANS FIRST!
FLICK
I'M NOT FIGHTING UNDER SOMEONE WHO'S ALREADY GOT THE BIRD!
SAY THAT AGAIN!
I'VE HAD ENOUGH OF THIS. LET'S GET THE BATTLE OVER BEFORE SIESTA TIME.
MACARONIX IS RIGHT.
CLIC!
I'VE GOT AN IDEA! LET'S HOLD AN ELECTION TO FIND OUT WHO'S CHIEF!
POTATOGNOCCHIX IS RIGHT!
ANYONE GOT A FULL BALLOT BOX?
NOTHING DOING!
GOOD IDEA!
WELL? MADE YOUR MINDS UP? I'M TIRED OF THIS!
SHALL WE GET THEM?
LET'S GET THEM!
36

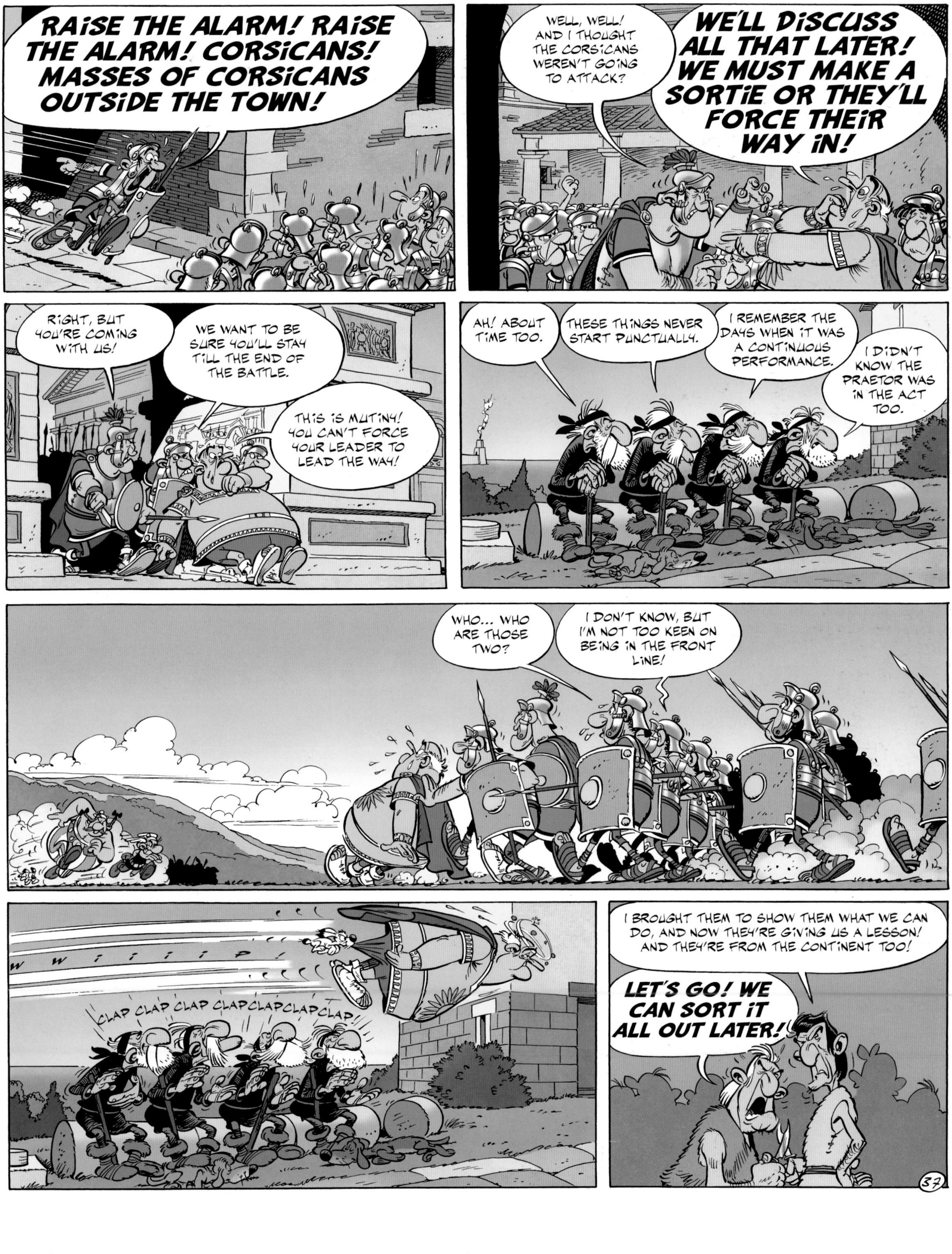
RAISE THE ALARM! RAISE THE ALARM! CORSICANS! MASSES OF CORSICANS OUTSIDE THE TOWN!
WELL, WELL! AND I THOUGHT THE CORSICANS WEREN'T GOING TO ATTACK?
WE'LL DISCUSS ALL THAT LATER! WE MUST MAKE A SORTIE OR THEY'LL FORCE THEIR WAY IN!
RIGHT, BUT YOU'RE COMING WITH US!
WE WANT TO BE SURE YOU'LL STAY TILL THE END OF THE BATTLE.
THIS IS MUTINY! YOU CAN'T FORCE YOUR LEADER TO LEAD THE WAY!
AH! ABOUT TIME TOO.
THESE THINGS NEVER START PUNCTUALLY.
I REMEMBER THE DAYS WHEN IT WAS A CONTINUOUS PERFORMANCE.
I DIDN'T KNOW THE PRAETOR WAS IN THE ACT TOO.
WHO... WHO ARE THOSE TWO?
I DON'T KNOW, BUT I'M NOT TOO KEEN ON BEING IN THE FRONT LINE!
WWIIIIIP!
CLAP CLAP CLAP CLAPCLAPCLAPCLAP!
I BROUGHT THEM TO SHOW THEM WHAT WE CAN DO, AND NOW THEY'RE GIVING US A LESSON! AND THEY'RE FROM THE CONTINENT TOO!
LET'S GO! WE CAN SORT IT ALL OUT LATER!
37

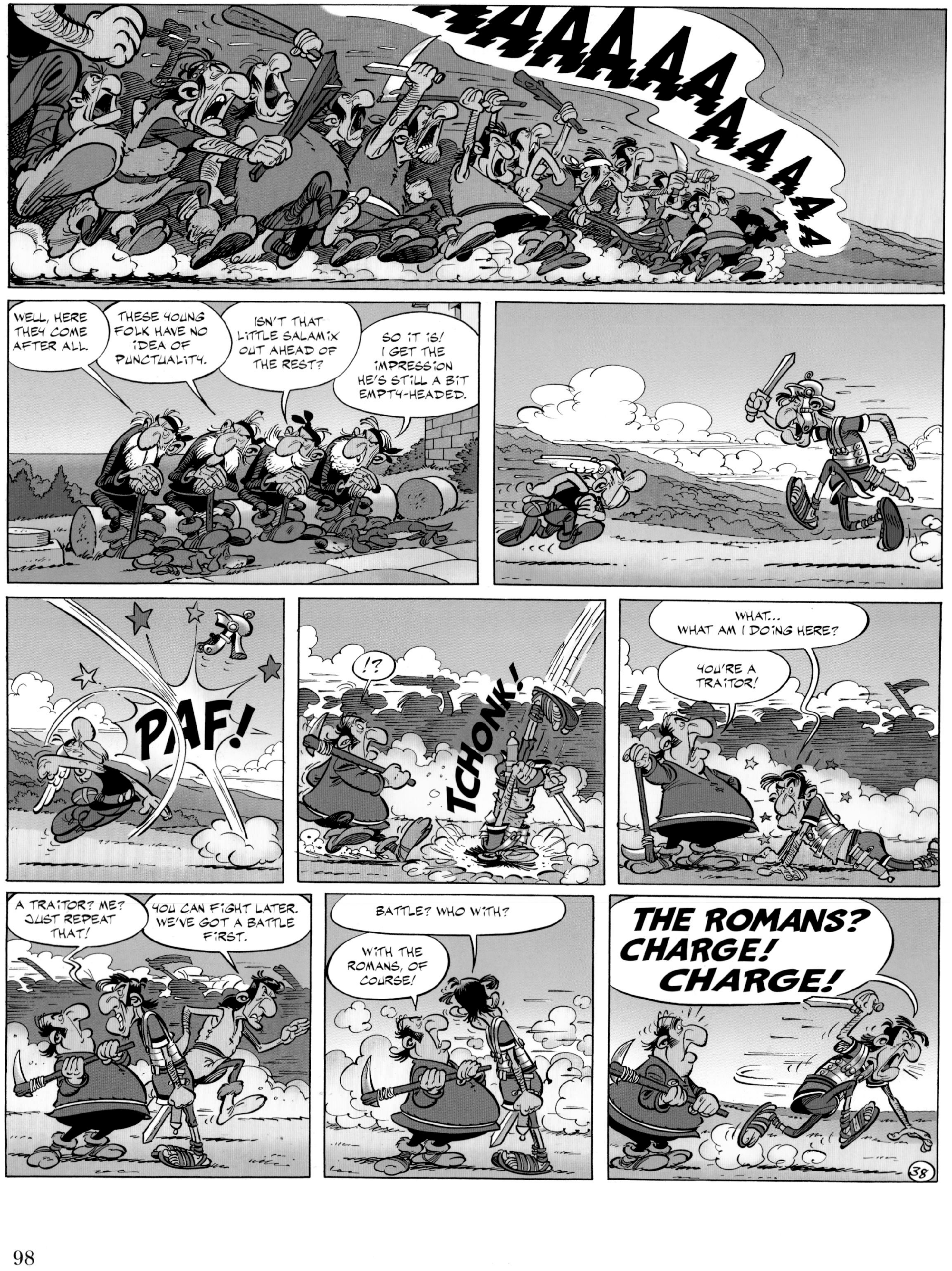
AAAAAAAAAAAAAAAAAA
WELL, HERE THEY COME AFTER ALL.
THESE YOUNG FOLK HAVE NO IDEA OF PUNCTUALITY.
ISN'T THAT LITTLE SALAMIX OUT AHEAD OF THE REST?
SO IT IS! I GET THE IMPRESSION HE'S STILL A BIT EMPTY-HEADED.
PAF!
!?
TCHONK!
WHAT... WHAT AM I DOING HERE?
YOU'RE A TRAITOR!
A TRAITOR? ME? JUST REPEAT THAT!
YOU CAN FIGHT LATER. WE'VE GOT A BATTLE FIRST.
BATTLE? WHO WITH?
WITH THE ROMANS, OF COURSE!
THE ROMANS? CHARGE! CHARGE!
38

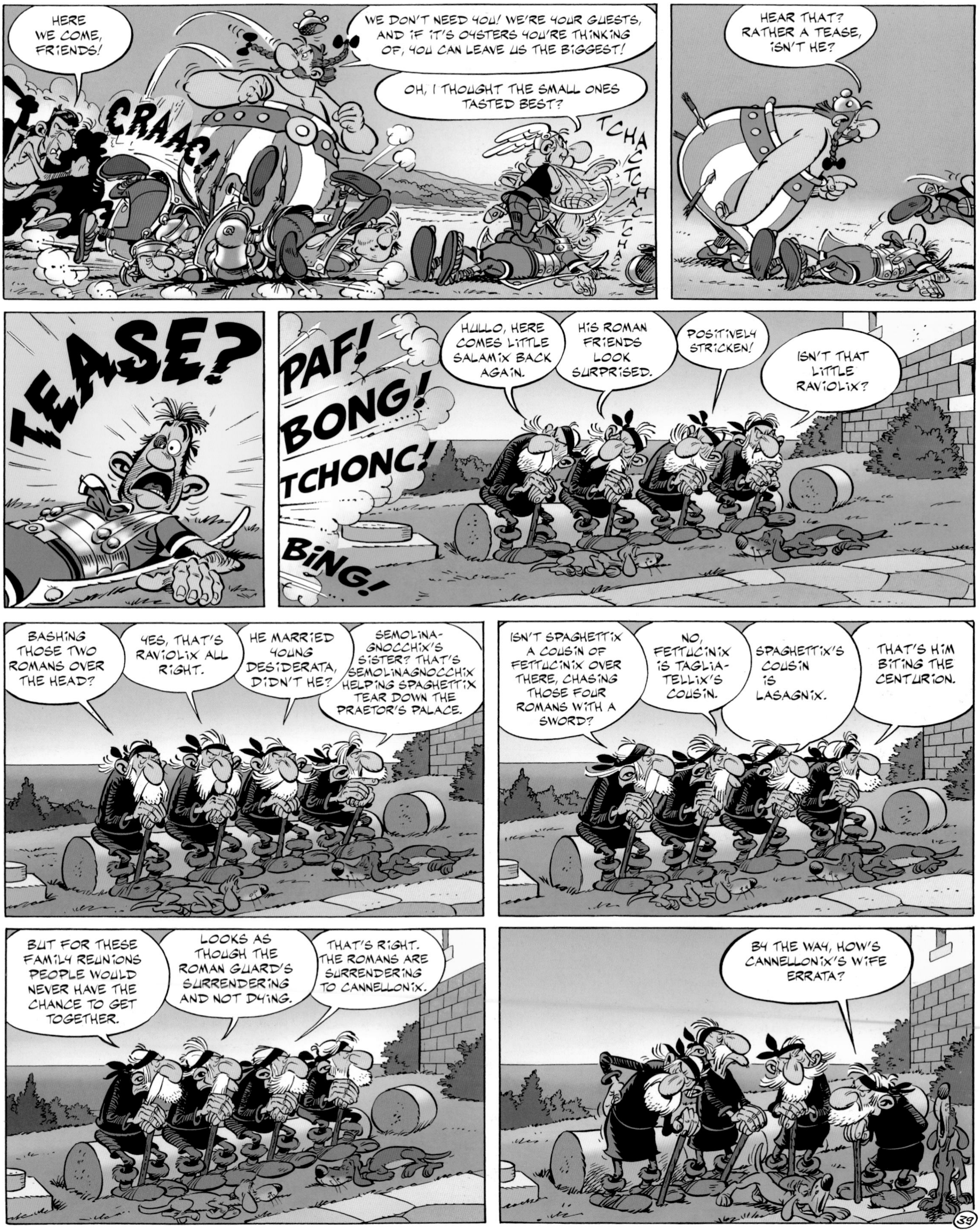
HERE WE COME, FRIENDS!
WE DON'T NEED YOU! WE'RE YOUR GUESTS, AND IF IT'S OYSTERS YOU'RE THINKING OF, YOU CAN LEAVE US THE BIGGEST!
OH, I THOUGHT THE SMALL ONES TASTED BEST?
CRAAAC!
TCHACTCHACTCHAC
HEAR THAT? RATHER A TEASE, ISN'T HE?
TEASE?
PAF! BONG! TCHONC! BING!
HULLO, HERE COMES LITTLE SALAMIX BACK AGAIN.
HIS ROMAN FRIENDS LOOK SURPRISED.
POSITIVELY STRICKEN!
ISN'T THAT LITTLE RAVIOLIX?
BASHING THOSE TWO ROMANS OVER THE HEAD?
YES, THAT'S RAVIOLIX ALL RIGHT.
HE MARRIED YOUNG DESIDERATA, DIDN'T HE?
SEMOLINA-GNOCCHIX'S SISTER? THAT'S SEMOLINAGNOCCHIX HELPING SPAGHETTIX TEAR DOWN THE PRAETOR'S PALACE.
ISN'T SPAGHETTIX A COUSIN OF FETTUCINIX OVER THERE, CHASING THOSE FOUR ROMANS WITH A SWORD?
NO, FETTUCINIX IS TAGLIATELLIX'S COUSIN.
SPAGHETTIX'S COUSIN IS LASAGNIX.
THAT'S HIM BITING THE CENTURION.
BUT FOR THESE FAMILY REUNIONS PEOPLE WOULD NEVER HAVE THE CHANCE TO GET TOGETHER.
LOOKS AS THOUGH THE ROMAN GUARD'S SURRENDERING AND NOT DYING.
THAT'S RIGHT. THE ROMANS ARE SURRENDERING TO CANNELLONIX.
BY THE WAY, HOW'S CANNELLONIX'S WIFE ERRATA?
39

LOST SOMETHING?
PRAETOR PERFIDIUS. I'VE GOT A WORD OR SO TO SAY TO HIM.
I KNOW WHERE HE IS! I REMEMBER NOW... HE WAS GOING TO ESCAPE, ON BOARD A SHIP!
SHOW US THE WAY. WE'LL BRING HIM BACK. OBELIX WILL COME TOO.
OOH, YES! WE'RE VERY GOOD ON SHIPS!
MEANWHILE, ON BOARD THE SHIP...
...AND THEN, DURING THE VOYAGE, WE'LL THROW THE ROMAN OVERBOARD AND SAIL OFF WITH THE LOOT!
CAST OFF! CAST OFF!
HE'LL GET A STITCH THAT WAY... DO WE CAST OFF?
GO SLOW...
QUICK! QUICK! CAST OFF!
A BIT OF PLAIN DEALING FIRST. WHERE'S THE LOOT YOU'VE PURLOINED? WE'VE ONLY GOT ONE AMPHORA ON BOARD SO FAR.
CAP'N! LOOK!
THE GAU... THE GAUGAU...
CAST OFF! QUICK! CAST OFF!!!
THAT'S JUST WHAT I WAS SAYING! CAST OFF!
40

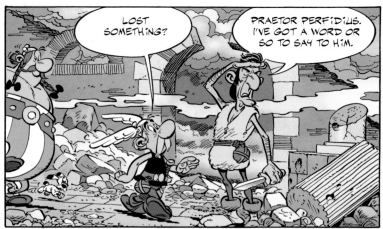

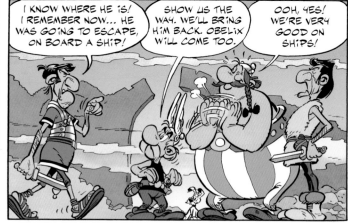

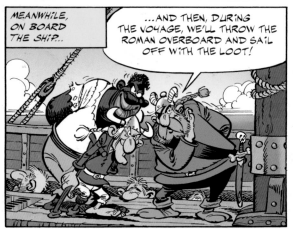

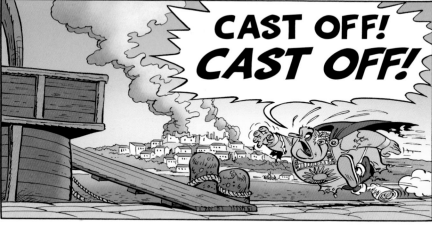

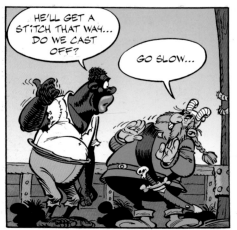

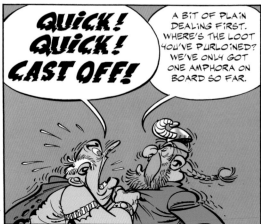

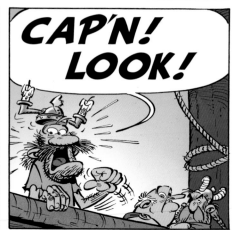

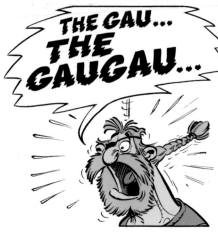

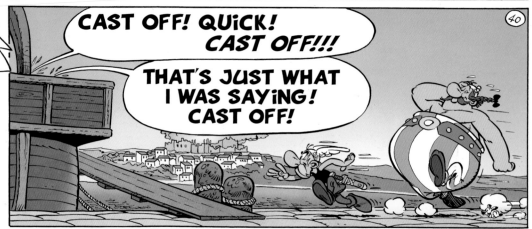

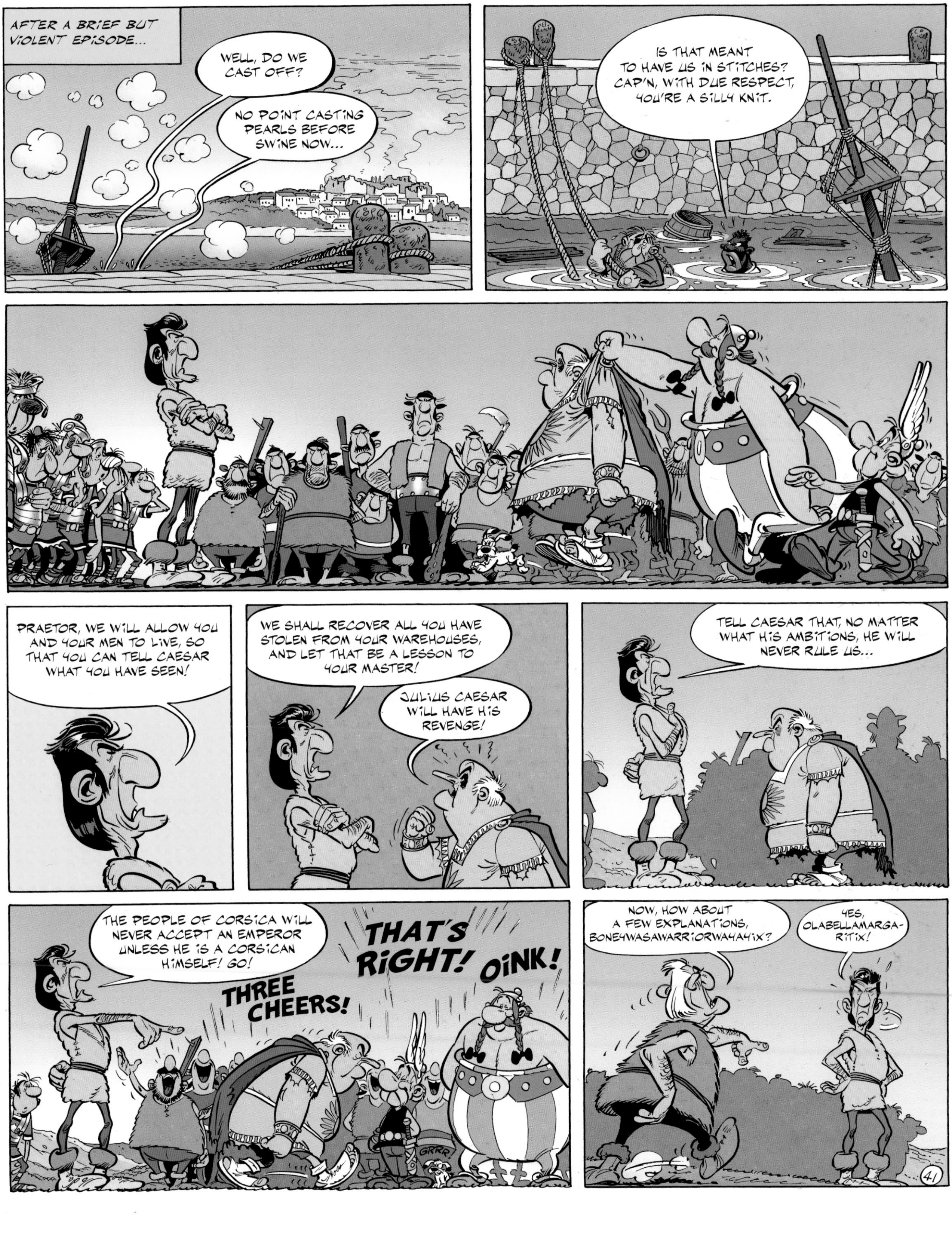
AFTER A BRIEF BUT VIOLENT EPISODE...
WELL, DO WE CAST OFF?
NO POINT CASTING PEARLS BEFORE SWINE NOW...
IS THAT MEANT TO HAVE US IN STITCHES? CAP'N, WITH DUE RESPECT, YOU'RE A SILLY KNIT.
PRAETOR, WE WILL ALLOW YOU AND YOUR MEN TO LIVE, SO THAT YOU CAN TELL CAESAR WHAT YOU HAVE SEEN!
WE SHALL RECOVER ALL YOU HAVE STOLEN FROM YOUR WAREHOUSES, AND LET THAT BE A LESSON TO YOUR MASTER!
JULIUS CAESAR WILL HAVE HIS REVENGE!
TELL CAESAR THAT, NO MATTER WHAT HIS AMBITIONS, HE WILL NEVER RULE US...
THE PEOPLE OF CORSICA WILL NEVER ACCEPT AN EMPEROR UNLESS HE IS A CORSICAN HIMSELF! GO!
THAT'S RIGHT!
OINK!
THREE CHEERS!
GRRR!
NOW, HOW ABOUT A FEW EXPLANATIONS, BONEYWASAWARRIORWAYAYIX?
YES, OLABELLAMARGA-RITIX!
41

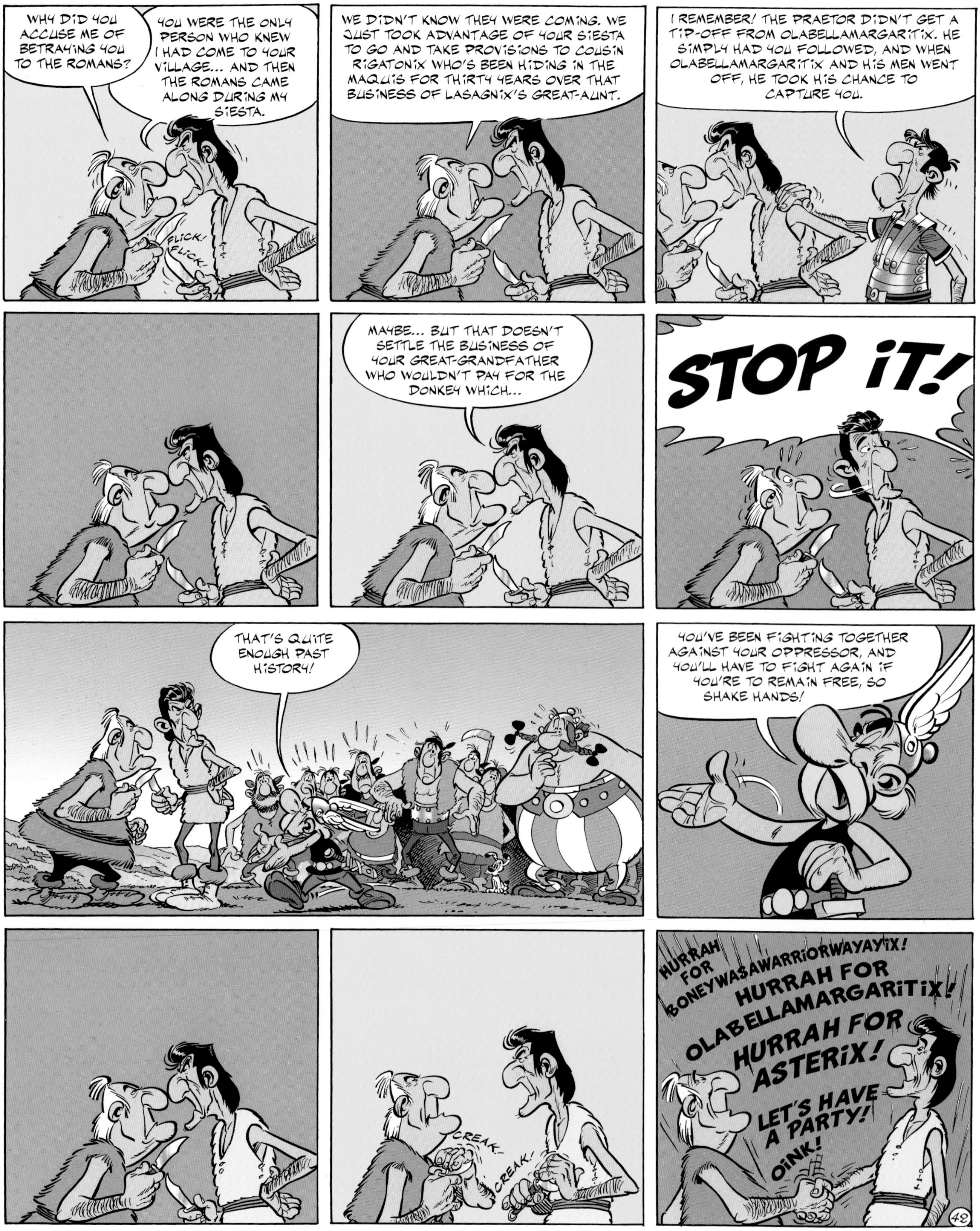
WHY DID YOU ACCUSE ME OF BETRAYING YOU TO THE ROMANS?
YOU WERE THE ONLY PERSON WHO KNEW I HAD COME TO YOUR VILLAGE... AND THEN THE ROMANS CAME ALONG DURING MY SIESTA.
FLICK! FLICK!
WE DIDN'T KNOW THEY WERE COMING. WE JUST TOOK ADVANTAGE OF YOUR SIESTA TO GO AND TAKE PROVISIONS TO COUSIN RIGATONIX WHO'S BEEN HIDING IN THE MAQUIS FOR THIRTY YEARS OVER THAT BUSINESS OF LASAGNIX'S GREAT-AUNT.
I REMEMBER! THE PRAETOR DIDN'T GET A TIP-OFF FROM OLABELLAMARGARITIX. HE SIMPLY HAD YOU FOLLOWED, AND WHEN OLABELLAMARGARITIX AND HIS MEN WENT OFF, HE TOOK HIS CHANCE TO CAPTURE YOU.
MAYBE... BUT THAT DOESN'T SETTLE THE BUSINESS OF YOUR GREAT-GRANDFATHER WHO WOULDN'T PAY FOR THE DONKEY WHICH...
STOP IT!
THAT'S QUITE ENOUGH PAST HISTORY!
YOU'VE BEEN FIGHTING TOGETHER AGAINST YOUR OPPRESSOR, AND YOU'LL HAVE TO FIGHT AGAIN IF YOU'RE TO REMAIN FREE, SO SHAKE HANDS!
CREAK! CREAK!
HURRAH FOR BONEYWASAWARRIORWAYAYIX!
HURRAH FOR OLABELLAMARGARITIX!
HURRAH FOR ASTERIX!
LET'S HAVE A PARTY!
OINK!
48

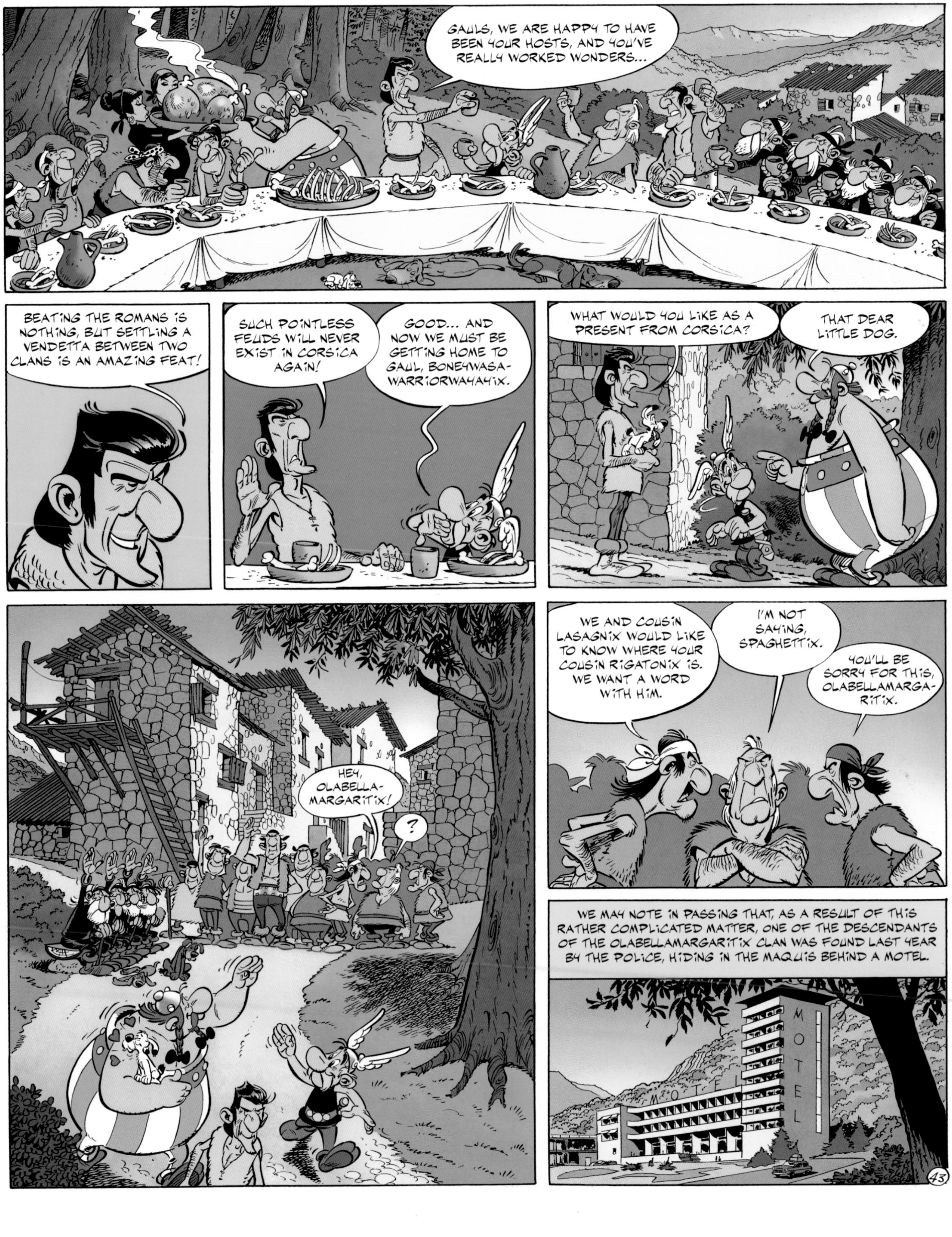
GAULS, WE ARE HAPPY TO HAVE BEEN YOUR HOSTS, AND YOU'VE REALLY WORKED WONDERS...
BEATING THE ROMANS IS NOTHING, BUT SETTLING A VENDETTA BETWEEN TWO CLANS IS AN AMAZING FEAT!
SUCH POINTLESS FEUDS WILL NEVER EXIST IN CORSICA AGAIN!
GOOD... AND NOW WE MUST BE GETTING HOME TO GAUL, BONEYWASAWARRIORWAYAYIX.
WHAT WOULD YOU LIKE AS A PRESENT FROM CORSICA?
THAT DEAR LITTLE DOG.
HEY, OLABELLAMARGARITIX!
?
WE AND COUSIN LASAGNIX WOULD LIKE TO KNOW WHERE YOUR COUSIN RIGATONIX IS. WE WANT A WORD WITH HIM.
I'M NOT SAYING, SPAGHETTIX.
YOU'LL BE SORRY FOR THIS, OLABELLAMARGARITIX.
WE MAY NOTE IN PASSING THAT, AS A RESULT OF THIS RATHER COMPLICATED MATTER, ONE OF THE DESCENDANTS OF THE OLABELLAMARGARITIX CLAN WAS FOUND LAST YEAR BY THE POLICE, HIDING IN THE MAQUIS BEHIND A MOTEL.
MOTEL
MOTEL
43

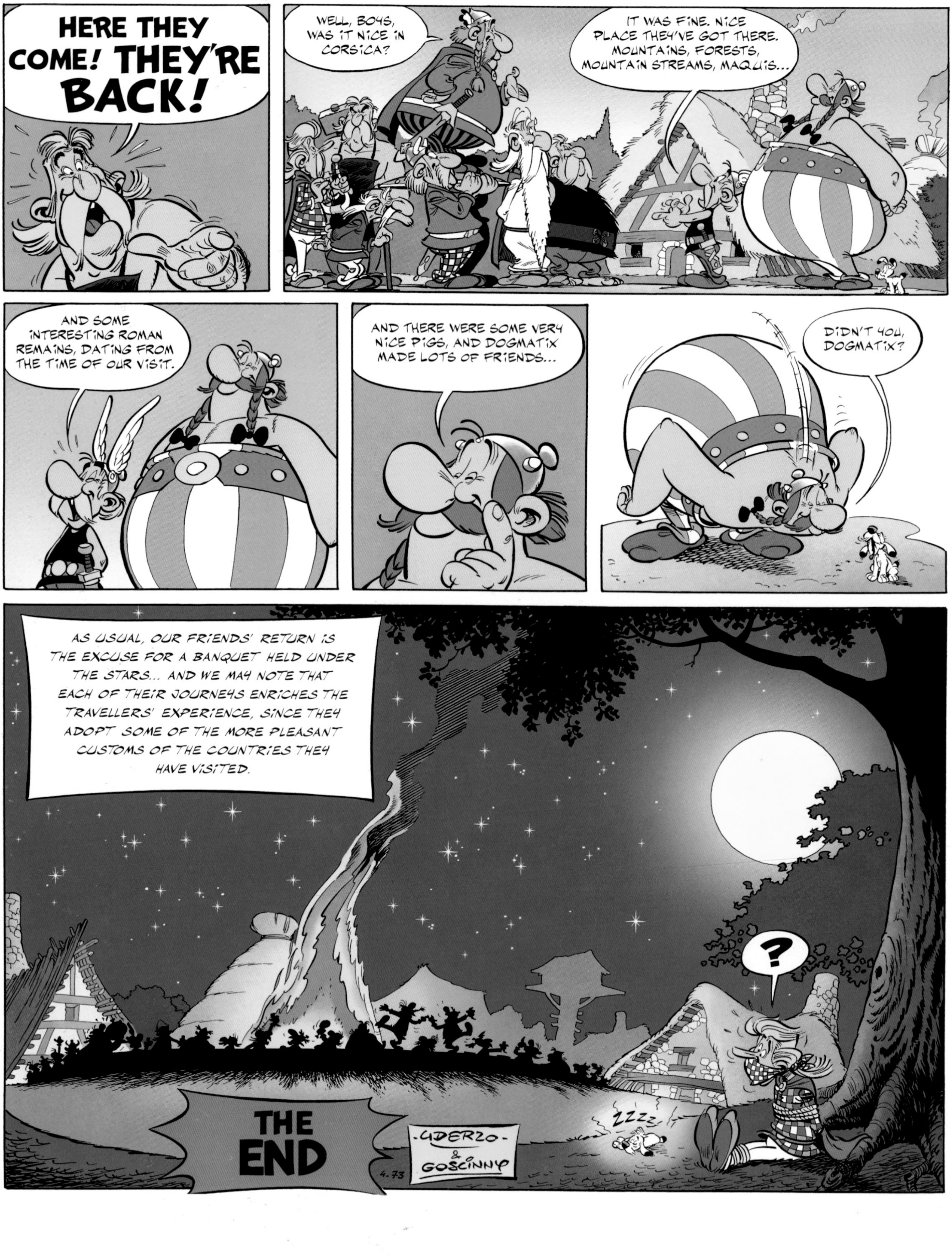
HERE THEY COME! THEY'RE BACK!
WELL, BOYS, WAS IT NICE IN CORSICA?
IT WAS FINE. NICE PLACE THEY'VE GOT THERE. MOUNTAINS, FORESTS, MOUNTAIN STREAMS, MAQUIS...
AND SOME INTERESTING ROMAN REMAINS, DATING FROM THE TIME OF OUR VISIT.
AND THERE WERE SOME VERY NICE PIGS, AND DOGMATIX MADE LOTS OF FRIENDS...
DIDN'T YOU, DOGMATIX?
AS USUAL, OUR FRIENDS' RETURN IS THE EXCUSE FOR A BANQUET HELD UNDER THE STARS... AND WE MAY NOTE THAT EACH OF THEIR JOURNEYS ENRICHES THE TRAVELLERS' EXPERIENCE, SINCE THEY ADOPT SOME OF THE MORE PLEASANT CUSTOMS OF THE COUNTRIES THEY HAVE VISITED.
?
ZZZZ
THE END
UDERZO & GOSCINNY
4.73

R. GOSCINNY Asterix A. UDERZO

Asterix and Caesar's Gift

Written by René GOSCINNY Illustrated by Albert UDERZO

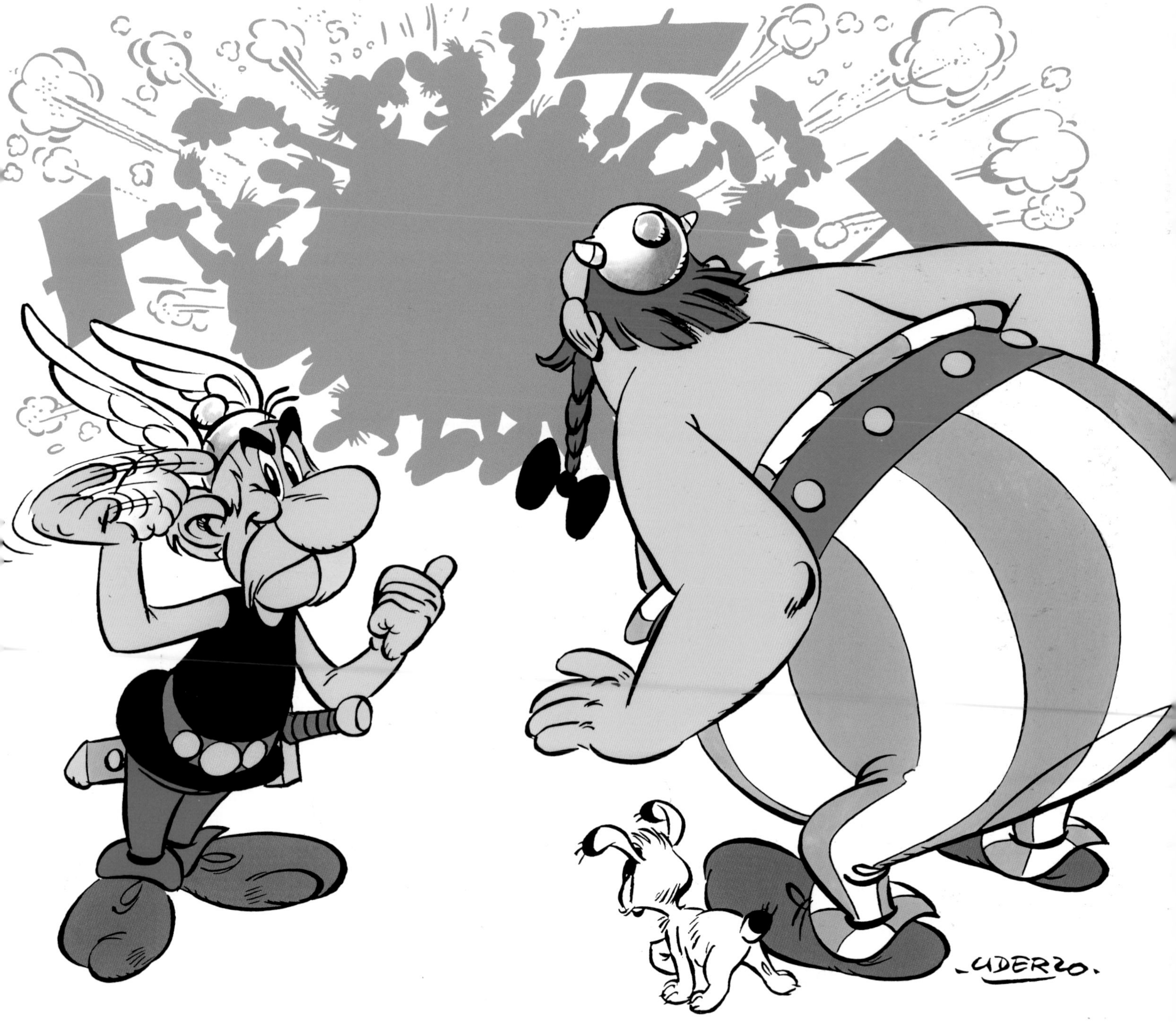
UDERZO

GOSCINNY AND UDERZO
PRESENT
An Asterix Adventure

ASTERIX
AND
CAESAR'S GIFT

Written by RENÉ GOSCINNY *and Illustrated by* ALBERT UDERZO

Translated by Anthea Bell *and* Derek Hockridge

Orion
Children's Books

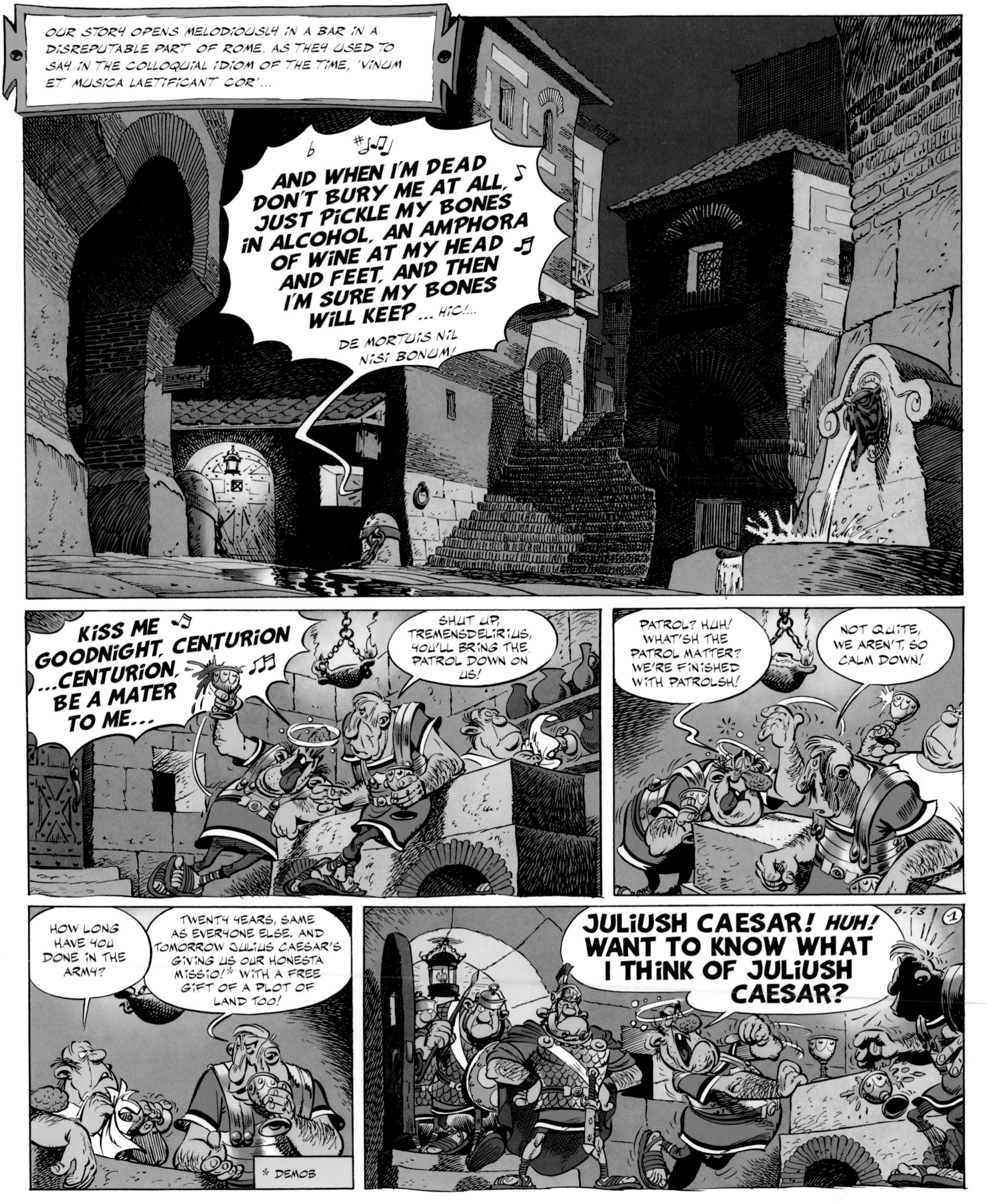
OUR STORY OPENS MELODIOUSLY IN A BAR IN A DISREPUTABLE PART OF ROME. AS THEY USED TO SAY IN THE COLLOQUIAL IDIOM OF THE TIME, 'VINUM ET MUSICA LAETIFICANT COR'...
AND WHEN I'M DEAD DON'T BURY ME AT ALL, JUST PICKLE MY BONES IN ALCOHOL, AN AMPHORA OF WINE AT MY HEAD AND FEET, AND THEN I'M SURE MY BONES WILL KEEP ... HIC!...
DE MORTUIS NIL NISI BONUM!
KISS ME GOODNIGHT, CENTURION ...CENTURION, BE A MATER TO ME...
SHUT UP, TREMENSDELIRIUS, YOU'LL BRING THE PATROL DOWN ON US!
PATROL? HUH! WHAT'SH THE PATROL MATTER? WE'RE FINISHED WITH PATROLSH!
NOT QUITE, WE AREN'T, SO CALM DOWN!
HOW LONG HAVE YOU DONE IN THE ARMY?
TWENTY YEARS, SAME AS EVERYONE ELSE. AND TOMORROW JULIUS CAESAR'S GIVING US OUR HONESTA MISSIO!* WITH A FREE GIFT OF A PLOT OF LAND TOO!
* DEMOB
6-73
1
JULIUSH CAESAR! HUH! WANT TO KNOW WHAT I THINK OF JULIUSH CAESAR?

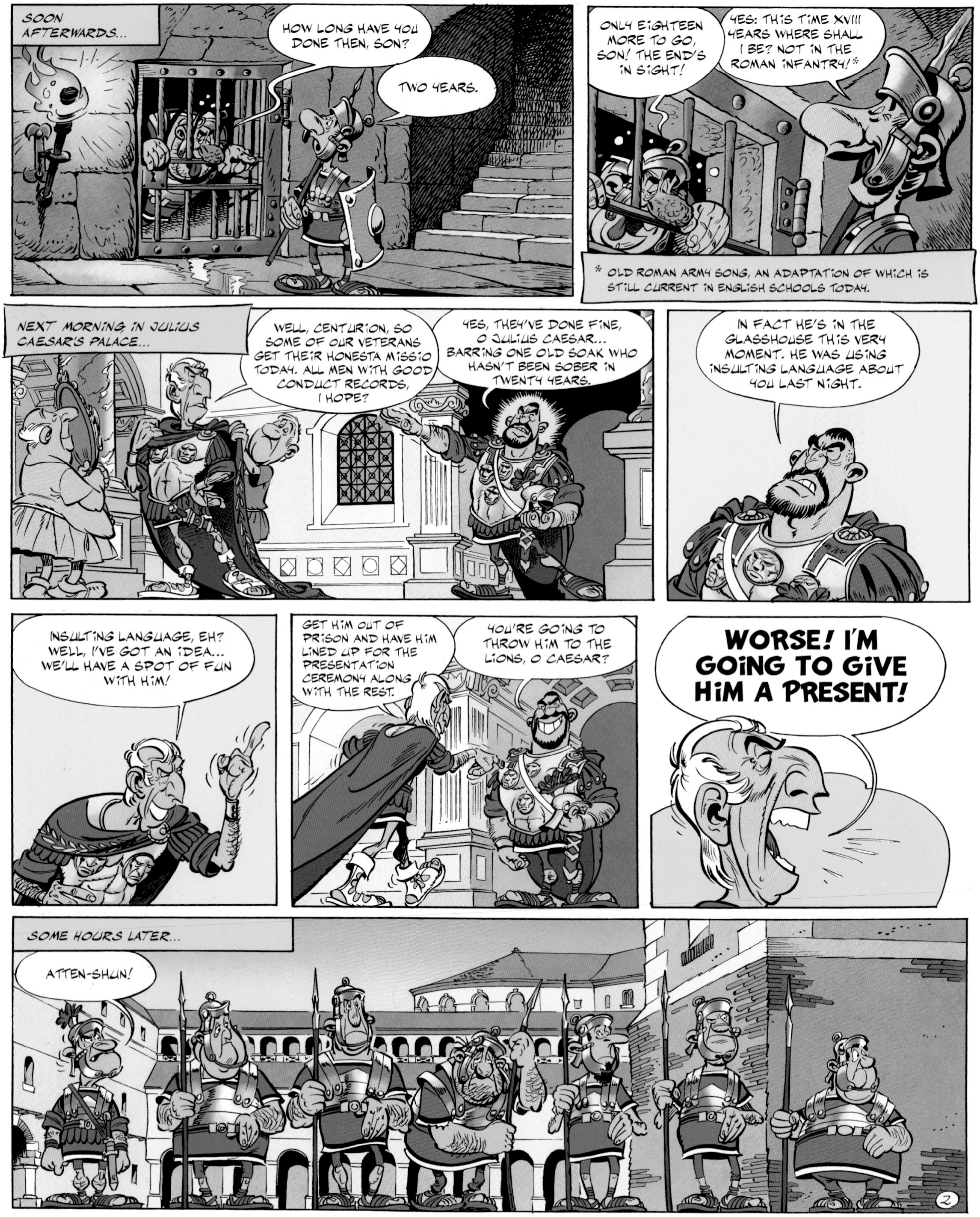
SOON AFTERWARDS...
HOW LONG HAVE YOU DONE THEN, SON?
TWO YEARS.
ONLY EIGHTEEN MORE TO GO, SON! THE END'S IN SIGHT!
YES: THIS TIME XVIII YEARS WHERE SHALL I BE? NOT IN THE ROMAN INFANTRY!*
* OLD ROMAN ARMY SONG, AN ADAPTATION OF WHICH IS STILL CURRENT IN ENGLISH SCHOOLS TODAY.
NEXT MORNING IN JULIUS CAESAR'S PALACE...
WELL, CENTURION, SO SOME OF OUR VETERANS GET THEIR HONESTA MISSIO TODAY. ALL MEN WITH GOOD CONDUCT RECORDS, I HOPE?
YES, THEY'VE DONE FINE, O JULIUS CAESAR... BARRING ONE OLD SOAK WHO HASN'T BEEN SOBER IN TWENTY YEARS.
IN FACT HE'S IN THE GLASSHOUSE THIS VERY MOMENT. HE WAS USING INSULTING LANGUAGE ABOUT YOU LAST NIGHT.
INSULTING LANGUAGE, EH? WELL, I'VE GOT AN IDEA... WE'LL HAVE A SPOT OF FUN WITH HIM!
GET HIM OUT OF PRISON AND HAVE HIM LINED UP FOR THE PRESENTATION CEREMONY ALONG WITH THE REST.
YOU'RE GOING TO THROW HIM TO THE LIONS, O CAESAR?
WORSE! I'M GOING TO GIVE HIM A PRESENT!
SOME HOURS LATER...
ATTEN-SHUN!
2

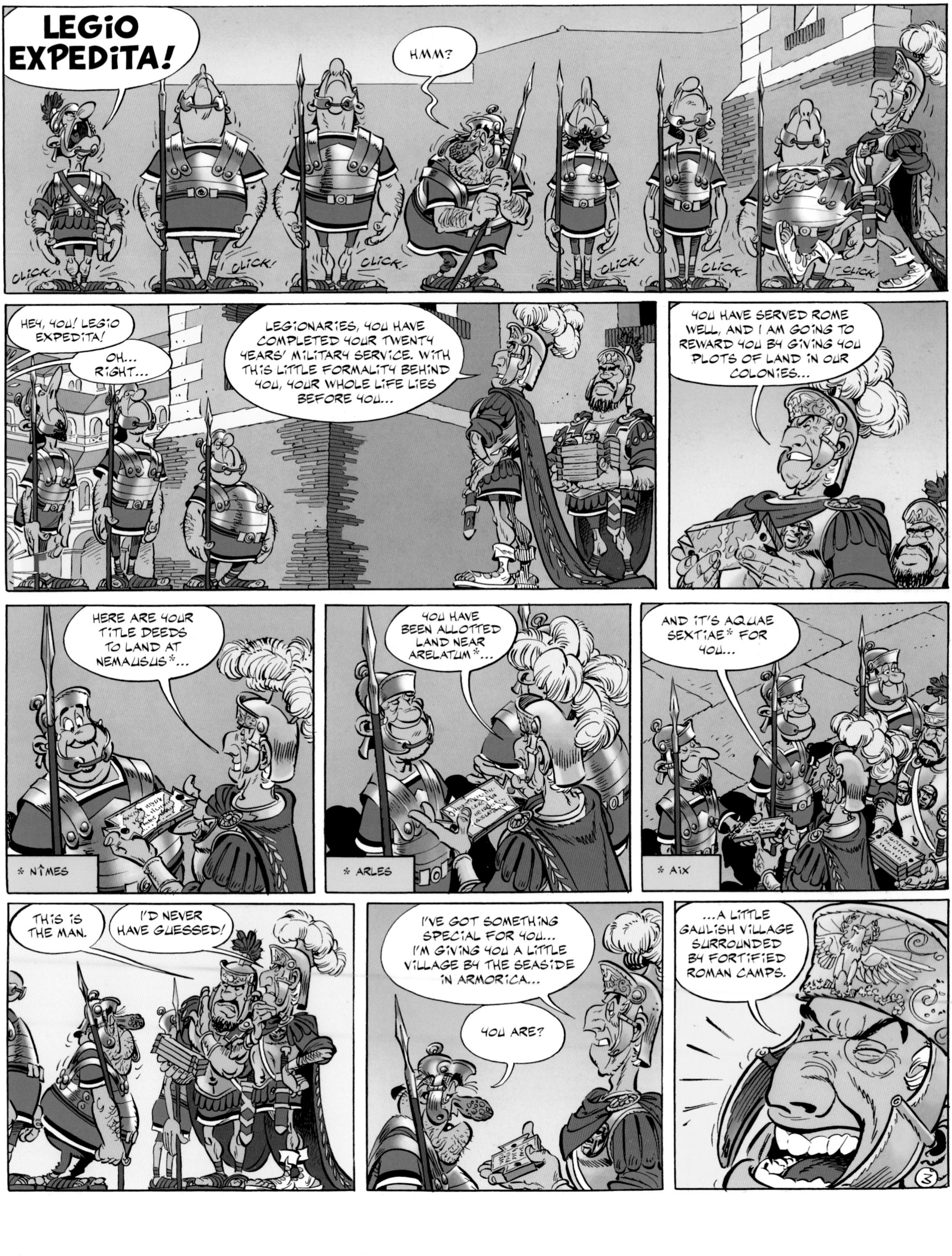

LEGIO EXPEDITA!
HMM?
CLICK! CLICK! CLICK! CLICK! CLICK! CLICK!
HEY, YOU! LEGIO EXPEDITA!
OH... RIGHT...
LEGIONARIES, YOU HAVE COMPLETED YOUR TWENTY YEARS' MILITARY SERVICE. WITH THIS LITTLE FORMALITY BEHIND YOU, YOUR WHOLE LIFE LIES BEFORE YOU...
YOU HAVE SERVED ROME WELL, AND I AM GOING TO REWARD YOU BY GIVING YOU PLOTS OF LAND IN OUR COLONIES...
HERE ARE YOUR TITLE DEEDS TO LAND AT NEMAUSUS*...
* NÎMES
YOU HAVE BEEN ALLOTTED LAND NEAR ARELATUM*...
* ARLES
AND IT'S AQUAE SEXTIAE* FOR YOU...
* AIX
THIS IS THE MAN.
I'D NEVER HAVE GUESSED!
I'VE GOT SOMETHING SPECIAL FOR YOU... I'M GIVING YOU A LITTLE VILLAGE BY THE SEASIDE IN ARMORICA...
YOU ARE?
...A LITTLE GAULISH VILLAGE SURROUNDED BY FORTIFIED ROMAN CAMPS.

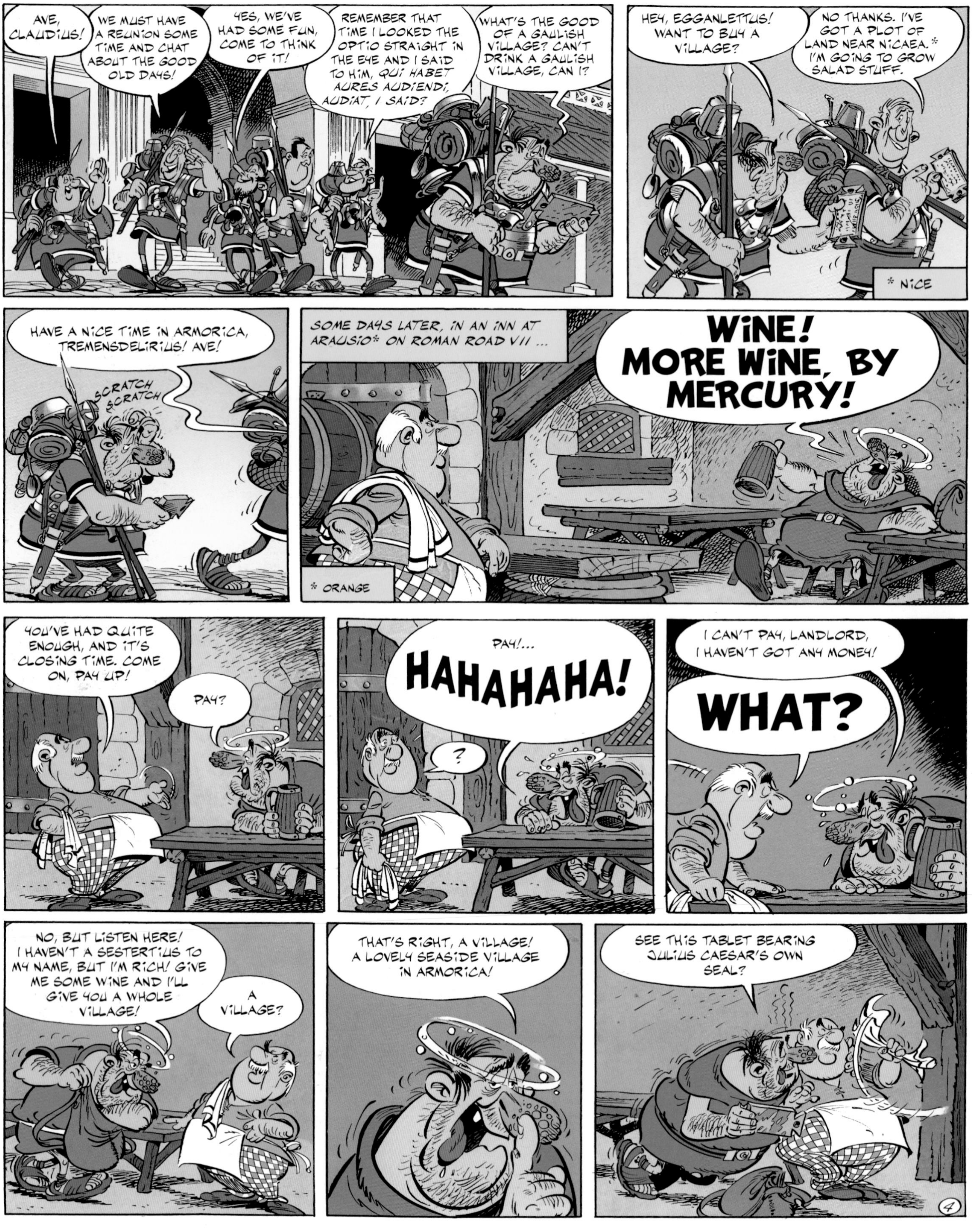
AVE, CLAUDIUS!
WE MUST HAVE A REUNION SOME TIME AND CHAT ABOUT THE GOOD OLD DAYS!
YES, WE'VE HAD SOME FUN, COME TO THINK OF IT!
REMEMBER THAT TIME I LOOKED THE OPTIO STRAIGHT IN THE EYE AND I SAID TO HIM, QUI HABET AURES AUDIENDI, AUDIAT, I SAID?
WHAT'S THE GOOD OF A GAULISH VILLAGE? CAN'T DRINK A GAULISH VILLAGE, CAN I?
HEY, EGGANLETTUS! WANT TO BUY A VILLAGE?
NO THANKS. I'VE GOT A PLOT OF LAND NEAR NICAEA.* I'M GOING TO GROW SALAD STUFF.
* NICE
HAVE A NICE TIME IN ARMORICA, TREMENSDELIRIUS! AVE!
SCRATCH SCRATCH
SOME DAYS LATER, IN AN INN AT ARAUSIO* ON ROMAN ROAD VII ...
WINE! MORE WINE, BY MERCURY!
* ORANGE
YOU'VE HAD QUITE ENOUGH, AND IT'S CLOSING TIME. COME ON, PAY UP!
PAY?
PAY!... HAHAHAHA!
?
I CAN'T PAY, LANDLORD, I HAVEN'T GOT ANY MONEY!
WHAT?
NO, BUT LISTEN HERE! I HAVEN'T A SESTERTIUS TO MY NAME, BUT I'M RICH! GIVE ME SOME WINE AND I'LL GIVE YOU A WHOLE VILLAGE!
A VILLAGE?
THAT'S RIGHT, A VILLAGE! A LOVELY SEASIDE VILLAGE IN ARMORICA!
SEE THIS TABLET BEARING JULIUS CAESAR'S OWN SEAL?
4

YOU MEAN YOU'D GIVE ME THIS VILLAGE, JUST FOR THE PRICE OF A MEAL AND A LITTLE WINE?
I MUST ASK MY WIFE.
DON'T FORGET THE WINE ON YOUR WAY BACK.
...AND LOOK AT THIS! AN OFFICIAL DOCUMENT! WITH JULIUS CAESAR'S OWN SEAL! I'VE ALWAYS DREAMT OF OWNING LAND...
WELL, ANGINA?
I MUST ADMIT, IT'S TEMPTING... THE CLIMATE HERE DOESN'T REALLY SUIT ME, SEASIDE AIR IS SO BRACING, AND WHAT'S MORE, AN INN IS NO FIT PLACE TO BRING UP A YOUNG GIRL...
SPECIALLY AS OUR LITTLE INFLUENZA WAS NEVER HAPPY ABOUT LEAVING LUTETIA TO COME HERE.
WE COULD SELL THIS INN...
WELL?
IT'S A DEAL!
FILL IT UP!
POP!
AS IT HAPPENS... THE LITTLE VILLAGE WHICH HAS CHANGED HANDS FOR A HUNK OF BREAD AND A FEW MUGS OF WINE...
...IS THIS VILLAGE!
GAULISH VILLAGE
COMPENDIUM
LAUDANUM
AQUARIUM
TOTORUM
5

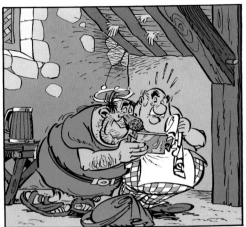

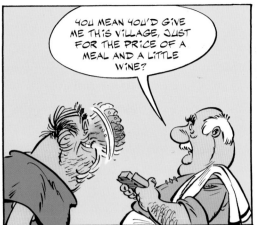

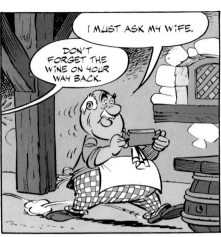

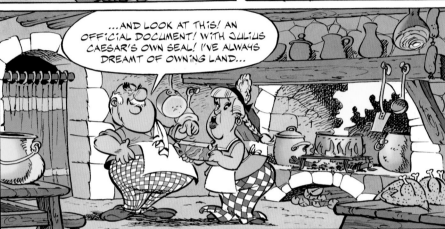

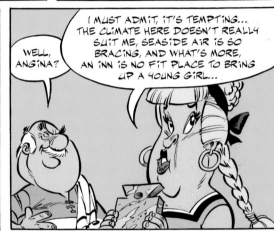

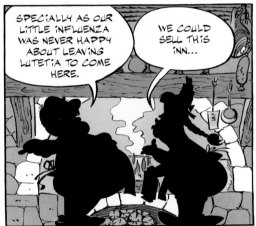

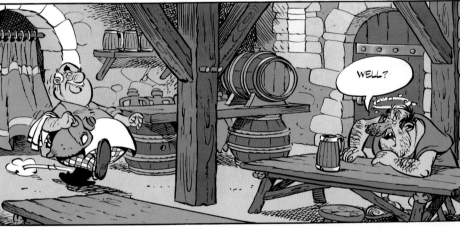

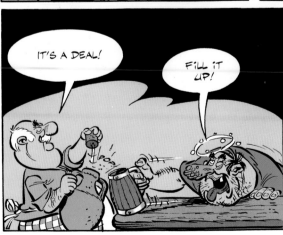

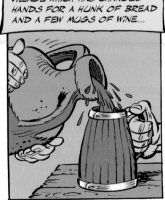

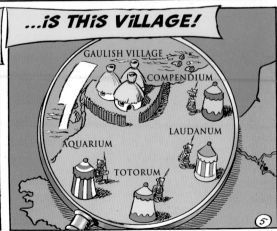

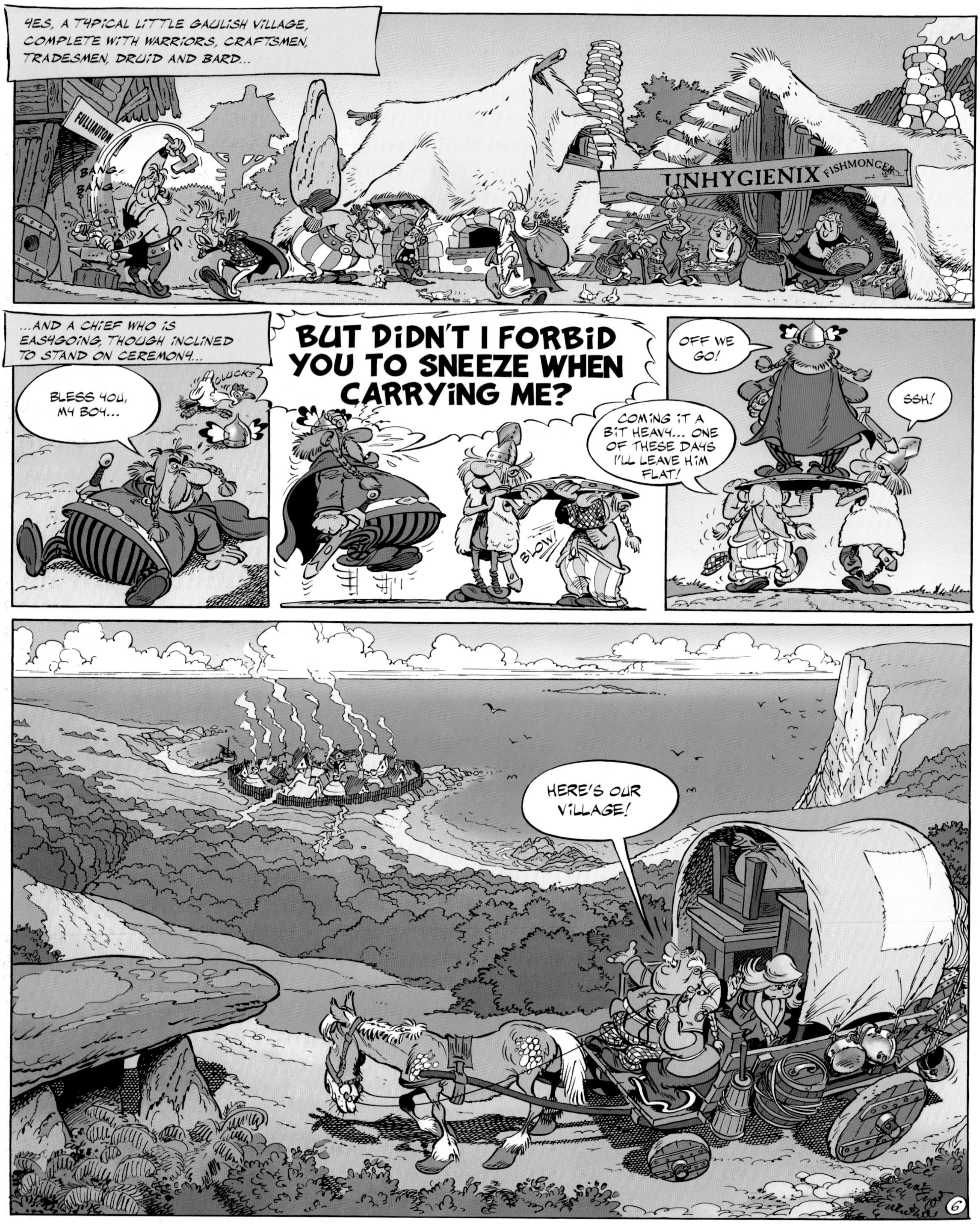
YES, A TYPICAL LITTLE GAULISH VILLAGE, COMPLETE WITH WARRIORS, CRAFTSMEN, TRADESMEN, DRUID AND BARD...
FULLIAUTOMATIX
BANG, BANG
UNHYGIENIX FISHMONGER
...AND A CHIEF WHO IS EASYGOING, THOUGH INCLINED TO STAND ON CEREMONY...
CLUCK?
BLESS YOU, MY BOY...
BUT DIDN'T I FORBID YOU TO SNEEZE WHEN CARRYING ME?
BLOW!
COMING IT A BIT HEAVY... ONE OF THESE DAYS I'LL LEAVE HIM FLAT!
OFF WE GO!
SSH!
HERE'S OUR VILLAGE!
6

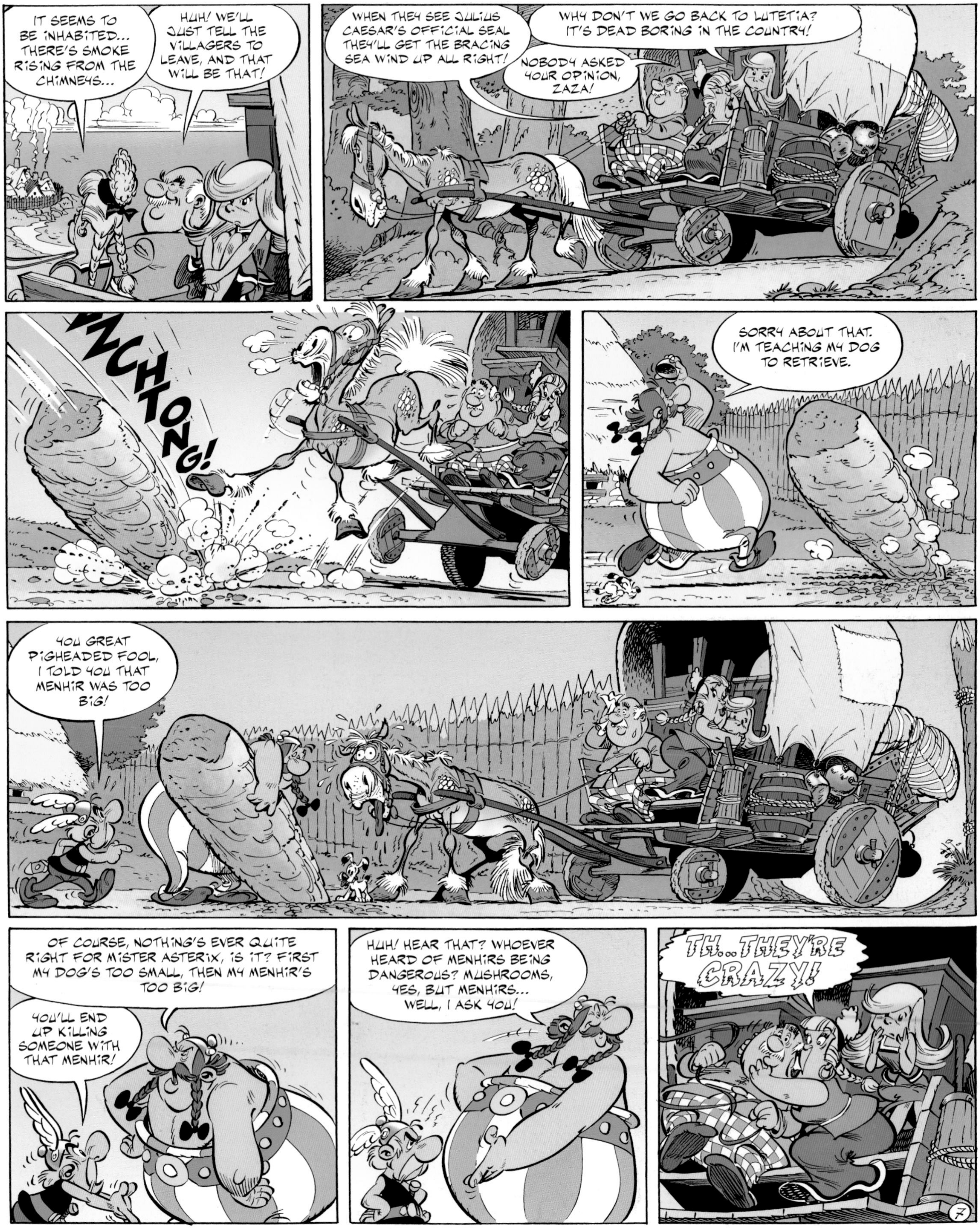
IT SEEMS TO BE INHABITED... THERE'S SMOKE RISING FROM THE CHIMNEYS...
HUH! WE'LL JUST TELL THE VILLAGERS TO LEAVE, AND THAT WILL BE THAT!
WHEN THEY SEE JULIUS CAESAR'S OFFICIAL SEAL THEY'LL GET THE BRACING SEA WIND UP ALL RIGHT!
WHY DON'T WE GO BACK TO LUTETIA? IT'S DEAD BORING IN THE COUNTRY!
NOBODY ASKED YOUR OPINION, ZAZA!
CHTONG!
SORRY ABOUT THAT. I'M TEACHING MY DOG TO RETRIEVE.
YOU GREAT PIGHEADED FOOL, I TOLD YOU THAT MENHIR WAS TOO BIG!
OF COURSE, NOTHING'S EVER QUITE RIGHT FOR MISTER ASTERIX, IS IT? FIRST MY DOG'S TOO SMALL, THEN MY MENHIR'S TOO BIG!
YOU'LL END UP KILLING SOMEONE WITH THAT MENHIR!
HUH! HEAR THAT? WHOEVER HEARD OF MENHIRS BEING DANGEROUS? MUSHROOMS, YES, BUT MENHIRS... WELL, I ASK YOU!
TH... THEY'RE CRAZY!
7

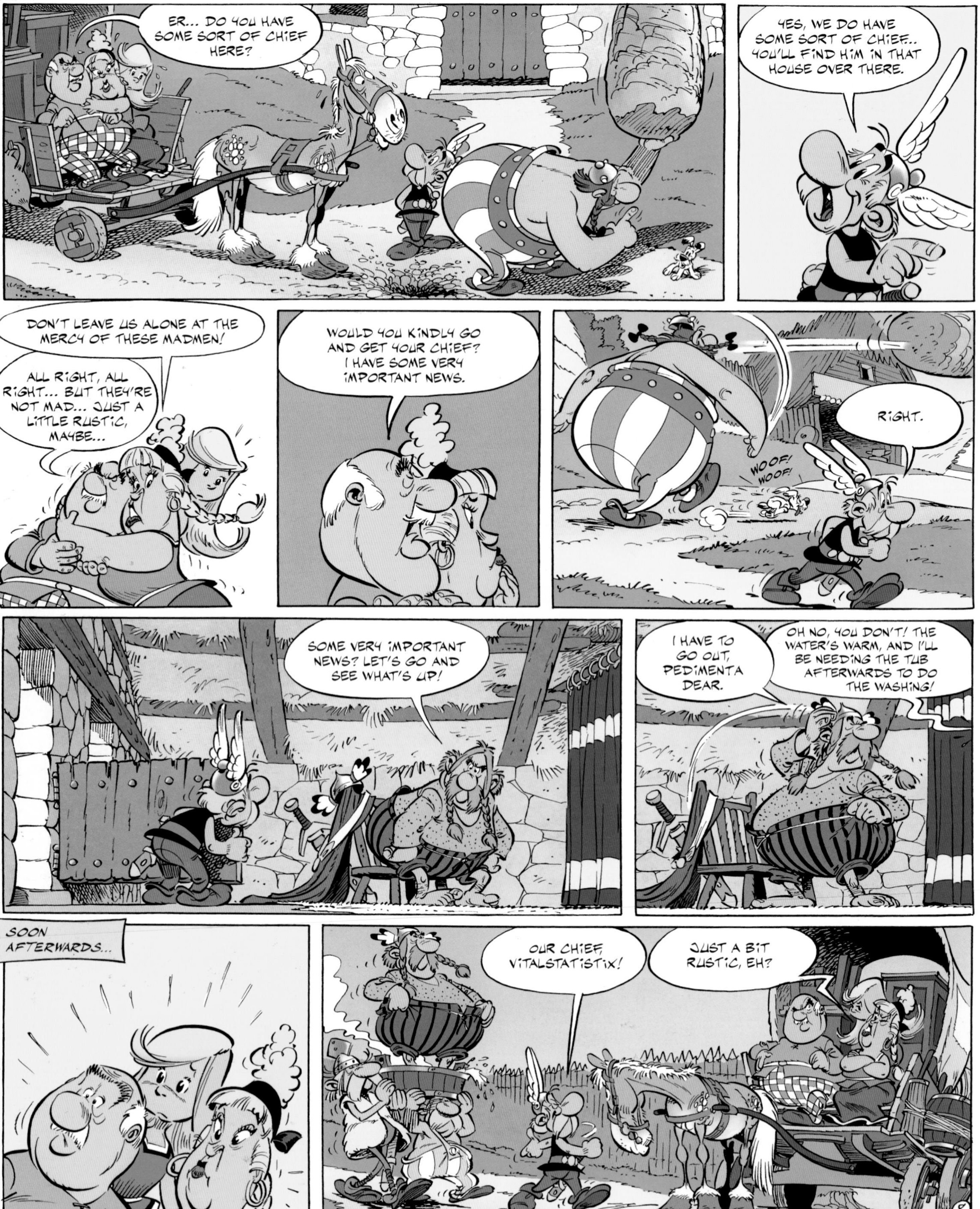
ER... DO YOU HAVE SOME SORT OF CHIEF HERE?
YES, WE DO HAVE SOME SORT OF CHIEF.. YOU'LL FIND HIM IN THAT HOUSE OVER THERE.
DON'T LEAVE US ALONE AT THE MERCY OF THESE MADMEN!
ALL RIGHT, ALL RIGHT... BUT THEY'RE NOT MAD... JUST A LITTLE RUSTIC, MAYBE...
WOULD YOU KINDLY GO AND GET YOUR CHIEF? I HAVE SOME VERY IMPORTANT NEWS.
RIGHT.
WOOF! WOOF!
SOME VERY IMPORTANT NEWS? LET'S GO AND SEE WHAT'S UP!
I HAVE TO GO OUT, PEDIMENTA DEAR.
OH NO, YOU DON'T! THE WATER'S WARM, AND I'LL BE NEEDING THE TUB AFTERWARDS TO DO THE WASHING!
SOON AFTERWARDS...
OUR CHIEF, VITALSTATISTIX!
JUST A BIT RUSTIC, EH?
8

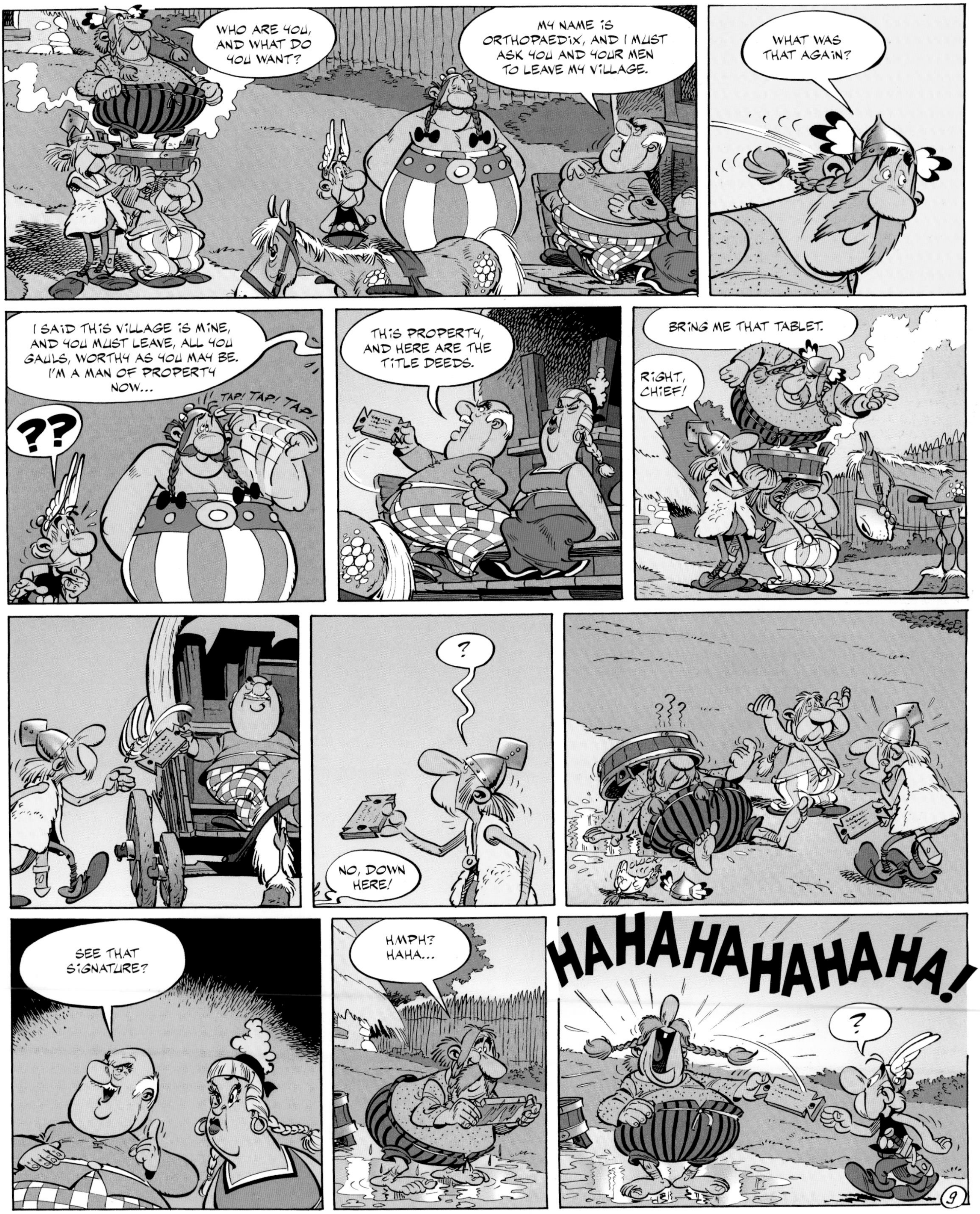
WHO ARE YOU, AND WHAT DO YOU WANT?
MY NAME IS ORTHOPAEDIX, AND I MUST ASK YOU AND YOUR MEN TO LEAVE MY VILLAGE.
WHAT WAS THAT AGAIN?
I SAID THIS VILLAGE IS MINE, AND YOU MUST LEAVE, ALL YOU GAULS, WORTHY AS YOU MAY BE. I'M A MAN OF PROPERTY NOW...
??
TAP! TAP! TAP!
THIS PROPERTY, AND HERE ARE THE TITLE DEEDS.
BRING ME THAT TABLET.
RIGHT, CHIEF!
?
NO, DOWN HERE!
???
CLUCK!
SEE THAT SIGNATURE?
HMPH? HAHA...
HAHAHAHAHAHAHA!
?
9

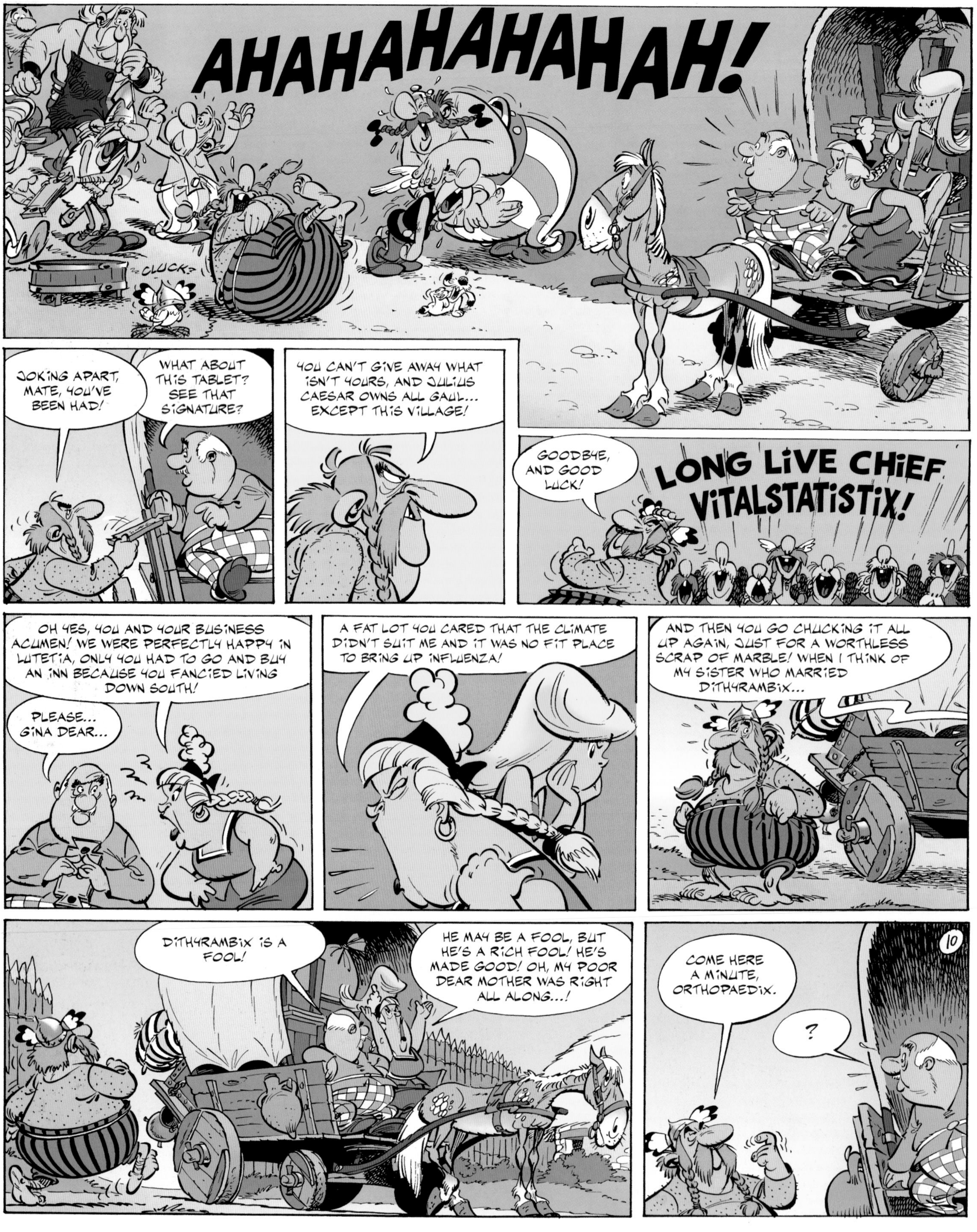
AHAHAHAHAHAHAH!
CLUCK?
JOKING APART, MATE, YOU'VE BEEN HAD!
WHAT ABOUT THIS TABLET? SEE THAT SIGNATURE?
YOU CAN'T GIVE AWAY WHAT ISN'T YOURS, AND JULIUS CAESAR OWNS ALL GAUL... EXCEPT THIS VILLAGE!
GOODBYE, AND GOOD LUCK!
LONG LIVE CHIEF VITALSTATISTIX!
OH YES, YOU AND YOUR BUSINESS ACUMEN! WE WERE PERFECTLY HAPPY IN LUTETIA, ONLY YOU HAD TO GO AND BUY AN INN BECAUSE YOU FANCIED LIVING DOWN SOUTH!
PLEASE... GINA DEAR...
A FAT LOT YOU CARED THAT THE CLIMATE DIDN'T SUIT ME AND IT WAS NO FIT PLACE TO BRING UP INFLUENZA!
AND THEN YOU GO CHUCKING IT ALL UP AGAIN, JUST FOR A WORTHLESS SCRAP OF MARBLE! WHEN I THINK OF MY SISTER WHO MARRIED DITHYRAMBIX...
DITHYRAMBIX IS A FOOL!
HE MAY BE A FOOL, BUT HE'S A RICH FOOL! HE'S MADE GOOD! OH, MY POOR DEAR MOTHER WAS RIGHT ALL ALONG...!
10
COME HERE A MINUTE, ORTHOPAEDIX.
?

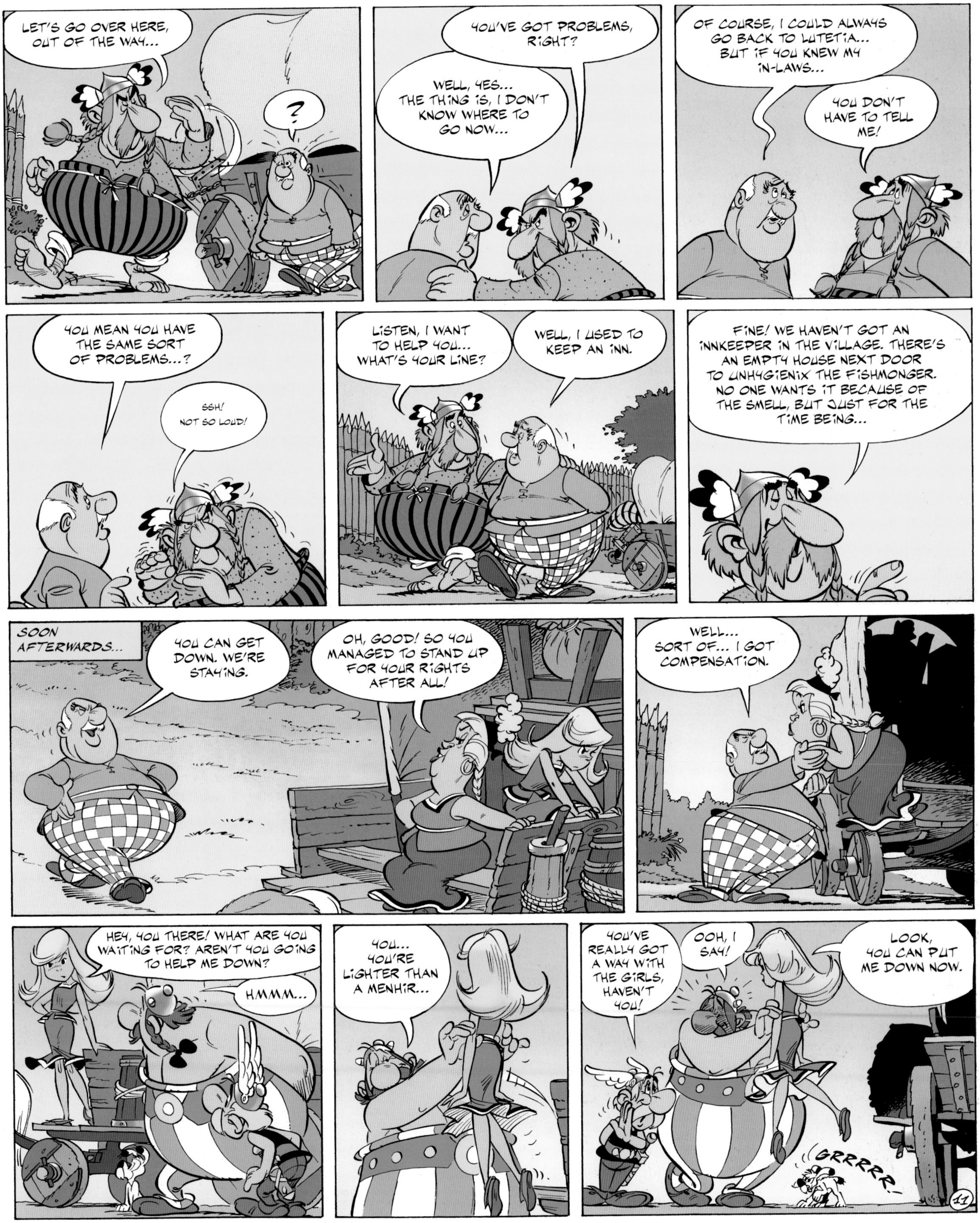
LET'S GO OVER HERE, OUT OF THE WAY...
?
YOU'VE GOT PROBLEMS, RIGHT?
WELL, YES... THE THING IS, I DON'T KNOW WHERE TO GO NOW...
OF COURSE, I COULD ALWAYS GO BACK TO LUTETIA... BUT IF YOU KNEW MY IN-LAWS...
YOU DON'T HAVE TO TELL ME!
YOU MEAN YOU HAVE THE SAME SORT OF PROBLEMS...?
SSH! NOT SO LOUD!
LISTEN, I WANT TO HELP YOU... WHAT'S YOUR LINE?
WELL, I USED TO KEEP AN INN.
FINE! WE HAVEN'T GOT AN INNKEEPER IN THE VILLAGE. THERE'S AN EMPTY HOUSE NEXT DOOR TO UNHYGIENIX THE FISHMONGER. NO ONE WANTS IT BECAUSE OF THE SMELL, BUT JUST FOR THE TIME BEING...
SOON AFTERWARDS...
YOU CAN GET DOWN. WE'RE STAYING.
OH, GOOD! SO YOU MANAGED TO STAND UP FOR YOUR RIGHTS AFTER ALL!
WELL... SORT OF... I GOT COMPENSATION.
HEY, YOU THERE! WHAT ARE YOU WAITING FOR? AREN'T YOU GOING TO HELP ME DOWN?
HMMM...
YOU... YOU'RE LIGHTER THAN A MENHIR...
YOU'VE REALLY GOT A WAY WITH THE GIRLS, HAVEN'T YOU!
OOH, I SAY!
LOOK, YOU CAN PUT ME DOWN NOW.
GRRRRR!
11

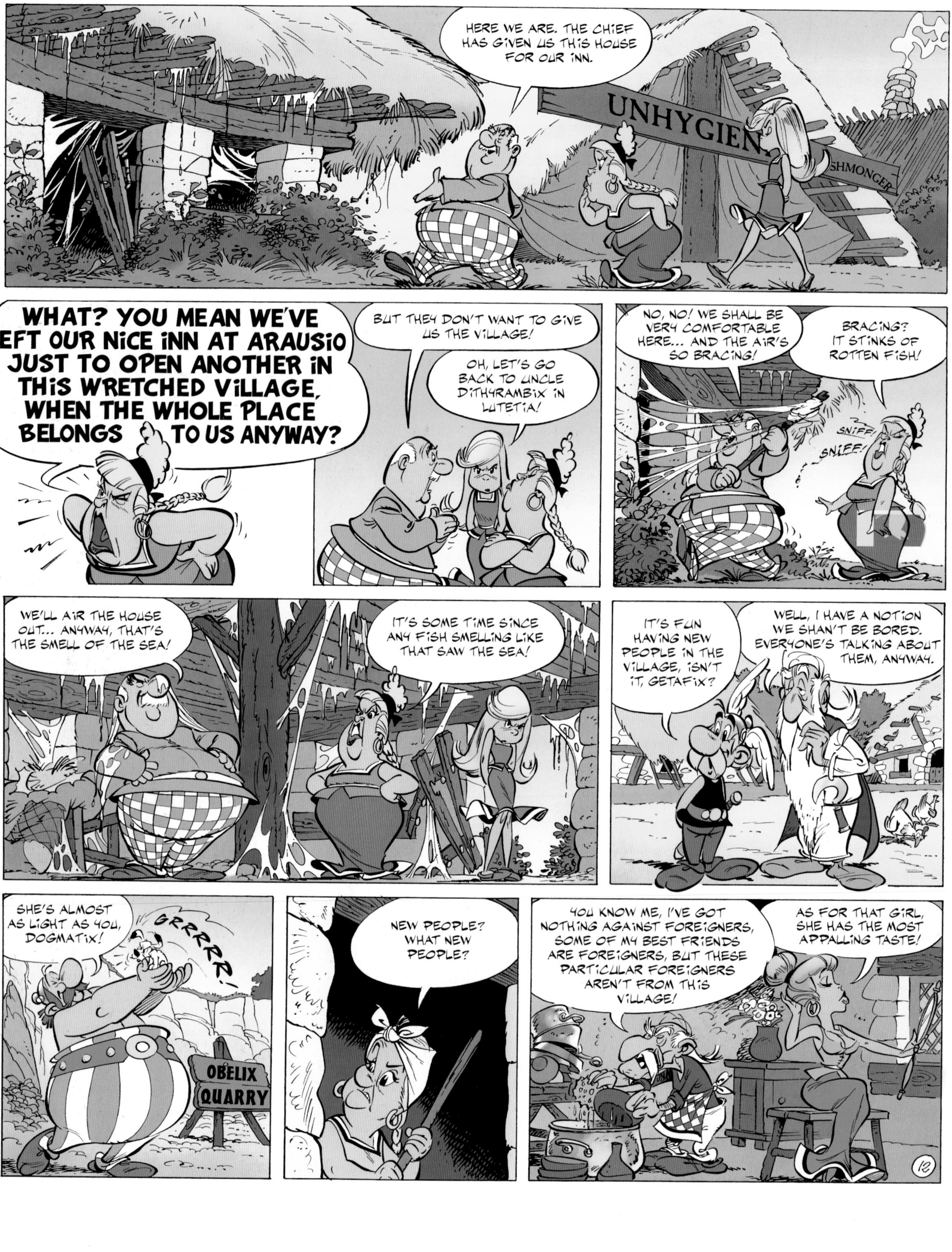

HERE WE ARE. THE CHIEF HAS GIVEN US THIS HOUSE FOR OUR INN.
UNHYGIEN
SHMONGER
WHAT? YOU MEAN WE'VE LEFT OUR NICE INN AT ARAUSIO JUST TO OPEN ANOTHER IN THIS WRETCHED VILLAGE, WHEN THE WHOLE PLACE BELONGS TO US ANYWAY?
BUT THEY DON'T WANT TO GIVE US THE VILLAGE!
OH, LET'S GO BACK TO UNCLE DITHYRAMBIX IN LUTETIA!
NO, NO! WE SHALL BE VERY COMFORTABLE HERE... AND THE AIR'S SO BRACING!
BRACING? IT STINKS OF ROTTEN FISH!
SNIFF!
SNIFF!
WE'LL AIR THE HOUSE OUT... ANYWAY, THAT'S THE SMELL OF THE SEA!
IT'S SOME TIME SINCE ANY FISH SMELLING LIKE THAT SAW THE SEA!
IT'S FUN HAVING NEW PEOPLE IN THE VILLAGE, ISN'T IT, GETAFIX?
WELL, I HAVE A NOTION WE SHAN'T BE BORED. EVERYONE'S TALKING ABOUT THEM, ANYWAY.
SHE'S ALMOST AS LIGHT AS YOU, DOGMATIX!
GRRRRR!
OBELIX QUARRY
NEW PEOPLE? WHAT NEW PEOPLE?
YOU KNOW ME, I'VE GOT NOTHING AGAINST FOREIGNERS, SOME OF MY BEST FRIENDS ARE FOREIGNERS, BUT THESE PARTICULAR FOREIGNERS AREN'T FROM THIS VILLAGE!
AS FOR THAT GIRL, SHE HAS THE MOST APPALLING TASTE!
12

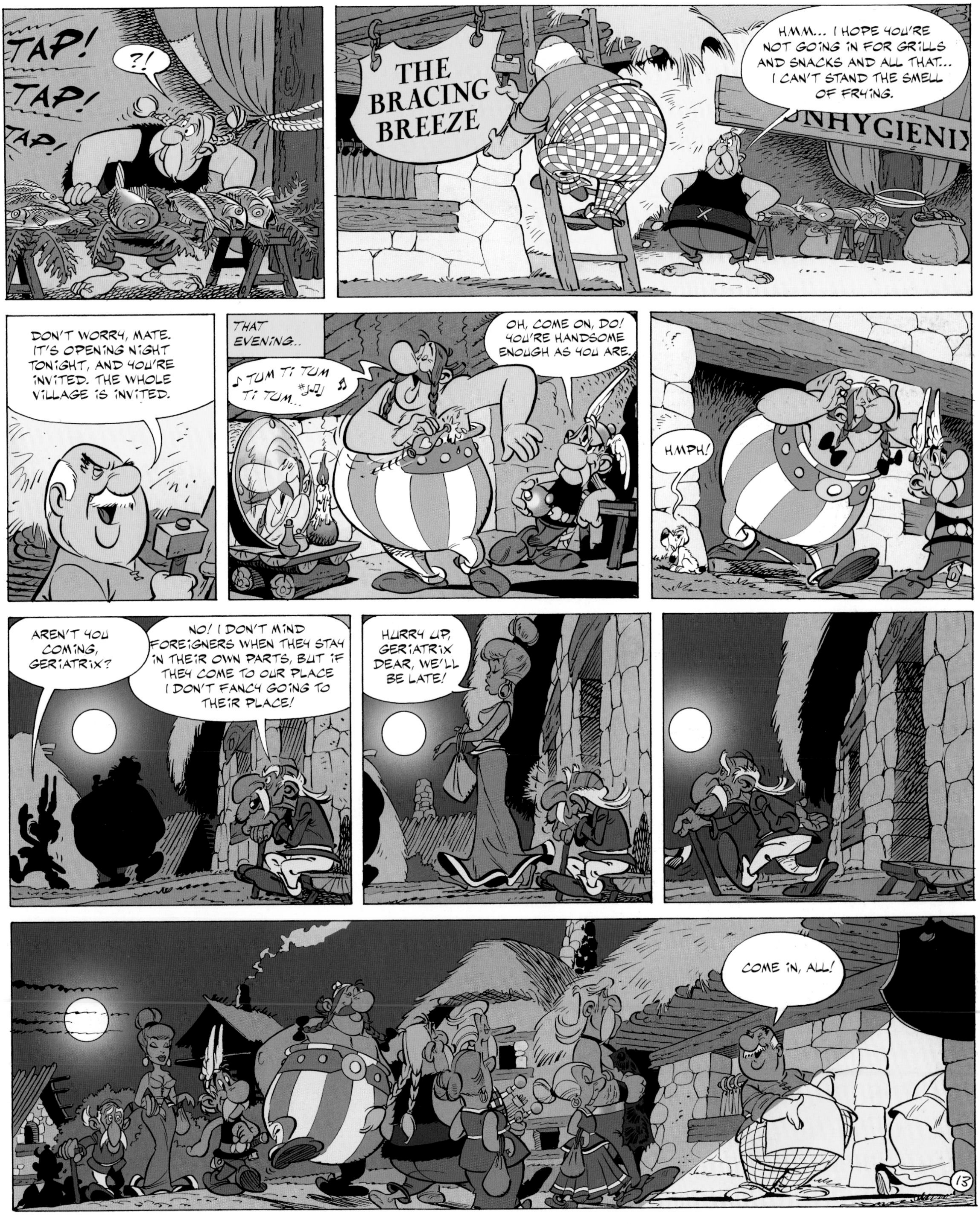
TAP!
TAP!
TAP!
?!
THE BRACING BREEZE
HMM... I HOPE YOU'RE NOT GOING IN FOR GRILLS AND SNACKS AND ALL THAT... I CAN'T STAND THE SMELL OF FRYING.
UNHYGIENIX
DON'T WORRY, MATE. IT'S OPENING NIGHT TONIGHT, AND YOU'RE INVITED. THE WHOLE VILLAGE IS INVITED.
THAT EVENING...
TUM TI TUM TI TUM...
OH, COME ON, DO! YOU'RE HANDSOME ENOUGH AS YOU ARE.
HMPH!
AREN'T YOU COMING, GERIATRIX?
NO! I DON'T MIND FOREIGNERS WHEN THEY STAY IN THEIR OWN PARTS, BUT IF THEY COME TO OUR PLACE I DON'T FANCY GOING TO THEIR PLACE!
HURRY UP, GERIATRIX DEAR, WE'LL BE LATE!
COME IN, ALL!
13

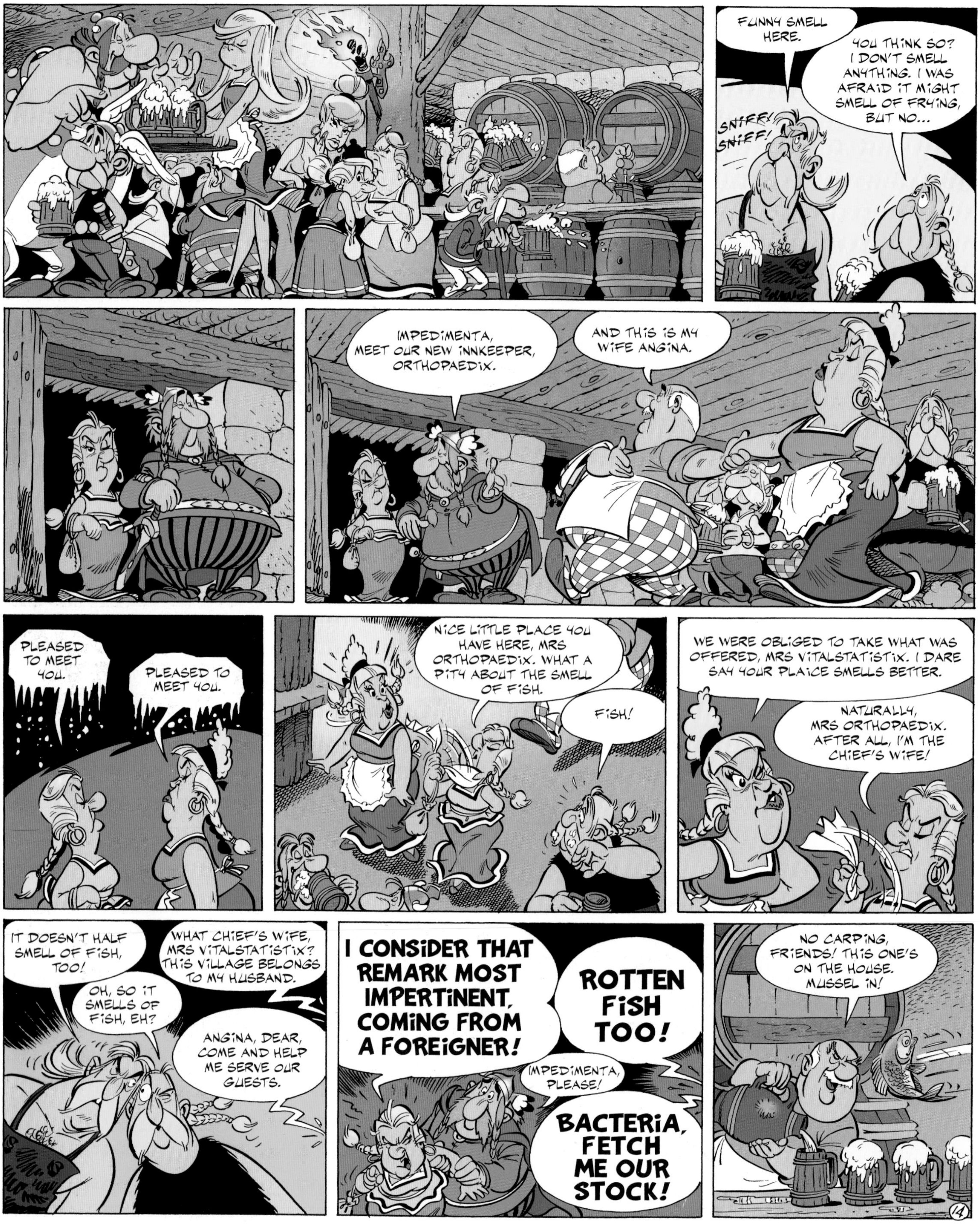

FUNNY SMELL HERE.
SNIFF! SNIFF!
YOU THINK SO? I DON'T SMELL ANYTHING. I WAS AFRAID IT MIGHT SMELL OF FRYING, BUT NO...
IMPEDIMENTA, MEET OUR NEW INNKEEPER, ORTHOPAEDIX.
AND THIS IS MY WIFE ANGINA.
PLEASED TO MEET YOU.
PLEASED TO MEET YOU.
NICE LITTLE PLACE YOU HAVE HERE, MRS ORTHOPAEDIX. WHAT A PITY ABOUT THE SMELL OF FISH.
FISH!
WE WERE OBLIGED TO TAKE WHAT WAS OFFERED, MRS VITALSTATISTIX. I DARE SAY YOUR PLAICE SMELLS BETTER.
NATURALLY, MRS ORTHOPAEDIX. AFTER ALL, I'M THE CHIEF'S WIFE!
IT DOESN'T HALF SMELL OF FISH, TOO!
WHAT CHIEF'S WIFE, MRS VITALSTATISTIX? THIS VILLAGE BELONGS TO MY HUSBAND.
OH, SO IT SMELLS OF FISH, EH?
ANGINA, DEAR, COME AND HELP ME SERVE OUR GUESTS.
I CONSIDER THAT REMARK MOST IMPERTINENT, COMING FROM A FOREIGNER!
ROTTEN FISH TOO!
IMPEDIMENTA, PLEASE!
BACTERIA, FETCH ME OUR STOCK!
NO CARPING, FRIENDS! THIS ONE'S ON THE HOUSE. MUSSEL IN!
14

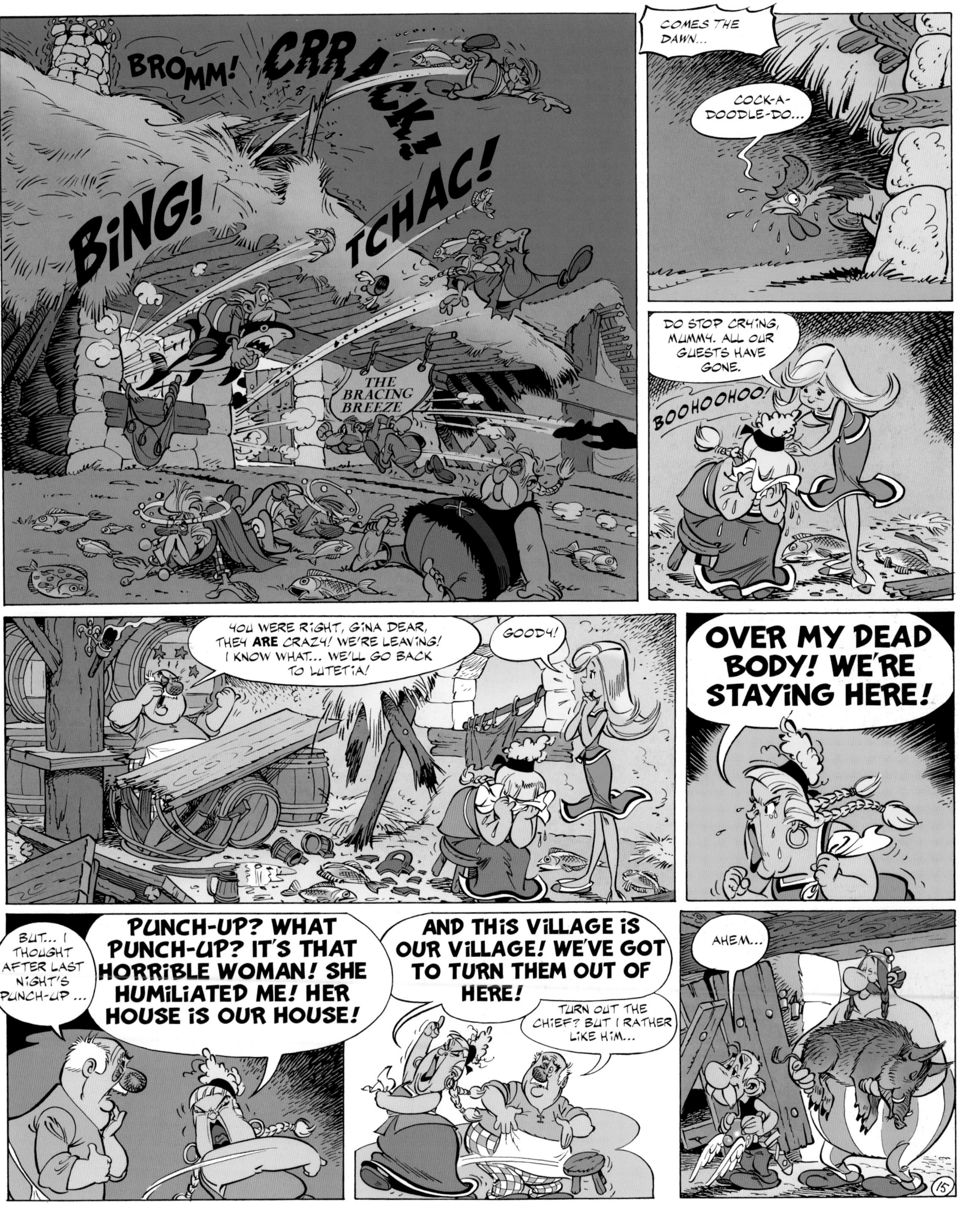

BROMM!
CRRACK!
BING!
TCHAC!
THE BRACING BREEZE
COMES THE DAWN...
COCK-A-DOODLE-DO...
DO STOP CRYING, MUMMY. ALL OUR GUESTS HAVE GONE.
BOOHOOHOO!
YOU WERE RIGHT, GINA DEAR, THEY ARE CRAZY! WE'RE LEAVING! I KNOW WHAT... WE'LL GO BACK TO LUTETIA!
GOODY!
OVER MY DEAD BODY! WE'RE STAYING HERE!
BUT... I THOUGHT AFTER LAST NIGHT'S PUNCH-UP...
PUNCH-UP? WHAT PUNCH-UP? IT'S THAT HORRIBLE WOMAN! SHE HUMILIATED ME! HER HOUSE IS OUR HOUSE!
AND THIS VILLAGE IS OUR VILLAGE! WE'VE GOT TO TURN THEM OUT OF HERE!
TURN OUT THE CHIEF? BUT I RATHER LIKE HIM...
AHEM...
15

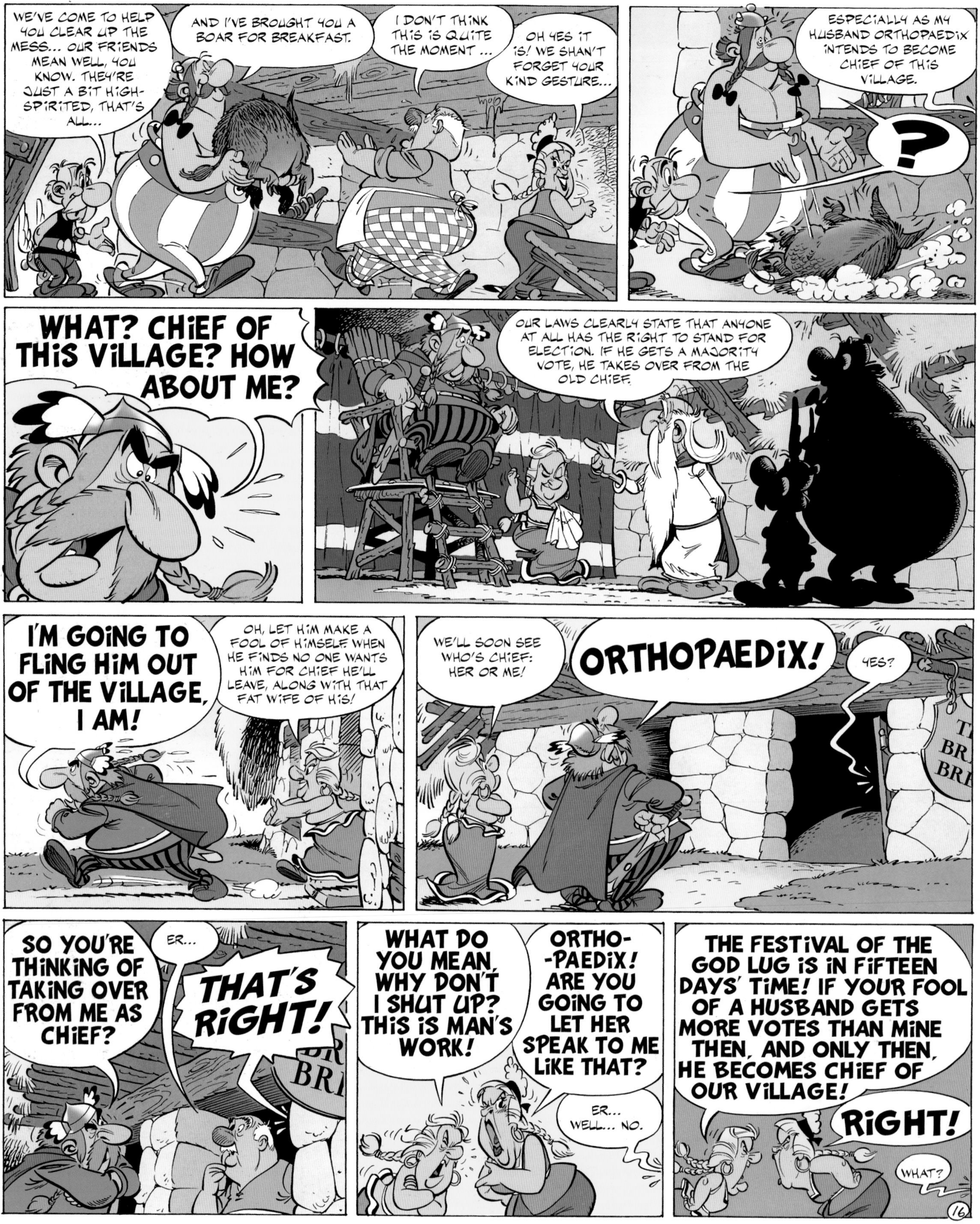
WE'VE COME TO HELP YOU CLEAR UP THE MESS... OUR FRIENDS MEAN WELL, YOU KNOW. THEY'RE JUST A BIT HIGH-SPIRITED, THAT'S ALL...
AND I'VE BROUGHT YOU A BOAR FOR BREAKFAST.
I DON'T THINK THIS IS QUITE THE MOMENT ...
OH YES IT IS! WE SHAN'T FORGET YOUR KIND GESTURE...
ESPECIALLY AS MY HUSBAND ORTHOPAEDIX INTENDS TO BECOME CHIEF OF THIS VILLAGE.
?
WHAT? CHIEF OF THIS VILLAGE? HOW ABOUT ME?
OUR LAWS CLEARLY STATE THAT ANYONE AT ALL HAS THE RIGHT TO STAND FOR ELECTION. IF HE GETS A MAJORITY VOTE, HE TAKES OVER FROM THE OLD CHIEF.
I'M GOING TO FLING HIM OUT OF THE VILLAGE, I AM!
OH, LET HIM MAKE A FOOL OF HIMSELF WHEN HE FINDS NO ONE WANTS HIM FOR CHIEF HE'LL LEAVE, ALONG WITH THAT FAT WIFE OF HIS!
WE'LL SOON SEE WHO'S CHIEF: HER OR ME!
ORTHOPAEDIX!
YES?
SO YOU'RE THINKING OF TAKING OVER FROM ME AS CHIEF?
ER...
THAT'S RIGHT!
WHAT DO YOU MEAN, WHY DON'T I SHUT UP? THIS IS MAN'S WORK!
ORTHO- -PAEDIX! ARE YOU GOING TO LET HER SPEAK TO ME LIKE THAT?
ER... WELL... NO.
THE FESTIVAL OF THE GOD LUG IS IN FIFTEEN DAYS' TIME! IF YOUR FOOL OF A HUSBAND GETS MORE VOTES THAN MINE THEN, AND ONLY THEN, HE BECOMES CHIEF OF OUR VILLAGE!
RIGHT!
WHAT?
16

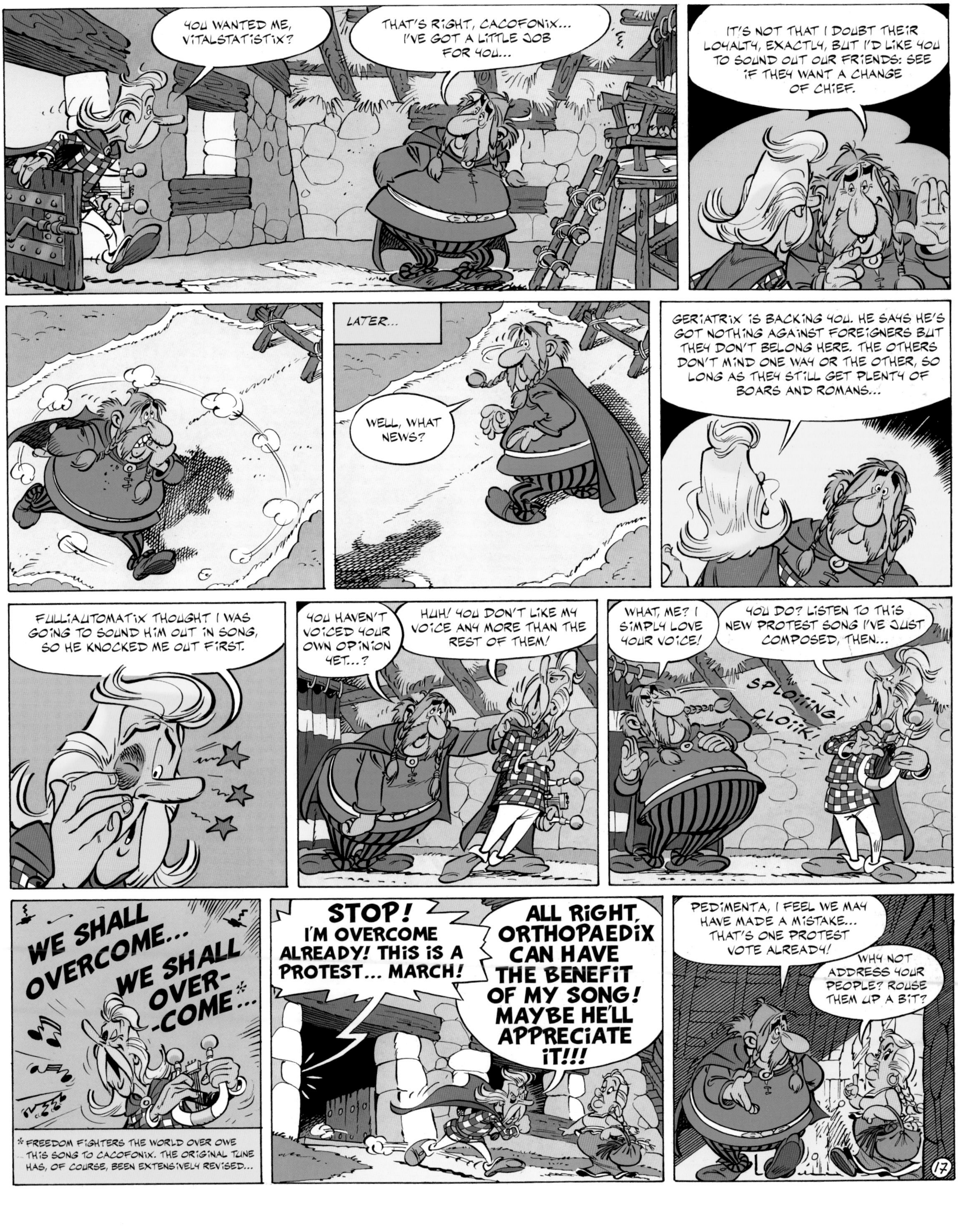
YOU WANTED ME, VITALSTATISTIX?
THAT'S RIGHT, CACOFONIX... I'VE GOT A LITTLE JOB FOR YOU...
IT'S NOT THAT I DOUBT THEIR LOYALTY, EXACTLY, BUT I'D LIKE YOU TO SOUND OUT OUR FRIENDS: SEE IF THEY WANT A CHANGE OF CHIEF.
LATER...
WELL, WHAT NEWS?
GERIATRIX IS BACKING YOU. HE SAYS HE'S GOT NOTHING AGAINST FOREIGNERS BUT THEY DON'T BELONG HERE. THE OTHERS DON'T MIND ONE WAY OR THE OTHER, SO LONG AS THEY STILL GET PLENTY OF BOARS AND ROMANS...
FULLIAUTOMATIX THOUGHT I WAS GOING TO SOUND HIM OUT IN SONG, SO HE KNOCKED ME OUT FIRST.
YOU HAVEN'T VOICED YOUR OWN OPINION YET...?
HUH! YOU DON'T LIKE MY VOICE ANY MORE THAN THE REST OF THEM!
WHAT, ME? I SIMPLY LOVE YOUR VOICE!
YOU DO? LISTEN TO THIS NEW PROTEST SONG I'VE JUST COMPOSED, THEN...
SPLOIIING!
CLOIIK!
WE SHALL OVERCOME... WE SHALL OVER-COME*...
* FREEDOM FIGHTERS THE WORLD OVER OWE THIS SONG TO CACOFONIX. THE ORIGINAL TUNE HAS, OF COURSE, BEEN EXTENSIVELY REVISED...
STOP! I'M OVERCOME ALREADY! THIS IS A PROTEST... MARCH!
ALL RIGHT, ORTHOPAEDIX CAN HAVE THE BENEFIT OF MY SONG! MAYBE HE'LL APPRECIATE IT!!!
PEDIMENTA, I FEEL WE MAY HAVE MADE A MISTAKE... THAT'S ONE PROTEST VOTE ALREADY!
WHY NOT ADDRESS YOUR PEOPLE? ROUSE THEM UP A BIT?
17

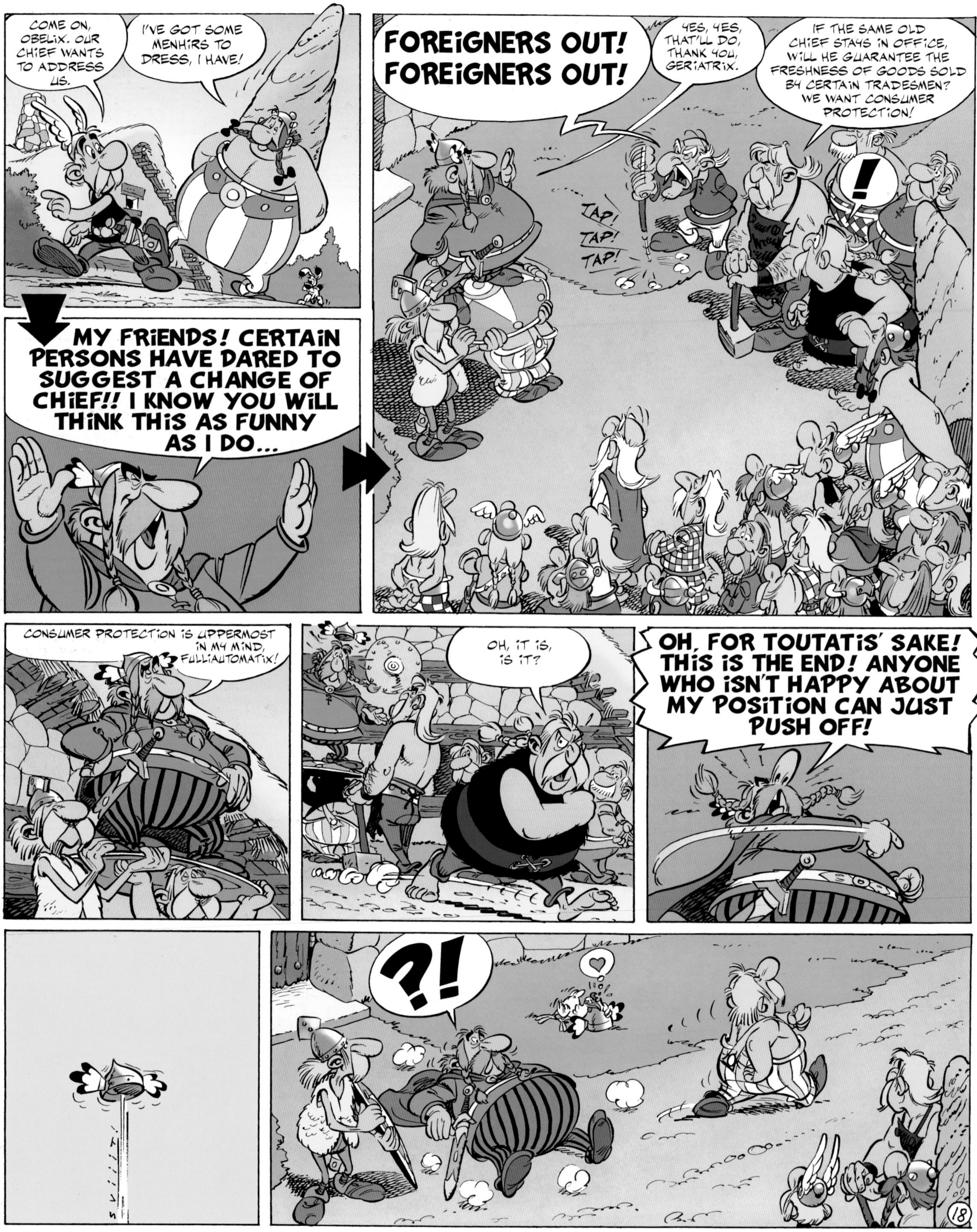
COME ON, OBELIX. OUR CHIEF WANTS TO ADDRESS US.
I'VE GOT SOME MENHIRS TO DRESS, I HAVE!
FOREIGNERS OUT! FOREIGNERS OUT!
YES, YES, THAT'LL DO, THANK YOU, GERIATRIX.
IF THE SAME OLD CHIEF STAYS IN OFFICE, WILL HE GUARANTEE THE FRESHNESS OF GOODS SOLD BY CERTAIN TRADESMEN? WE WANT CONSUMER PROTECTION!
!
TAP! TAP! TAP!
MY FRIENDS! CERTAIN PERSONS HAVE DARED TO SUGGEST A CHANGE OF CHIEF!! I KNOW YOU WILL THINK THIS AS FUNNY AS I DO...
CONSUMER PROTECTION IS UPPERMOST IN MY MIND, FULLIAUTOMATIX!
OH, IT IS, IS IT?
OH, FOR TOUTATIS' SAKE! THIS IS THE END! ANYONE WHO ISN'T HAPPY ABOUT MY POSITION CAN JUST PUSH OFF!
?!
18

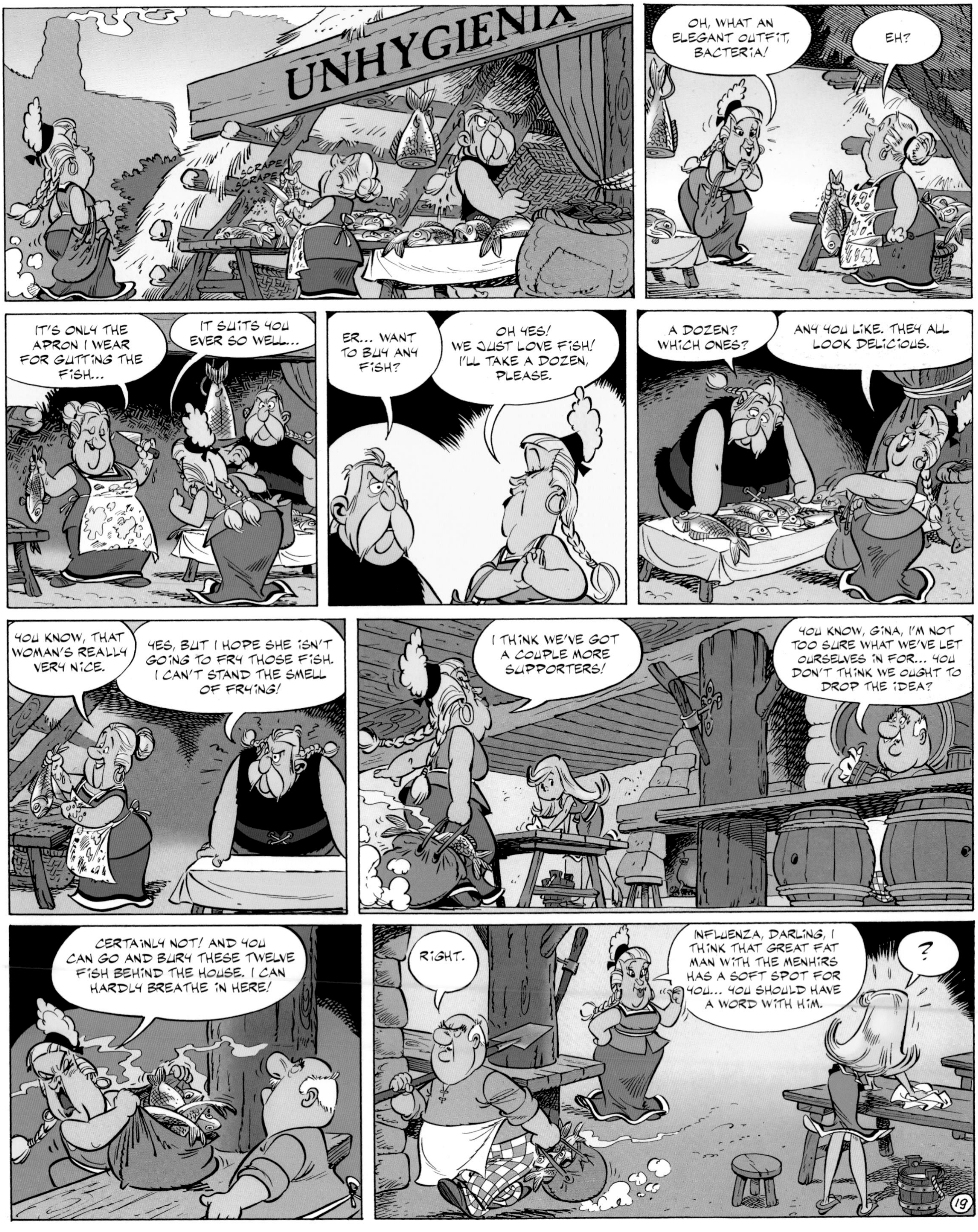
UNHYGIENIX
SCRAPE! SCRAPE!
OH, WHAT AN ELEGANT OUTFIT, BACTERIA!
EH?
IT'S ONLY THE APRON I WEAR FOR GUTTING THE FISH...
IT SUITS YOU EVER SO WELL...
ER... WANT TO BUY ANY FISH?
OH YES! WE JUST LOVE FISH! I'LL TAKE A DOZEN, PLEASE.
A DOZEN? WHICH ONES?
ANY YOU LIKE. THEY ALL LOOK DELICIOUS.
YOU KNOW, THAT WOMAN'S REALLY VERY NICE.
YES, BUT I HOPE SHE ISN'T GOING TO FRY THOSE FISH. I CAN'T STAND THE SMELL OF FRYING!
I THINK WE'VE GOT A COUPLE MORE SUPPORTERS!
YOU KNOW, GINA, I'M NOT TOO SURE WHAT WE'VE LET OURSELVES IN FOR... YOU DON'T THINK WE OUGHT TO DROP THE IDEA?
CERTAINLY NOT! AND YOU CAN GO AND BURY THESE TWELVE FISH BEHIND THE HOUSE. I CAN HARDLY BREATHE IN HERE!
RIGHT.
INFLUENZA, DARLING, I THINK THAT GREAT FAT MAN WITH THE MENHIRS HAS A SOFT SPOT FOR YOU... YOU SHOULD HAVE A WORD WITH HIM.
?
19

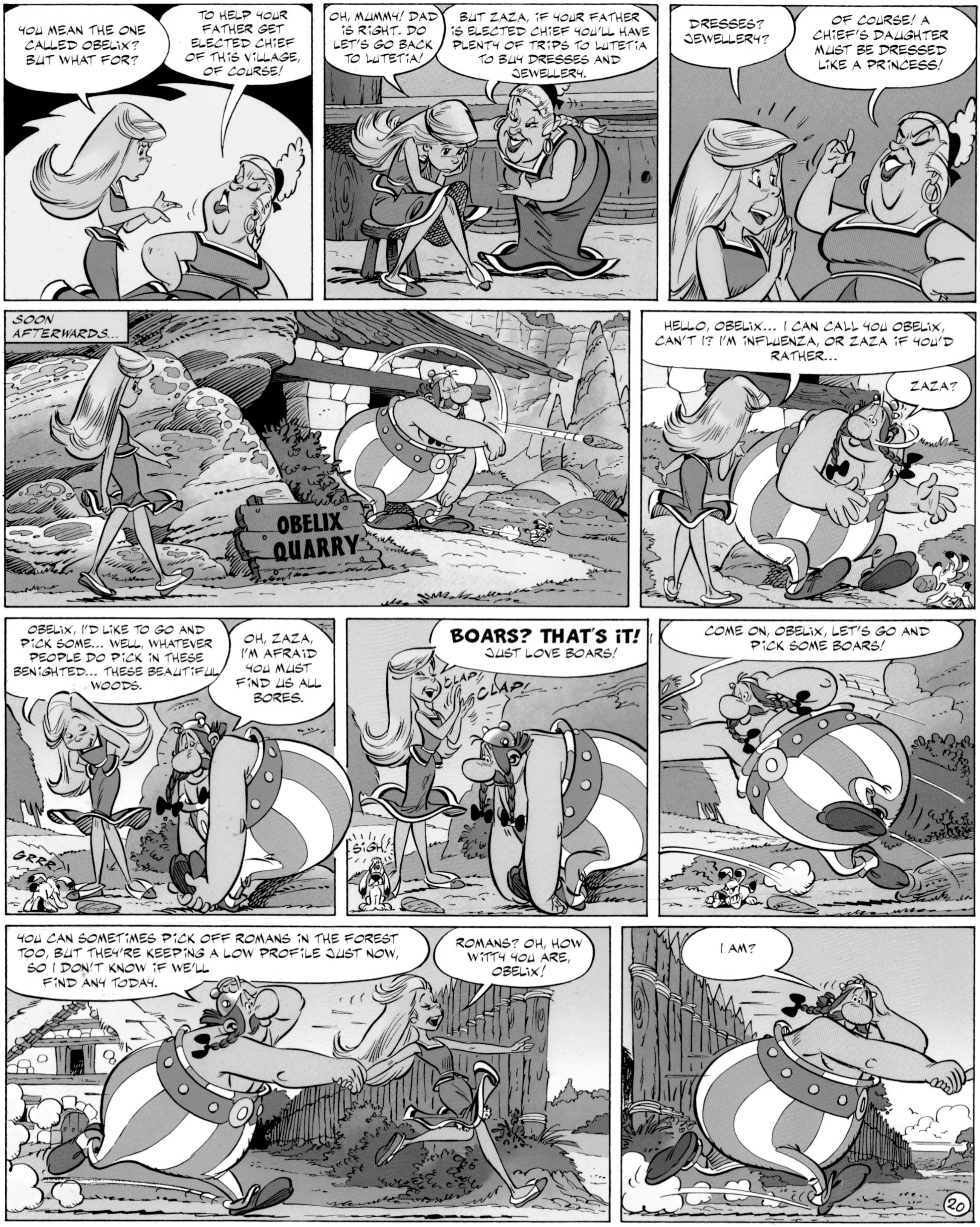
YOU MEAN THE ONE CALLED OBELIX? BUT WHAT FOR?
TO HELP YOUR FATHER GET ELECTED CHIEF OF THIS VILLAGE, OF COURSE!
OH, MUMMY! DAD IS RIGHT. DO LET'S GO BACK TO LUTETIA!
BUT ZAZA, IF YOUR FATHER IS ELECTED CHIEF YOU'LL HAVE PLENTY OF TRIPS TO LUTETIA TO BUY DRESSES AND JEWELLERY.
DRESSES? JEWELLERY?
OF COURSE! A CHIEF'S DAUGHTER MUST BE DRESSED LIKE A PRINCESS!
SOON AFTERWARDS...
OBELIX QUARRY
HELLO, OBELIX... I CAN CALL YOU OBELIX, CAN'T I? I'M INFLUENZA, OR ZAZA IF YOU'D RATHER...
ZAZA?
OBELIX, I'D LIKE TO GO AND PICK SOME... WELL, WHATEVER PEOPLE DO PICK IN THESE BENIGHTED... THESE BEAUTIFUL WOODS.
OH, ZAZA, I'M AFRAID YOU MUST FIND US ALL BORES.
GRRR
BOARS? THAT'S IT! JUST LOVE BOARS!
CLAP! CLAP!
SIGH!
COME ON, OBELIX, LET'S GO AND PICK SOME BOARS!
YOU CAN SOMETIMES PICK OFF ROMANS IN THE FOREST TOO, BUT THEY'RE KEEPING A LOW PROFILE JUST NOW, SO I DON'T KNOW IF WE'LL FIND ANY TODAY.
ROMANS? OH, HOW WITTY YOU ARE, OBELIX!
I AM?
20

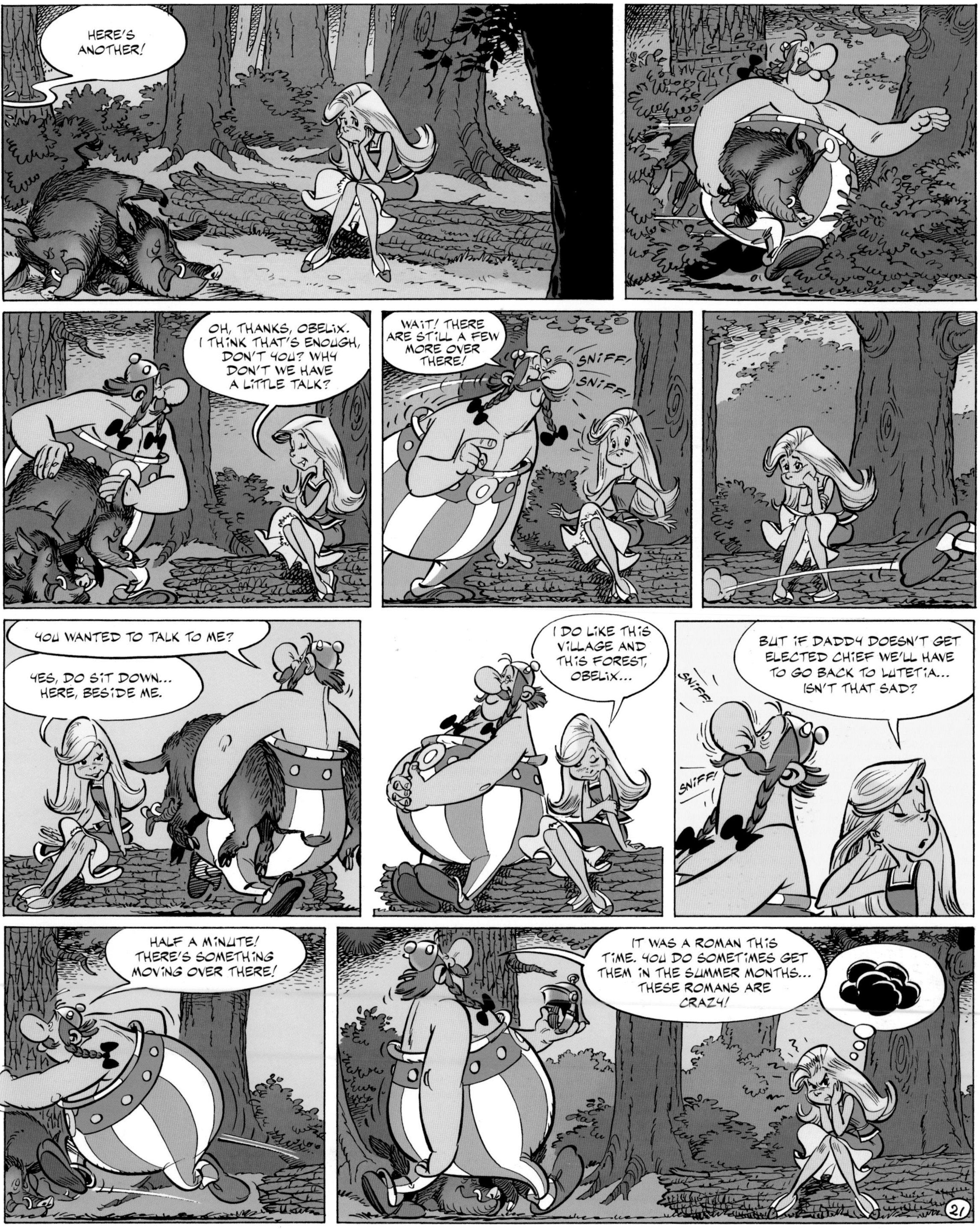
HERE'S ANOTHER!
OH, THANKS, OBELIX. I THINK THAT'S ENOUGH, DON'T YOU? WHY DON'T WE HAVE A LITTLE TALK?
WAIT! THERE ARE STILL A FEW MORE OVER THERE!
SNIFF! SNIFF!
YOU WANTED TO TALK TO ME?
YES, DO SIT DOWN... HERE, BESIDE ME.
I DO LIKE THIS VILLAGE AND THIS FOREST, OBELIX...
BUT IF DADDY DOESN'T GET ELECTED CHIEF WE'LL HAVE TO GO BACK TO LUTETIA... ISN'T THAT SAD?
SNIFF! SNIFF!
HALF A MINUTE! THERE'S SOMETHING MOVING OVER THERE!
IT WAS A ROMAN THIS TIME. YOU DO SOMETIMES GET THEM IN THE SUMMER MONTHS... THESE ROMANS ARE CRAZY!
21

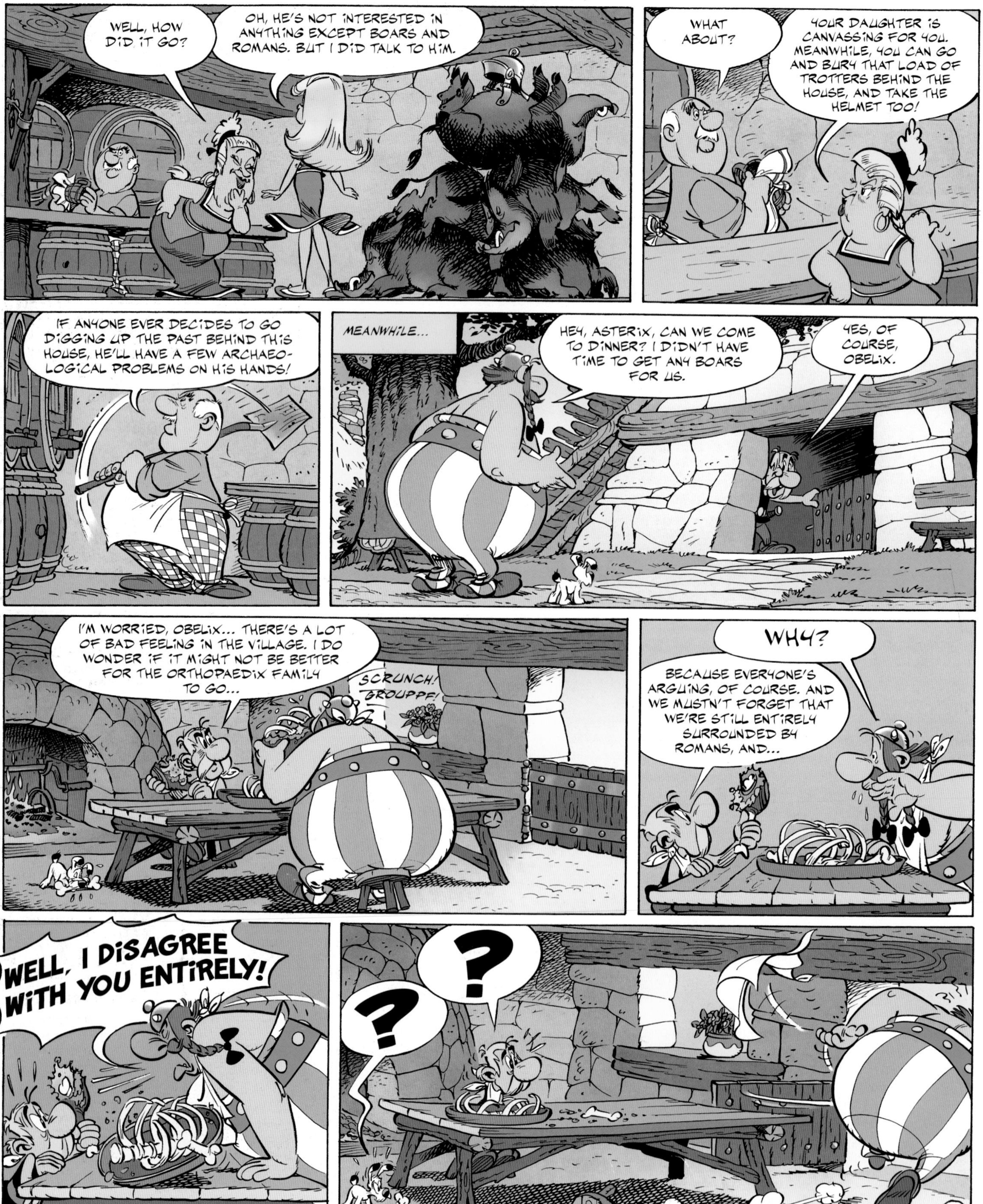

WELL, HOW DID IT GO?
OH, HE'S NOT INTERESTED IN ANYTHING EXCEPT BOARS AND ROMANS. BUT I DID TALK TO HIM.
WHAT ABOUT?
YOUR DAUGHTER IS CANVASSING FOR YOU. MEANWHILE, YOU CAN GO AND BURY THAT LOAD OF TROTTERS BEHIND THE HOUSE, AND TAKE THE HELMET TOO!
IF ANYONE EVER DECIDES TO GO DIGGING UP THE PAST BEHIND THIS HOUSE, HE'LL HAVE A FEW ARCHAEOLOGICAL PROBLEMS ON HIS HANDS!
MEANWHILE...
HEY, ASTERIX, CAN WE COME TO DINNER? I DIDN'T HAVE TIME TO GET ANY BOARS FOR US.
YES, OF COURSE, OBELIX.
I'M WORRIED, OBELIX... THERE'S A LOT OF BAD FEELING IN THE VILLAGE. I DO WONDER IF IT MIGHT NOT BE BETTER FOR THE ORTHOPAEDIX FAMILY TO GO...
SCRUNCH! GROUPPF!
WHY?
BECAUSE EVERYONE'S ARGUING, OF COURSE. AND WE MUSTN'T FORGET THAT WE'RE STILL ENTIRELY SURROUNDED BY ROMANS, AND...
WELL, I DISAGREE WITH YOU ENTIRELY!
?
?
22

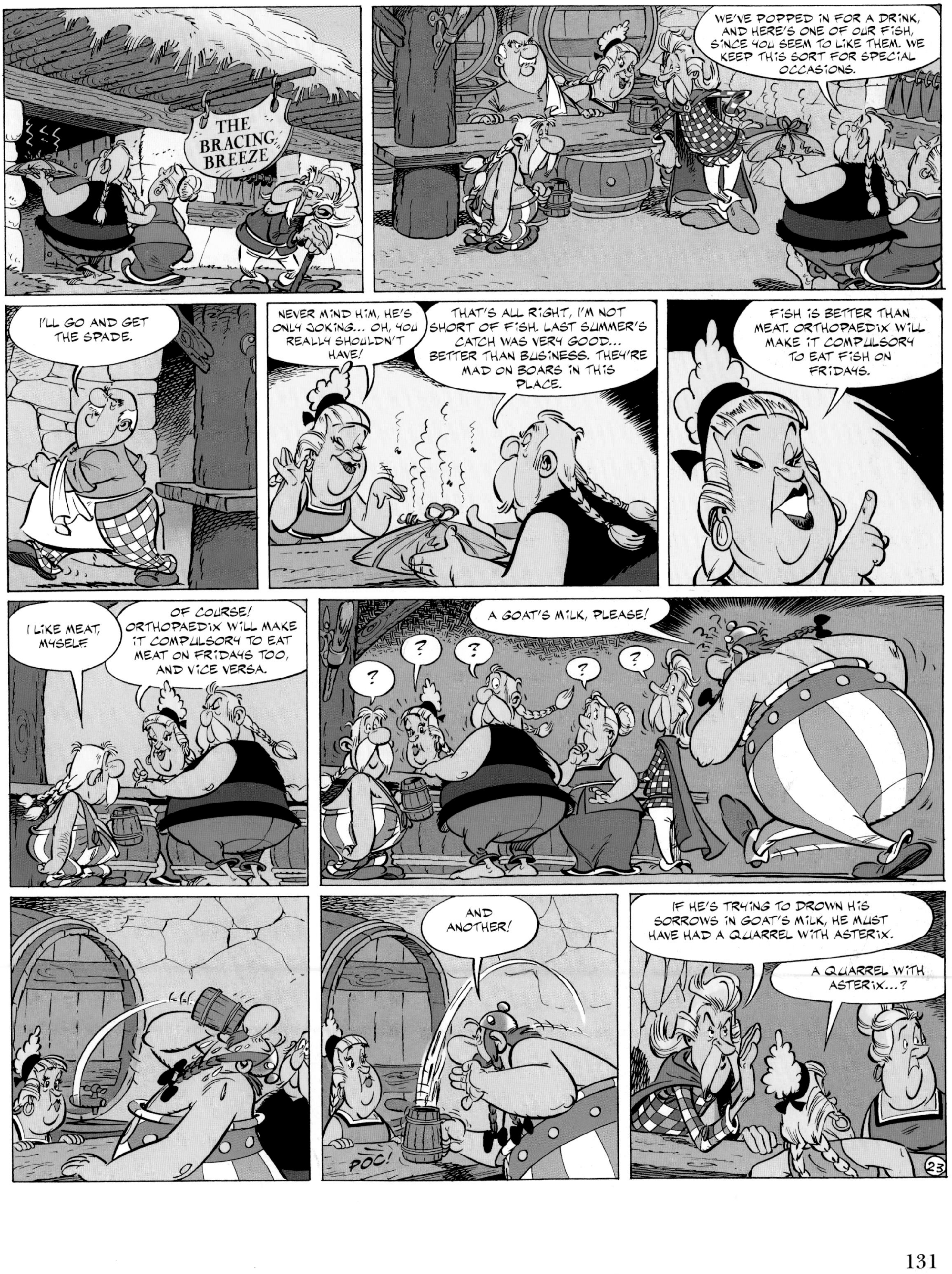
THE BRACING BREEZE
WE'VE POPPED IN FOR A DRINK, AND HERE'S ONE OF OUR FISH, SINCE YOU SEEM TO LIKE THEM. WE KEEP THIS SORT FOR SPECIAL OCCASIONS.
I'LL GO AND GET THE SPADE.
NEVER MIND HIM, HE'S ONLY JOKING... OH, YOU REALLY SHOULDN'T HAVE!
THAT'S ALL RIGHT, I'M NOT SHORT OF FISH. LAST SUMMER'S CATCH WAS VERY GOOD... BETTER THAN BUSINESS. THEY'RE MAD ON BOARS IN THIS PLACE.
FISH IS BETTER THAN MEAT. ORTHOPAEDIX WILL MAKE IT COMPULSORY TO EAT FISH ON FRIDAYS.
I LIKE MEAT, MYSELF.
OF COURSE! ORTHOPAEDIX WILL MAKE IT COMPULSORY TO EAT MEAT ON FRIDAYS TOO, AND VICE VERSA.
A GOAT'S MILK, PLEASE!
?
?
?
?
?
AND ANOTHER!
POC!
IF HE'S TRYING TO DROWN HIS SORROWS IN GOAT'S MILK, HE MUST HAVE HAD A QUARREL WITH ASTERIX.
A QUARREL WITH ASTERIX...?
23

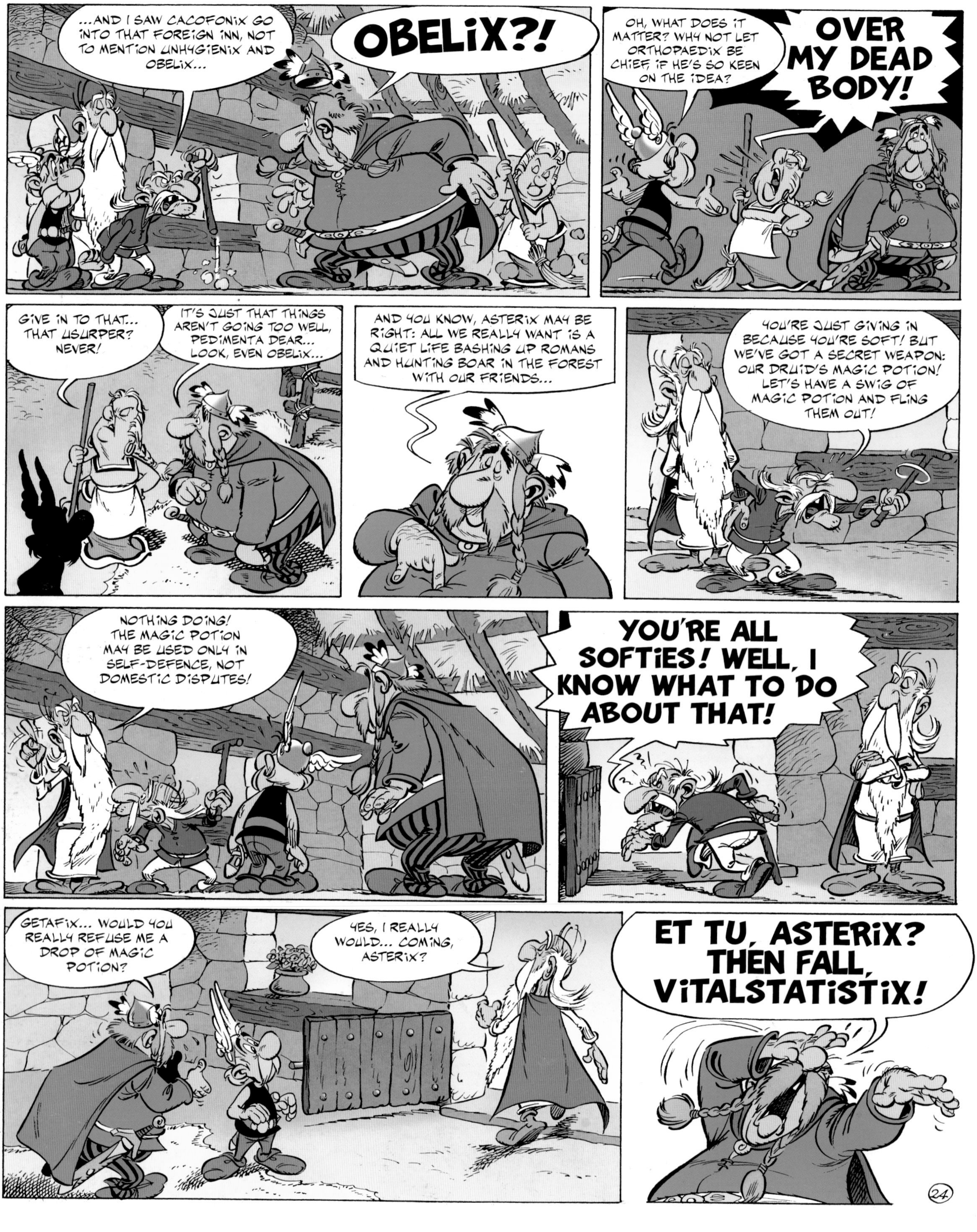
...AND I SAW CACOFONIX GO INTO THAT FOREIGN INN, NOT TO MENTION UNHYGIENIX AND OBELIX...
OBELIX?!
OH, WHAT DOES IT MATTER? WHY NOT LET ORTHOPAEDIX BE CHIEF, IF HE'S SO KEEN ON THE IDEA?
OVER MY DEAD BODY!
GIVE IN TO THAT... THAT USURPER? NEVER!
IT'S JUST THAT THINGS AREN'T GOING TOO WELL, PEDIMENTA DEAR... LOOK, EVEN OBELIX...
AND YOU KNOW, ASTERIX MAY BE RIGHT: ALL WE REALLY WANT IS A QUIET LIFE BASHING UP ROMANS AND HUNTING BOAR IN THE FOREST WITH OUR FRIENDS...
YOU'RE JUST GIVING IN BECAUSE YOU'RE SOFT! BUT WE'VE GOT A SECRET WEAPON: OUR DRUID'S MAGIC POTION! LET'S HAVE A SWIG OF MAGIC POTION AND FLING THEM OUT!
NOTHING DOING! THE MAGIC POTION MAY BE USED ONLY IN SELF-DEFENCE, NOT DOMESTIC DISPUTES!
YOU'RE ALL SOFTIES! WELL, I KNOW WHAT TO DO ABOUT THAT!
GETAFIX... WOULD YOU REALLY REFUSE ME A DROP OF MAGIC POTION?
YES, I REALLY WOULD... COMING, ASTERIX?
ET TU, ASTERIX? THEN FALL, VITALSTATISTIX!
24

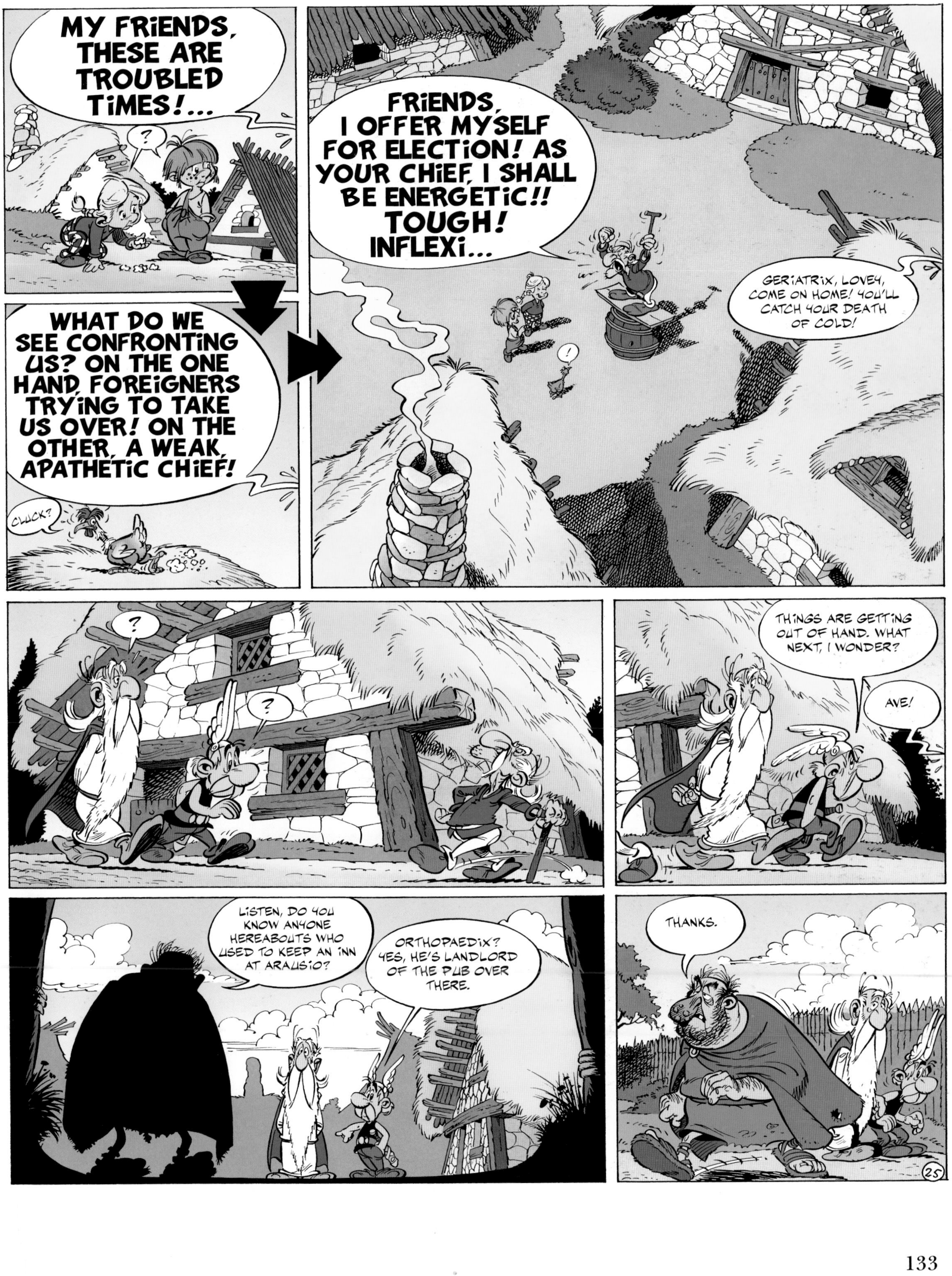
MY FRIENDS, THESE ARE TROUBLED TIMES!...
?
WHAT DO WE SEE CONFRONTING US? ON THE ONE HAND, FOREIGNERS TRYING TO TAKE US OVER! ON THE OTHER, A WEAK, APATHETIC CHIEF!
CLUCK?
FRIENDS, I OFFER MYSELF FOR ELECTION! AS YOUR CHIEF, I SHALL BE ENERGETIC!! TOUGH! INFLEXI...
!
GERIATRIX, LOVEY, COME ON HOME! YOU'LL CATCH YOUR DEATH OF COLD!
?
?
THINGS ARE GETTING OUT OF HAND. WHAT NEXT, I WONDER?
AVE!
LISTEN, DO YOU KNOW ANYONE HEREABOUTS WHO USED TO KEEP AN INN AT ARAUSIO?
ORTHOPAEDIX? YES, HE'S LANDLORD OF THE PUB OVER THERE.
THANKS.
25

THE BRACING BREEZE

AVE, ALL!

IT'S THE MAN WHO SOLD ME THE VILLAGE!

'SRIGHT. TREMENSDELIRIUS, AT YOUR SERVICE!

WH...WHAT DO YOU WANT?

A DRINK, FOR A START!

WE ONLY HAVE GOAT'S MILK.

BANG!

AH, SO THAT'S WHY YOU LOOK SO GLUM... BUT I CAN CHANGE ALL THAT.

OH? AND HOW, MAY I ASK?

WELL, I HAVEN'T HAD MUCH LUCK SINCE WE LAST MET... I'VE TRIED ALL SORTS OF JOBS... I EVEN SIGNED ON AS A PIRATE, ONLY UNFORTUNATELY THE PIRATE SHIP GOT SUNK...

NOW I WANT MY VILLAGE BACK, CAESAR GAVE IT TO ME!

BUT YOU SOLD IT TO ME!

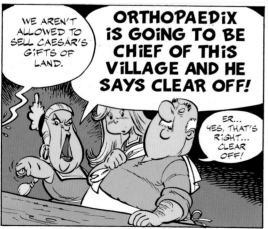

WE AREN'T ALLOWED TO SELL CAESAR'S GIFTS OF LAND.

ORTHOPAEDIX IS GOING TO BE CHIEF OF THIS VILLAGE AND HE SAYS CLEAR OFF!

ER... YES, THAT'S RIGHT... CLEAR OFF!

LOOK HERE, YOU... SEE THIS LITTLE MEMENTO OF MY ARMY SERVICE?

EEEEEK!

26

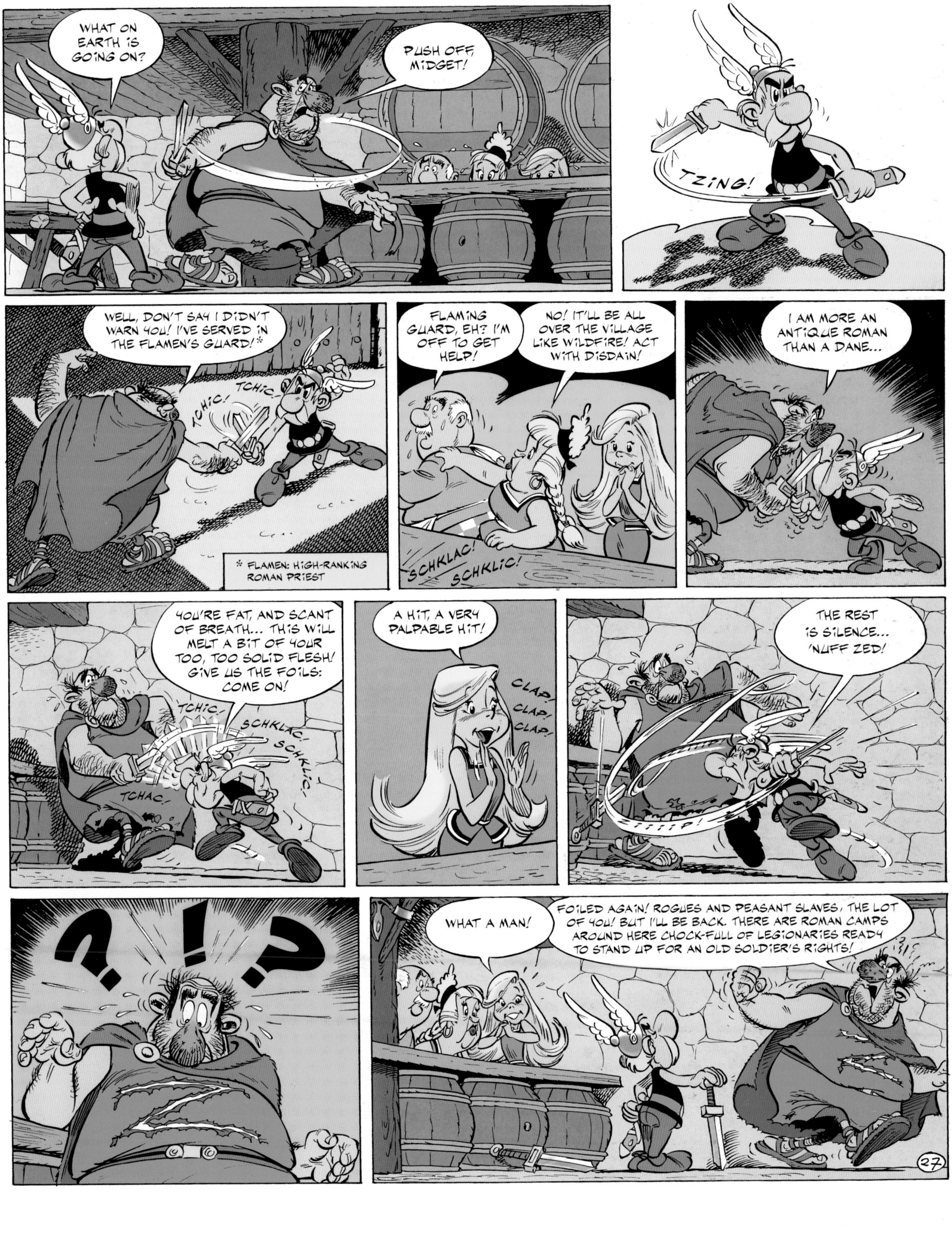
WHAT ON EARTH IS GOING ON?
PUSH OFF, MIDGET!
TZING!
WELL, DON'T SAY I DIDN'T WARN YOU! I'VE SERVED IN THE FLAMEN'S GUARD!*
TCHIC
TCHIC!
* FLAMEN: HIGH-RANKING ROMAN PRIEST
FLAMING GUARD, EH? I'M OFF TO GET HELP!
NO! IT'LL BE ALL OVER THE VILLAGE LIKE WILDFIRE! ACT WITH DISDAIN!
SCHKLAC!
SCHKLIC!
I AM MORE AN ANTIQUE ROMAN THAN A DANE...
YOU'RE FAT, AND SCANT OF BREATH... THIS WILL MELT A BIT OF YOUR TOO, TOO SOLID FLESH! GIVE US THE FOILS: COME ON!
TCHIC!
SCHKLAC!
SCHKLIC!
TCHAC!
A HIT, A VERY PALPABLE HIT!
CLAP! CLAP! CLAP!
THE REST IS SILENCE... 'NUFF ZED!
ZIIIIIP!
?!?
WHAT A MAN!
FOILED AGAIN! ROGUES AND PEASANT SLAVES, THE LOT OF YOU! BUT I'LL BE BACK. THERE ARE ROMAN CAMPS AROUND HERE CHOCK-FULL OF LEGIONARIES READY TO STAND UP FOR AN OLD SOLDIER'S RIGHTS!
27

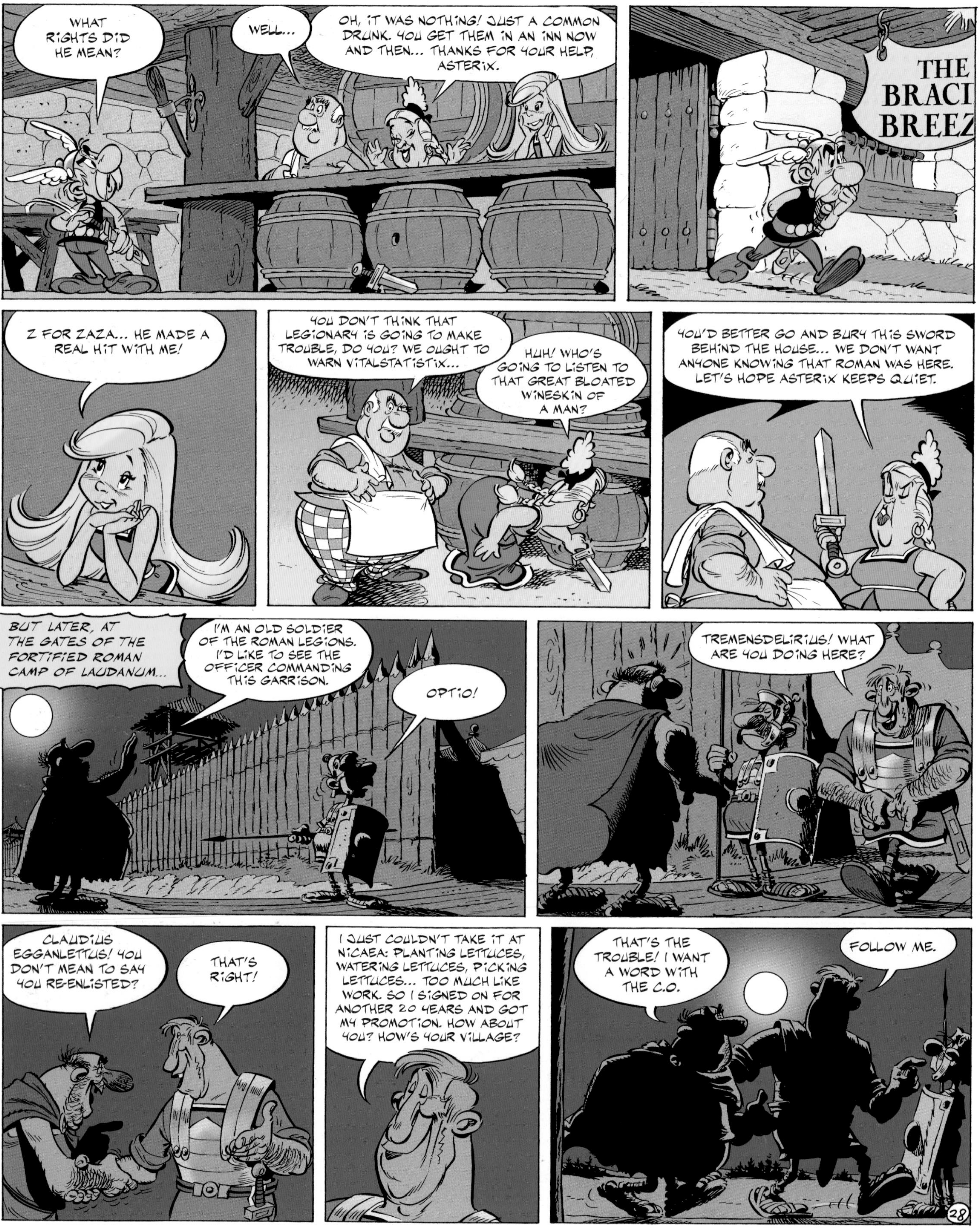

WHAT RIGHTS DID HE MEAN?
WELL...
OH, IT WAS NOTHING! JUST A COMMON DRUNK. YOU GET THEM IN AN INN NOW AND THEN... THANKS FOR YOUR HELP, ASTERIX.
THE BRACI BREEZ
Z FOR ZAZA... HE MADE A REAL HIT WITH ME!
YOU DON'T THINK THAT LEGIONARY IS GOING TO MAKE TROUBLE, DO YOU? WE OUGHT TO WARN VITALSTATISTIX...
HUH! WHO'S GOING TO LISTEN TO THAT GREAT BLOATED WINESKIN OF A MAN?
YOU'D BETTER GO AND BURY THIS SWORD BEHIND THE HOUSE... WE DON'T WANT ANYONE KNOWING THAT ROMAN WAS HERE. LET'S HOPE ASTERIX KEEPS QUIET.
BUT LATER, AT THE GATES OF THE FORTIFIED ROMAN CAMP OF LAUDANUM...
I'M AN OLD SOLDIER OF THE ROMAN LEGIONS. I'D LIKE TO SEE THE OFFICER COMMANDING THIS GARRISON.
OPTIO!
TREMENSDELIRIUS! WHAT ARE YOU DOING HERE?
CLAUDIUS EGGANLETTUS! YOU DON'T MEAN TO SAY YOU RE-ENLISTED?
THAT'S RIGHT!
I JUST COULDN'T TAKE IT AT NICAEA: PLANTING LETTUCES, WATERING LETTUCES, PICKING LETTUCES... TOO MUCH LIKE WORK. SO I SIGNED ON FOR ANOTHER 20 YEARS AND GOT MY PROMOTION. HOW ABOUT YOU? HOW'S YOUR VILLAGE?
THAT'S THE TROUBLE! I WANT A WORD WITH THE C.O.
FOLLOW ME.
28

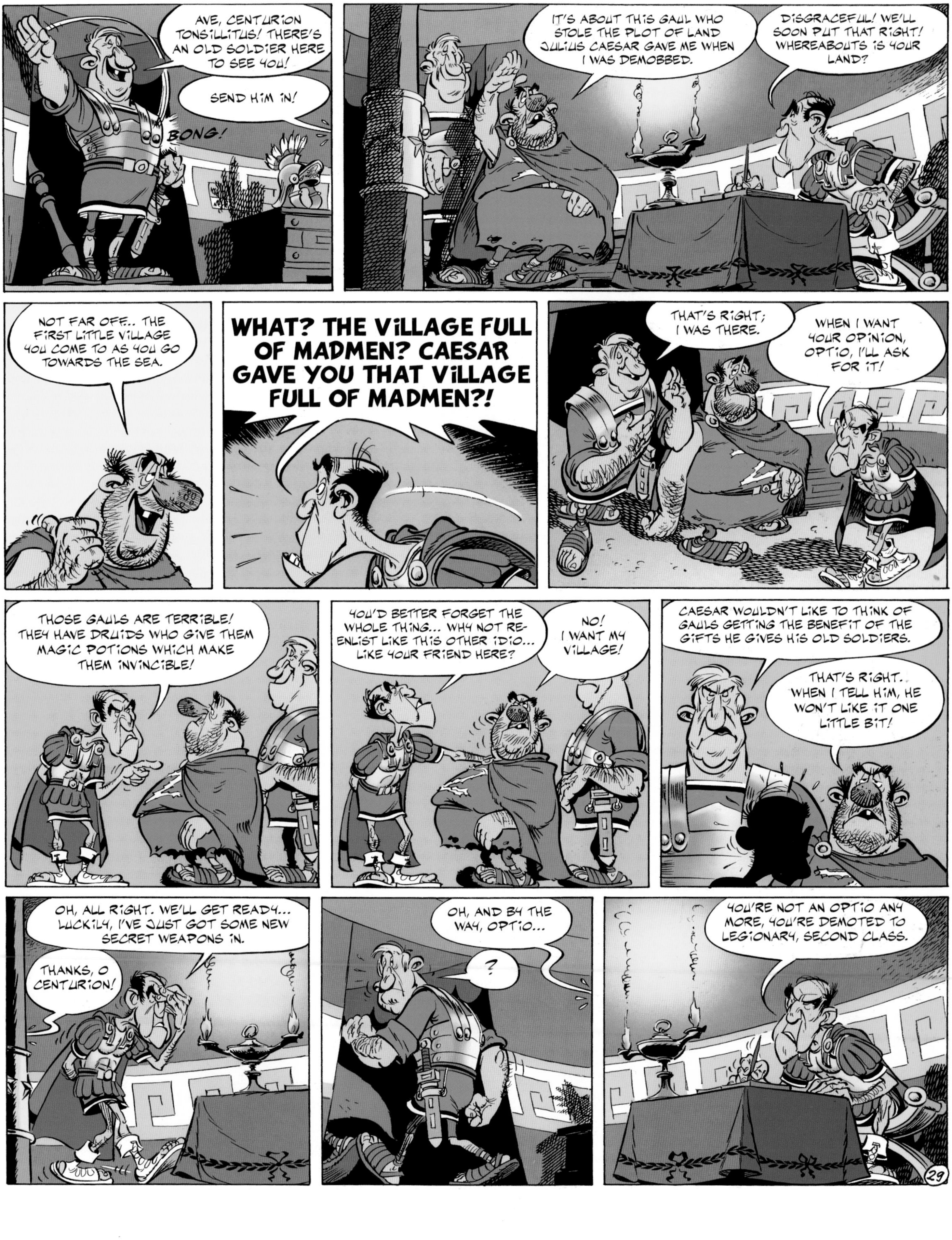
AVE, CENTURION TONSILLITUS! THERE'S AN OLD SOLDIER HERE TO SEE YOU!
SEND HIM IN!
BONG!
IT'S ABOUT THIS GAUL WHO STOLE THE PLOT OF LAND JULIUS CAESAR GAVE ME WHEN I WAS DEMOBBED.
DISGRACEFUL! WE'LL SOON PUT THAT RIGHT! WHEREABOUTS IS YOUR LAND?
NOT FAR OFF.. THE FIRST LITTLE VILLAGE YOU COME TO AS YOU GO TOWARDS THE SEA.
WHAT? THE VILLAGE FULL OF MADMEN? CAESAR GAVE YOU THAT VILLAGE FULL OF MADMEN?!
THAT'S RIGHT; I WAS THERE.
WHEN I WANT YOUR OPINION, OPTIO, I'LL ASK FOR IT!
THOSE GAULS ARE TERRIBLE! THEY HAVE DRUIDS WHO GIVE THEM MAGIC POTIONS WHICH MAKE THEM INVINCIBLE!
YOU'D BETTER FORGET THE WHOLE THING... WHY NOT RE-ENLIST LIKE THIS OTHER IDIO... LIKE YOUR FRIEND HERE?
NO! I WANT MY VILLAGE!
CAESAR WOULDN'T LIKE TO THINK OF GAULS GETTING THE BENEFIT OF THE GIFTS HE GIVES HIS OLD SOLDIERS.
THAT'S RIGHT.. WHEN I TELL HIM, HE WON'T LIKE IT ONE LITTLE BIT!
OH, ALL RIGHT. WE'LL GET READY... LUCKILY, I'VE JUST GOT SOME NEW SECRET WEAPONS IN.
THANKS, O CENTURION!
OH, AND BY THE WAY, OPTIO...
?
YOU'RE NOT AN OPTIO ANY MORE, YOU'RE DEMOTED TO LEGIONARY, SECOND CLASS.
29

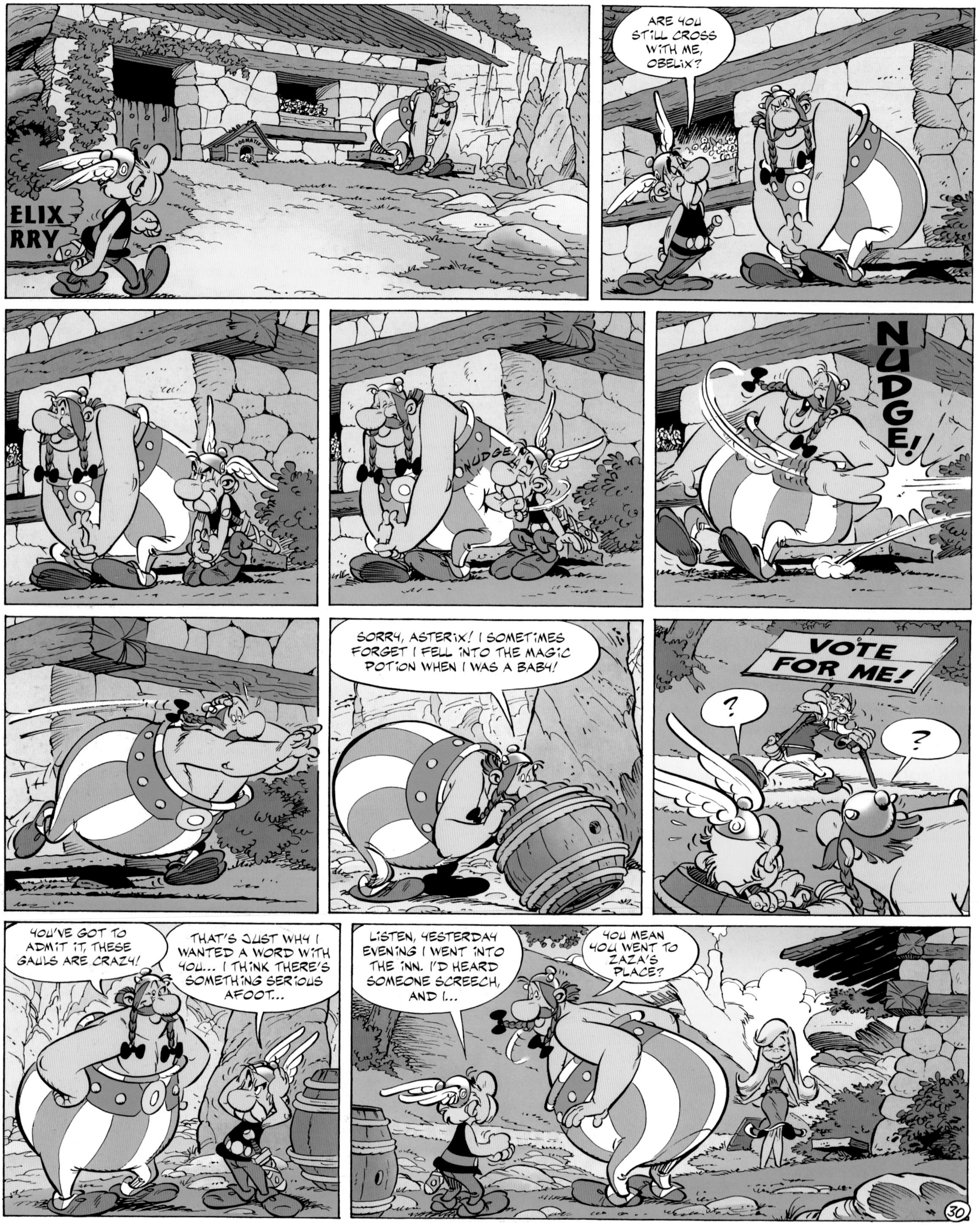
ELIX
RRY
DOGMATIX
ARE YOU STILL CROSS WITH ME, OBELIX?
NUDGE
NUDGE!
SORRY, ASTERIX! I SOMETIMES FORGET I FELL INTO THE MAGIC POTION WHEN I WAS A BABY!
VOTE FOR ME!
?
?
YOU'VE GOT TO ADMIT IT, THESE GAULS ARE CRAZY!
THAT'S JUST WHY I WANTED A WORD WITH YOU... I THINK THERE'S SOMETHING SERIOUS AFOOT...
LISTEN, YESTERDAY EVENING I WENT INTO THE INN. I'D HEARD SOMEONE SCREECH, AND I...
YOU MEAN YOU WENT TO ZAZA'S PLACE?
30

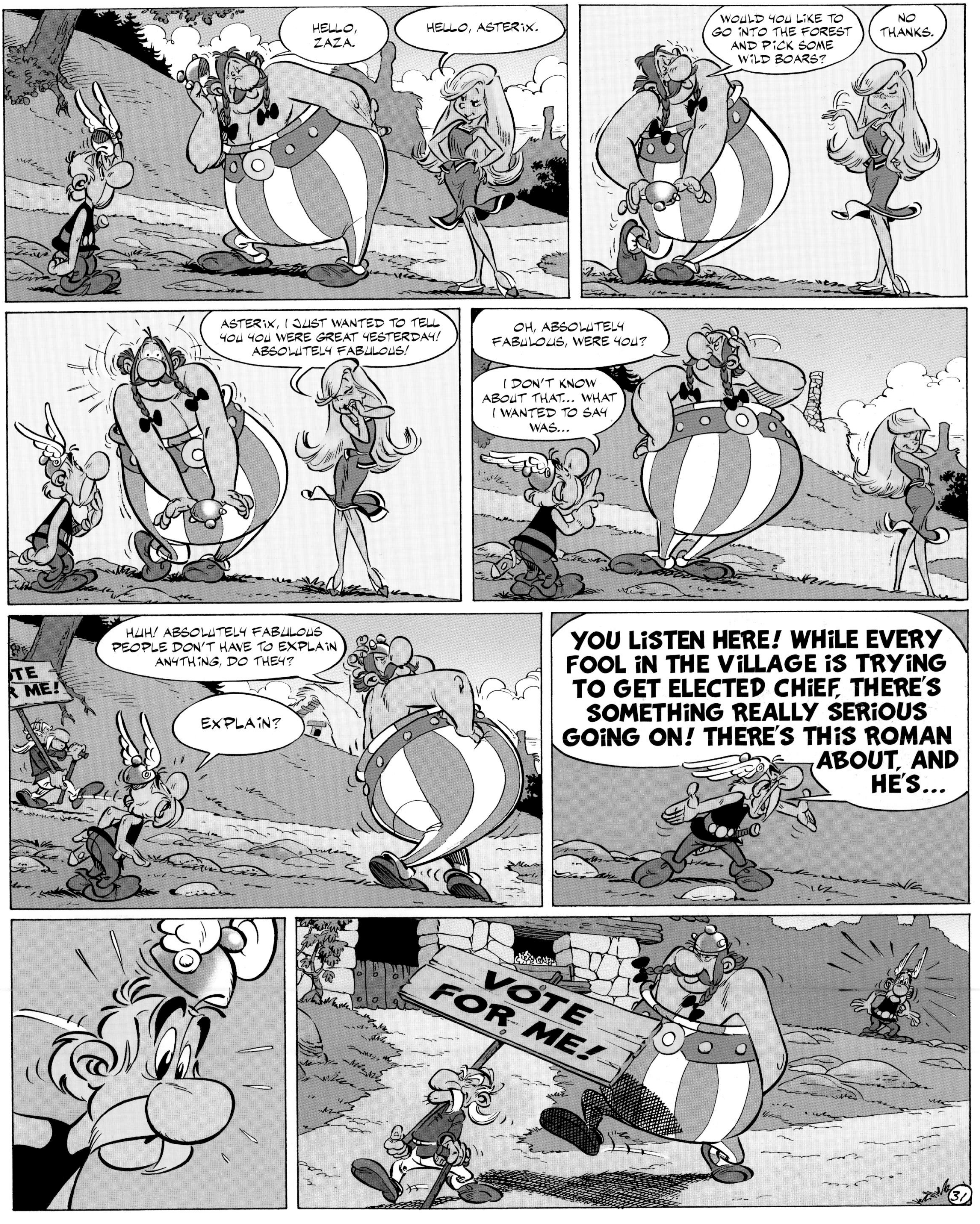
HELLO, ZAZA.
HELLO, ASTERIX.
WOULD YOU LIKE TO GO INTO THE FOREST AND PICK SOME WILD BOARS?
NO THANKS.
ASTERIX, I JUST WANTED TO TELL YOU YOU WERE GREAT YESTERDAY! ABSOLUTELY FABULOUS!
OH, ABSOLUTELY FABULOUS, WERE YOU?
I DON'T KNOW ABOUT THAT... WHAT I WANTED TO SAY WAS...
HUH! ABSOLUTELY FABULOUS PEOPLE DON'T HAVE TO EXPLAIN ANYTHING, DO THEY?
EXPLAIN?
YOU LISTEN HERE! WHILE EVERY FOOL IN THE VILLAGE IS TRYING TO GET ELECTED CHIEF, THERE'S SOMETHING REALLY SERIOUS GOING ON! THERE'S THIS ROMAN ABOUT, AND HE'S...
VOTE FOR ME!
31

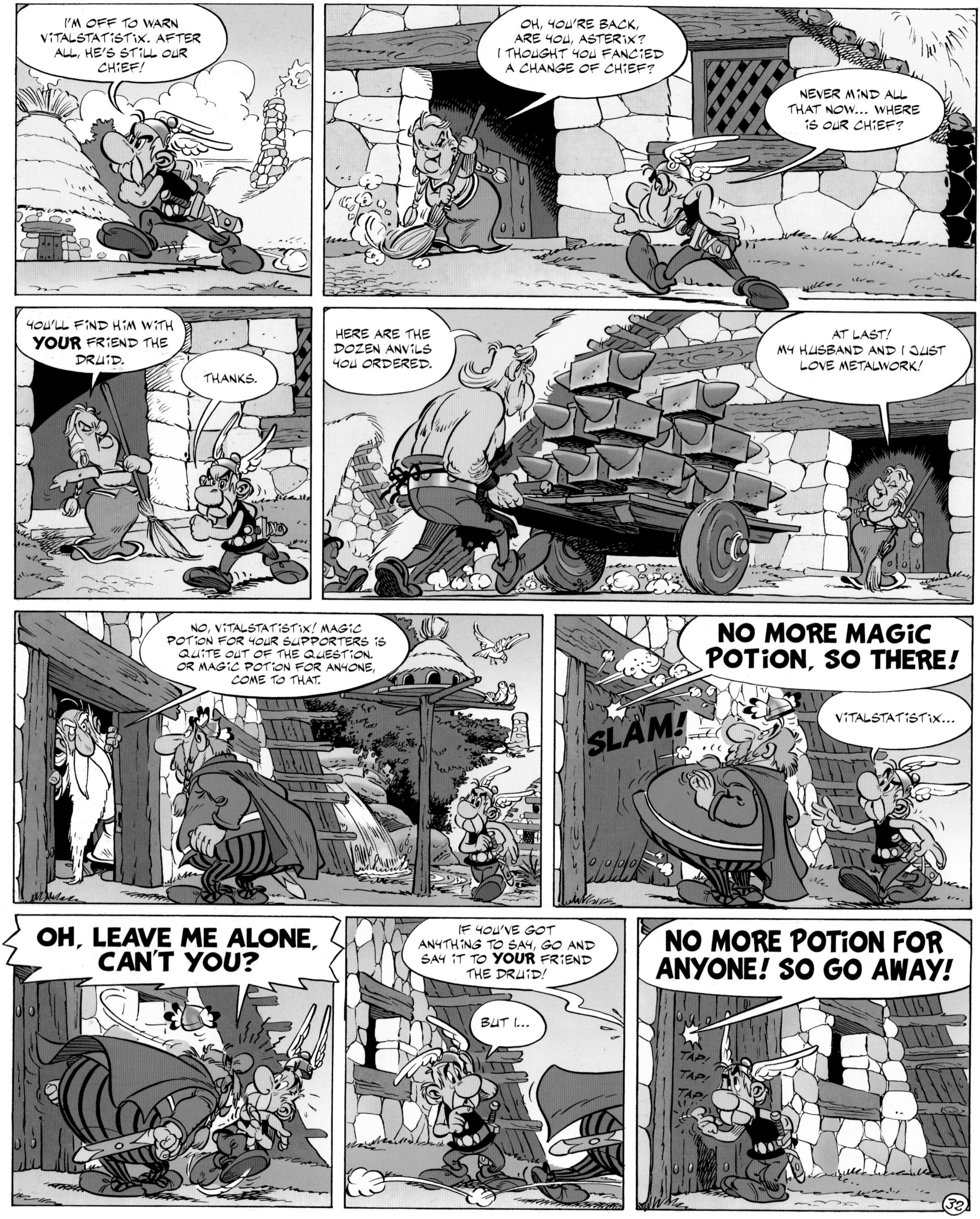

I'M OFF TO WARN VITALSTATISTIX. AFTER ALL, HE'S STILL OUR CHIEF!
OH, YOU'RE BACK, ARE YOU, ASTERIX? I THOUGHT YOU FANCIED A CHANGE OF CHIEF?
NEVER MIND ALL THAT NOW... WHERE IS OUR CHIEF?
YOU'LL FIND HIM WITH YOUR FRIEND THE DRUID.
THANKS.
HERE ARE THE DOZEN ANVILS YOU ORDERED.
AT LAST! MY HUSBAND AND I JUST LOVE METALWORK!
NO, VITALSTATISTIX! MAGIC POTION FOR YOUR SUPPORTERS IS QUITE OUT OF THE QUESTION. OR MAGIC POTION FOR ANYONE, COME TO THAT.
NO MORE MAGIC POTION, SO THERE!
SLAM!
VITALSTATISTIX...
OH, LEAVE ME ALONE, CAN'T YOU?
IF YOU'VE GOT ANYTHING TO SAY, GO AND SAY IT TO YOUR FRIEND THE DRUID!
BUT I...
NO MORE POTION FOR ANYONE! SO GO AWAY!
TAP! TAP! TAP!
32

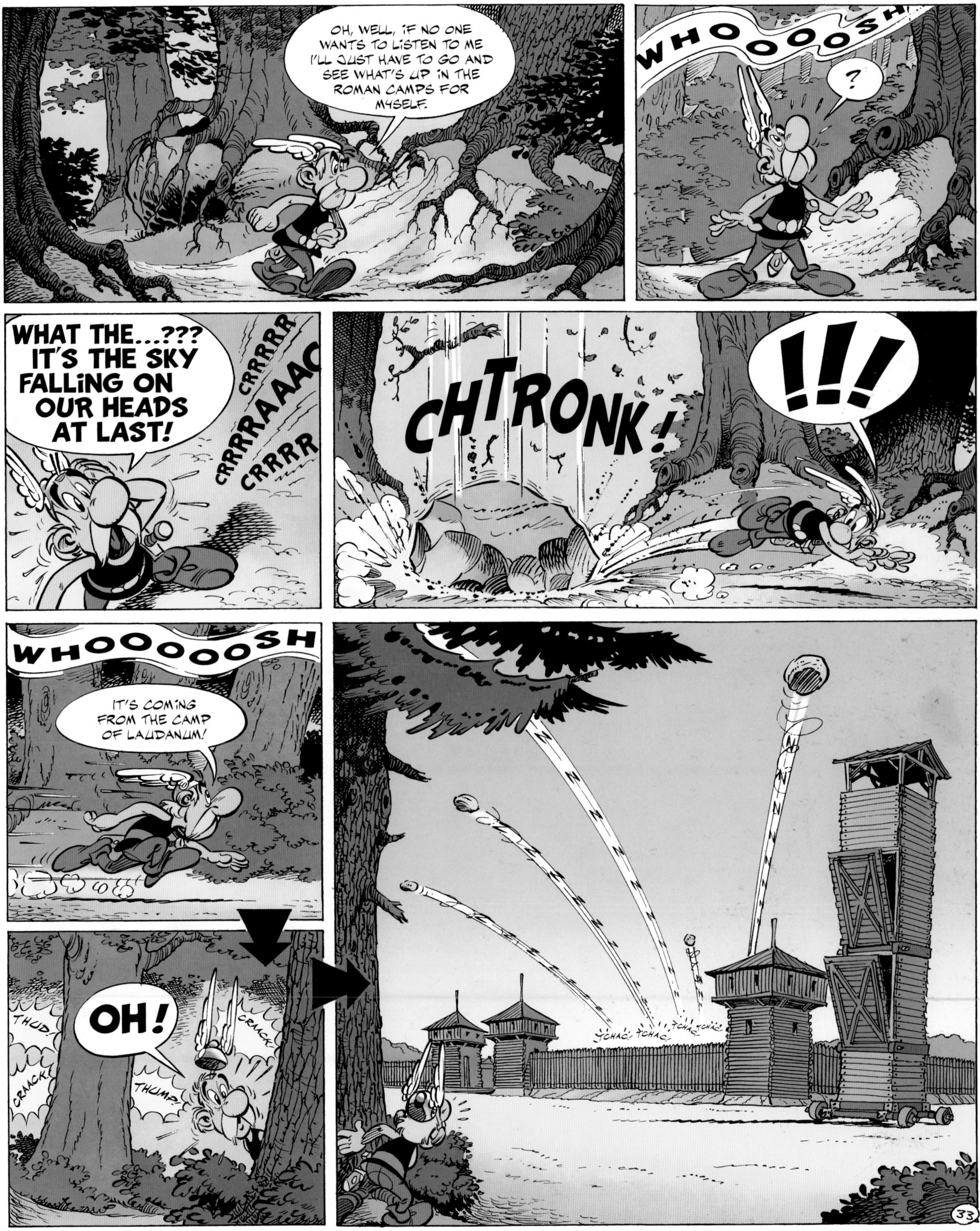
OH, WELL, IF NO ONE WANTS TO LISTEN TO ME I'LL JUST HAVE TO GO AND SEE WHAT'S UP IN THE ROMAN CAMPS FOR MYSELF.
WHOOOOOSH
?
WHAT THE...??? IT'S THE SKY FALLING ON OUR HEADS AT LAST!
CRRRRRR
CRRRRAAAC
CRRRRR
CRRRR
CHTRONK!
!!!
WHOOOOOOSH
IT'S COMING FROM THE CAMP OF LAUDANUM!
THUD!
CRAACK!
OH!
CRAACK!
THUMP!
TCHAC! TCHAC! TCHAC! TCHAC!
33

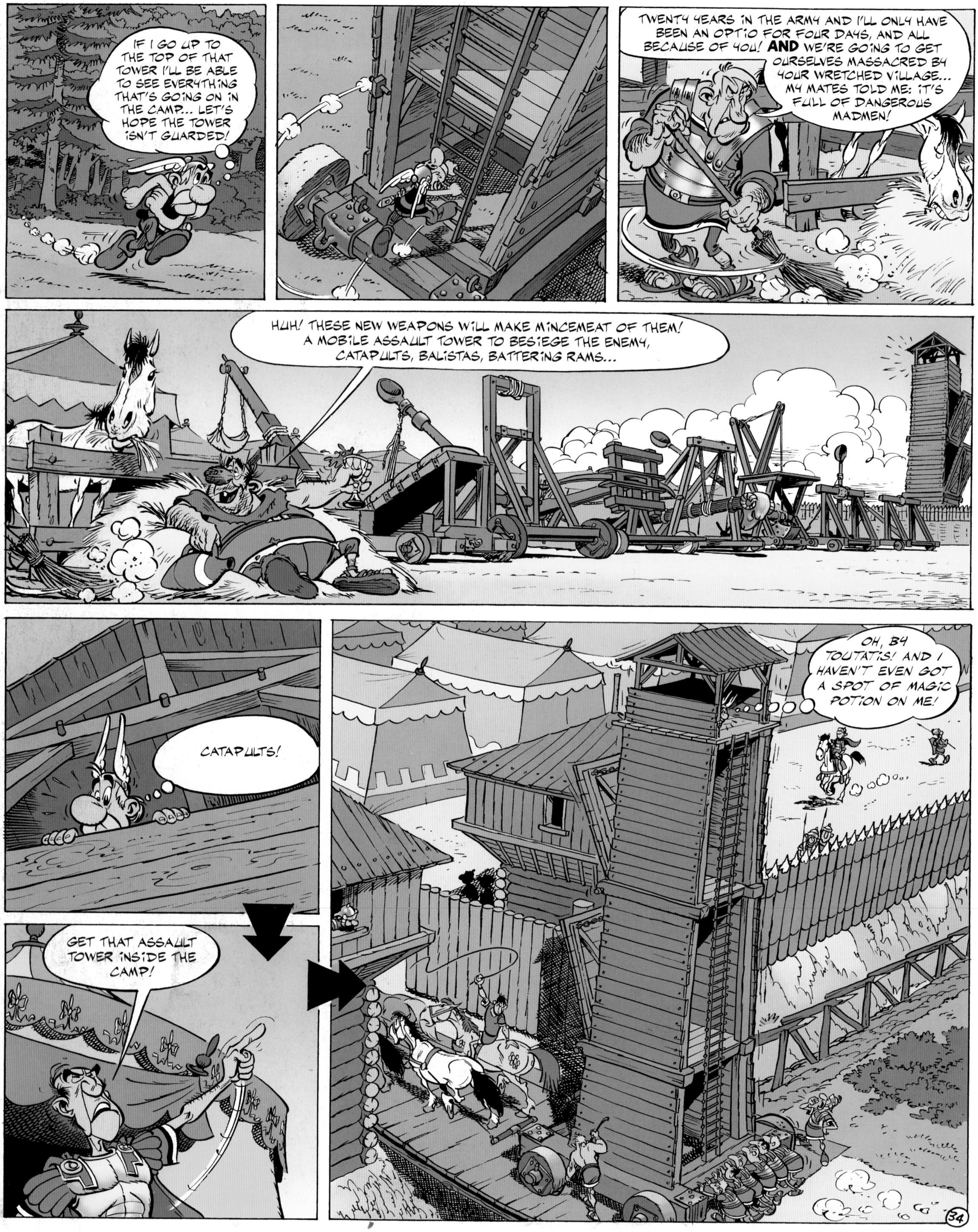
IF I GO UP TO THE TOP OF THAT TOWER I'LL BE ABLE TO SEE EVERYTHING THAT'S GOING ON IN THE CAMP... LET'S HOPE THE TOWER ISN'T GUARDED!
TWENTY YEARS IN THE ARMY AND I'LL ONLY HAVE BEEN AN OPTIO FOR FOUR DAYS, AND ALL BECAUSE OF YOU! AND WE'RE GOING TO GET OURSELVES MASSACRED BY YOUR WRETCHED VILLAGE... MY MATES TOLD ME: IT'S FULL OF DANGEROUS MADMEN!
HUH! THESE NEW WEAPONS WILL MAKE MINCEMEAT OF THEM! A MOBILE ASSAULT TOWER TO BESIEGE THE ENEMY, CATAPULTS, BALISTAS, BATTERING RAMS...
CATAPULTS!
GET THAT ASSAULT TOWER INSIDE THE CAMP!
OH, BY TOUTATIS! AND I HAVEN'T EVEN GOT A SPOT OF MAGIC POTION ON ME!
34

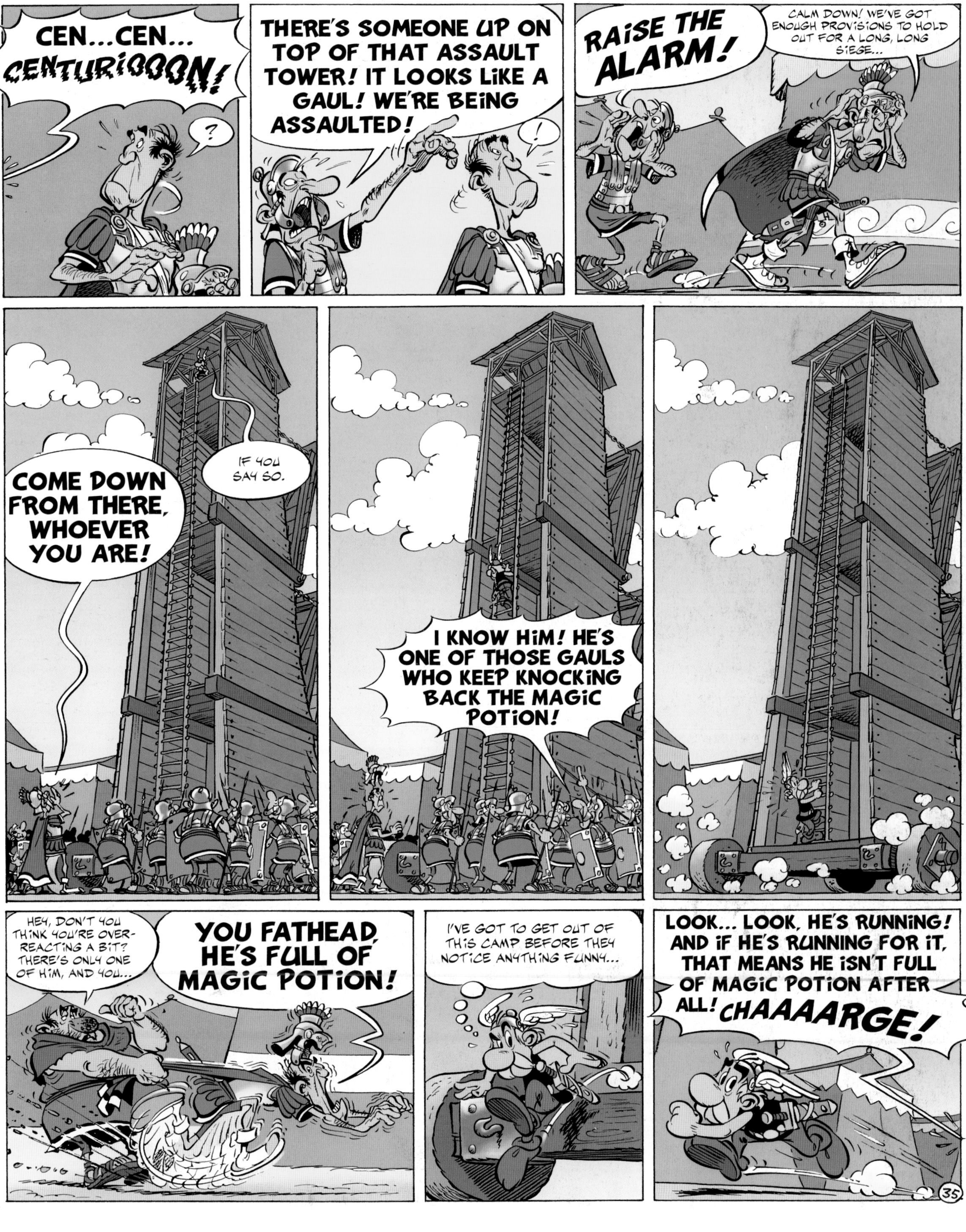
CEN...CEN... CENTURIOOON!
?
THERE'S SOMEONE UP ON TOP OF THAT ASSAULT TOWER! IT LOOKS LIKE A GAUL! WE'RE BEING ASSAULTED!
!
RAISE THE ALARM!
CALM DOWN! WE'VE GOT ENOUGH PROVISIONS TO HOLD OUT FOR A LONG, LONG SIEGE...
COME DOWN FROM THERE, WHOEVER YOU ARE!
IF YOU SAY SO.
I KNOW HIM! HE'S ONE OF THOSE GAULS WHO KEEP KNOCKING BACK THE MAGIC POTION!
HEY, DON'T YOU THINK YOU'RE OVER-REACTING A BIT? THERE'S ONLY ONE OF HIM, AND YOU...
YOU FATHEAD, HE'S FULL OF MAGIC POTION!
I'VE GOT TO GET OUT OF THIS CAMP BEFORE THEY NOTICE ANYTHING FUNNY...
LOOK... LOOK, HE'S RUNNING! AND IF HE'S RUNNING FOR IT, THAT MEANS HE ISN'T FULL OF MAGIC POTION AFTER ALL! CHAAAARGE!
35

HE'S CORNERED! WE'VE GOT HIM!

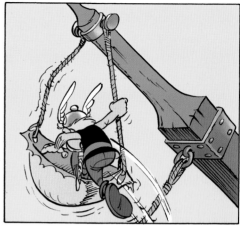

SLASH! SLASH!

SCHTONNK!

WE'VE LITERALLY SLUNG HIM OUT!

WHOOSH

YES, AND IT LOOKS AS IF THEY'VE RUN OUT OF MAGIC POTION! BY JUPITER, THERE'S A GREAT VICTORY AHEAD OF US! JULIUS CAESAR WON'T HALF BE PLEASED!

WHERE ARE YOU OFF TO?

WELL, I HAVEN'T FINISHED SWEEPING THE BARRACKS YARD YET.

SWEEPING THE BARRACKS YARD? SINCE WHEN WAS THAT A JOB FOR AN OPTIO?

FIRST STONES, THEN PEOPLE... THERE'S NO LIVING IN THIS FOREST ANY MORE!

THAT'S RIGHT! HOW ABOUT ECOLOGY, EH? NO RESPECT FOR THE ENVIRONMENT!

36.

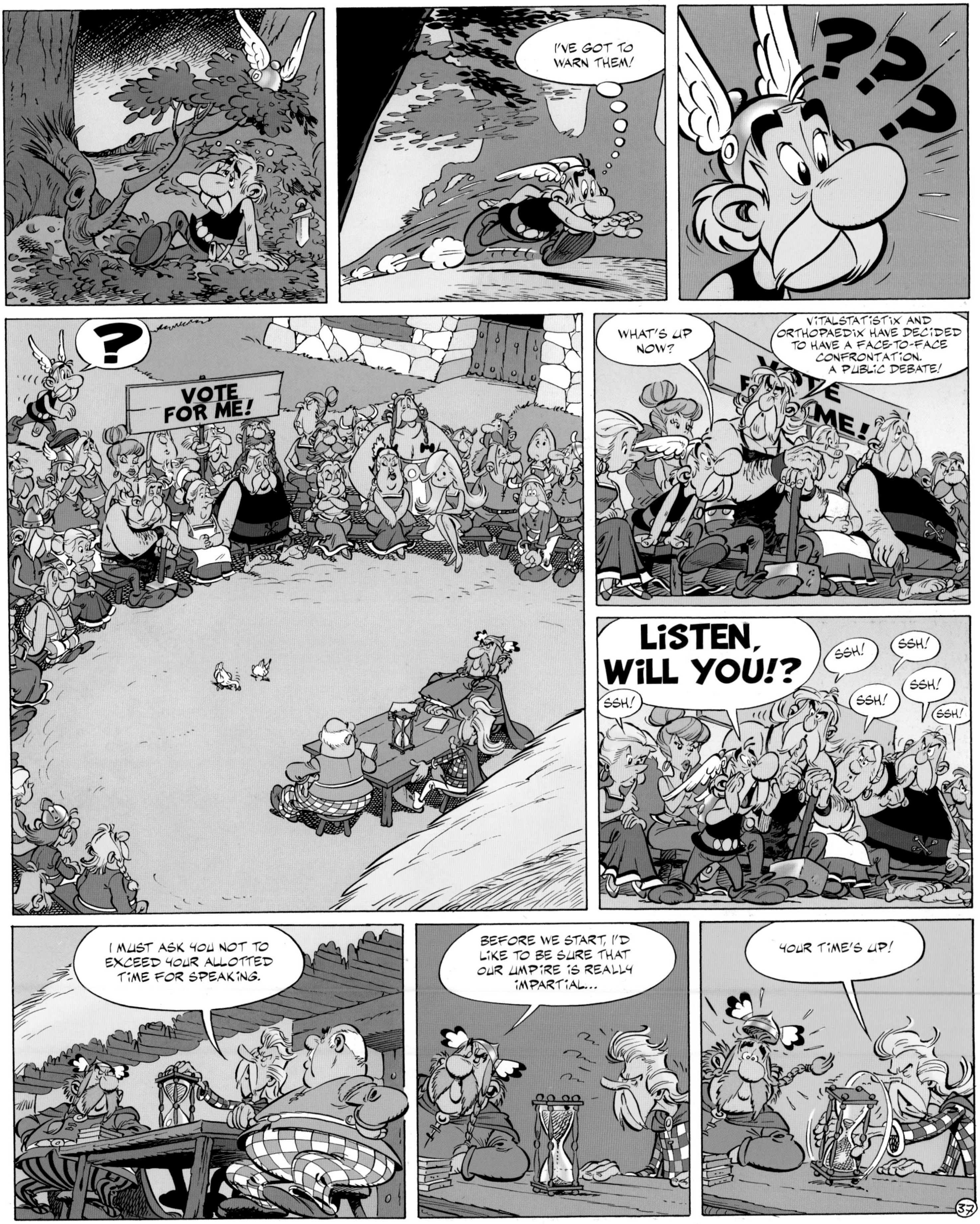

I'VE GOT TO WARN THEM!
VOTE FOR ME!
WHAT'S UP NOW?
VITALSTATISTIX AND ORTHOPAEDIX HAVE DECIDED TO HAVE A FACE-TO-FACE CONFRONTATION. A PUBLIC DEBATE!
LISTEN, WILL YOU!?
SSH!
SSH!
SSH!
SSH!
SSH!
SSH!
I MUST ASK YOU NOT TO EXCEED YOUR ALLOTTED TIME FOR SPEAKING.
BEFORE WE START, I'D LIKE TO BE SURE THAT OUR UMPIRE IS REALLY IMPARTIAL...
YOUR TIME'S UP!
37

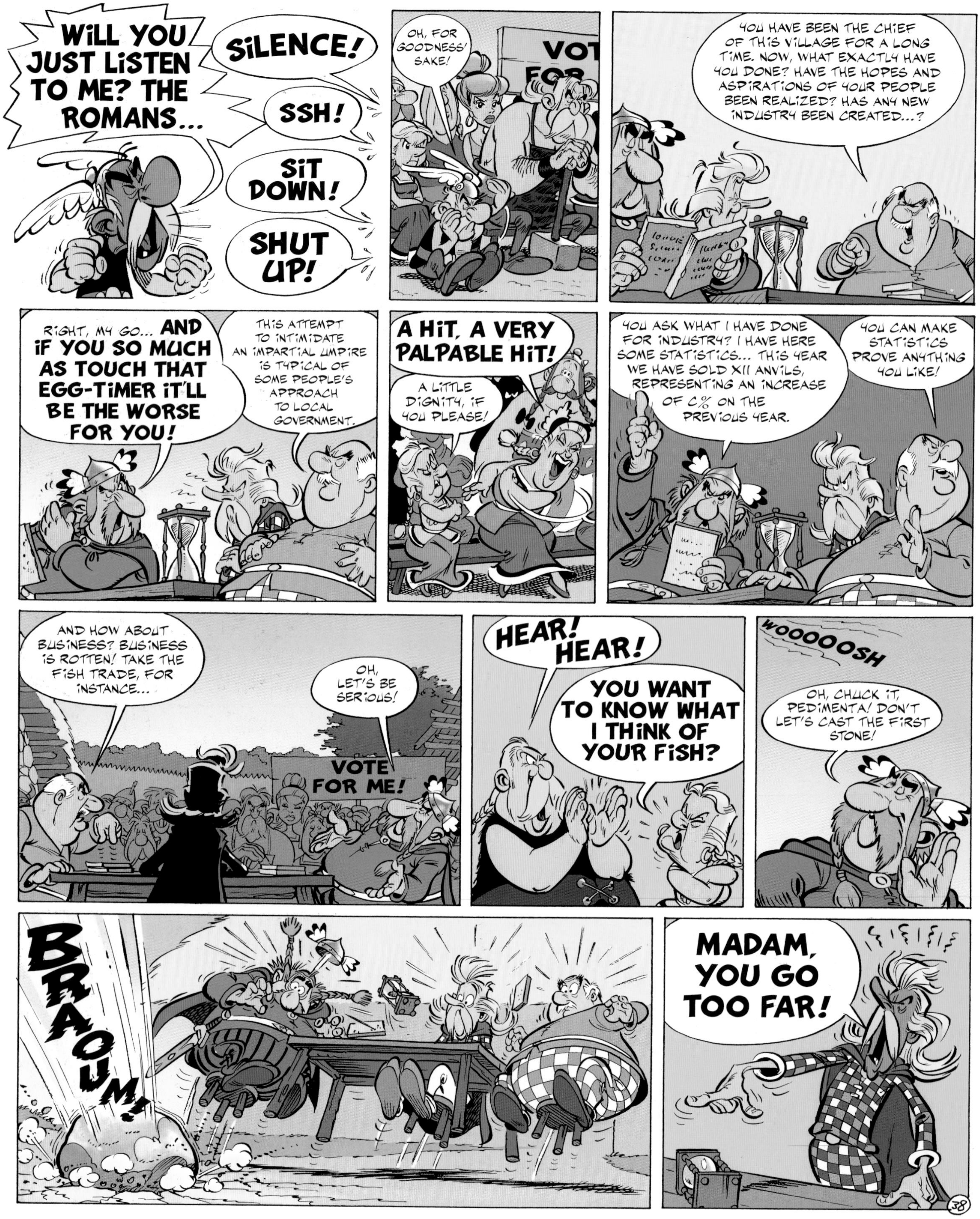
WILL YOU JUST LISTEN TO ME? THE ROMANS...
SILENCE!
SSH!
SIT DOWN!
SHUT UP!
OH, FOR GOODNESS' SAKE!
VOTE FOR
YOU HAVE BEEN THE CHIEF OF THIS VILLAGE FOR A LONG TIME. NOW, WHAT EXACTLY HAVE YOU DONE? HAVE THE HOPES AND ASPIRATIONS OF YOUR PEOPLE BEEN REALIZED? HAS ANY NEW INDUSTRY BEEN CREATED...?
RIGHT, MY GO... AND IF YOU SO MUCH AS TOUCH THAT EGG-TIMER IT'LL BE THE WORSE FOR YOU!
THIS ATTEMPT TO INTIMIDATE AN IMPARTIAL UMPIRE IS TYPICAL OF SOME PEOPLE'S APPROACH TO LOCAL GOVERNMENT.
A HIT, A VERY PALPABLE HIT!
A LITTLE DIGNITY, IF YOU PLEASE!
YOU ASK WHAT I HAVE DONE FOR INDUSTRY? I HAVE HERE SOME STATISTICS... THIS YEAR WE HAVE SOLD XII ANVILS, REPRESENTING AN INCREASE OF C% ON THE PREVIOUS YEAR.
YOU CAN MAKE STATISTICS PROVE ANYTHING YOU LIKE!
AND HOW ABOUT BUSINESS? BUSINESS IS ROTTEN! TAKE THE FISH TRADE, FOR INSTANCE...
OH, LET'S BE SERIOUS!
VOTE FOR ME!
HEAR! HEAR!
YOU WANT TO KNOW WHAT I THINK OF YOUR FISH?
WOOOOOOSH
OH, CHUCK IT, PEDIMENTA! DON'T LET'S CAST THE FIRST STONE!
BRAOUM!
MADAM, YOU GO TOO FAR!
38

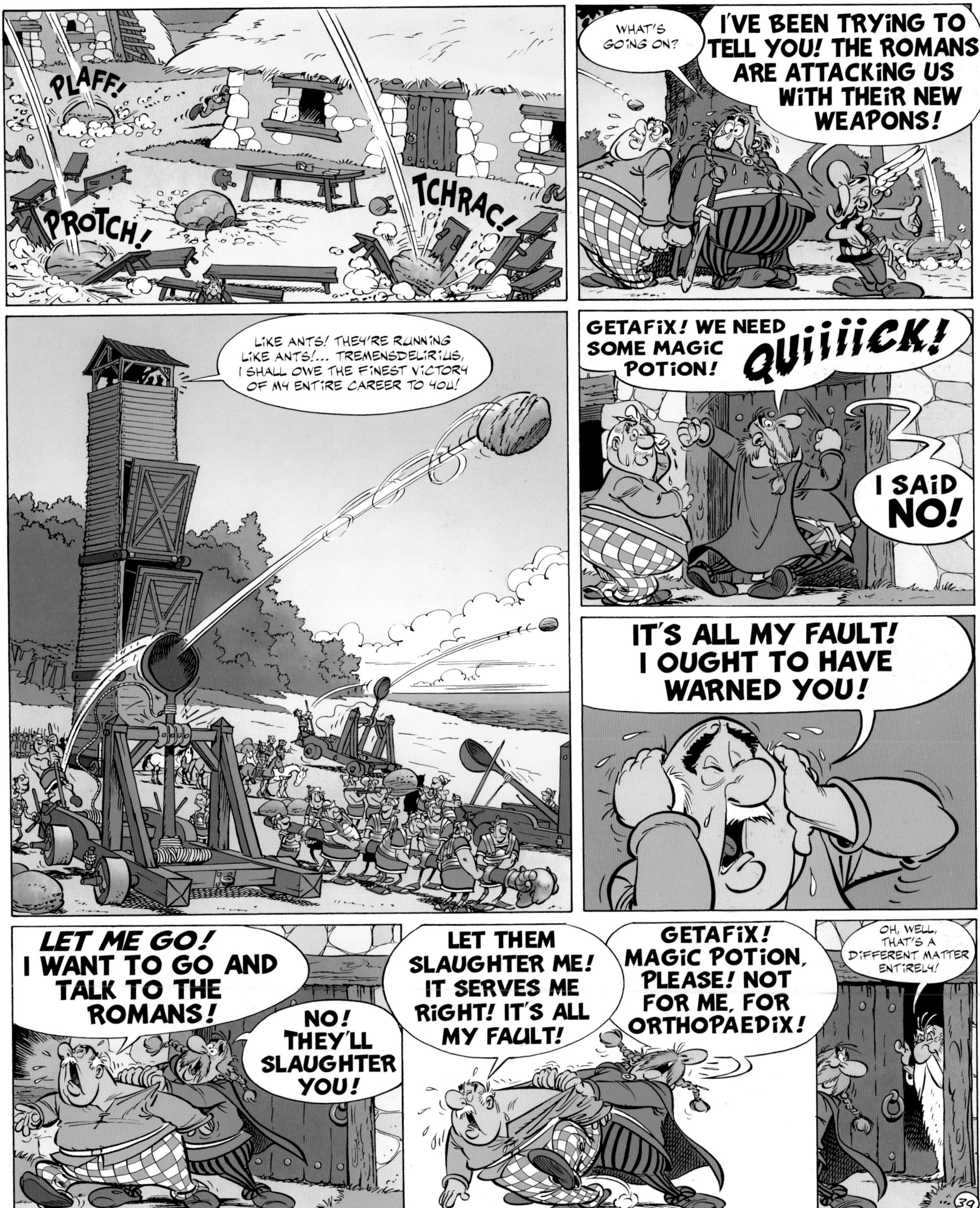
PLAFF!
PROTCH!
TCHRAC!
WHAT'S GOING ON?
I'VE BEEN TRYING TO TELL YOU! THE ROMANS ARE ATTACKING US WITH THEIR NEW WEAPONS!
LIKE ANTS! THEY'RE RUNNING LIKE ANTS!... TREMENSDELIRIUS, I SHALL OWE THE FINEST VICTORY OF MY ENTIRE CAREER TO YOU!
GETAFIX! WE NEED SOME MAGIC POTION!
QUIIIICK!
I SAID NO!
IT'S ALL MY FAULT! I OUGHT TO HAVE WARNED YOU!
LET ME GO! I WANT TO GO AND TALK TO THE ROMANS!
NO! THEY'LL SLAUGHTER YOU!
LET THEM SLAUGHTER ME! IT SERVES ME RIGHT! IT'S ALL MY FAULT!
GETAFIX! MAGIC POTION, PLEASE! NOT FOR ME, FOR ORTHOPAEDIX!
OH, WELL, THAT'S A DIFFERENT MATTER ENTIRELY!
39

ASTERIX, TRY TO KEEP THE ROMANS HAPPY WHILE I COOK SOMETHING UP...
SHALL WE GET THEM, OBELIX?
LET'S PLAY THEM AT THEIR OWN GAME!
WOOF! WOOF!
CRAAAAASH!
HULLO, HAVE THEY GOT ENGINES OF WAR TOO? WE'LL HAVE TO DO SOMETHING ABOUT THAT... BREAK DOWN THE GATE WITH THE BATTERING RAM!
NO, DOGMATIX! DON'T FETCH THAT MENHIR!
HEEL, DOGMATIX!
CRAAAASH!
BONG!
?
40

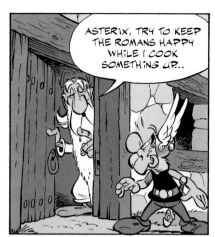

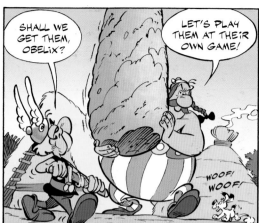

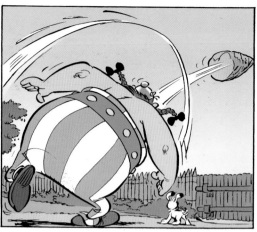

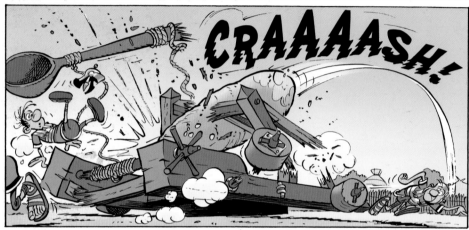

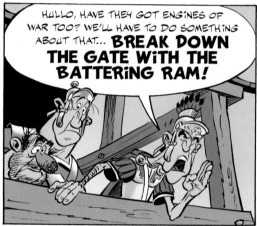

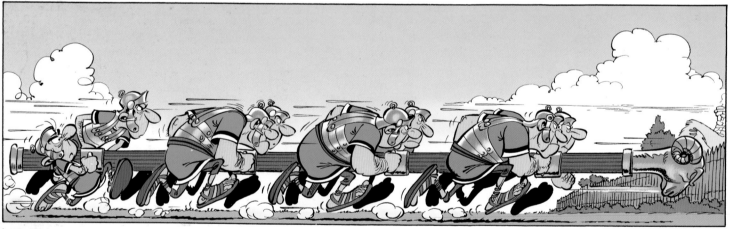

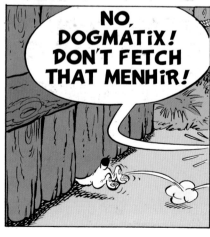

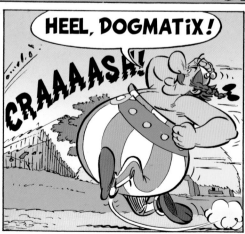

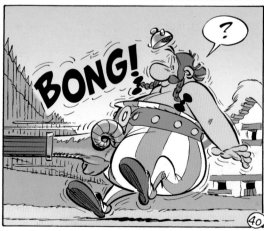

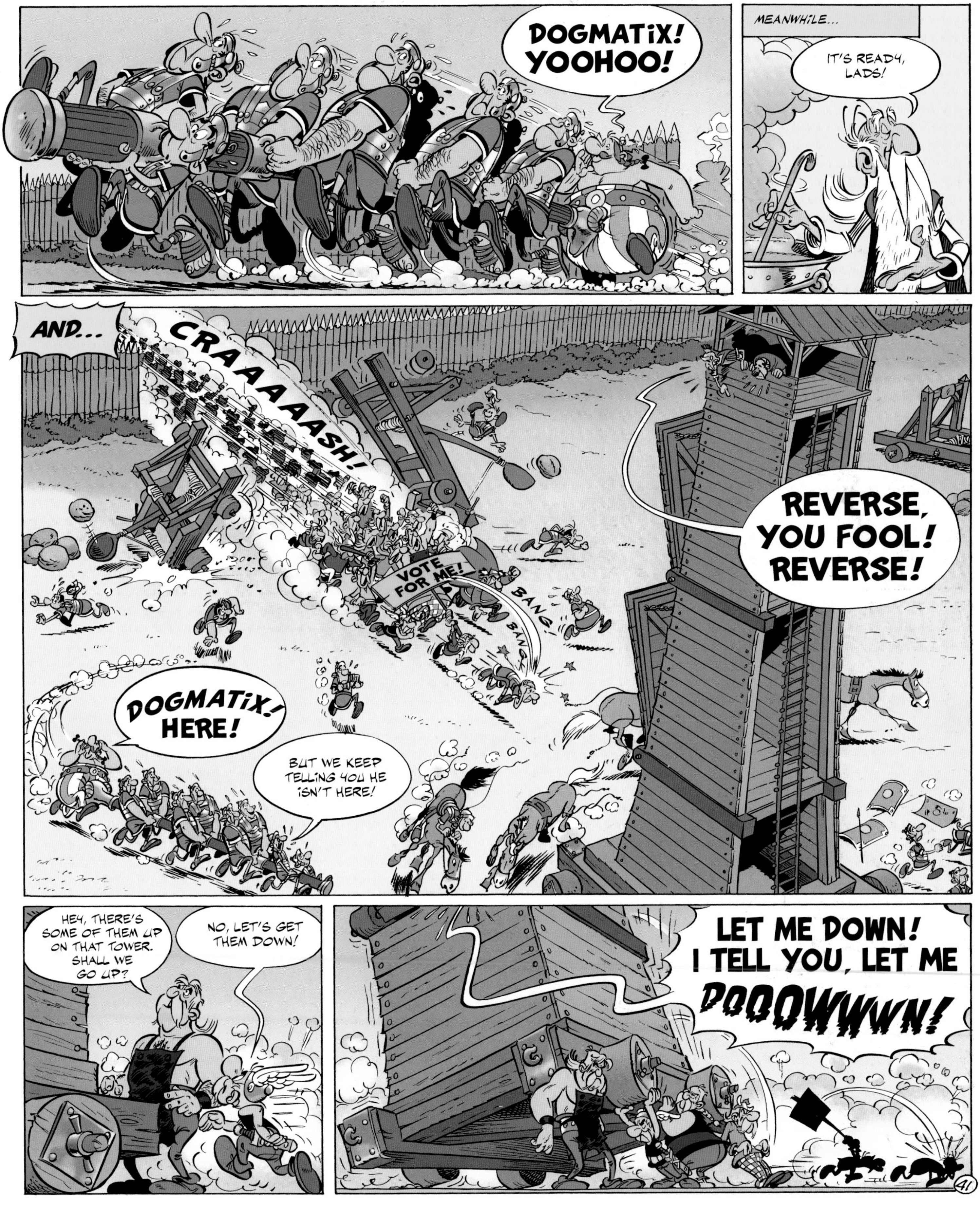
DOGMATiX! YOOHOO!
MEANWHiLE...
iT'S READY, LADS!
AND...
CRAAAAAASH!
VOTE FOR ME!
BANG
BANG
REVERSE, YOU FOOL! REVERSE!
DOGMATiX! HERE!
BUT WE KEEP TELLiNG YOU HE iSN'T HERE!
HEY, THERE'S SOME OF THEM UP ON THAT TOWER. SHALL WE GO UP?
NO, LET'S GET THEM DOWN!
LET ME DOWN! I TELL YOU, LET ME DOOOWWWN!
41

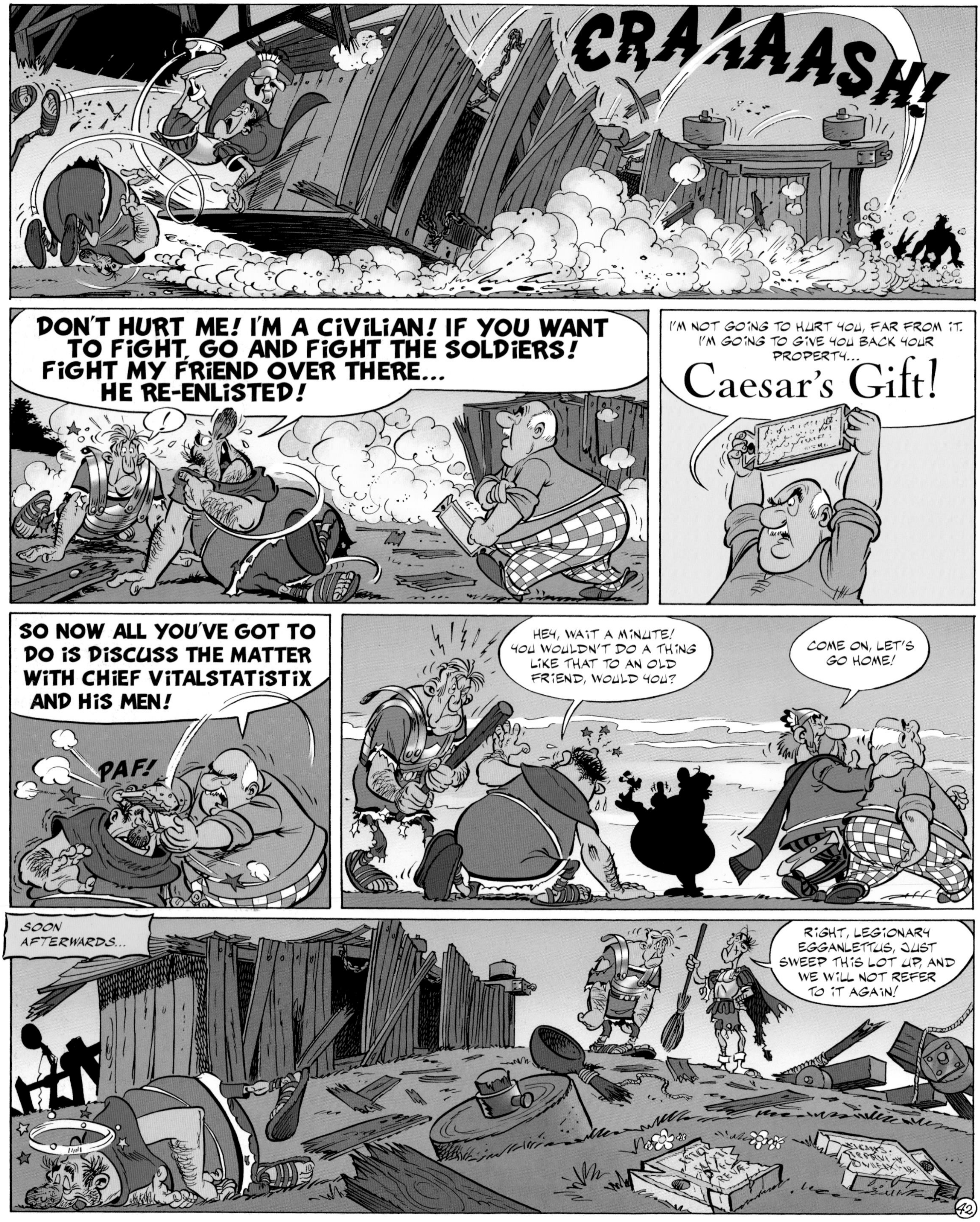
CRAAAASH!
DON'T HURT ME! I'M A CIVILIAN! IF YOU WANT TO FIGHT, GO AND FIGHT THE SOLDIERS! FIGHT MY FRIEND OVER THERE... HE RE-ENLISTED!
!
I'M NOT GOING TO HURT YOU, FAR FROM IT. I'M GOING TO GIVE YOU BACK YOUR PROPERTY...
Caesar's Gift!
SO NOW ALL YOU'VE GOT TO DO IS DISCUSS THE MATTER WITH CHIEF VITALSTATISTIX AND HIS MEN!
PAF!
HEY, WAIT A MINUTE! YOU WOULDN'T DO A THING LIKE THAT TO AN OLD FRIEND, WOULD YOU?
COME ON, LET'S GO HOME!
SOON AFTERWARDS...
RIGHT, LEGIONARY EGGANLETTUS, JUST SWEEP THIS LOT UP, AND WE WILL NOT REFER TO IT AGAIN!
42

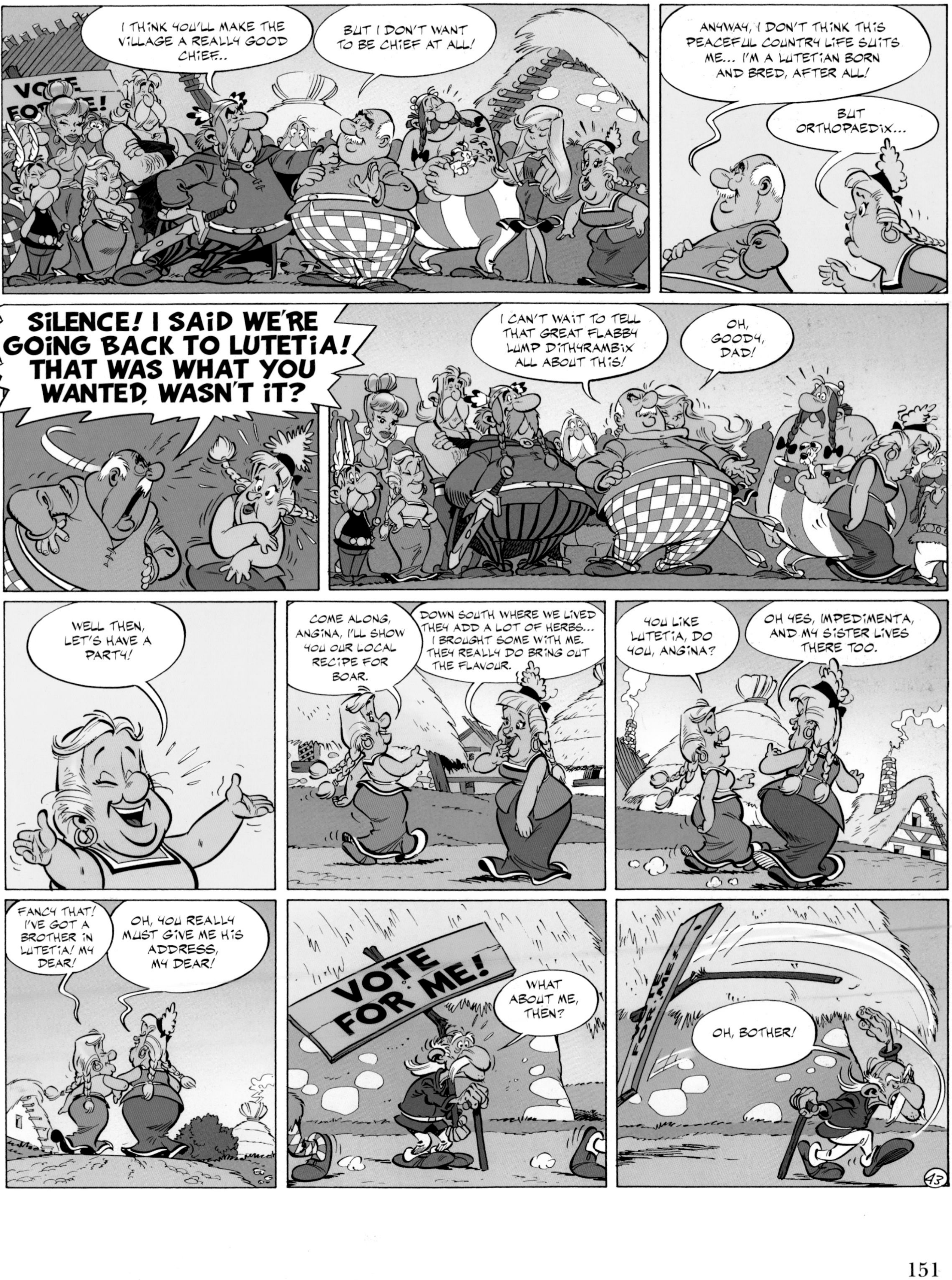
VOTE FOR ME!
I THINK YOU'LL MAKE THE VILLAGE A REALLY GOOD CHIEF..
BUT I DON'T WANT TO BE CHIEF AT ALL!
ANYWAY, I DON'T THINK THIS PEACEFUL COUNTRY LIFE SUITS ME... I'M A LUTETIAN BORN AND BRED, AFTER ALL!
BUT ORTHOPAEDIX...
SILENCE! I SAID WE'RE GOING BACK TO LUTETIA! THAT WAS WHAT YOU WANTED, WASN'T IT?
I CAN'T WAIT TO TELL THAT GREAT FLABBY LUMP DITHYRAMBIX ALL ABOUT THIS!
OH, GOODY, DAD!
WELL THEN, LET'S HAVE A PARTY!
COME ALONG, ANGINA, I'LL SHOW YOU OUR LOCAL RECIPE FOR BOAR.
DOWN SOUTH WHERE WE LIVED THEY ADD A LOT OF HERBS... I BROUGHT SOME WITH ME. THEY REALLY DO BRING OUT THE FLAVOUR.
YOU LIKE LUTETIA, DO YOU, ANGINA?
OH YES, IMPEDIMENTA, AND MY SISTER LIVES THERE TOO.
FANCY THAT! I'VE GOT A BROTHER IN LUTETIA! MY DEAR!
OH, YOU REALLY MUST GIVE ME HIS ADDRESS, MY DEAR!
VOTE FOR ME!
WHAT ABOUT ME, THEN?
OH, BOTHER!
43

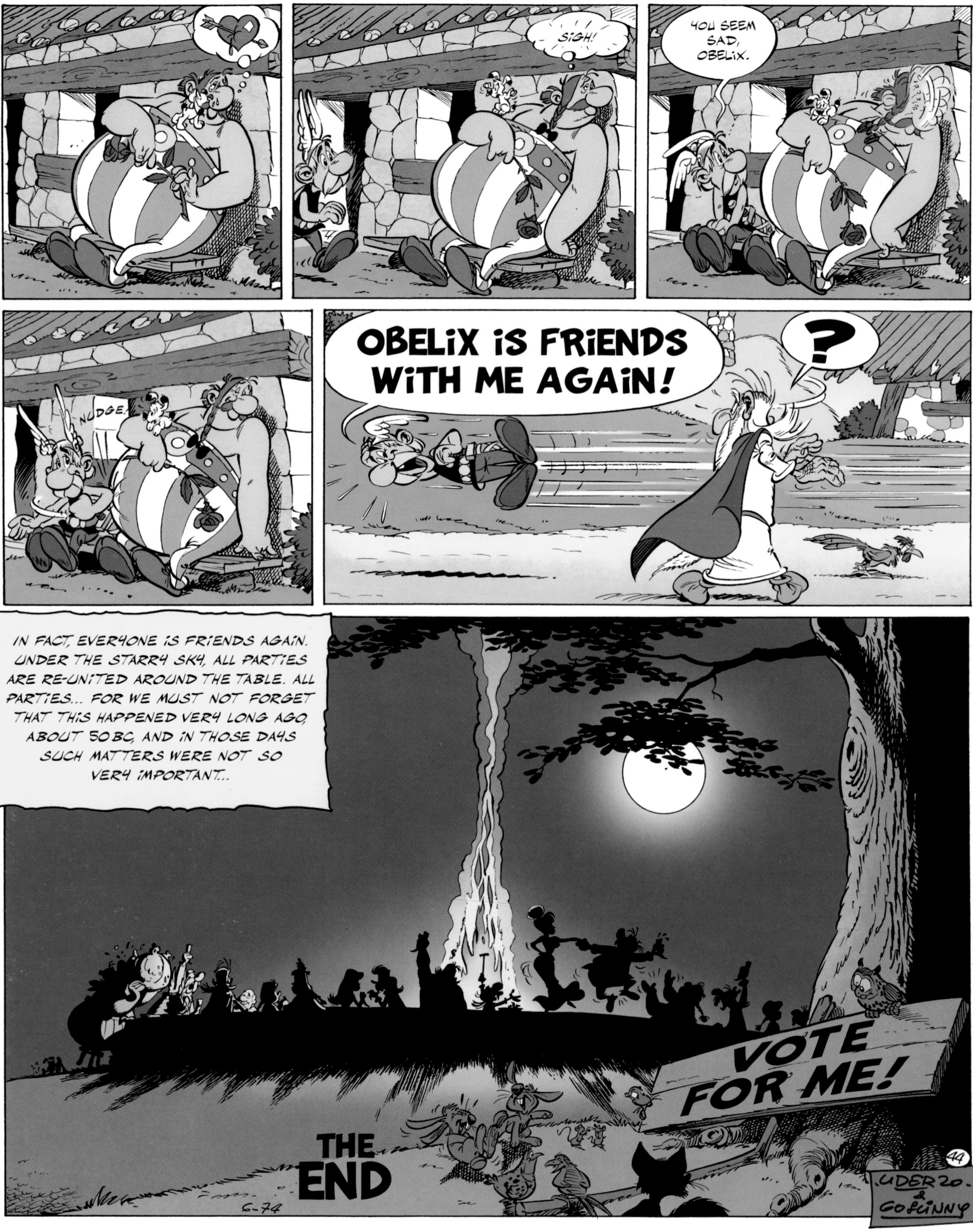
SIGH!
YOU SEEM SAD, OBELIX.
NUDGE!
OBELIX IS FRIENDS WITH ME AGAIN!
?
IN FACT, EVERYONE IS FRIENDS AGAIN. UNDER THE STARRY SKY, ALL PARTIES ARE RE-UNITED AROUND THE TABLE. ALL PARTIES... FOR WE MUST NOT FORGET THAT THIS HAPPENED VERY LONG AGO, ABOUT 50 BC, AND IN THOSE DAYS SUCH MATTERS WERE NOT SO VERY IMPORTANT...
VOTE FOR ME!
THE END
6-74
44
UDERZO & GOSCINNY

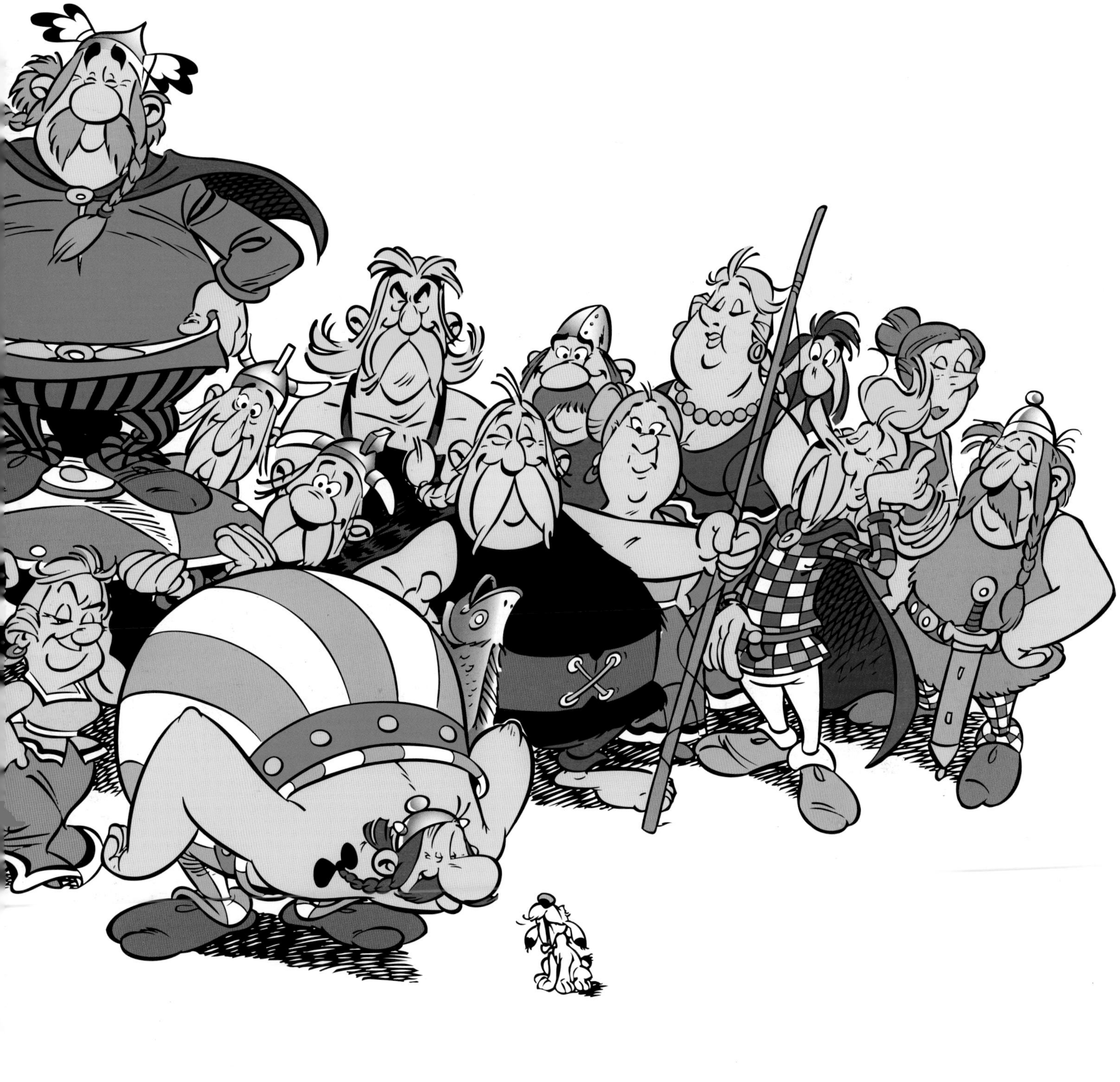